Virginia Andrew [illegible]
USA, studied a [illegible]
worked as a fash [illegible]
and later as a po [illegible] painter.

Flowers in the Attic, based on a true story, was her first novel and became an immediate best-seller. Published in 1979, it received tremendous acclaim on both sides of the Atlantic, and was made into a feature film. It was followed by three more books about the Dollanganger family – *Petals on the Wind*, *If There be Thorns* and *Seeds of Yesterday* – as well as by the prequel to *Flowers in the Attic*, *Garden of Shadows*. In addition to these novels, she is also author of *My Sweet Audrina*, and the novels in the Casteel family saga – *Heaven*, *Dark Angel*, *Fallen Hearts*, *Gates of Paradise* and *Web of Dreams* – set in Virginia, and in Boston.

Virginia Andrews died in December 1986, but left a considerable amount of unpublished work.

By the same author

FLOWERS IN THE ATTIC
PETALS ON THE WIND
IF THERE BE THORNS
MY SWEET AUDRINA
SEEDS OF YESTERDAY
DARK ANGEL
GARDEN OF SHADOWS
FALLEN HEARTS
GATES OF PARADISE
WEB OF DREAMS

VIRGINIA ANDREWS

Heaven

HarperCollins*Publishers*

HarperCollins*Publishers*
77–85 Fulham Palace Road,
Hammersmith, London W6 8JB

Special edition 1995

Previously published in paperback by Fontana 1985
Reprinted twelve times

First published in the USA by
Pocket Books 1985

ISBN 0 286 15133 2

Set in Plantin

Printed in Great Britain by
HarperCollinsManufacturing Glasgow

PART ONE

In the Willies

Prologue

Whenever the summer winds blow I hear the flowers whispering, and the leaves singing in the forest, and I see again the birds on wing, the river fish jumping. I remember, too, the winters: how the bare tree branches made tortured sounds as the cold winds whipped them about, forcing limbs to scrape the shedlike cabin that clung precariously to the steep mountainside of a range called by the West Virginian natives the Willies.

The wind didn't just blow in the Willies, it howled and shrieked, so everyone living in the Willies had good reason for looking anxiously out their small dirty windows. Living on the mountainsides was enough to give anyone the willies – especially when the wolves howled like the wind and the bobcats screeched and the wild things of the forest roamed at will. Often small pets would vanish, and once every decade or so an infant disappeared or a toddler wandered off and was never seen again.

With special clarity I remember one particular cold February night that revealed to me my own beginning. It was the eve of my tenth birthday. I lay close to the wood stove on my floor pallet, tossing and turning, hearing the wolves yowl at the moon. I had the unfortunate habit of sleeping lightly, so the slightest movement in the tiny cabin jolted me awake. Every sound was magnified in our isolated cabin. Granny and Grandpa snored. Pa staggered home drunk, bumping into furniture as he stumbled over sleeping bodies on the floor before he crashed down on the squealing springs of his big brass bed waking up Ma and making her angry again so she raised her voice in shrill complaint because again he'd spent too much time in Winnerrow, in Shirley's Place. At that time I didn't even know why Shirley's Place was such a bad place, and why Pa's going there caused so much trouble.

Our cabin floor, with half-inch spacings between each crookedly laid board, let in not only cold air but also the snortings of the sleeping pigs, dogs, cats, and whatever else took retreat under it.

Suddenly out of the black came a different kind of noise. Who was moving in the darkness of the dim red glow near the stove? I strained to see. It was Granny, bent over, her long grey hair streaming, making her seem like a witch, sliding along the rough wooden planks as quietly as possible. It couldn't be the outhouse she was heading for; Granny was the only one of us allowed to use the 'hockeypot' when nature called. The rest of us had to trek two hundred yards to the outhouse. Granny was in her mid-fifties. Chronic arthritis and various other undiagnosed aches and pains made life miserable for Granny, and the loss of most of her teeth made her seem twice her age. Once, so I had been told by those old enough to remember, Annie Brandywine had been the beauty queen of the hills.

'Come, girl,' Granny whispered hoarsely, her gnarled hand on my shoulder, 'it's time ya stopped crying out in the night. I'm hoping maybe ya won't be doing it no more once ya know the truth about yourself. So, before your pa wakes up again, you and me are going somewheres, an before we come back, ya'll have something to cling to when he glares his eyes and slings his fists.' She sighed like the south wind blowing gently, whispering the tendrils of hair around my face to make them tickle like ghosts that were coming – through her.

'You mean we're going outside? Granny, it's miserably cold out there,' I warned even as I got up and pulled on a cast-off pair of Tom's too-big shoes. 'You aren't planning on going far, are you?'

'Gotta,' said Granny, 'Hurts bad to hear the words my Luke yells at his own firstborn. Even worse, it makes my blood run cold to hear ya scream right back when he can strike out and end what ain't hardly begun yet. Girl, why do ya have to answer back?'

'You know, you know,' I whispered. 'Pa hates me, Granny, and I don't know why. Why does he hate me so much?'

There was enough moonlight coming through a window to allow me to see her dear old wrinkled face.

'Yes, yes, time ya knew,' she mumbled, tossing me a heavy black shawl she'd knitted herself, then wrapping her own narrow, bent shoulders in another just as dark and drab. She led me to the door, swung it open, letting in the cold wind before she shut it again. In their bed beyond the tattered, faded red curtain, Ma and Pa grumbled as if the wind half-woke them. 'We got a trip to make, ya and me, down to where we plant our kinfolk. Been trying to make it with ya for many a year. Can't keep putting it off. Time runs out, it does. Then it's too late.'

So on this cold, snowy, miserable, dark night she and I set off through the black pine woods. A solid sheet of ice lay rippling on the river, and the wolves sounded closer now. 'Yep, Annie Brandywine Casteel sure knows how to keep secrets,' Granny said as if to herself. 'Not many do, ya know, not many born like me . . . ya listening, girl, are ya?'

'Can't help but hear you, Granny. You're shouting directly in my ear.'

She had me by the hand, leading me a far way from home. Crazy to be out here, it was. Why, on this freezing winter's night, was she going to give up one of her precious secrets, and to me? Why me? But I loved her enough to assist her down the rough mountain trail. It seemed like miles we travelled in the dark cold of night, that old moon overhead shining down on us with evil intentions.

The treat she had in store for me was a graveyard, stark and eerie in the light of the pale, bluish, winter moon. The wind blew wild and fierce and snapped her thin white hair and blended it with my own before she spoke again. 'Onliest thing I can give ya, child, onliest thing worth having, is what I'm gonna tell ya.'

'Couldn't you have told me in the cabin?'

'Nah,' she scoffed, stubborn as she could sometimes be, set in her ways like an old tree with too many roots. 'Ya wouldn't pay no attention if I told ya there. Here, ya'll always remember.'

She hesitated as her eyes fixed on a slim little tombstone. She raised her arm and pointed her gnarled finger at that granite headstone. I stared at it and tried to read what was engraved there. How very odd for Granny to bring me here during the night, where maybe the ghosts of those who lay here roamed about looking for living bodies to inhabit.

'Ya gotta forgive yer pa for being what he is,' intoned Granny, huddling close to me for warmth. 'He's what he is, and he can't help it no more than the sun can help from rising or setting, no more than the skunks can help from making their stinks, and no more than ya can help being what ya are.'

Oh, that was an easy thing for Granny to say. Old people didn't remember what it was like to be young and afraid.

'Let's go home,' I said, shivering and pulling at Granny. 'I've heard and read tales about what goes on in graveyards on nights when the moon is full and the hour is after midnight.'

'Know better than to be scared of dead things that can't move or speak.'

Yet she drew me tighter into her embrace and forced me to stare again at the narrow sunken grave. 'Ya just listen and don't say nothing till I'm finished. I got a tale to tell that's gonna make ya feel better. There's a good reason why yer pa speaks mean when he looks at ya. He don't really hate ya. In my mind I done put the pieces together and when my Luke looks at ya he sees *not* ya, but someone else . . . and chile, he really is a loving man. A good man underneath it all. Why, he had a first wife he loved so much he near died when she did. He met her down in Atlanta. He was seventeen and she was only fourteen and three days, so she told me later.' Her thin voice dropped an octave. 'Beautiful as an angel, she was, and oh, yer pa did love her so. Why, he swept her off her feet, when she was running away from home. Heading for Texas, she was. Running from Boston. Had a fancy suitcase with her, full of clothes the likes of what ya've never seen. All kinds of pretty stuff in that suitcase, suits an silky things, silvery brush, comb and mirror, and rings for her fingers, and jewels for her ears, and she come here to live, because she went and made the mistake of marrying up with a man not her kind . . . because she loved him.'

'Granny, I've never heard of Pa having a first wife. I thought Ma was his first and only wife.'

'Didn't I tell ya to stay quiet? Ya let me finish telling this in my own way. . . She was from a rich Boston family. Came to live with Luke and Toby and me. I didn't want her when she come. Didn't like her at first. Knew she wouldn't last, right from the first, knew that. Too good for the likes of us, and the hills, and the hardships. Thought we had bathrooms, she did. Shocked her when she knew she'd have to trek to the outhouse, and sit on a board with two holes. Then durn if Luke didn't go and build her a pretty lil' outhouse all her own, painted it white, he did, and she put in fancy rolled paper on a spindle, and even offered to let me use her pink shop-bought paper. Her *bathroom*, she called it. She hugged and kissed Luke for doing that for her.'

'You mean Pa wasn't mean to her like he is to Ma?'

'Shut up, girl. Yer making me lose track. . . . she came, she stole my heart, maybe Toby's, too. She tried so hard to do her best. Helping out with the cooking. Trying to make our cabin pretty. And Toby and me, we gave them our bed, so they could start their babies in the right way and not on the floor. She'd have slept on the floor, she would have, but I wouldn't let her. All Casteels are made in beds . . . I'm hoping and praying anyways that's true. Well . . . one day she's laughing and happy because she's gonna have a baby. My Luke's baby. And I feel so sorry, so blessed sorry. Was always hoping she'd go back to where she come from before the hills took her, the way they do delicate folks. But she made him happy when she was here. Made him happier than he's been since.' Granny stopped talking abruptly.

'How did she die, Granny? Is this her grave?'

She sighed before she continued. 'Yer pa was only eighteen when she passed on, and she was still only fourteen when he had to bury her in this cold ground and walk away and leave her alone in the night. He knew she hated the cold nights without him. Why, chile, he laid on her grave all the first night to keep her warm, and it was February. . . and that's my tale of her who came as an angel to the hills, to live and love yer pa, and make him happier than he's ever been, and likely he'll never be that happy again, from the looks of it.'

'But why did you have to bring me out here to tell me all of this, Granny? You could have told me in the cabin. Even if it is a sad and kind sweet story . . . still, Pa's meaner than hell, and she must have taken all the best of him into the grave with her, and left only the worst for the rest of us. Why didn't she teach him how to love others? Granny, I wish she'd never come! Not ever come! Then Pa would love Ma, and he'd love me, and not her so much.'

'Oh,' said Granny, appearing stunned. 'What's wrong with ya, girl, what's wrong? Ain't ya done guessed? That girl that yer pa called his angel, she was yer ma! She's the one who birthed ya, and by the time ya come, she could hardly speak . . . and she named ya Heaven Leigh, she did. And ya can't truly say, can ya, that ya ain't proud of that name that everybody says suits ya just fine, just fine.'

I forgot the wind. I forgot my hair snapping around my face. Forgot everything in the wonder of finding out just what and who I was.

When the moon slipped from behind a dark cloud, a random beam of light shone for an instant on the engraved name:

Angel
Beloved wife of Thomas Luke Casteel

Strange how it made me feel to see that grave. 'But where did Pa find Sarah? And how did he do it so quickly?'

Granny, as if eager to spill it all out while she had the chance, began to talk faster. 'Well, yer pa needed a wife to fill his empty bed. He hated his lonely nights, and men gets cravings, chile, physical cravings you're gonna find out about one day when you're old enough. He wanted a wife to give him what his angel had, and she tried, give Sarah credit for that. She made ya a good mother, treated ya like ya were her own. Nursed ya, loved ya. And Sarah gave Luke her body willingly enough, but she had nothing of his angel's spirit to give him, and that leaves him still yearning for the girl who would have made him a better man. He was better then, chile Heaven – even if ya don't believe it. Why, in the days when yer angel ma were alive he'd set out for work early each morning, driving his old pick-up truck down to Winnerrow where he was learnig all about carpentry and how to build houses and such. He used to come home full of nice talk about building us all a new house down in the valley, and when he had that house, he were gonna work the land, raise cows, pigs, and horses . . . yer pa, he's always had a keenness for animals. Loves 'em, he does, like ya do, chile Heaven. Ya get that from him.'

Odd how I felt when Granny took me back to the cabin, and from a clutter of old junk, and many old cardboard boxes in which we kept our pitifully few clothes, she dragged out something wrapped about in an old quilt. From that she extracted an elegant suitcase, the kind mountain-folks like us could never afford.

'Yours,' she whispered so the others wouldn't wake up and intrude on this most private moment. 'Belonged to your ma. Promised her I'd give it to ya when the time were right. Figure it's as right as it'll ever be tonight, now . . . so look, girl, look. See what kind of ma ya had.'

As if a dead mother could be compressed and put into a fancy, expensive suitcase!

But when I looked, I gasped.

There before me in the dim, firelit room were the most beautiful clothes I'd ever seen. Such delicate lacy things I hadn't dreamed existed . . . and at the very bottom I found something long, and carefully wrapped in dozens of sheets of tissue paper. I could tell from Granny's expression she was tense, watching me closely, as if to savour my reaction.

In the dim glow of the woodfire burning I stared at a doll. A doll? What I'd least expected to find. I gazed and gazed at the doll with the silvery-gold hair bound up in a fancy way. She wore a wedding veil, the filmy mist flowing out from a tiny, jewelled cap. Her face was exceptionally pretty, with beautifully shaped, bowed lips, the upper cleft ridge fitting so precisely into the bottom centre indentation. Her long dress was made of white lace, lavishly embroidered with tiny pearls and sparkling beads. A bride doll . . . veil and everything. Even her white shoes were lace and white satin, with sheer stockings fastened to a tiny suspender belt, as I saw when I took a peek under the skirts and veil.

'It's her. Yer ma. Luke's angel that was named Leigh,' whispered Granny, 'just the way yer ma looked when she came here after she married up with yer pa. Last thing she said before she died was, "Give what I brought with me to my little girl . . ." And now I have.'

Yes, now she had.

And in doing so, she'd changed the course of my life.

One

The Way It Used to Be

If Jesus died almost two thousand years ago to save us all from the worst we had in us, he'd failed in our area, except on Sundays between the hours of ten a.m. and noon. At least in my opinion.

But what was my opinion? Worthy as onion peelings, I thought, as I ponderd how Pa had married Sarah two months after my mother died in childbirth – and he'd loved his 'angel' so much. And four months after I was born and my mother was buried, Sarah gave birth to the son Pa had so wanted when I had come along and ended my mother's brief stay on earth.

I was too young to remember the birth of this first son, who was christened Thomas Luke Casteel the Second, and they put him, so I've been told, in the cradle with me, and like twins we were rocked, nursed, held, but not equally loved. No one had to tell me that.

I loved Tom, with his fire-red hair inherited from Sarah, and his flashing green eyes, also inherited from his mother. There was nothing in him at all to remind me of Pa, except later he did grow very tall.

After hearing Granny's tale of my true mother on the eve of my tenth birthday, I determined never, so help me God, never would I tell my brother Tom any different from what he already believed, that Heaven Leigh Casteel was his own true whole-blooded sister. I wanted to keep that special something that made us almost one person. His thoughts and my thoughts were very much alike because we'd shared the same cradle, and had communicated silently soon after we were born, and that had to make us special. Being special was of great importance to both of us, I guess because we feared so much we weren't.

Sarah stood six feet tall without shoes – an Amazon mate very suitable for a man as tall and powerful as Pa. Sarah was never sick. According to Granny (whom Tom sometimes jokingly called Wisdom Mouth), the birth of Tom gave Sarah a mature bustline, so full it appeared matronly when she was still fourteen.

'And,' informed Granny, 'even after giving birth, Sarah would get up soon as it was over, pick up what chore she'd left unfinished, just as if she hadn't undergone the most awful ordeal we women have to suffer through without complaint. Why, Sarah could cook while trying to encourage a newborn baby to suckle.' Yeah, thought I, her robust good health must be her main attraction for Pa. He didn't seem to admire Sarah's type of beauty much, but at least she wasn't likely to die in childbirth and leave him in a pit of black despair.

One year after Tom came Fanny, with her jet-black hair like Pa's, her dark blue eyes turning almost black before she was a year old. An Indian girl was our Fanny, browner than a berry, but very seldom happy about anything.

Four years after Fanny came Keith, named after Sarah's long-dead father. Keith had the sweetest, pale auburn hair, you just had to love him right from the beginning – especially when he turned out to be very quiet, hardly any bother at all, not wailing, screaming, and demanding all the time as Fanny had – and still did. Eventually Keith's blue eyes turned topaz, his skin rivalled the peaches-and-cream complexion lots of people said I had, though I didn't truly know since I wasn't given much to peering into our cracked and poorly reflecting mirror.

Keith grew to be an exceptionally good little boy who appreciated beauty so much that when a new baby came along the year after he was born, he would sit for hours and hours just gazing at the delicate little girl who was sickly from the very beginning. Pretty as a tiny doll was this new little sister that Sarah allowed me to name, and Jane she became, since at that time I'd seen Jane on a magazine cover, too pretty to believe.

Jane had soft wisps of pale golden-red hair, huge aquamarine eyes, long, dark, curling lashes that she'd flutter as she lay discontentedly in the cradle gazing at Keith. Occasionally Keith would reach to rock the cradle, and that would make her smile, a smile of such disarming sweetness you'd do anything just to see that smile come out like sunshine after the rain.

After Jane was born, she began to dominate our lives. To bring a smile to Jane's angelic face became the loving and dutiful obligation of all of us. To make her laugh instead of wail was my own special delight. Time to rejoice when Jane could smile instead of whine from mysterious aches and pains she couldn't name. And in this, as in everything else, what I enjoyed doing was what Fanny had to spoil.

'Ya give her to me!' screamed Fanny, running to kick my shins with her long skinny legs before she darted away and called from a safe place in our dirt yard, 'She's *our* Jane – not yers! Not Tom's! Not Keith's! Ours! Everything here is *ours*, not yers alone! Heaven Leigh Casteel!'

From then on Jane became *Our Jane*, and was called that until eventually all of us forgot that once upon a time our youngest sweetest, frailest, had only one name.

I knew about names and what they could do.

My own name was both a blessing and a curse. I tried to make myself believe such a 'spiritual' name had to be a blessing – why, who else in the whole wide world had a name like Heaven Leigh? No one, no one, whispered the little bluebird of happiness who lived now and then in my brain, singing me to sleep and telling me that everything, in the long run, would work out just fine . . . just fine. Trouble was, I had an old black crow roosting in my brain as well, telling me such a name tempted fate to do its worst.

Then there was Pa.

In my secret and putaway heart there were times when I wanted more than anything in the world to love the lonely father who sat so often staring into space, looking as if life had cheated him. He had ebony-dark hair, inherited from a true Indian ancestor who'd stolen a white girl and mated with her. His eyes were as black as his hair, and his skin kept a deep bronze colour winter and summer; his beard didn't show through shadowy dark the way most beards did on men with such dark hair. His shoulders were wonderfully wide. Why, you could watch him in the yard swinging an axe, chopping wood, and see the most complicated display of muscles all big and strong, so that Sarah, bending over a washtub, would look up and stare at him with such love and yearning in her eyes it would almost break my heart to know he never seemed to care whether or not she admired and loved him, or cried every time he didn't come home until early morning.

Sometimes his moody, melancholy air made me doubt my mean thoughts. I watched him the spring when I was thirteen, knowing about my own true mother, and saw him sitting slouched in a chair, staring into space, as if dreaming of something; I, in the shadows, longed to reach out and touch his cheek, wondering if it would be bristly – I'd never touched his face. What would he do if I dared? Slap my face? Yell, shout, no doubt that's exactly what he'd do – and yet, yet, there was in me a deep need to love him and be loved by him. All the time that aching need was there, waiting to ignite and burst into a bonfire of love and affection.

If only he'd see me, do or say one thing to encourage me to believe he did love me at least a little.

But he never even looked at me. He never spoke to me. He treated me as if I weren't there.

But when Fanny came flying up the rickety steps of the porch and hurled herself onto his lap, shouting out how glad she was to see him, he kissed her. My heart ached to see the way he cuddled her close so he could stroke her long, shiny, dark hair. 'How ya been, Fanny girl?'

'Missing ya, Pa! Hate it when ya don't come home. Ain't good here without ya! Please, Pa, this time stay!'

'Sweet,' he murmered, 'nice to be missed – maybe that's why I stay away.'

Oh, the pain my father delivered when he stroked Fanny's hair and ignored mine. Worse than the pain he gave from the slaps and ugly words when once in a while I made him see me, and forced him to respond to me. Deliberately I strode forward, coming out of the shadows into the light, carrying balanced on my hips a huge basket of clothes I'd just taken from the rope lines and folded. Fanny smirked my way. Pa didn't move his eyes to indicate he knew how hard I worked, though a muscle near his lips twitched. I didn't speak but passed on, as if he hadn't been gone two weeks and I'd seen him only minutes ago. It did shrivel me some to be ignored, even as I ignored him.

Fanny never did any work. Sarah and I did that. Granny did the talking; Grandpa whittled; and Pa came and went as he pleased, selling booze for the moonshiners, and sometimes helping them make it, but it was outwitting the Federals that gave Pa his greatest pleasure, and made him his biggest money – according to Sarah, who was terrified he'd be caught and thrown in jail, because the professional liquor brewers didn't care for the competition which overproof alchohol gave them. Often he'd go and stay away for a week or two, and when he was gone Sarah allowed her hair to go dirty, and her meals were worse than usual. But when Pa walked in the door and threw her a careless smile or word, she came alive, to hurry and bathe, to put on the best she had (a choice of three dresses, none really good). It was her fervent desire to have makeup to wear when Pa was home, and a green silk dress to match the colour of her eyes. Oh, it was easy to see that Sarah had all her hopes and dreams pinned on that day when real cosmetics and a green silk dress came into her life and made Pa love her as much as he'd loved that poor dead girl who'd been my mother.

Our cabin near the sky was made of old wood full of knotholes to let in the cold and heat, or let out our cold or heat, whichever would make us most miserable. It had never known paint, and never would. Our roof was made of tin that had turned rusty long before I was born, and had wept a million tears to stain the old silvery wood. We had drainpipes and rain barrels to catch the water in which we took baths and washed our hair once we had heated it on the cast-iron stove we nicknamed Ole Smokey. It belched and spat out so much vile smoke we were always half crying and coughing when we were shut up in there with the windows down and the door to the outside closed.

Across the front of our mountain cabin was the obligatory front porch. Each spring saw Granny and Grandpa leave the cabin, to decorate our sagging, dilapidated porch with their twin rockers. Granny knitting, crochetting, weaving, making braided rugs, as Grandpa whittled. Sometimes Grandpa fiddled for the barn dances held once a week, but the older Grandpa grew the less he liked to fiddle and the more he liked to whittle.

Inside were two small rooms, with a tattered curtain to form a kind of flimsy door for the 'bedroom.' Our stove not only heated our place but, also cooked our food, baked our biscuits, heated our bathwater. Once a week before we went to church on Sundays, we took baths and washed our hair.

Next to Ole Smokey sat an ancient kitchen cabinet outfitted with metal bins for flour, sugar, coffee, and tea. We couldn't afford real sugar, coffee, or tea but we did use gallon cans of lard for our gravy and biscuits. When we were extraordinarily lucky we had honey for our wild berries. When we were blessed beyond belief we had a cow to give us milk, and always there were chickens, ducks and geese to supply us with eggs, and fresh meat on Sundays. Hogs and pigs roamed at will, to snuggle down under our house and keep us awake with all their bad dreams. Inside, Pa's hunting hounds had the run of our home, since all mountain folk knew dogs were durn important when it came to supplying a steady flow of meat other than domestic fowl.

Animals we had in plenty when you counted the stray cats and dogs who came to give us hundreds of kittens and puppies. Why, our dirt yard was full of wandering animals, and anything else that could stand the clutter and noise of living with Casteels – the scum of the hills.

In what we called our bedroom was one big brass bed with a saggy, old, stained mattress over coiled springs that squeaked and squealed whenever there was activity on that bed. Sometimes what went on in there was embarrassingly close and loud; the curtain did little to muffle sound.

In town and in school they called us hill scum, hill filth, and scumbags. Hillbillies was the nicest thing they ever called us. Of all the folks in the mountain shacks, there wasn't one family more despised than ours, the Casteels, the worst of the lot. Despised not only by valley folk but by our own kind, for some reason I never understood. But . . . we were the family with five Casteel sons in prison for major and minor crimes. No wonder Granny cried at night; all her sons had been so disappointing. She had only her youngest left, Pa, and if he gave her joy I never knew it. On him she'd placed all her expectations, waiting for that wonderful someday when he proved to the world that Casteels were not the worst scum of the hills.

Now, I've heard tell, though it's hard to believe, that there are kids in the world who hate school, but Tom and I couldn't wait for Mondays to roll around, just so we could escape the confines of our small, mountain cabin with its smelly, cramped two rooms, its far walk to the stinking old outhouse.

Our school was made of red brick and sat smack in the heart of Winnerrow, the nearest valley village, set deep in the Willies. We walked seven miles to and seven miles fro as if they were nothing, always with Tom close at my side, Fanny tagging along behind, meaner than ten vipers, with Pa's black eyes and Pa's own temper. She was pretty as a picture, but mad at the world because her family was so 'stinking rotten poor,' as Fanny succinctly put it.

'. . . and we don't live in a pretty, painted house like they do in Winnerrow, where they got real bathrooms,' Fanny shrilled, always complaining about things the rest of us accepted lest we be miserable. 'Inside bathrooms, can ya imagine? Heard tell some houses got two, each with hot and cold running water, can ya believe such as that?'

'Can believe most anything about Winnerrow,' answered Tom, skipping a pebble over the river water that was our bathing hole in the summers. Without that river running we'd have been much dirtier than we were. The river and its little ponds, pools, and freshwater springs made life better in a thousand ways, making up a little for all that would have been intolerable but for cool, tasty, spring water, and a swimming hole as good as any city pool.

'Heaven, ya ain't listening!' yelled Fanny, who had to have centre stage all of the time. 'And what's more, they got kitchen sinks in Winnerrow. Double sinks! Central heating . . . Tom, what's central heating?'

'Fanny, we got the same thing in Ole Smokey that sets clean smack in the middle of our cabin.'

'Tom,' I said, 'I don't think that's really what central heating means.'

'As far as I'm concerned, that's exactly what I want it to mean.'

If I seldom agreed with Fanny about anything else, I did agree that it would be paradise unlimited to live in a painted house with four or five rooms, to have all the hot and cold water at one's will just by turning on a tap, and a toilet that flushed.

Oh, gosh, to think of central heating, double sinks, and flushing toilets made me realize just how poor we really were. I didn't like to think about it, to feel sorry for myself, to be inundated with worries about Keith and Our Jane. Now, if Fanny would only wash her clothes, that would help a little. But Fanny would never do anything, not even sweep the front porch, though she was pretty crazy about sweeping the dirt yard free of leaves. Because it was a fun thing to do, was my sour reasoning. Out there she could watch Tom playing ball with his buddies, while Sarah and I did the work, and Granny did the talking.

Granny had good reasons for not working as hard as Sarah. Granny had her own problems getting up once she was down, and getting down once she was up. The time it took for her to get from here to there seemed an eternity as she held on to what furniture we had. There just wasn't enough furniture to take Granny everywhere she wanted to go easily.

Sarah taught me when I was old enough, and Granny was too feeble to help (and Fanny flatly refused to do anything even when she was three, four, or five), how to change babies, how to feed them, give them baths in a small metal washtub. Sarah taught me a thousand things. By the time I was eight, I knew how to make biscuits, melt the lard for the gravy, add the flour with water before I blended it into the hot grease. She taught me how to clean windows and scrub floors and use the washboard to force dirt out of filthy clothes. She also taught Tom to do as much as he could to help me, even if other boys did call him a sissy for doing 'women's work.' If Tom had not loved me so much, he might have objected more.

A week came when Pa was home every night. Sarah was as happy as a bluebird, humming under her breath and shyly glancing at Pa often, as if he'd come courting and wasn't just a husband tired of running moonshine. Maybe somewhere out on a lonely highway a Federal revenue man was waiting for Luke Casteel, ready to pitch him into jail along with his brothers.

Out in the yard I scrubbed away on dirty clothes, as usual, while Fanny skipped and Pa pitched the ball for Tom to swing at with his one and only plaything, a bat left over from Pa's childhood. Keith and Our Jane hung around me, wanting to hang up the washed clothes – neither one could reach the rope lines.

'Fanny, why don't you help Heavenly?' yelled Tom, throwing me a worried glance.

'Don't want to!' was Fanny's answer.

'Pa, why don't you make Fanny help Heavenly?'

Pa hurled the ball so hard it almost hit Tom, who took a wild swing and, off balance, fell to the ground. 'Don't ever pay attention to women's work,' said Pa with a gruff laugh. He turned toward the house, in time to hear Sarah bellow our evening meal was ready: 'Come and get it!'

Painfully Granny rose from her porch rocker. Grandpa struggled to rise from his. 'Getting old is worse than I thought it would be,' groaned Granny once she was on her feet and trying to make it to the table before all the food was gone. Our Jane ran to her to be led by the hand, for Granny could do that if not much else. She groaned again. 'Makes me think that dying ain't so bad after all.'

'Stop saying that!' stormed Pa. 'I'm home to enjoy myself, not hear talk about death and dying!' And in no time at all, almost before Granny and Grandpa were comfortable in their chairs at the table, he got up, finished with the meal that had taken Sarah hours to prepare, and out into the yard he went, jumping into his pickup truck to head to God knows where.

Sarah, wearing a dress she'd ripped apart, then sewn back together in a different fashion, with new sleeves and pockets added from her bag of scrap fabrics, stood in the doorway staring out, softly crying. Her freshly washed hair scented with the last of her lilac water shone rich and red in the moonlight, and all for nothing when those girls in Shirley's Place wore real French pefume, and real makeup, not just the rice powder that Sarah used to take the shine from her nose.

I determined I was not going to be another Sarah or another angel found in Atlanta. Not me. Not ever me.

Two

School and Church

The cock-a-doodle-do of our solitary rooster with his harem of thirty hens woke us all. The sun was only a hazy rim of rose in the eastern sky. With the crow of the cock came the mumbling of Ma waking up, of Granny and Grandpa turning over, of Our Jane beginning to wail because her tummy always ached in the mornings. Fanny sat up and rubbed at her eyes. 'Ain't gonna go to school today,' she informed grouchily.

Keith sprang immediately to his feet and ran to fetch Our Jane a cold biscuit she could nibble on to calm those hunger pains that hurt her more than they hurt any of the rest of us. Placated, she sat on her floor pallet and nibbled on her biscuit, her pretty eyes watching each one of us hopefully for the milk she'd soon be crying for.

'Hey, Ma,' said Tom coming in the door, 'cow's gone. Went out early to milk her . . . she's gone.'

'Damn Luke to hell and back!' shrieked Sarah. 'He knows we need that cow for milk!'

'Ma, maybe Pa didn't sell her. Somebody could have stolen her.'

'He sold her,' she said flatly. 'Said yesterday he might have to. Go and see if ya can round up that goat.'

'Milk, milk, milk!' wailed Our Jane.

I hurried to Our Jane, drawing her into my arms. 'Don't cry, darling. Why in ten minutes flat you'll be drinking the best kind of milk, fresh from a nanny goat.'

Our morning meal consisted of hot biscuits made fresh each day, covered with lard gravy. Today we were also having grits. Our Jane wanted her milk more than she wanted anything else. 'Where is it, Hev-lee?' she kept asking.

'It's coming,' said I, hoping and praying it was.

It took Tom half an hour to come back with a pail of milk. His face was flushed and hot-looking, as if he'd run a long, long way. 'Here ya are, Our Jane,' he said with triumph, pouring milk into her glass, and then into the pitcher so Keith could enjoy the milk as well.

'Where'd ya get it?' asked Ma suspiciously, sniffing the milk. 'That goat belongs now to Skeeter Burl, ya know that . . . and he's mean, real mean.'

'What he don't know won't hurt him,' answered Tom, sitting down to dig into his food. 'When Our Jane and Keith need milk, I go stealing. And yer right, Ma. Our cow is now pastured in Skeeter Burl's meadow.'

Sarah threw me a hard look. 'Well, that's the wager, ain't it? And yer pa lost, like always.'

Pa was a gambling man, and when Pa lost, we all lost, not only the cow. Each day for the past several weeks, one by one our barnyard fowl had been disappearing. I tried to convince myself that they'd come back once Pa had a winning streak. 'I'll collect the eggs,' called Sarah, heading for the door while I dressed for school. 'Got to before he wagers all our hens! One day we'll wake up to no eggs, no nothing!'

Sarah was given to pessimism, whereas Tom and I were always thinking somehow our lives would turn out fine, even without cows, goats, or chickens and ducks.

It seemed to take forever for Our Jane to grow old enough to go with us to Winnerrow and attend the first class. But finally, this autumn, she was six, and she was going if Tom and I had to drag her there every day. And that's what we had to do, literally drag her along, holding fast to her small hand so she couldn't escape and dash back to the cabin. Even as I tried to tug her along at a faster pace, she dragged her small feet, resisting in every way she could, as Keith encouraged and assured her, 'It's not so bad, not so bad,' and that's all he could say in favour of school. The cabin was where Our Jane wanted to stay, with Sarah, with her ragged old doll with the stuffing half fallen out. Right from the beginning she hated school, the hard seats without cushions, sitting still, having to pay attention, though she loved being with other children her age. Our Jane's attendance at school was irregular because of her frail health and her determination to stay home with her ma.

Our Jane was a dear, darling doll, but she could wear on your nerves with her caterwauling, and all the food she spat up that smelled sickly sour. I turned to scold her, knowing that she was going to make us late, and that again everyone in the school would mock us for not even knowing how to tell time. Our Jane smiled, stretched out her frail, slender arms, and immediately my chastising words froze unspoken on my tongue. I picked her up and lavished on her pretty face all the kisses she had to have.

'Feeling better, Our Jane?'

'Yes,' she whispered in the smallest voice possible, 'but don't like walking. Makes my legs hurt.'

'Give her to me,' said Tom, reaching to take her from my arms. Even Tom, loud-mouthed, brash, and tough, proud to be all boy, turned sweet and tender with Our Jane. Definitely my smallest sister was gifted in ways of grabbing your heart and never giving it back.

Tom held her in his arms, staring down at her pretty little face, all screwed up to yell if he dared to put her down. 'You're just like a tiny, pretty doll,' Tom said to her before he turned to me. 'You know, Heavenly, even if Pa can't afford to give you or Fanny dolls for Christmas or birthdays, you have something even better, Our Jane.'

I could have disagreed with that. Dolls could be put away and forgotten. No one could ever forget Our Jane. Our Jane saw to it that you didn't forget her.

Keith and Our Jane had a special relationship, as if they too, were 'heartfelt twins.' Sturdy and strong, Keith ran beside Tom, staring up at his small sister with adoration, just as he ran home to wait on his little sister who'd immediately smile through her tears when he turned over to her whatever she wanted. And she wanted whatever he had. Keith, kindly, sweetly, gave in to her demands, never complaining even when too many 'wants' of Our Jane would have had Tom openly rebellious.

'You're a dope, Tom, and ya too, Keith,' stated Fanny. 'Durn if I would carry no girl who can walk as good as I can.'

Our Jane began to wail. 'Fanny don't like me . . . Fanny don't like me . . . Fanny don't like me . . . Fanny don't like me . . . ' and it might have gone on all the way to school if Fanny hadn't reluctantly reached out and taken Our Jane from Tom's arms. 'Aw, ya ain't so bad. But why can't ya learn to walk, Our Jane, why can't ya?'

'Don't wanna walk,' said Our Jane, hugging her arms tight around Fanny's neck, and kissing Fanny's cheek.

'See,' said Fanny proudly, 'she loves me best . . . not ya, Heaven, nor ya, Tom . . . loves me best, don't ya, Our Jane?'

Disconcerted, Our Jane looked down at Keith, at me, at Tom, then screamed: 'Put me down! Down! Down!'

Our Jane was dropped into a mud puddle! She screamed, then started to cry, and Tom chased after Fanny to give her a good wallop. I tried to calm Our Jane and dry her off with a rag I had for a handkerchief. Keith broke into tears. 'Don't cry, Keith. She's not hurt . . . are you, darling? And see, now you're all dry, and Fanny will say she's sorry . . . but you really should try to walk. It's good for your legs. Now catch hold of Keith's hand, and we'll all sing as we go to school.'

Magic words. If Our Jane didn't like walking, she did like to sing as much as we all did, and together she, Keith, and I sang until we caught up with Tom, who had chased Fanny into the schoolyard. Six boys had formed a line for Fanny to hide behind – and Tom was outclassed by boys much older and taller. Fanny laughed, not at all sorry she'd dropped Our Jane and soiled her best school dress so it clung damply to her thin legs.

With Keith waiting patiently, in the school rest room I again dried off Our Jane; then I saw Keith to his classroom, pried him loose from Our Jane, then led Our Jane to the first class. Seated at the table with five other little girls her age, she was the smallest there. What a shame all the other girls had nicer clothes, though not one had such pretty hair, or such a sweet smile. 'See you later, darling,' I called. Her huge scared eyes stared woefully back at me.

Tom was waiting for me outside Miss Deale's classroom. Together we entered. Every student in there turned to stare at our clothes and our feet; whether we were clean or dirty, it didn't matter. They always snickered. Day in and day out, we had to wear the same clothes, and every day they looked us over scornfully. It always hurt, but we both tried to ignore them as we took our seats near the back of the class.

Seated in front of our classroom was the most wonderful woman in the entire world – the very kind of beautiful lady I hoped and prayed I would be like when I grew up. While all her students turned to mock us, Miss Marianne Deale lifted her head to smile her welcome. Her smile couldn't have been warmer if we'd come adorned in the best clothes the world had to offer. She knew we had to walk farther than any of the others, and that Tom and I were responsible for seeing that Keith and Our Jane made it safely to school. She said a million nice things with her eyes. With some other teacher perhaps Tom and I wouldn't have developed such a love for school. She was the one who made our school days a real adventure, a quest for knowledge that would take us, eventually, out of the mountains, out of a poverty-ridden shack, into the bigger, richer world.

Tom and my eyes met, both of us thrilled to be again in the presence of our radiant teacher who had already given us a bit of the world when she inspired in us the love of reading. I was nearer the window than Tom, since looking outside always gave Tom compelling itches to play hooky, despite his desire to finish school and earn a scholarship that would take him through college. If we couldn't win our way to college with good marks, we'd work our way through. We had it all planned. I sighed as I sat. Each day we managed to go to school was another small battle won, taking us closer to our goals. Mine was to be a teacher just like Miss Deale.

My idol's hair was very much the texture and colour of Our Jane's, pale, reddish blonde; her eyes were light blue, her figure slim and curvy. Miss Deale was from Baltimore and spoke with a different accent than any of her students. Truthfully, I thought Miss Deale was absolutely perfect. Miss Deale glanced at a few empty seats before she looked again at the clock, sighing as she stood up and made the roll call. 'Let us all stand and salute the flag,' she said, 'and before we sit again, we will all say silent prayers of gratitude to be alive and healthy and young, with all the world waiting for us to discover, and to improve.'

Boy, if she didn't know how to start the day off right no one did. Just to see her, to be with her, gave both Tom and me reason to feel the future did hold something special for both of us. She had respect for her students, even us in our shabby clothes, but she never gave an inch when it came to order, neatness, politeness.

First we had to hand in our homework. Since our parents couldn't afford to buy our books, we had to use the schoolbooks to complete our homework during school hours. Sometimes this was just too much, especially when the days grew shorter and darkness fell before we reached home.

I was scribbling like mad from the chalkboard when Miss Deale stopped at my desk and whispered, 'Heaven, you and Tom please stay after class. I have something to discuss with the two of you.'

'Have we done something wrong?' I asked worriedly.

'No, of course not. You always ask that. Heaven, just because I single out you and Tom does not always mean I plan to reprimand you.'

The only times Miss Deale seemed to be disappointed in either Tom or me was when we turned sullen and quiet from her questioning about how we lived. We became defensive about both Ma and Pa, not wanting her to know how poorly we were housed, and how pitiful were our meals compared to what we heard the city kids describing.

Lunchtimes in school were the worst. Half the valley kids brought brown lunch bags, and the other half ate in the cafeteria. Only we from the hills brought nothing, not even the change it took to buy a hot dog and a drink. In our high mountain home we ate breakfast at dawn, a second meal before darkness drove us into bed. Never lunch.

'What do you think she wants?' Tom asked as we met briefly during the lunch hour, before he went to play ball and I went out to join the skipping.

'Don't know.'

Miss Deale was busy checking papers as Tom and I hung back after school, worried about Keith and Our Jane, who wouldn't know what to do if we weren't there when they were dismissed from their classrooms. 'You explain,' Tom whispered, and then dashed off to collect Keith and Our Jane. We couldn't depend on Fanny to look out for them.

Suddenly Miss Deale looked up. 'Oh, I'm sorry, Heaven . . . have you been standing there long?'

'Only a few seconds,' I lied, for it had been more than that. 'Tom ran to fetch Our Jane and Keith and bring them here. They'll be afraid if one or the other of us doesn't show up to walk them home.'

'What about Fanny? Doesn't she do her share?'

'Well,' I began falteringly, trying to be protective of Fanny just because she was my sister, 'sometimes Fanny gets distracted and forgets.'

Miss Deale smiled. 'I realize you have a long walk home, so I won't wait for Tom to return. I've spoken to the school-board members about the two of you, hoping to convince them to allow you to take books home to study, but they are adamant, and said if they give you two special privileges, they will have to give all the students free books. So I am going to allow you to use my books.'

I stared at her in surprise. 'But won't you need them?'

'No . . . there are others I can use. From now on, you can use them, and please take as many books from the library as you care to read in one week. Of course you'll have to respect those books and keep them clean, and return them when they're due.'

I was so thrilled I could have shouted. 'All the books we can read in a week? Miss Deale, we won't have arms strong enough to carry so many!'

She laughed, and, strangely, tears came to her eyes. 'I could have guessed you'd say something like that.' She beamed at Tom as he came in carrying Our Jane, who appeared exhausted, and leading Keith by the hand. 'Tom, I think you already have your arms full, and won't be able to carry home books.'

Dazed-looking, he stared at her. 'Ya mean we can take home books? Not have to pay for them?'

'That's right, Tom. And pick up a few for Our Jane and Keith, and even Fanny.'

'Fanny won't read 'em,' said Tom, his eyes lighting up, 'but Heaven and I sure will!'

We went home that day with five books to read, and four to study. Keith did his bit by carrying two books so neither Tom nor I would refuse to carry Our Jane when she grew tired. It worried me to see how white she grew after only a few steps uphill.

Tagging along behind came Fanny with her boyfriends swarming like bees aroung the sweetest flower. I had only a devoted brother. Keith lagged about twenty yards behind Fanny and her friends, reluctant to stay with us, but not for the same reasons as Fanny. Keith was in love with nature, with the sights, sounds, and smells of earth, wind, forest, and, most of all animals. I glanced behind to check, and saw he was so absorbed in studying the bark of a tree he didn't hear me calling his name. 'Keith, hurry up!'

He ran a short way before he stopped to pick up a dead bird, examining it with careful hands and obsevant eyes. If we didn't constantly remind him where he was he would be left far behind, and never find his way home. Strange how absentminded Keith was, never noticing where he was, only where the objects of his interests grew, lived, or visited.

'Which is heavier, Tom, the books or Our Jane?' I asked, lugging along six.

'The books,' he said quickly, setting down our frail sister so I could empty my arms of books and pick up Our Jane.

'What are we gonna do, Ma?' Tom asked when we reached our cabin, where the smoke belched out and reddened our eyes immediately. 'She gets so tired, yet she needs to go to school.'

Sarah looked deep into Our Jane's tired eyes, touched her pale face, then gently picked up her youngest and carried her into the big bed and laid her down. 'What she needs is a doctor, but we can't afford it. That's what makes me so damned mad with yer pa. He's got money for booze, and money for women . . . but none for doctors to heal his own.'

How bitter she sounded.

Every Sunday night I had nightmares. The same one repeated over and over, until I grew to hate Sunday nights. I dreamed I was all alone in the cabin, snowed in and alone. Every time the dream came I woke up crying.

'It's all right,' comforted Tom, crawling from his place on the floor near the stove and throwing his arms about me after one of my worst nightmares. 'I get those bad dreams, too, once in a while. Don't cry, we're all here. Ain't no place for us to go but to school and back, and to church and back. Wouldn't it be nice if we never had to come back?'

'Pa doesn't love me like he loves you, Fanny, Keith, and Our Jane,' I sobbed, and even that made me feel weak and ashamed. 'Am I so ugly and unbearable, Tom? Is that why Pa hates me so?'

'Naw,' scoffed Tom, looking embarrassed, 'it's something about yer hair he dislikes. Heard him tell Sarah that once. But I think yer hair is beautiful, really do. Not so hatefully red as mine, nor so pale as Our Jane's. Or so black and straight as Fanny's. You've got an angel look, even if it is black. I think you are, no doubt, the prettiest girl in all the hills, and Winnerrow as well.'

There were many pretty girls in the hills and in the valley. I hugged Tom and turned away. What did Tom know about judging beautiful girls? Already I knew there was a world beyond the hills – a huge, wonderful world I was going to know one day.

'I'm sure glad I'm not a girl,' shouted Tom the next day, shaking his head in wonder at a sister who went so easily from frowns to laughter, 'made happy by silly compliments!'

'You didn't mean what you said last night?' I asked, crestfallen. 'You're not gonna like me either?'

He whirled about and made an ugly face. 'See – yer almost as pretty as this face of mine – and I'd marry ya when I grow up – if I could.'

'You've been saying that since you learned how to talk.'

'How would ya know?' he shouted back.

'Tom, you know Miss Deale doesn't want you to say *yer* or *ya*. You must remember your diction and your grammar. Say instead *you are* or *you*. You must learn to speak properly, Tom.'

'Why?' he asked, his green eyes sparkling with mischief. He tugged the red ribbon from my ponytail and set my hair free to blow in the wind. 'Nobody round here cares about grammar and diction, not Ma, not Pa, not anybody but ya and Miss Deale.'

'And who do you love most in the whole wide world?' I asked.

'Love you first, Miss Deale second,' Tom said with a laugh. 'Can't have you, so I'll settle for Miss Deale. I'm gonna order God to stop her growing old and ugly. Then I can catch up and marry her, and she'll read to me every book in the whole wide world.'

'You'll read your own books, Thomas Luke Casteel!'

'Heavenly,' (he was the only one to combine my two names in this flattering way), 'the others in the school whisper about you, thinking you know more than you should at your age, and that's my age too. I don't know as much. How come?'

'I get the A's, and you get the B's and C's because you play hooky too much – and I don't play hooky at all.' Tom was as thirsty for knowledge as I was, but he had to be like others of his sex once in a while, or fight them each day so they wouldn't call him teacher's pet. When he came back to the cabin from his wild days of fun in the woods or on the river, he'd spend twice as much of his free time poring over the books Miss Deale allowed us to bring home.

Other words Miss Deale had said to Tom and me lingered in my head, to comfort me when my pride was injured, my self-confidence wounded. 'Look,' she'd said, her pretty face smiling, 'you and Tom are my very best students. The very kind every teacher hopes for.'

The day Miss Deale gave us permission to take books home, she gave us the world and all it contained.

She gave us treasures beyond belief when she put in our hands her favourite classics. *Alice's Adventures in Wonderland*, *Through the Looking Glass*, *Moby Dick*, *A Tale of Two Cities*, and three Jane Austen novels – and they were all for me. On the days that followed Tom had his own selection, boy's books, *The Hardy Boys* series, seven of them, and just when I'd begun to think he'd select nothing but fun books, he picked up a thick volume of Shakespeare, and that made Miss Deale's blue eyes glow.

'You don't, perchance, hope to be a writer one day, do you, Tom?' she asked.

'Don't know yet what I want to be,' he said in his most careful diction, nervous as he always was around someone as educated and pretty as Miss Marianne Deale. 'Get all kinds of notions about being a pilot; then next day I want to be a lawyer so I can get to be president one day.'

'President of our country, or of a corporation?'

He blushed and looked down at his large feet that kept shuffling about. How awful his shoes looked. They were too big, too old and worn. 'I guess President Casteel would sound kinda stupid, wouldn't it?'

'No,' she said seriously, 'I think it sounds fine. You just set your mind on what you want to be, and take your time about it. If you work to obtain your goal, and realize from the very beginning that nothing valuable comes easily, and still forge ahead, without a doubt you'll reach your goal, whatever it is.'

Because of Miss Marianne Deale's generosity (we learned later she put down her own money as deposit so we could take those books home), in books we had the chance to look at pictures of the ancient world, and in books we travelled together to Egypt and India. In books we lived in palaces and strode the narrow crooked lanes in London. Why, we both felt that when we got there eventually, we wouldn't :ven feel strange in a foreign land, because we'd been there before.

I loved historical novels that brought the past to life much better than history books did. Until I read a novel about George Washington I thought him a dull, stodgy sort of president . . . and to think he'd once been young and handsome enough to cause girls to think he was charming and sexy.

We read books by Victor Hugo, by Alexandre Dumas, and thrilled to know adventures like that were possible, even if they were horrible. We read classics, and we read junk; we read everything, anything that would take us out of that godforsaken cabin in the hills. Maybe if we'd had movies, our own TV set, and other forms of entertainment, we wouldn't have grown so fond of those books Miss Deale allowed us to take home. Or maybe it was only Miss Deale, being clever when she 'allowed' only us to take home precious, expensive books that she said others wouldn't respect as much as we did.

And that was true enough. We read our books only after we washed our hands.

I suspected that Miss Marianne Deale liked our pa more than a little. God knows she should have better taste. According to Granny, his 'angel' had taught Pa to speak proper English, and with his natural good looks, many an aristocratic woman fell for the charms of Luke Casteel, when he cared enough to be charming.

Every Sunday Pa went with us to church, sat in the midst of his large family, next to Sarah. Petite and dainty Miss Deale sat primly across the aisle and stared at Pa. I could guess she was marvelling at Pa's dark good looks, but surely she should consider his lack of knowledge. From all I'd heard from Granny, Pa had quit school before he was finished with the fifth class.

Sundays rolled around so fast when you didn't have the kind of good clothes you needed, and I was always thinking I'd have a pretty new dress before another Sunday showed up; but new garments of any kind were difficult to come by, when Sarah had so much to do. So there we were again, in the very last pew, all in our best rags that others would throw out for trash. We'd stand, and we'd sing along with the best and richest in Winnerrow, along with all the other hillbillies dressed no better or worse than we were, who revelled in coming to church.

In God you had to trust, and in God you had to believe or feel a fool.

On this particular Sunday after church services were over, I tried to keep Our Jane neat while she licked the ice cream just outside the chemist, not so far from where Pa had parked his truck. Miss Deale had bought cones for all five of the Casteel children. She stood about ten yards away, staring at where Ma and Pa were having a tiff about something, which meant any moment Pa might whack her, or Sarah would belt him one. I swallowed nervously, wishing Miss Deale would move on, or look somewhere else, but she stood watching, listening, almost transfixed.

It made me wonder what she was thinking, though I never found out.

Not a week passed without her writing at least one note to Pa concerning Tom or me. He was seldom home, and when he was, he couldn't read her neat, small handwriting; even if he could, he wouldn't have responded. Last week she had written:

Dear Mr Casteel,

Surely you must be very proud of Tom and Heaven, my two best students. I would like very much, at a time convenient for both of us, to meet to discuss the possibilities of seeing that they both win scholarships.

Yours sincerely,
Marianne Deale

The very next day she asked me, 'Didn't you give it to him, Heaven? Surely he wouldn't be so rude as not to respond. He's such a handsome man. You must adore him.'

'Sure do adore him,' I said cynically. 'Sure could chisel him into a fine museum piece. Put him in a cave with a club in his hand, and a red-haired woman at his feet. Yep, that's where Pa belongs, in the Smithsonian Museum.'

Miss Deale narrowed her sky-blue eyes, stared at me with the oddest expression. 'Why, I'm shocked, really shocked. Don't you love your father, Heaven?'

'I just adore him, Miss Deale, I really do. Specially when he's visiting Shirley's Place.'

'Heaven! You shouldn't say things like that. What can you possibly know about a house of ill-rep – ' She broke off and looked embarrassed. Her eyes lowered before she asked, 'Does he really go there?'

'Every chance he gets, according to Ma.'

The next Sunday Miss Deale didn't look at Pa with admiration; in fact, she didn't cast her eyes his way one time.

But even if Pa had fallen from Miss Deale's grace, she still was waiting for all five of us in the chemist while Ma and Pa chatted with their hill friends. Our Jane ran to our teacher with wide-open arms, hurling herself at Miss Deale's pretty blue skirt. 'Here I am!' she cried out in delight. 'Ready for ice cream!'

'That's not nice, Our Jane,' I immediately corrected. 'You should wait and allow Miss Deale to offer you ice cream.'

Our Jane pouted, and so did Fanny, both with wide,

pleading eyes fixed doglike on our teacher. 'It's all right, Heaven, really,' Miss Deale said, smiling. 'Why do you think I come here? I like ice cream cones, too, and hate to eat one all alone . . . so, come, tell me which flavours you want this week.'

It was easy to see Miss Deale pitied us, and wanted to give us treats, at least on Sundays. In a way it wasn't fair, to her or to us, for we were so damned needing of treats, but we also needed to have pride in ourselves. Time after time pride went down in defeat when it came to choosing between chocolate, vanilla, or strawberry. Lord knows how long it would have taken us if there had been more flavours.

Easily Tom could say vanilla; easily I could say chocolate; but Fanny wanted strawberry, chocolate, and vanilla, and Keith wanted what Our Jane was having, and Our Jane couldn't make up her mind. She looked at the man behind the soda fountain, stared wistfully at the huge jars of penny candy, eyed a boy and a girl sitting down to enjoy an ice-cream soda, and hesitated. 'Look at her,' whispered Fanny; 'Can't make up her mind 'cause she wants it all. Miss Deale, don't give it all to her – unless ya give it all to us, too.'

'Why, of course I'll give Our Jane anything she wants, all three flavours if she can manage a triple cone, and a chocolate candy bar for later, and a bag of sweets for all of you to take home. Is there anything else you'd like?'

Fanny opened her mouth wide, as if to blab out all we wanted and needed. I quickly intervened. 'You do too much already, Miss Deale. Give Our Jane her small vanilla cone, which will drip all over her before she eats it anyway, and a chocolate bar that she and Keith can share. That's more than enough. We have plenty of what we need at home.'

What an ugly face Fanny made behind Miss Deale's back. She groaned, moaned, and made a terrible fuss before Tom hushed her up with his hands over her mouth.

'Perhaps one day you'll all have lunch with me,' Miss Deale said casually after a short silence, as all of us watched Our Jane and Keith lick their cones with so much rapture it could make you cry. No wonder they loved Sundays so much; Sunday brought them the only treats they'd known so far in life.

We'd no sooner finished our cones than Ma and Pa showed up in the doorway of the drugstore. 'C'mon,' called Pa, 'leaving for home now – unless you want to walk.'

Then he spied Miss Deale, who was hurriedly buying penny sweets that Our Jane and Fanny were selecting with the greatest possible care, pointing to this piece, and that piece. He strode toward us, wearing a cream-coloured suit that Granny said my mother had bought for him on their two-week honeymoon in Atlanta. If I hadn't known differently, I would have thought Pa a handsome gentleman with culture, the way he looked in that suit.

'You must be the teacher my kids talk about all the time,' he said to her, putting out his hand. She pulled away, as if all my information about his visiting Shirley's Place had killed her admiration for him.

'Your eldest son and daughter are my best students,' she said coolly, 'as you should know, since I've written you many times about them.' She didn't mention Fanny or Keith or Our Jane, since they weren't in her class. 'I hope you are proud of both Heaven and Tom.'

Pa looked totally astounded as he glanced at Tom, then flicked his eyes my way. For two solid years Miss Deale had been writing him notes to tell him how bright she thought we were. The Winnerrow school was so delighted with what Miss Deale was doing for deprived hill kids (sometimes considered half-wits) they were allowing her to 'advance' along with us, from grade to grade.

'Why, that's a very nice thing to hear on a beautiful Sunday afternoon,' said Pa, trying to meet her eyes and hold them. She refused to look at him, as if afraid once she did, she couldn't look away. 'I always wanted to go on to acquire a higher education myself, but never had the chance,' extolled Pa.

'Pa,' said I, speaking up loud and sharp, 'we've decided

to walk home . . . so you and Ma can leave and forget about us.'

'Don't wanna walk home!' cried Our Jane. 'Wanna ride!'

Near the doorway of the store, Sarah stood watching with her eyes narrowed suspiciously. Pa bowed slightly to Miss Deale and said, 'It's been a pleasure to meet you, Miss Deale.' He leaned to sweep Our Jane up in one arm, lifted Keith with the other, and out the door he strode, seeming to everyone in the shop the only cultivated, charming Casteel the world had ever seen. Not one pair of lips was left together, all gaping as if at a miracle not to believed.

And again, despite all I'd said to warn her, something admiring lit up the gullible sky-blue eyes of my teacher.

It was a rare kind of perfect day, with birds flying overhead, and autumn leaves softly falling. I was like Keith, caught up in nature. I only half heard what Tom was saying until I saw Fanny's dark eyes widen with surprise. 'No! Yer wrong. Weren't Heaven that good-looking new boy was staring at! It was me!'

'What boy?' I asked.

'The son of the new pharmacist who's come to run the drugstore,' explained Tom. 'Didn't ya notice the name Stonewall? He was in the store when Miss Deale bought us the cones, and by gosh, he sure seemed taken by ya, Heavenly, he sure did.'

'Liar!' yelled Fanny. 'Nobody ever stares at Heaven when I'm there, they don't!'

Tom and I ignored Fanny and her screaming voice. 'Heard tell he's gonna be coming to our school tomorrow,' Tom continued. 'Made me feel funny the way he looked at ya,' he went on in an embarrassed way. 'Sure will hate the day when ya marry up and we're not close anymore.'

'We'll always be close,' I said quickly. 'No boy is ever going to convince me I need him more than I need an education.'

Yet, in bed that night, curled up on the floor near Ole Smokey, I stared through the dimness to where I could imagine seeing a brand-new pretty blue dress, never worn by anyone else, hanging on a wall nail. Foolishly, as only the young can believe, I believed that if I wore beauty it would somehow change the world about me. I woke up knowing I wanted a new dress more than anything – and wondering, too, if that new boy would like me even if I never had anything new to wear.

Three

Logan Stonewall

Tom, Fanny, Our Jane, Keith, and I had hardly hit the schoolyard on Monday morning when Tom was pointing out the new boy, the very one he'd spotted staring at me in church. When I turned to look toward the field where boys were already playing, my breath caught. He stood out from all the others, this new boy in better clothes than the valley boys wore. The morning sun behind him put a sort of fiery halo above his dark hair, so I couldn't really see his face that was in the shadow, yet I knew from the way he stood, tall and straight, not slouched like some mountain boys who were ashamed of their height, that I liked him right from the beginning. It was silly, of course, to like a complete stranger just because he had a certain kind of confidence that wasn't arrogance, only visible strength and poise. I glanced at Tom, and knew why I immediately liked a boy I'd never seen before. Logan and Tom both had the same kind of natural grace and ease with themselves that came from knowing who and what they were. I looked again at Tom. How could he stride so proudly beside me when he was a Casteel?

I longingly wished I had his poise, his confidence, his ability to accept, though I might have if I'd had my father's love – as he had.

'He's staring at you again,' whispered Tom, giving me a sharp nudge, causing Fanny to shrill in her too-loud voice, 'He is not staring at Heaven! He's staring at me!'

Fanny embarrassed me again. But if that new boy heard, he didn't show any signs. He stood out like a Christmas tree in his sharply creased grey flannel slacks and his bright green sweater worn over a white shirt and a green-and-grey striped tie. He had on regular Sunday hard shoes, polished to a shine. All the valley boys wore jeans and knit tops, and sneakers. No one, ever, came to school dressed up as Logan Stonewall was.

Did he see us staring? He must have, for suddenly, alarmingly, he came our way! What would I say to someone so dressed up? I tried to shrink into my shoes. Each step that brought him closer put panic in my heart. I wasn't ready yet to meet anyone wearing grey flannel slacks (something I wouldn't have known if Miss Deale hadn't once worn a grey suit to school of the same fabric; she was always trying to educate me on fabrics, clothes, and such). I tried to scurry away with Keith and Our Jane before he saw the shabbiness of my worn, colourless dress with the hem half-out and scuffed, almost soleless shoes, but Our Jane resisted.

'Don't feel good,' she wailed. 'Wanna go home, Hev-lee.'

'You can't go home again,' I whispered. 'You'll never finish the first class if you stay out sick all the time. Maybe I can bring you and Keith a sandwich this noon – and some milk.'

'Tuna fish!' Keith sang out happily, and with thoughts of half a tuna fish sandwich, Our Jane let go of my hand and with slow, small steps entered the classroom where all the first class seemed to have fun – all but Our Jane.

I hurried after my two charges, but not so fast that Logan Stonewall didn't catch up in the hall just outside the first class. I turned to see him shaking hands with Tom. Logan was good-looking in the kind of way I'd seen in books and magazines, like someone with years and years of cultured background that had given him what none of us in the hills had – quality. His nose was slender and straight, his lower lip much fuller and more shapely than his upper one, and even from six feet away I could see his dark blue eyes smiling warmly at me. His jaw was squarish and strong, and a dimple in his left cheek played in and out as he smiled my way. His demeanour of assurance made me feel awkward, afraid I'd do and say everything wrong, and then he'd turn for sure to Fanny, and if she said and did everything wrong, it wouldn't matter. Boys always fell for Fanny.

'Hi there, stranger,' greeted Fanny, skipping forward and smiling up into his face. Fanny had never bothered to accompany Our Jane or Keith to their respective classrooms before. 'Yer the best-looking boy I ever did see.'

'That's Fanny, my sister,' explained Tom.

'Hi, Fanny. . .' But Logan Stonewall didn't do more than glance at Fanny. He waited for Tom to introduce me.

'And this is my sister, Heaven Leigh.' There was so much pride in Tom's voice, as if he didn't see my shapeless ugly dress, or think I had any reason to be ashamed of my shoes. 'And that small girl who's peeking out of the first class door is my youngest sister, who we call Our Jane, and across the hall, that amber-haired boy grinning at us is my brother, Keith. Go sit down, Keith; you too, Our Jane.'

How could Tom act so natural around a boy as citified and well-dressed as Logan Stonewall? I was all aflutter with excitement as those smiling, sapphire eyes looked at me as I'd never been looked at before. 'What a pretty name,' said Logan, his eyes meeting mine. 'It suits you very well. I don't think I've ever seen more heavenly blue eyes.'

'I've got black eyes,' shouted Fanny, stepping in front of me to block his view. 'Anybody can have blue eyes . . . like Heaven's. I like yer colour blue better.'

'Cornflower-blue eyes, Miss Deale calls the colour of Heavenly's eyes,' informed Tom with evident pride, 'and there isn't another girl for ten miles around with eyes that same shade of blue that I call heavenly blue.'

'I believe you . . . ' murmured Logan Stonewall, still staring at me.

I was only thirteen; he couldn't have been more than fifteen, or at the most sixteen, yet our eyes seemed to cling and strike a gong that would resound throughout the rest of our lives.

It was only the schoolbell ringing.

I was saved from having to say anything by the bustling scurry of kids rushing to their classrooms and seating themselves before the teacher came in. Tom was laughing when he sat behind his desk. 'Heavenly, I never saw you turn so many shades of red. Logan Stonewall is just another boy. Better dressed than most, and better looking, but only another boy.'

He wasn't feeling what I was feeling, yet he narrowed his eyes and stared at me in an odd way, until he turned and bowed his head, and I bowed mine.

Miss Deale came in, and before I could figure out what I'd say to Logan when next I saw him, it was lunchtime. I had to keep my promise about the sandwich and milk. I sat at my desk as all the others left for lunch. Miss Deale looked up. 'Why, Heaven, do you want to speak to me about something?'

I wanted to plead for a sandwich to give to Keith and Our Jane, but somehow I just couldn't. Standing, I smiled and hurried out, staring at the floor of the corridor, just praying to find a quarter. . . and that's when Logan's grey shoes came into view. 'I waited for you to come out with Tom.' He looked earnest even as his eyes still smiled. 'Will you have lunch with me?'

'I never eat lunch.'

My answer made him frown. 'Everybody eats lunch. So come along, and we'll have hamburgers, shakes, and french fries.'

Did that mean he was going to pay for my lunch as well as his own? My pride reared high. 'I have to take care of Our Jane and Keith during the lunch hour . . .'

'Okay, they're invited, too,' he said nonchalantly, 'and I might as well include Tom and Fanny, in case you're thinking of them.'

'We can afford to pay for our own lunches.'

For a second he didn't seem to know what to say. He shot me another quick glance, then shrugged. 'All right, if you want it that way.'

Oh, gosh . . . I didn't want it that way! But my pride was as high as any mountain in the Willies.

He walked beside me toward the lower-grade classroom.

Any moment, I thought, he'd regret his invitation. Both Our Jane and Keith were waiting near the first class, each seeming terribly anxious before Our Jane came flying into my arms, half sobbing. 'Can we eat now, Hev-lee? My tummy hurts.'

About the same time, Keith began jabbering about the tuna fish sandwich I'd promised. 'Did Miss Deale send us another one?' he asked, his small face bright and eager. 'Is it Monday today? Did she send us milk?'

I tried to smile at Logan, who was taking all of this in and looking thoughtfully at Our Jane, then at Keith. Finally he turned to me and smiled. 'If you'd rather have tuna fish sandwiches, maybe the cafeteria will have a few left if we hurry there.'

There wasn't anything I could do now that Keith and Our Jane began running toward the cafeteria like foxes on the scent of chickens. 'Heaven,' said Logan with earnestness, 'I've never allowed a girl to pay for her own lunch when I invite her. Please allow me to treat you.'

We no sooner entered the cafeteria than I could hear the whispers and speculations – what was Logan doing with the crummy Casteels? Tom was there, as if Logan had invited him earlier, and for some reason that made me feel much better. Now I could smile and help Our Jane sit at a long table. Keith crowded as close to her side as possible and looked around shyly.

'Everybody still want tuna fish sandwiches and milk?' asked Logan, who had asked Tom to go with him to help bring back our lunches. Our Jane and Keith stuck to their preference, while I agreed to try the hamburger and cola drink. I looked around while Tom and Logan were gone, trying to see Fanny. She wasn't in the cafeteria. That gave me another worry. Fanny had her own ways of gaining a meal.

All about us, people kept whispering, not seeming to care if I heard or not. 'What's he doing with her? She's just a hillbilly. And his family has to be rich.'

Logan Stonewall drew many an eye as he came back with

Tom, both of them smiling and happy to deliver tuna sandwiches, hamburgers, french fries, and shakes, and milk too. Both Our Jane and Keith were overwhelmed by all the food, wanting to sip my cola, taste my hamburger, try the french fries, so I ended up with the milk and Our Jane drank my cola, closing her eyes tight with delight. 'I'll buy you another,' Logan offered, but I refused to allow him to do that. He'd already done more than enough.

I found out he really was fifteen. He smiled with pleasure when I whispered my age. He had to know my birthdate, as if that mattered, and it seemed it did; his mother believed in astrology. He told me how he'd managed to have himself assigned to the study hall where I sat each day to do my homework. I always tried to finish it there so I could take novels home instead of schoolbooks.

For the first time in my life I had a real boyfriend, one who didn't presume I was easy just because I lived in the hills. Logan didn't mock my clothes or my background. However, from day one Logan made enemies in our school, because he was different, too good-looking, his clothes too 'citified.' His poise was too annoying, his family too rich, his father too educated, his mother too haughty. It was presumed by the other boys he was a sissy. Even that first day Tom said that one day Logan would have to prove himself. The other boys tried all their silly, but not so harmless, pranks. They put tacks in his shoes in the gym; they tied his shoelaces together so he'd be late to his next class after gym; they put glue in his shoes, and backed away when he grew angry and threatened to beat the culprit.

Before his first week was over Logan was placed two classes above Tom's and my level. By that time he, too, wore jeans and plaid shirts, but more expensive designer jeans, and shirts that came from some place in New England called Bean's. He still stuck out despite the clothes. He was too soft-spoken and polite when others were rude, loud, and rough. He refused to act like the other boys, refused to use their foul language.

On Friday I skipped the study period, much to Tom's amazement. He couldn't stop questioning me as we strolled home in bright September sunshine. It was still warm enough so Tom could dive into the river, clothes and all – though he did pull off his worn sneakers. I fell on the grassy bank with Our Jane cuddled near my side, and Keith gazed up at a squirrel perched on a tree limb. I said without thought to Tom as he splashed around, 'I wish to God I'd been born with silvery-gold hair'; then I bit down hard on my tongue from the way Tom turned to stare at me. He shook his head to throw off the water as a dog would. Fortunately, Fanny had dropped far, far behind as we trudged home, and even from where we were, we could hear her faint lilting giggles coming over the hills and through the woods.

'Heavenly, do ya know now?' Tom asked in the oddest hesitant whisper.

'Know what?'

'Why ya want silvery-blonde hair when what ya got is fine, just fine?'

'Just a crazy wish, I guess.'

'Now wait a minute, Heavenly. If ya and me are gonna stay friends, and more than just brother and sister, ya gotta be on the square. Do ya or don't ya know who had that silvery-gold colour of hair – ?'

'Do you know?' I tried to evade.

'Sure I know.' He came out of the water, and we headed toward home. 'Always have known,' he said softly, 'since the first time I went to school. Boys told me about Pa's first city wife from Boston with her long silvery-gold hair, and how everybody just knew she couldn't last living up in the hills. Just kept on hoping ya'd never find out, and stop thinking I was durn wonderful. 'Cause I ain't that wonderful. Got no Boston blood in me, no rich genes that's been cultured and civilized – like you got. I got one hundred percent dumb hillbilly genes, despite what you and Miss Deale think.'

It hurt to hear him say such things. 'Don't you talk like that, Thomas Luke Casteel! You heard Miss Deale talk on that subject the other day. The most brilliant parents in the world often give birth to idiots . . . and idiots can give birth to genius! Didn't she say that it was nature's way to equalize? Didn't she say that sometimes when parents are too smart, they seem to use up all the brain fodder on themselves and leave none of it for their children? Remember all she said about nothing in nature being predictable? The only reason you don't get all the A's I do is because you play hooky too much! You must keep on believing what Miss Deale said about all of us being unique, born for a purpose only we can fulfill. Thomas Luke, you keep remembering that.'

'You keep remembering it too,' he said gruffly, turning to give me a hard look, 'and stop crying out in the night to be different than what you are. I like what you are now.' His green eyes were soft and luminous in the dim shade of the piney woods. 'You're my fair, gypsy sister, ten times more important to me than my whole sister, Fanny, who doesn't really give a damn about anybody but herself. She doesn't love me as you do, and I can't love her as much as I can love you. You're the only sister I got who can put her mind on a star in another universe.' He looked so sad then, making me hurt inside.

'Tom, I'm gonna cry if you say one more thing! It makes me ache to think someday you might go away and I'll never see you again.'

He shook his head, making his red hair ruffle in layers. 'I'd never go anywhere you didn't want me to go, Heavenly. It's you and me together, all our lives through. You know, like they say in books, through thick and thin, through rain and snow . . . through the dark of night.'

Laughing, I answered, 'That's the mail, silly.' Tears were in my eyes as I reached to take his hand and squeeze it. 'Let's just promise never, so help us God, will we ever go separate ways, or be angry with one another, or feel differently about each other than we feel now.'

He had me then in his arms, holding me as if I were made of spun glass and any second I'd break. He choked when he said, 'Someday you'll get married – I know you say you won't, but Logan Stonewall is already looking with calf eyes at you.'

'How can he love me when he doesn't know me?'

His face bowed into my hair. 'All he needs to do is look at your face, your eyes – that's enough. Everything about you is written on your face, shining in your eyes.'

I pulled away and brushed at my tears. 'Pa never sees what you do, does he?'

'Why do you let him hurt you so much?'

'Oh, Tom . . . !' I wailed, falling into his arms and really beginning to cry. 'How am I ever going to have any confidence in myself when my own father can't stand to look at me? There must be something evil he sees in me that makes him hate me.'

He stroked my hair, my back, and there were tears in his eyes when I looked, as if my pain were his. 'Someday Pa's gonna find out he don't hate ya, Heavenly. I know that day's coming soon.'

I yanked my hair away.

'No, it's not ever coming! You know it as much as I know it. Pa thinks I killed his angel by being born, and in a thousand years he won't forgive me! And if you want to know what I think, I think my mother was damned lucky to escape him! For sooner or later he'd have been mean to her as he is to Sarah now!'

We were both shaken by this kind of frankness. He pulled me back and tried to smile, but he only looked sad. 'Pa doesn't love Ma, Heavenly. He's miserable with Ma. From all I've heard, he did love your mother. He married mine only because she was pregnant with me, and he tried for once to do the right thing.'

'Because Granny made him do the right thing!' I flared with hot bitterness.

'Nobody can make Pa do what he sets his mind against, remember that.'

'I'm remembering,' I said, with thoughts of how Pa

refused to let himself really look at me.

Again it was Monday, and we were all at school. Miss Deale expounded on the joys of reading Shakespeare's plays and sonnets, but I was dying to get on to study hall.

'Heaven,' said Miss Deale, her baby-blue eyes fixed on me, 'are you listening, or daydreaming?'

'Listening!'

'What was the poem I just discussed?'

For the life of me I couldn't remember one word she'd said in the last half hour, and that was not my way. Oh, I had to stop thinking of that darn Logan. Yet, when I was in the study hall and Logan was seated to my right, I began feeling the strangest kind of sensations whenever our eyes met. His hair wasn't a true brown or black, but a blend with auburn highlights, with a little gold where the summer sun had streaked it. Really, I had to force myself not to glance his way again, since every time I did he was staring at me.

Logan smiled before he whispered: 'Who in the world was ingenuous enough to give you such a name as Heaven? I've never known anyone with that name before.'

I had to swallow twice so I could say it just right. 'My father's first wife named me minutes after I was born, and then Leigh because that was her Christian name. Granny said she wanted to give me something uplifting, and Heaven is about as uplifting as a name can get.'

'It's the most beautiful name I have ever heard. Where is your mother now?'

'Dead in a cemetery,' I said bluntly, forgetting to be charming and coquettish, something Fanny never forgot. 'She died minutes after I was born, and because she did, my father can't forgive me for taking her life.'

'Absolutely no talking in this room!' shouted Mr Prakins. 'The next one who speaks will receive fifteen hours' detention after school!

Logan's eyes softened with compassion and sympathy. And the minute Mr Prakins left the room, Logan again whispered: 'I'm sorry it happened that way, but you said it wrong. Your mother isn't dead in a cemetery – she's passed into the great beyond, into a better place, into heaven.'

'If there is a heaven or a hell, I've been thinking it's right here on earth.'

'How old are you anyway, one hundred and twenty?'

'You know I'm thirteen!' I flared angrily. 'Just feeling two hundred and fifty today.'

'Why?'

'Because it's better than feeling thirteen, that's why!'

Logan cleared his throat, glanced at Mr Prakins, who kept his eyes on us through a glass wall, and risked another whisper.

'Would it be all right if I walked you home today? I've never talked to anyone as old as two hundred and fifty, and you've got my curiosity aroused. I'd sure like to hear what you have to say.'

I nodded, feeling a bit sick as well as exuberant. Now I'd tricked myself into a situation that might disappoint him with only ordinary answers. What did I know about wisdom, old age, or anything else?

Still, he showed up on the edge of the schoolyard, where all the boys walking home with hill girls waited until their choices showed up. And there stood Fanny.

She spun about, flinging her hair over her face, then tossed it back, whipping around to make it fan out in circle, grinning broadly when she saw Logan, as if she thought he was coming for her. A short distance from Fanny stood Tom and Keith. Tom seemed surprised to find Logan waiting near our trail. Ours was just a faint path through the underbush that led to the woods, and eventually to only our cabin nearest the sky. The minute Fanny saw Logan and me heading for our trail she let out a whoop so loud and embarrassing I wanted to drop dead.

'Heaven, what are you doing with that new boy? Ya know ya don't like boys! Ain't ya done said a million times yer never gonna be nothing but a dried-up ole schoolteacher?'

I tried to ignore Fanny, though my face turned beet-red. What kind of sisterly loyalty was she showing anyway? I knew better than to expect tact. I tried to smile at Logan. It was always best to ignore Fanny, if possible.

Logan stared at her with disapproval, as did Tom.

'Fanny, please don't say one more word,' I said uncomfortably. 'Just run along home, and start the wash for a change.'

'I never have to walk home with only a brother,' Fanny said to Logan in a sneering way before she turned on her most brilliant smile. 'Boys don't like Heaven, they always like me. Ya'll like me too. Ya wanna hold my hand?'

Logan glanced at me, at Tom, and then said seriously to Fanny, 'Thank you, but right now I'm intent on seeing Heaven home, and hearing all that she has to tell me.'

'Ya should hear me sing!'

'Another time, Fanny, I'll listen to you sing.'

'Our Jane sings . . .' said Keith faintly.

'She sure does!' exclaimed Tom, seizing Fanny by the arm and pulling her along with him. 'Come along, Keith. Our Jane is home waiting for you.' That's all Keith needed to hear to hurry after Tom, for Our Jane had missed school today due to another tummyache and a fever.

Fanny broke away from Tom and came running back to scowl and yell before she stuck out her tongue. 'Yer selfish, Heaven Leigh Casteel! Mean, skinny, an ugly too! Hate yer hair! Hate yer silly name! *Hate yer everything!* I do! Ya just wait till I tell Pa what yer doing Pa won't like ya for taking charity from some strange city boy who pities ya – eating his hamburgers and stuff, and teaching Our Jane and Keith to beg!'

Oh, now Fanny was at her worst, jealous, spiteful, and apt to do just what she threatened, and Pa would punish me!

'Fanny,' called Tom, running to catch her. 'You can have my new watercolour set if you keep yer trap shut about Logan taking us all to lunch . . .'

Instantly Fanny smiled. 'All right! I want that colouring

book Miss Deale gave ya, too! Don't know why she don't give me nothing!'

'You don't know why?' sneered Tom, giving her what she asked for even though I knew he wanted that paint set and that colouring book so much it hurt. He'd never had a box of brand-new watercolours before, or a colouring book about Robin Hood. Robin Hood, this year, was his favourite hero from a book. 'When you learn to behave yerself in the cloakroom, maybe Miss Deale will be generous with you, for a change.'

Again I could have died from embarrassment!

Crying, Fanny fell down on the mountain trail that was gradually spiraling upward through tall trees that appeared to touch the sky. She pounded her small fists on the grass, screamed because a stone was hidden there and it drew blood. Sucking on that, she sat up and stared at Tom with huge pleading eyes. 'Don't tell Pa, please, please.'

Tom promised.

I promised. Though I still wanted to vanish and not see Logan's wide eyes drinking all this in, as if never in his life had he witnessed such a stupid, ill-mannered scene. I tried to avoid meeting his eyes until he smiled and I saw understanding. 'You sure got one family that might age you dramatically inside – outside, you look younger than springtime.'

'Yer stealing words from a song!' yelled Fanny. 'Ya ain't supposed to court a gal with song words!'

'Oh, dry up!' ordered Tom, seizing her arms again and running so she had to race with him or have her arm pulled off. This gave me my chance to be alone with Logan.

Keith was again bringing up the rear of our little parade, though he'd stopped to stare up at a robin, mesmerized and not likely to move for a least ten minutes – if the bird didn't fly away.

'Your sister is really something else,' said Logan when finally we were as good as alone on the trail. Keith was far behind us and so quiet. I kept my thoughts to myself. Valley boys thought all hill girls were easy for any boy hoping to experiment with sex. As young as she was, Fanny had caught the hill spirit and its easy sexuality that came much earlier than it did in low places. Perhaps it was due to all the copulating we saw going on in our yards and in our one-or two-room shacks; there was no need for sex education in our hills, sex hit you in the face the moment you knew man from woman.

Logan cleared his throat to remind me he was there. 'I'm ready to hear all your years of accumulated wisdom. I'd take notes, but I find it difficult to write while walking. But next time, I could bring along a tape recorder.'

'You're making fun of me,' I complained before I justified myself. 'We happen to live with our grandparents. Grandpa never says anything that's not absolutely necessary, and seldom does he find words necessary. My granny rambles on and on incessantly, talking about how good all the old times were, and how rotten things are now. My stepmother fusses and fumes because she's got more than she can do . . . and sometimes when I go home to that cabin, and face up to all the problems, I feel not two hundred and fifty but one thousand years old – only without any wisdom from living that long.'

'Hey,' he said with a smile, 'a girl who knows how to talk honestly. I like that. I understand. I'm an only child, and I've grown up with uncles, aunts, and grandparents, too, so I do understand. But you've got the edge on me with two brothers and two sisters.'

'Is it an edge of advantage or disadvantage?'

'Whatever you make it. From my point of view, Heaven Leigh, it's an advantage to have a large family so you're never lonely. Lots of time I'm lonely, wishing I had brothers, sisters. I think Tom's great, loads of fun and a good sport; and Keith and Our Jane are beautiful kids.'

'And Fanny, what do you think of her?'

He blushed and looked uncomfortable before he spoke slowly, cautiously. 'I think she's going to grow up to be an exotic beauty.'

'That's all you think?' He had to know about Fanny and all her promiscuous ways with the boys in the cloakroom.

'No, it's not all I think. I think of all the girls I've ever seen, and all the girls I hope to see, the one I see named Heaven Leigh is the one with the potential to be more beautiful than any other. I think Heaven is exceptionally honest and forthright . . . so if you don't mind, and I hope you don't, I'd like to walk you home every day from now on.'

I felt so happy! Soaring high, laughing before I ran on ahead and called back, 'Logan, see you tomorrow. Thanks for seeing me home.'

'But we haven't reached there yet!' he called, taken aback by my abrupt flight.

I couldn't let his see where we lived, how we lived. Why, he'd never want to speak to me again if he really knew our circumstances. 'On another day, a better day, I'll invite you in,' I called, standing at the edge of a clearing in the dappled sunlight. He was across the small bridge covering our narrow stream. Behind him was a field of wild yellow grass, and the sun had caught in his hair and eyes. If I live to be a thousand, I'll never forget the way he smiled, then waved and called back, 'Okay. I've staked my claim. Heaven Leigh Casteel is, from this day on, mine.'

All the rest of the way home I sang to myself, happier than I'd ever been, forgetting all about my promise to myself that I positively would not fall in love until I was thirty.

'Yer looking mighty happy,' commented Sarah, glancing up from the washboard with a weary sigh. 'Day gone good?'

'Oh, yes, Ma, it went fine.'

Fanny stuck her head out of the cabin door. 'Ma, Heaven's gone and got herself a valley boyfriend – and ya know what kind they are.'

Again Sarah sighed. 'Heaven, ya ain't gone an let him . . . have ya?'

'Ma!' I cried out in protest. 'You know I wouldn't!'

'She would too!' screamed Fanny from the doorway.

'She's shameful in the cloakroom with the boys, really shameful!'

'Why, you big liar!' I started to go for her, but Tom shoved Fanny out onto the porch, where she fell and immediately started howling. 'Ma, it's not Heavenly who carries on. Fanny's the most indecent-acting girl in the entire school, and that's saying a whole lot.'

'Yeah,' muttered Sarah, turning the wash over to me, 'sure would be saying a lot. Guess I know who's the one who's the worst, without yer having to tell me. It's my Indian Fanny with her wild devil ways, her flirting eyes that's gonna get her into the same mess I'm in sooner or later. Heaven ya stick to yer guns, and say no, no, no . . . Now take off that dress, and get to work on the wash. Ain't feeling so good lately. Just don't understand why I'm tired all the time.'

'Maybe you should see a doctor, Ma.'

'Will, when they got free ones.'

I finished the wash, and with Tom's willing help hung the clothes up to dry. When we finished it looked like a yard rag sale. 'Ya like Logan Stonewall?' asked Tom.

'Yes, I think so . . .' I answered, blushing several times.

He looked sad, as if Logan might put a wall of difference between us, when nothing could, not ever.

'Tom, maybe Miss Deale will give you another watercolouring set . . .'

'It doesn't matter. I'm not gonna be an artist. Probably won't end up much of nothing, if you're not there to help me believe in myself.'

'But we're always going to be together, Tom. Didn't we swear to stay together through thick and thin?'

His green eyes looked happier, then shaded. 'But that was before Logan Stonewall walked you home.'

'You walk Sally Browne home sometimes, don't you?'

'Once,' he admitted, blushing, as if he didn't know I knew about that, 'but only because she's something like you are, not silly and giggly.'

I didn't know what to say then. Sometimes I wished to be

like the other girls, full of silly laughter about nothing at all, and not always so burdened down with responsibilities that made me feel older than my years.

Later that same night I gave Fanny a good scolding about her behaviour and the consequences. She didn't have to explain again. Already she'd confessed to me, on a rare occasion when we were like sisters needing each other, that she hated school and the time it took from having fun with the other girls her age. Even at the tender age of not quite twelve, she wanted to make out with boys much older who might have ignored her but for her insistence. She liked the boys to undress her, to slip their hands into her panties and start those exciting sensations only they could give her. It had distressed me to hear her say that, and distressed me even more to witness how she acted in the cloakroom with boys.

'Won't do it no more, really I won't let them,' promised Fanny, who was sleepy and agreeable to any suggestion, even an order from me to stop.

The very next day, despite Fanny's vow, it happened all over again when I went to Fanny's class to pick her up and head her back home. I forced my way into the cloakroom and tore Fanny away from her pimply-faced valley boy.

'Yer sister ain't stuck-up and prissy like ya!' the boy hissed.

And all the time I could hear Fanny giggling.

'Ya leave me alone!' Fanny screamed as I dragged her away. 'Pa treats ya like yer invisible, so naturally ya can't know how good it feels to like boys and men, and if ya keep on pestering me not to do this and not to do that, I'm gonna let em do anything they want – and I won't give a damn if ya tell Pa. He loves me and hates ya anyway!'

That stung, and if Fanny hadn't come running to throw her slender arms about my neck, crying and pleading for my forgiveness, I might have turned my back on such a hateful, insensitive sister. 'I'm sorry, Heaven, really sorry. I love ya, I do, I do. I just like what they do. Can't help it, Heaven. Don't want to help it. Ain't it natural, Heaven, ain't it?'

'Yer sister Fanny is gonna be a whore,' said Sarah later, her voice dull and without hope as she pulled bed pallets from boxes for us to put on the floor. 'Ya can't do nothing about Fanny, Heaven. Ya just look out for yerself.'

Pa came home only three or four times a week, as if timing how long our food would last, and he'd come in bringing as much as he could afford to buy at one time. Just last week I'd heard Granny telling Sarah that Grandpa had taken Pa out of school when he was only eleven in order to put him to work in the coal mines – and Pa had hated that so much he'd run away and hadn't come back until Grandpa found him hiding out in a cave. 'And Toby swore to Luke he'd never have to go down into them mines again, but he sure would make more money if he did once in a while . . .'

'Don't want him down there,' Sarah said dully. 'Ain't right to make a man do something he hates. Even if the Feds catch him sooner or later peddling moonshine, he'd die before he'd let 'em lock him up. Rather see him dead than shut up like his brothers . . .'

It made me look at the coal miners differently than I had before.

Many of them lived beyond Winnerrow, scattered a bit higher on the hills, but not really in the mountains like we were. Often at night when the wind was still, I'd lie awake and think I could hear the pickaxes of those dead miners who'd been trapped underground, all trying to dig their way out of the very mountain that was topped by our own cabin.

'Can you hear them, Tom?' I asked the night when Sarah went to bed crying because Pa hadn't been home in five days. 'Chop, chop, chop . . . don't you hear 'em?'

Tom sat up and looked around. 'Don't hear nothing.'

But I did. Faint and far away, chop chop chop. Even fainter, help help help! I got up and went out to the porch, and the sound was louder. I shivered, then called to Tom. Together we drifted to where the sound came from – and there was Pa in the moonlight, shirtless and sweaty, swinging an axe to fell another tree so we could have firewood, come this winter.

For the first time in my life I looked at him with a kind of wondering pity. *Help help help* echoed in my brain – had it been him crying out, had it been? What kind of a man was he anyway, that he would come in the night to chop wood without even stopping in the cabin to say hello to his wife and children?'

'Pa,' called out Tom, 'I can help ya do that.'

Pa didn't pause in his swing that sent wood chips flying, just yelled: 'Go back and get your rest, boy. Tell your ma I've got a new job that keeps me busy all day, and the only spare time I have is at night, and that's why I'm chopping down trees for you to chop into logs later on.' He didn't say a word to indicate he saw me beside Tom.

'What kind of a job have ya got now, Pa?'

'Working on a railroad, boy. Learning how to drive one of them big engines. Pulling coal on the railway . . . come down to the tracks tomorrow about seven and you'll see me pull out . . .'

'Ma sure would like to see ya, Pa.'

I thought he paused then, the axe hesitating before it slammed again into the pine. 'She'll see me . . . when she sees me.' And that was all he said before I turned and ran back to the cabin.

On my coarse pillow stuffed with chicken feathers I cried. Didn't know why I cried, except all of a sudden I was sorry for Pa – and even sorrier for Sarah.

Four

Sarah

Another Christmas came and went without real gifts to make it memorable. We were given only small necessities like toothbrushes and soap. If Logan hadn't given me a gold bracelet set with a small sapphire I wouldn't even have remembered that Christmas. I had nothing to give him but a cap I'd knitted.

'It's a terrific cap,' he said, pulling it down over his head. 'I've always wanted a bright red hand-knitted cap. Thank you very much, Heaven Leigh. Sure would be nice if you'd knit me a red scarf for my birthday that's coming up in March.'

It surprised me that he wore the cap. It was much too large, and he didn't seem to notice that I'd dropped a couple of stitches and that the wool had been handled so much it was more than a bit soiled. No sooner was Christmas over than I started on the scarf. I had it finished by Valentine's Day. 'It's too late for a red scarf in March,' I said with a smile when he wrapped it around his neck – and he was still wearing that red cap to school every day. If anything could have made me like him more than his devotion to that awful red cap, I don't know what it would have been.

I turned fourteen in late February. Logan gave me another gift, a lovely white sweater set that made Fanny's dark eyes blaze with envy. The day after my birthday Logan met me after school where the mountain trail ended; he walked me to the clearing before the cabin, and every day after until it was spring. Keith and Our Jane learned to love and trust him, and all the time Fanny plied her charms, Logan continued to ignore her. Oh, falling in love at age fourteen was so exhilarating I could have laughed and cried at the same time I was so happy.

The glorious, spring days sailed by too quickly now that love was in the air, and I wanted time for romancing, but Granny and Sarah were relentless in their demands for my time. There was planting to do as well as all the other chores that were my duty, but not Fanny's. Without the large garden in the back of our cabin we wouldn't have been as well nourished as we were. We had cabbages, potatoes, cucumbers, carrots, collards for the autumn, and turnip greens, and, best of all, tomatoes.

On Sunday I looked forward to seeing Logan again in church. When we were in church and he was seated across the aisle from me, meeting and holding my eyes and sending so many silent messages, how could I help but forget the desperate poverty of our lives? Logan shared so much of what was in his father's pharmacy with us; small things he thought commonplace filled all of us with delight, like shampoo in a bottle, perfume we could spray on, and a razor and blade for Tom, who began to grow more than auburn fuzz over his lips.

One Sunday afternoon we planned to go fishing after church, though Logan didn't tell his parents who he was friendly with. I could tell from their stony faces when we occasionally met on the streets of Winnerrow that his parents didn't want me, or any Casteel, in their son's life. What they wanted didn't seem to matter nearly as much to Logan as it did to me. I wanted them to like me, and yet they always managed, somehow, to avoid the introductions Logan wanted to make.

I was thinking about Logan's parents as I furtively brushed my hair while Fanny was in the yard tormenting Snapper, Pa's favourite hound. Sarah sat down heavily behind me and pushed back long strands of red hair from her face before she sighed. 'I'm really tired. So blessed tired all the time. And yer Pa's never home. When he is, he don't even look to see my condition.'

What she said made me start, made me want to look and see what Pa was missing. I whirled around to stare at her, realizing that I very seldom really looked at Sarah, or else I would have seen before this that she was pregnant . . . again.

'Ma!' I cried. 'Haven't you told Pa?'

'If he really looked at me, he'd know, wouldn't he?' Irridescent tears of self-pity formed in her eyes. 'Last thing in the world we need is another mouth to feed. Yet we're gonna have another come fall.'

'What month, Ma what day?' I cried unsettled by the thoughts of another baby to take care of, just when Our Jane was finally in school and not quite as troublesome as she'd been, and Lord knows it had been difficult enough with only a year separating her and Keith.

'I don't count days to tell doctors. Don't see a doctor,' whispered Sarah, as if her strong voice were weakened by the coming baby.

'Ma! You've got to tell me when so I can be here if you need me!'

'I just hope and pray this one will be black-haired,' she mumbled as if to herself. 'The dark-eyed boy yer pa's been wanting – a boy like him. Oh, God, hear me this time and give to me and Luke his look-alike son, and then he will love me, like he loved her.'

It made me hurt to think about that. What good did it do for a man to grieve too long – and when had he started that baby? Most of the time I could tell what they were doing, and it had been a long time since the bedsprings had creaked in that rhythmical, telling way.

Gravely I told Tom the news while we were on the path to the lake where we would meet Logan to fish. Tom tried to smile, to look happy, and finally managed a weak grin. 'Well, since there's nothing we can do about it, we'll make the best of it, won't we? Maybe it will be the kind of boy that will make Pa a happier man. And that would be nice.'

'Tom, I didn't mean to hurt you by repeating that.'

'I ain't hurt. I know every time he looks at me he wishes I looked more like him than Ma. But as long as you like my looks, I'll be satisfied.'

'Oh, Tom, all the girls think you're devilishly handsome.'

'Ain't it funny how girls always put devilishly up front to make handsome not quite so meaningful?'

I turned to hug him. 'It's those teasing green eyes, Tom.' I bowed my head so my forehead rested on his chest just under his chin. 'I feel so sorry for Ma, all worn out and so big and clumsy-looking, and you know, up until today, I never even noticed. I feel so ashamed. I could have done so much to help her.'

'Ya do enough already,' Tom mumbled, pulling away when Logan stepped into view. 'Now smile, act happy, for boys don't like girls with too many problems.'

All of a sudden Fanny appeared, darting out from the shadows of the trees. She ran straight to Logan and threw herself at him as if she were six instead of a girl of thirteen, already beginning to develop rapidly. Logan was forced to catch her in his arms or be bowled over backward.

'My, yer getting more handsome by the day,' crooned Fanny, trying to kiss him, but Logan put her down and shoved her forcefully away, then came over to me. But Fanny was everywhere that day with her loud voice to scare off the fish, with her incessant demands for attention, so the Sunday afternoon that could have been fun was spoiled, until finally around twilight Fanny took off for parts unknown, leaving Logan, Tom, and me standing with three small fish not worth carrying home. Logan threw them back into the water, and we watched them swim away.

'I'll see ya at the cabin,' said Tom before he darted off, leaving me alone with Logan.

'What's wrong?' asked Logan as I sat staring at the way the setting sun was reflecting all sorts of rosy colours on the lake. I knew it would soon turn crimson as the blood that would spill when Sarah's newest baby came into the world. Memories of other births came fleetingly into the dark crevices of my mind. 'Heaven, you're not listening to me.'

I didn't know if I should or should not tell Logan about something so personal, yet it came out voluntarily, as if I couldn't keep anything secret from him. 'I'm scared, Logan, not just for Sarah and her baby, but for all of us. Sometimes when I look at Sarah and see how desperate she is, I don't know how long she can put up with her kind of life and if she goes – and she's always talking about leaving Pa – then she'll leave behind a new baby for me to take care of. Granny can't do anything much but knit or crochet, or sew braided rugs together.'

'And already you have more than enough to do, I understand. But, Heaven, don't you know everything always works out? Didn't you hear Reverend Wise's sermon today about the crosses we all have to carry? Didn't he say God never gives us one too heavy?'

That's what he'd said, all right, but right now Sarah was feeling that her cross weighed a ton, and I could hardly blame her.

We walked slowly toward the cabin, reluctant to part.

'You're not going to ask me in . . . again?' asked Logan in a stiff way.

'Next time . . . maybe.'

He stopped walking. 'I'd like to take you home with me, Heaven. I've told my parents how wonderful you are, and how pretty, but they'll have to see you and know you to appreciate the truth of what I've been saying.'

I backed off, sad for him and sad for me, wondering why he didn't let the poverty and shame of the Casteels drive him away. That's when he stepped up very quickly, grabbed me, and gave me a peck on my mouth. I was startled by the feel of his lips, by the way he looked in the strange light of the early evening.

'Good night . . . and don't worry, for I'll be here when you need me.' And with that he was off down the trail, heading for the clean and pretty streets of Winnerrow, where he'd climb stairs to the apartment over Stonewall's Pharmacy. In bright, cheerful modern rooms with running water and flushing toilets, two of them, he'd watch television this evening with his parents. I stared at the place where he had disappeared, wondering what it would be like to live in clean rooms, with a colour television. Oh, a thousand times better than here, I knew that, just knew that.

If I hadn't been thinking romantically of Logan, thinking about his kiss, I wouldn't have drifted so unaware into the cabin – and been so surprised when it exploded all around me.

Pa was home.

He paced the small space of the front room, throwing Sarah glares hard enough to drive knives through her. 'Why did you let yourself get pregnant again?' he bellowed, slamming his fist into the palm of his other hand; then he whirled round to bang his fist on the nearest wall, causing cups to jump from the shelf nearby and fall to the floor and break. And we had just enough cups, none to spare.

Pa was terrible in his anger – frightening as he whipped around with energy too great to confine in such a small space. 'I'm working night and day to keep you and your kids going . . .' he stormed.

'Ya had nothing to do with 'em, did ya?' screamed Sarah, her long, red hair loose from the ribbon that usually held it back.

'But I gave you those pills to take!' yelled Pa. 'I paid good money for those things, hoping you'd have sense enough to read the directions!'

'I took 'em! Didn't I tell ya I took 'em? Took 'em all, waiting for ya to come home, and ya didn't – and when ya did, all the pills were gone!'

'You mean you took them all at one time?'

She jumped up, started to speak, and then fell back into the chair she'd just left, one of the six hard straight chairs that gave no one real comfort. 'I forgot . . . kept forgetting, so I swallowed them all so I wouldn't forget . . . '

'Oh, God!' Pa moaned. His dark eyes glared at her with scorn and contempt. 'Dumb! And I read the directions to you!' With that he slammed out the door, leaving me to sit on the floor near Tom, who held Keith and Our Jane on his lap. Our Jane had her small face hidden against Tom, crying as she always cried when her parents fought. Fanny was on her bed pallet rolled up in a tight knot, her hands over her ears, and her eyes shut tight. Granny and Grandpa just sat rocking on and on, staring blankly into space, as if they'd heard all this many times before and they'd hear it many times again in the future.

'Luke'll come back and take care of ya,' Granny comforted weakly when Sarah continued to cry. 'He's a good boy. He'll forgive ya when he sees his new baby.'

Groaning, Sarah got up and began to prepare our last meal of the day. I hurried to assist. 'Sit down, Ma, or go and rest on the bed. I can handle this meal by myself.'

'Thank ya, Heaven . . . but I gotta do something to keep from thinking. And I used to love him so much. Oh, God, how I used to love and want Luke Casteel, never knowing or guessing he don't know how to love anyone better than himself . . .'

Fanny hissed at me that night, soon after supper was over: 'Gonna hate that new baby! We don't need it. Ma's too old to have babies . . . it's me who needs my own baby.'

'You don't need your own baby!' I flared sharply. 'Fanny, you're just brainwashing yourself to think having a baby means you'll be grown-up and free – a baby will tie you down worse than youth, so watch out how you play with your boyfriends.'

'You don't know nothing! It don't happen the first time! Yer ten times more a kid than me or else ya'd know what I really mean.'

'What do you really mean?'

She sobbed, clutching at me. 'Don't know. . . just want so much we don't have it hurts. There's gotta be something I can do to make my life better. Don't have no real boyfriend like ya got. They don't love me like Logan loves ya. Heaven, help me, please help me.'

'I will, I will,' I pledged as we clung together, not knowing what I could do but pray.

*

Hot August days seemed to grow shorter much too fast. The last weeks of Sarah's pregnancy passed more or less painfully for her, and for all of us, even though Pa showed up more often than he had, and he'd stopped yelling and pacing, and seemed resigned to the fact that Sarah might have five or six more kids before she was through.

She clumped heavily around the mountain cabin, her red, calloused hands often clasped over the mound that carried her fifth baby, which she was not anticipating with much joy. Mumbled prayers stayed on her lips, or else she bellowed out orders. The sweetness of Sarah at her best seldom showed anymore. Then, worse than anything, the loud mouthed meanness we'd unhappily grown accustomed to was replaced by an alarming silence.

Instead of yelling and screaming abuse at Pa, at all of us, she just shuffled along, like an old lady, and Sarah wasn't more than twenty-eight. She hardly glanced at Pa when he came home, not even bothering to ask where he'd been, forgetting about Shirley's Place: forgetting to ask if he was still earning 'clean' money, or selling that moonshine which was 'dirty' money. Sarah seemed locked up in herself, struggling to make some decision.

Day by day Sarah grew quieter, more withdrawn, less devoted to all of us. That hurt, to have no mother at all now, especially when Our Jane and Keith needed her so badly. Her glare hardened whenever Pa came in the door once or twice a week. He was working in Winnerrow, doing honest work, but she refused to believe that, as if she were looking for a reason to hate and distrust him. Sometimes I heard him telling Sarah about his work, looking uneasy because she didn't ask. 'Doing odd jobs for the church and the rich ladies with banker husbands who don't wanna dirty their lily-white hands.'

Sure, many a dollar Pa earned doing handyman chores for rich folks, and Sarah shouldn't dispute him. Pa could do any sort of handyman job.

*

Our Jane felt Sarah's depression, and seemed to get sick even more than usual that summer. She was the one who caught all the colds the rest of us easily threw off; she had chicken pox; and no sooner was that over than Our Jane fell into a patch of poison ivy and cried for one solid week night and day – driving Pa out in the middle of the night, again, to visit Shirley's Place.

There were good days when Our Jane felt well. When she was smiling and happy, there wasn't a more beautiful child in the whole wide world than Our Jane, the supreme ruler in the cabin of the Casteels. Oh, indeed, all the valley folks said, how beautiful were all the children of the wicked, cruel, sullen, and stormy Luke Casteel, and his wife Sarah, who according to jealous women, was not just plain but huge downright ugly.

One day when Keith, who seldom wanted anything, asked for crayons, it happened that the only ones in the cabin at the time were the ones given to Fanny by Miss Deale months ago. (So far Fanny had not once opened the box to colour anything.)

'No!' Fanny screeched. 'Keith can't have my brand-new crayons!'

'Give him your crayons or he might not speak again,' I urged, keeping a wary eye on the little quiet brother who had Grandpa's own silent way of sitting and doing nothing much. Still, Grandpa saw so much more than the rest of us. Who else could whittle each hair on a squirrel's tail? Who else had eyes that didn't just look, but really saw?

'I don't care if he never says nothing!' yelled Fanny.

Tom took her crayons and gave them to Keith as Fanny screamed and threatened to drown herself in the well.

'Shut up!' bellowed Pa, striding in the door and surveying his raucous children. He winced as if the noise we made pained his head.

'Ya made 'em, didn't ya?' was Sarah's only welcome. She clamped her lips together and didn't say another word. Pa glowered in her direction and dumped his supply of food on our scrubbed plank table. I hurriedly checked it over, trying to calculate how long that fifty-pound sack of flour would last, that five-gallon tin of lard, the bags of pinto and navy beans. I'd make soup to stretch the cabbage and ham . . .

Bang went the front door. Dismayed, I looked up. Pa was striding across the yard toward his old truck. Gone again.

My heart sank.

Every time Pa walked out and left Sarah needing him, she did something terrible to one of us, or to herself. And I could hardly blame him sometimes for not wanting to stay. Not only did Our Jane and the rest of us wear on Pa's nerves, he and Sarah wore on each other's nerves too. Sarah had lost not only what looks she had but her sweet personality as well.

Early mornings turned winterlike and squirrels raced around, hurrying to store their nuts for the winter, and Tom was helping Grandpa find the wood he needed to whittle, and that was no easy chore, for it had to be a certain kind, not too hard, and not so soft it would break easily with much handling. Both Pa and I were in the yard, alone for a change. 'Pa,' I began in a tentative way, 'I'm doing the best I can for this family . . . can't you do at least one thing for me, like say a kind word now and then?'

'Haven't I told ya before to leave me alone!' His piercing eyes glared my way before he turned his back. 'Now git before I give you what you deserve.'

'What do I deserve?' I asked fearlessly, my eyes no doubt an everlasting reminder of all he'd had once and lost. *Her*.

Starlings sat like miniature dark soldiers on the clotheslines. Puffy, sleepy birds, eyes closed, anticipating the coming cold and waiting for the warm sun. Mountain snow would be falling in the nights. I sighed as I stacked the wood, knowing no matter how we tried we'd never have enough to keep really warm. There was an axe half jutting from a felled tree trunk, an axe I thought Pa might use on me if I said one more word. I shut up and hefted the logs he'd split neatly onto the pile.

'There,' Pa said to Sarah when she came to the door, 'that should hold you until I'm home again.'

'Where ya going this time, so late?' called Sarah, who'd washed her hair and tried to make herself pretty for a change. 'Luke, gets mighty lonesome for a woman without a man, just ole folk and kids for company.'

'See ya soon,' Pa called back, hurrying toward his pickup truck. 'Got me a job to finish, and then I'll come home to stay all night.'

He didn't come home for an entire week. I sat on the porch late one night and stared at the grim, stormy sky. Sour thoughts made me miserable. There had to be a better place than here for me. Somewhere, a better place. An owl hooted, followed by the howl of a roaming wolf. The night held a thousand sounds. The autumn wind from the north shrieked and whistled around the forest trees, whipped around the trembling cabin and tried to blow it away, but all the people huddled close together for warmth held the house down, or so I thought.

I stared at the horned moon half hidden by dark clouds – the same moon that rode high over Hollywood and New York City, London and Paris. I blinked my eyes and tried to see across the hills, the ocean, then closed my eyes the better to see my future. Someday I'd like to have a real bed of my own to sleep in, with goosedown pillows and satin comforters.

I'd have closets, too, full of new dresses I'd wear once, like Queen Elizabeth, and I'd burn them as she had hers burned, so she'd never see them worn by anybody else. And shoes by the dozens I'd have, in all colours, and I'd eat in fancy restaurants where tall slim candles glowed . . . but right now I had only a hard, cold step to sit on. And tears were freezing on my cheeks and eyelashes.

I began to shiver, to cough; still, I wouldn't go inside and lay in that crowded room between Fanny and Our Jane. Tom and Keith slept next to the pallet used by Granny and Grandpa.

While the others lay sleeping more or less peacefully, there came the whisper of old feet moving slowly. Raspy breathing, grunts and groans, as Granny settled down by my side on the step.

'Ya'll catch yer death in this night cold, and maybe ya'll think that will make yer pa sorry, but is that gonna make ya happy in yer grave?'

'Granny, Pa doesn't have to hate me like he does. Why can't you make him understand it wasn't my fault my mother died?'

'He knows it ain't yer fault – down underneath he knows it. But if he admits it, he's gotta blame himself for marrying up with her, and bringing a gal like her to this kind of place she weren't used to. She tried, oh, she did try to do her best, and I'd see her out here scrubbing, ruining her pretty white hands, brushing back that hair of hers that was something to see . . . and she'd go running to that suitcase of hers, full of all sort of pretties, and she'd rub on cream from a tube, trying always to keep those hands young and pretty.'

'Granny, you know I can't bear to look in that suitcase and see all her pretty things. What good are clothes like that way up here where nobody ever comes? But I had a dream about the doll the other night – that she was me, and I was her. Someday I'm going to Boston and find my mother's family. I owe it to them to let them know what happened to their daughter, for surely they must think she's alive, living happily somewhere.'

'Yer right. Never thought of it myself, but yer right.' Her thin old arms hugged me briefly, and there was no strength in them none at all. 'Ya just set yer mind on what ya want, and ya'll get it, ya will.'

Life in the mountains was harder on Granny than on any of us. Nobody seemed to notice how much more difficult it had become for Granny to get up and down. Often she'd stop walking to clutch her heart. Sometimes her face would go chalky grey, and she'd gasp. It didn't do any good to suggest a doctor; she didn't believe in doctors, or any medicine she didn't concoct herself from roots and herbs she sent me out to find.

With Sarah acting glum and grim, each day was an ordeal to survive, except when I was with Logan, and then one terrible day when the sun was truly hot, I found him down by the river and Fanny was racing up and down the riverbank without a stitch on! Laughing and teasing him to try and catch her. 'And when ya do . . . I'll be yers, all yers,' she taunted. I stood frozen, horrified by Fanny's actions, as I turned my eyes on Logan and waited to see what he'd do.

'Shame on you, Fanny!' he called to her. 'You're just a kid who deserves a good spanking.'

'Then ya catch me and give it to me!' she challenged.

'No, Fanny,' he yelled, 'you're just not my type.' He turned to head back toward Winnerrow, or so I thought, and that's when I stepped out from behind the tree that had shielded me from his view.

He tried to smile and succeeded only in looking embarrassed. 'I wish you hadn't seen and heard that. I was waiting for you when Fanny showed up, and she just tore off her dress, and she wore nothing underneath . . . it wasn't my fault, Heaven, I swear it wasn't.'

'Why are you explaining?'

'It's not my fault!' he cried, his face red.

'I know it wasn't . . .' I said stiffly. I knew Fanny and her need to take from me anything I really wanted for myself. Still, from all I'd heard, most boys wanted loose girls with no modesty and no inhibitions, like my younger sister Fanny, who would undoubtedly live ten exciting lives while I struggled through one.

'Hey,' said Logan, reaching to tilt my bowed head so my lips were near his, 'it's your type I want, and your type I need. Fanny's pretty and bold . . . but I like my girls shy, beautiful, and sweet, and if I don't manage somehow to marry Heaven, I don't want to go there, not ever.'

This kiss he gave me did ring a few bells. I could hear them chiming like wedding bells ringing in the future.

Mrs Logan Grant Stonewall . . . me.

Instantly I was happy. In some things Fanny was right. Life did have to go on. Everybody needed a chance at living and loving. Now it was my turn.

Now Sarah took to talking to herself, walking in some unhappy dream.

'Gotta escape, gotta get away from this hell,' she mumbled. 'Ain't nothin but work, eat, sleep, wait and wait fer him t'come home – and when he does, ain't no satisfaction, ain't none at all.'

Don't say that, Sarah, please don't . . . what would we do without you?

'Done dug my own grave with my own desire,' Sarah confessed to herself on another day. 'Coulda had some otha man, coulda . . .'

'I'd leave, but for the kids.' She said this to herself day and night; then she'd stare hard at Pa when he came home on weekends, only to see he'd grown more handsome (damn him, she'd mutter), and her heart would jump up in her emerald eyes, and like a stupid, stopped clock whose hands had to say the same thing over and over again, back came her love for him.

Only too obviously, too painfully, Sarah's small world grew darker, grimmer. And it was I who bore most of the brunt of Sarah's frustration. Exhausted at the end of the day, I fell to my floor pallet and sobbed silent tears into my hard pillow. Granny heard, and Granny laid a comforting hand on my shoulder. 'Sssh, don't cry. Sarah don't hate ya none, chile. It's yer pa that makes her mad, but yer here and he's not. She can't yell out at him when he's not here, or hit out at him – couldn't even if he was here. Nobody ya don't love can be hurt if ya yell and scream – and she's been yelling and screaming for years and years, and he don't hear or care – and she don't go nowhere, so she's striking out at ya.'

'But why did he marry her in the first place if he didn't

love her, Granny?' I sobbed. 'Just so I'd have a stepmother to hate me?'

'Aw, Lawdy knows the whys and the wherefores of what makes men like they are,' wheezed Granny, turning over and hugging Grandpa, whom she called Toby, with great affection. Giving him more love with one kiss and one stroking hand on his grizzly face than any of us ever did. 'Ya just make sure to marry the right one, like I did, that's all. And wait till yer old enough to have good sense. Say fifteen.'

In the hills, a girl who reached sixteen without being engaged was almost bound beyond hope to be an old maid.

'Listen to them whispering,' mumbled Sarah, straining her ears from behind the faded thin red curtain, 'talking about me. Girl's crying again. Why am I so mean to her, why not Fanny who causes all the trouble? He likes Fanny, hates her – why not jump on Fanny? Our Jane, Keith? And most of all, Tom.'

I pulled in a deep fearful breath. Oh, the pity of Sarah thinking about turning against Tom!

It was terrible the day when Sarah lashed Tom with a whip, as if in striking him she could get back at Pa for never being what she wanted him to be. 'Didn't I tell ya to go into town and earn money? Didn't I?'

'But, Ma, nobody wanted to hire me! They got boys who have riding lawn mowers, with vacums that pull in the leaves. They don't need a hill boy who hasn't got even a push mower!'

'Excuses! I need money, Tom, money!'

'Ma . . . I'll try again tomorrow,' cried Tom, throwing up his arms and trying to protect his face. 'I'll never get a job if I look swollen and bloody, will I?'

Frustrated momentarily, Sarah stared down at the floor – unfortunately. Tom had forgotten to wipe his feet. 'Didn't look, did ya? The floors clean! Just scrubbed it! And look at it now, all muddy!'

Wham! She slammed her heavy fist into Tom's astonished face, spun him back against the wall, jarring from the shelf above, our precious jar of stolen honey that fell on his head and spilled the sticky stuff all over him.

'Thanks a heap, Ma,' said Tom with a funny grin. 'Now I got all the honey I can eat.'

'Oh, Tommy . . .' she sobbed, immediately ashamed. 'I'm sorry. Don't know what gets into me . . . don't ya go hating yer ma who loves ya.'

A nightmare with a capricious red-haired witch included had come to live in our house. A nightmare that didn't go when the sun dawned, when noon flared bright and cheerful; The stringy-haired, loud mouthed, ugly witch showed no mercy, not even to her own.

It was September. Soon we'd be going back to school, and any day Sarah's baby could come, any day. Still Sarah didn't go as she threatened time and again, thinking she'd really hurt Pa when she took away his look-alike dark-haired son. Pa stayed more and more in town.

All the hours blurred one into the other, horrible hours less than hell but far from paradise. Over the summer, we had grown noticeably larger, older, needing more, asking more questions, But as, Sarah's unborn child swelled out her front, the oldest among us grew weaker, quieter, less demanding.

It was building, building toward something. That something kept me tossing and turning all night, so when I got up in the morning it was as if I hadn't slept at all.

Five

Bitter Season

Logan was waiting for me halfway down the trail to the valley to walk me to the first day of school. The weather was turning chilly in the hills, but it was pleasantly warm in the valley. Miss Deale was still our teacher, since the school board continued to allow her to advance with her class. I was enchanted by her, as always; still, I kept drifting off . . .

'Heaven Leigh,' called the sweet voice of Miss Deale, 'are you day dreaming again?'

'No, Miss Deale. I don't day dream in class, only at home.' Why did everyone always titter – as if I did day dream?

It thrilled me to be back in school where I'd see Logan every day, and he'd walk me home and hold my hand, and with him I could momentarily forget all the problems that beset me in the cabin.

He walked beside me on the way home, both of us eagerly discussing our plans for the future, as Tom led the way with Our Jane and Keith, and Fanny lagged way back, accompanied by her many boyfriends.

All I had to do was to look around and see that soon our mountain nights would be freezing the water in the rain barrels, and all of us needed new coats and sweaters and boots that we couldn't afford. Logan held my hand, glancing at me often, as if he couldn't stop admiring me. Slowly, slowly, we strolled. Now Our Jane and Keith were skipping, laughing, as Tom ran back to check on what Fanny was doing with those boys.

'You're not talking to me,' Logan complained, stopping to pull me down on to a rotten log. 'Before we know it we'll reach your cabin yard, and you'll dash ahead, turn to me, and wave good-bye, and I'll never get to see the inside of your home.'

'There's nothing to see,' I said with my eyes lowered.

'There's nothing to be ashamed of, either,' he said softly, squeezing my fingers before he released my hand and tilted my face toward his. 'If you're going to stay in my life, and I can't picture life without you, someday you'll have to let me in, won't you?'

'Someday . . . when I'm braver.'

'You're the bravest person I've ever known! Heaven, I've been thinking about us a lot lately; about how much fun we have together, and how lonely the hours are when we're not together. When I'm finished with college, I'm thinking about becoming a scientist, a brilliant one, of course. Wouldn't you be interested in delving into the mysteries of life along with me? We could work as a team like Madame Curie and her husband. You'd like that, wouldn't you?'

'Sure,' I said without thought, 'but wouldn't it be boring, shut up in a lab day in and day out? Is it possible to have an outdoor lab?'

He thought me silly, and hugged me close. I put my arms around his neck and pressed my cheek against his. It felt so good to be held like this. 'We'll have a glass lab,' he said in a low, husky voice, with his lips close to mine, 'full of live plants . . . will that make you happy?'

'Yes . . . I think so . . .' Was he going to kiss me again? If I tilted my head just a little to the right, would that eliminate the problem of his nose bumping against mine?

If I didn't know how to manage a kiss, he sure did. It was sweet, thrilling. But the moment I was home all my elation was lost in the tempestuous seas of Sarah's miseries.

That Saturday dawned a bit brighter, a little warmer, and, eager to escape the sour hatefulness of Sarah at her worst, Tom and I went to meet Logan, and behind us tagged Our Jane and Keith. We were all good friends, trying to make Keith and Our Jane as happy as possible.

Hardly had we reached the river where we intended to

fish when over the hills came Sarah's bellowing hog call, beckoning us back. 'Good-bye Logan!' I cried anxiously. 'I have to get back to Sarah, she might need me! Tom, you stay and take care of Our Jane and Keith.'

I saw Logan's disappointment before I sped away to respond to Sarah's demand that I wash clothes instead of wasting my time playing around with a no-good village boy who'd only ruin my life. No good to love playing games and having fun when Sarah couldn't sit comfortably or stand for longer than seconds, and the work never ended. Feeling guilty to have escaped for a few minutes, I lifted the washtub onto the bench, carried hot water there from the stove, and began scrubbing on the old rippled board. Through the open window that tried to let out the stench from Ole Smokey, inside the cabin I could hear Sarah talking to Granny.

'Used to think it were good growing up in these hills. Felt freer than being some city gal who'd have to lock away all her sexual feelings till she was sixteen or so. Went to school only three years, hardly ever learned anything. Didn't like spelling, reading, writing, didn't like nothing but the boys. Fanny and me, no different. Couldn't keep my eyes off boys. When I first saw yer son, my heart did likketty-splits and flip-flops, and he were a man, almost. I were just a kid. Used to go to all the barn dances, every last one, and I'd hear yer Toby playing his fiddle, and see yer son dancing with all the prettiest gals, and something deep inside me told me I just had to have Luke Casteel or die trying.' Sarah paused and sighed, and when I took a peek in the window, I saw a tear coursing its way down her reddened face.

'Then there goes Luke off to Atlanta and meets up with that city gal, and he ups and marries her. My face, when I saw it sometimes in mirrors, looked coarse as a horse as compared to hers. But didn't make no difference, Annie, it didn't. Married or not, I still wanted Luke Casteel . . . wanted him so bad I'd do just anything to get him.'

Grandpa was on the porch, rocking, whittling, paying no

mind. Granny was rocking, not even seeming to be listening as Sarah talked on and on. 'Luke, he didn't look at me, though I tried to make him.'

I kept on scrubbing dirty clothes, stretching my ears to hear better. Near me was a rain barrel full of frogs croaking. Clothes I'd already washed were flapping on the line drying. Another peek inside showed me that Sarah was working near the stove, cutting biscuits with an inverted small glass, and in her low monotone she continued as if she had to tell someone or burst – and Granny was the best kind of listener. Never asking questions, just accepting, as if nothing she said would change anything. And no doubt it wouldn't.

I was all ears, and I kept sliding closer and closer to the window in order to hear better.

'I hated everything about her, that frail gal he called his angel; hated how she walked and how she talked – like she was better than us – and he doted on her like some jackass fool; trying to act fancypants like she did. Still, we all went running after, specially when she got herself knocked up; we thought he'd want to screw around on the side, and he paid us no mind at all. I decided I'd get him one way or another. He couldn't have her then, so he took me three times, and what I prayed for happened. He put a baby in me. He didn't love me, I knew that. Maybe he didn't even like me. He seemed bothered every time he were with me, and even called me angel once when he was riding me. When I told him I had his kid coming, he started turning money over to me for the baby I had in my womb. And just when I thought I'd have to up and marry some other man, that city girl obliged me by dying . . .'

Oh, oh! How awful for Sarah to be glad my mother died!

Sarah talked on in her flat, emotionless way, and I could hear the faint squeak of Granny's rocker going back and forth, back and forth.

'When he came to ask me to marry him so his baby could have its father, I thought in a month or so he'd forget all about her – but he didn't. He ain't yet. I tried to make him love me, Annie, truly I did. Was good to his baby, named Heaven. Gave him Tom, then Fanny, Keith, and Our Jane. Ain't had no other man since I married up. Would never have another if only he'd love me like he loved her – but he won't do it – and I can't talk to him no more. He won't listen. He's got his mind set on doing something crazy, and won't let me say nothing to keep him from trying. Gonna go and leave us all, that's what he's planning to do someday soon. Leave me here to wash, cook, clean, suffer . . . and take care of another baby. I'd stay forever if only he'd love me. But when he turns on me and shouts out ugly words, they eat on my soul, tellin me I'm sending him to his ruin, making him a mean, ugly animal that hits out at his own kids – wishing they were hers, not mine. I know. I see it in his eyes. He won't ever love me, not even like me. Ain't nothing I got that he admires. Except my good health, and he's ruining that. By God, he's ruining that!'

'Why ya keep saying that, Sarah? Ya seem healthy enough.'

'Never thought that dead wife would take his heart in the grave with her, never did think that,' Sarah whispered brokenly, as if she hadn't heard Granny's question. 'Don't care no more about him, Annie. Don't care no more about nothing. Not even my own kids. I'm just here, putting in time . . .'

What did she mean? Panic hit me hard. I almost tipped over the washtub and the scrubbing board I was leaning so hard against the rim.

The next day Sarah paced the floor again, mumbling to herself and anyone who chose to listen. 'Gotta escape, gotta get away from this kind of hell. Ain't nothing but work, eat, sleep, wait and wait for him to come home – and when he does, ain't no joy, no happiness, no satisfaction.'

She'd said all that a thousand times, and she was still here. It had been building so long I thought it could never happen, though I'd had ugly dreams of seeing Sarah murdered and bloody. I dreamed of Pa in his coffin, shot through the heart.

Many times I wakened suddenly, thinking I'd heard a gunshot. I'd glance at the walls, see the three long rifles, and shudder again. Death and killings and secret burials were all part of mountain living, which was always close to mountain dying.

Then the day came . . . what we'd all been nervously anticipating. It started early on a Sunday September morning when I was up and putting on water so we'd have some hot water for quick washups before going to church. Out of the bedroom came howls of distress, loud, sharp, full of pain. 'Annie, it's coming! Annie, it's Luke's dark-haired son coming!'

Granny scuttled around lamely, but her legs hurt and her breath came in short gasps, making my help more than necessary. And right from the first pain she seemed to know this birthing was going to be different, and more complicated than the others. Tom ran to hunt up Pa and bring him home as Grandpa reluctantly got up from his porch rocker and set off in the direction of the river, and I ordered Fanny to take care of Keith and Our Jane, but not to take them too far from the cabin. Granny and Sarah needed my help. This labour was taking much longer than it had when Our Jane came into the world on the same bed where all of us had been born.

Exhausted, Granny fell into a chair and gasped out instructions while I boiled the water to sterilize a knife to cut the umbilical cord. I tried to stop all the blood that flowed from Sarah like a red river of death.

And finally, after hours and hours of trying, with Pa in the yard waiting with Grandpa, Tom, Keith, and Our Jane, and Fanny nowhere to be found, while Sarah's face was white as paper, through all that blood emerged painfully, and slowly, a baby. A little bluish baby lying exceptionally still and strange-looking.

'A boy . . . a girl?' wheezed Granny, her voice as weak and thin as the wind that fanned our worn curtains. 'Tell me, girl, is it Luke's look-alike son?'

I didn't know what to say.

Sarah propped herself up to look. She stared and stared, trying to brush back her hair that was wet with sweat. Her colour came back as if she had gallons of blood to spare. I gingerly carried the baby over to Granny so she could tell me just what kind of baby this was.

Granny looked where some type of sex parts should be, and she nor I saw any.

I could hardly accept what my eyes told me. Shocking to see a baby with nothing between its legs. But what did it matter that this child was neither girl nor boy when it was dead and the top of its head was missing? A monster baby, sticky with running sores.

'Stillborn!' screamed Sarah, jumping out of bed and seizing the baby from my arms. She hugged it close, kissed its poor half-face a dozen or more times before she threw back her head and howled out her anguish like one of those mountain wolves that screamed at the moon.

'It's Luke and his damned whores!' Wild and crazy, she ran like a fury to where Pa sat outside, and she called his name just once before she shoved the baby into his arms. He held the baby with expertise, then stared down with incredulity and horror.

'See what ya did!' yelled Sarah, her single shapeless garment stained with the fluids of childbirth. 'Ya and yer rotten blood and whorin ways done killed yer own child! And made it a freak, too!'

Pa yelled out his rage. 'You're the mother! What you produce ain't got a damn thing to do with me!' He threw the dead child onto the ground, then ordered Grandpa to give it a decent burial before the hogs and dogs got to it. And away he strode, to jump into his truck and head to Winnerrow to drown his sorrows, if he had any, in moonshine, and later he'd no doubt stagger into Shirley's Place.

Oh, how terrible was this Sunday when I had to bathe a dead child in the tin tub, and get it ready for burying while Granny took care of Sarah, who suddenly lost all her strength and began to cry like any ordinary woman would. Gone was the Amazon fighting strength, only a woman after all, a sobbing bereaved mother on her knees asking God why a baby had to be cursed by his father's sins

Poor little thing, I kept thinking as I washed away all the blood and froth of birth from the pitiful, tiny body that lay so limp and still. I didn't even have to be careful to keep its half-head above water, but I did just the same. I dressed it in clothes that Our Jane and Keith had worn, maybe Fanny, Tom, and me as well.

Sarah finally fell flat on her face on the soiled bed, gripping the mattress in her clawing fingers, crying as I'd never known her to cry before.

I didn't even notice Granny until I was finished with the dead baby. Not until I looked at her two or three times did I realize that she wasn't knitting, crocheting, darning, braiding, weaving, or even rocking. She was just sitting very still with her eyes half closed. On her thin white lips was a faint smile. It scared me, that funny happy smile; she should be looking sad and mournful.

'Granny . . .' I whispered fearfully, laying down the stillborn child all dressed and clean, 'are you all right?'

I touched her. She fell to one side. I felt her face, and she was already turning cold, her flesh hardening.

Granny was dead!

Shocked into death by the birth of a monster baby, or by years and years of struggling to endure a life of hardships! I cried out, and felt an awful blow to my own heart. I knelt by her rocking chair to hold her close. 'Granny, when you get to heaven, please tell my mother I'm really trying hard to be like her. Tell her that, will you, please?'

A scraping sound moved our way, drifting in from the porch. 'What ya doing with my Annie?' asked Grandpa, coming back from the river where he'd gone to avoid knowing what men never wanted to know – only fitting for men to disappear until birthing was over. The way of the men of the hills, to flee from women's screams of suffering, and pretend to themselves they never suffered at all.

I looked up, my face streaked with tears, not knowing how to tell him. 'Grandpa . . .'

His faded blue eyes widened as he stared at Grandma. 'Annie . . . yer all right, ain't ya? Get up, Annie . . . why don't ya get up?' Of course he had to know when her eyes were staring backwards into her head. He stumbled forward, all his agility fleeing as if his life had flown the moment he knew his better half was dead.

On his knees he took Granny from my arms and cuddled her against his heart. 'Oh, Annie,' he sobbed, 'been so long since I loved ya . . . can ya hear me, Annie, can ya? Meant to do better by ya. Had me the best intentions. Never knew it'd turn out this way . . . Annie.'

It was awful to see his suffering, his terrible grief to lose a good and faithful wife who'd been with him since he was fourteen years old. How strange to know I'd never see him and Grandma cuddled up together on their bed pallet, with her long white hair spread out to pillow his face.

It took both Tom and me to pry Granny's body from Grandpa's arms, and all the time Sarah just lay on her back, tears gone now as she stared blankly at a wall.

We all cried at the funeral, even Fanny, all but Sarah, who stood frozen as stiff and empty-eyed as any cigar-store Indian.

Pa wasn't even there.

Dead drunk at Shirley's Place I had to presume, when his last child and his only mother were buried. Reverend Wayland Wise was there with his poker-faced wife, Rosalynn, to say the words for an old woman whom everybody had liked, if not respected.

Not one of ours would go into the ground without a proper funeral, with all the right words said to see this old woman and this stillborn child into heaven.

'And the Lord giveth, and the Lord taketh away,' intoned the Reverend. He tilted his face toward the sun. 'Lord God, hear my prayer. Accept this beloved wife, mother, grandmother and true believer, along with this tiny new soul, into heaven – fling wide your pearly gates, throw them open! Gather in this Christian woman, Lord, this child, Lord, for she was honest, plain, true to her faith, and the child is innocent, pure and divine!'

We trudged home in single file, still crying.

The people of the mountains were there to grieve with us. to suffer the departure of Annie Brandywine Casteel, one of their own, and with us they trooped back to the house, and sat with us, and sang with us, and prayed with us for hours on end. And when it was done, they brought out the moonshine, the guitars and banjos and fiddles, and they struck up a lively tune as the hill women brought out the treats to serve.

The next day when the sun was shining, I went to the graveyard to stand with Tom and stare down at Granny's raw grave, and that tiny one barely a foot long. My heart was broken to see 'Child Casteel' buried near my own mother. There wasn't a date put on her tombstone.

'Don't look at it,' whispered Tom. 'Your mother's been dead so long, and it's Granny we're going to miss most. Didn't know until her chair was empty just how much she added to our lives – did ya know?'

'No,' I whisperd, shamefaced. 'I just accepted her presence like she'd live forever. We're going to have to do more for Grandpa, he's so lost and alone-looking.'

'Yeah,' agreed Tom, catching my hand and leading me away from a sorrowful place that did little to communicate love to us. 'We gotta appreciate Grandpa while he's still with us, and not save our caring for his funeral day.'

A week later Pa came home looking sober and very grim. He pushed Sarah into a chair, pulled up a second one, and spoke in a strained voice while Tom and I paused outside the window to spy and eavesdrop. 'Went to see a doctor in the city, Sarah. That's where I been. He told me I was sick, real sick. Told me I was spreading my disease all over, and I'd have to stop what I was doing or I'd go insane before I die too young. Told me I can't have sexual relationships with any woman, not even my wife. Told me I needed shots to cure what I got, but we don't have that kind of money.'

'What ya got?' demanded Sarah in a cold, hard voice, not at all sympathetic.

'Got syphillis in its first stages,' Pa confessed in a hollow voice. 'Wasn't yer fault ya lost that baby, was mine. And so I'll say this one time, and that's all. I'm sorry.'

'Too late to be sorry!' yelled Sarah. 'Too late to save my baby! Ya killed yer ma when ya killed my last little one! Hear that! Yer ma is dead!'

Even I, who hated him, was shocked at how Sarah yelled that out, for if Pa loved anyone but himself, it had been Granny. I heard him suck in his breath, kind of groan, and then he sat down heavily enough to make the chair crack . . . and Sarah hadn't even finished punishing him.

'Ya had to play around, when I were here all the time, just yearning for ya to need me. I hate ya, Luke Casteel! Hate ya even more for never letting go a dead woman ya should have let alone anyway!'

'Yer turning against me?' he said bitterly. 'Now – when my ma is gone and I'm sick?'

'Yer damned right!' she screamed, jumping up and beginning to throw his clothes into a cardboard carton. 'Here's all yer rotten, stinking clothes – now git! Git before ya make all of us as rotten sick as ya are! Never want to see ya again! Not ever!'

He stood up, seeming humbled, glancing around the cabin as if he'd never see it again, and I was scared, so darn scared. I trembled as Pa stopped by Grandpa's chair and laid a gentle hand on his shoulder. 'Sorry, Pa. Real sorry I wasn't here on her funeral day.'

Grandpa said nothing, only bowed his head lower, and the tears from his eyes fell slowly, slowly, to wet his knees.

I watched silently as Pa again got into his old truck and sped off, kicking up dry dirt and scattering dead leaves, creating a whirl of dust and litter. He was gone, and he'd taken his dogs with him. Now we had only cats who hunted just for themselves.

When I ran to tell Sarah that Pa had really gone and this time he'd taken his dogs, she cried out and sank slowly to the floor. I knelt beside her. 'Ma, it's what you wanted, isn't it? You drove him out. You said you hated him . . . why are you crying when it's too late?'

'Shut up!' she roared in Pa's own ugly way. 'Don't care! It's better so, better so!'

Better so? Then why did she cry even more?

Who did I have to talk to now but Tom? Not Grandpa whom I'd never loved as much as Granny, mainly because he was so content in his locked-in, small world, and he didn't seem to need anyone but his wife, and she was gone.

Still, I helped him to the table each morning when Sarah stayed in bed, and each evening, and said what I could to ease him along until he grew accustomed to being without a wife. 'Your Annie has gone to heaven, Grandpa. She told me many a time to look out for you after she was gone, and I will. And think of this, Grandpa. Now she doesn't ache and pain anymore, and in paradise she can eat anything she wants, and not feel sick after every meal. I guess that's her reward . . . isn't it, Grandpa?'

Poor Grandpa . . . he couldn't speak. Tears streaked from his pale, tired eyes. When he had eaten a little, I helped him back to the rocker Granny had used, the one with the best cushions to make it more bearable for painful hips and joints. 'Ain't nobody to call me Toby no more,' he said in the saddest way.

'I'll call you Toby,' I said quickly.

'So will I,' volunteered Tom.

Grandpa said more after Granny died than I'd heard him say since I was born.

'Oh, God, life's getting dreary!' cried Fanny. 'If somebody else dies, I'm taking off!'

Sarah looked up, stared at Fanny for the longest time before she disappeared into the second room, where I heard the bedsprings squeal in protest as she threw herself down and cried again.

For when Granny's spirit left our cabin, all the love that held us together seemed to go with her.

Six

The End of the Road

For the first time since Granny had given it to me, when everyone was fast asleep I tiptoed to that secret place where I had hidden my mother's suitcase. I pulled it out from under all the old boxes full of junk and carefully, while sitting behind Ole Smokey so Fanny couldn't wake up and see, I took out the doll: The magical, beautiful bride doll that represented to me my mother.

I held that long, hard bundle for a long time, thinking back to the winter's night when Granny had given it to me. I'd been in and out of the suitcase a dozen times to fondle this or that, but I'd not unwrapped the doll since. Many a time I'd wanted to stare at the pretty face surrounded by all that lovely pale hair, but I'd feared doing so would make me feel sick inside for a mother who must have deserved better than she got. Granny's frail voice came as a whispery ghost to echo in my ears:

'Go on, chile. Ain't it time ya looked good to see what's inside? Been wondering many a year why ya don't want to play with it, and wear the fancy clothes.'

I felt her thin white hair whispering across my face, felt the cold winter winds blowing as I took out the fancy bride doll and unwrapped her. In the glow of the fire I stared at her face. How lovely she was in her marvellous white lace gown and veil, with tiny buttons that fastened right up to the chin, with white, filmy stockings, white satin-and-lace shoes that could be taken off and put back on. She wore a blue satin garter, for something blue, and held a tiny white-and-gold Bible with silk orange blossoms and white satin ribbons dangling, for something new.

Even her underwear was exquisitely made, a tiny bra to cup small hard breasts, and defiantly there was a cleft where most dolls remained neutered between the thighs.

Why was this doll made differently, more realistically?

It was part of the mystery of my mother, the doll and what it had to signify in her life. Someday I'd find out. I kissed her small face and saw the cornflower-blue eyes up so close there were faint specks of green and grey and violet – like my own eyes! My very own eyes!

In the morning, while Fanny was visiting a friend, and Tom was out showing Keith and Our Jane how to fish with more skill, I remembered when Granny told me how Pa wanted to chop up everything my mother had left behind, so she'd taken the suitcase and its contents and hidden them away. Now I'd lost Granny. My best connection to the past. Pa would never talk to me the way she had. Grandpa no doubt hadn't even taken notice of the girl his son called angel.

'Oh,' I sighed as Tom came in. 'Look, Tom, here is a doll that Granny said belonged to my real mother. A bride doll to look like her when she was only a girl the same as me. See what's written on her bare foot.' I held it so he could see, once I had her decently dressed again, but for stockings and shoes.

A Tatterton Original Portrait Doll
Issue, One

'Put her stockings and shoes on, and hide her quick,' whispered Tom. 'Fanny's coming with Our Jane and Keith, and that's your face if I ever saw it. No good letting Fanny ruin something so beautiful.'

'You're not surprised?'

'Sure, but I found it long ago, and put it back like Granny told me to do. . . . Now quick, before Fanny comes in.'

As fast as I could I pulled on the stockings, stuffed on the shoes, and rewrapped the suitcase in the filthy old quilt, and in the nick of time hid it again, only then brushing away the tears from my cheeks.

'Still crying for Granny?' asked Fanny, who could display

grieving emotions one second and be laughing the next. 'She's better off, she is, than sitting in here all day and doing nothing but hurting and complaining. Anywhere but here is a better place.'

My doll made up for so much. Made up, I thought at the time, for Sarah's meanness, for Pa's illness, for the fact that I hadn't seen Logan for a week. Where was he? Why didn't he wait to walk me home anymore? Why hadn't he come to say he was sorry about Granny? Why didn't he and his parents go to church anymore? What kind of devotion was he showing now that he'd kissed me?

Then I guessed. His parents had to know about Pa's disease, and they didn't want their one and only son coming to see hill scum like me. I wasn't good enough, even if I didn't have syphilis.

Put away thoughts. Better to think about the doll, and the secret of why my mother, at such a late age, would want a doll made to look like herself.

Nothing short of death would keep us from church, and proudly we trudged onward, wearing our old rags, the best we had, with Sarah leading the way now that Pa had the truck, and didn't come to drive us there. I held Grandpa's large bony hand in mine, and actually pulled him along, just as I had to tug on Our Jane, who held with her other hand to Keith.

Every head in the church turned to stare our way, as if one family with so much trouble had to be unworthy sinners.

They were singing as we entered, singing in their glorious voices that had so much practice when they attended church three times a week, and we only went on Sundays.

'Rock of Ages, cleft for me,
Let me hide myself in thee . . .'

Hide, how appropriate that word was. We should all run away and hide until Pa was well again, and Sarah could laugh once more, and Our Jane stopped crying for a granny who'd gone away and didn't give her hugs anymore. But there was no place to hide.

Then, the next day, Logan showed up by my locker, smiling at me with his eyes even when his lips stayed in a straight line. 'Did you miss me the week I was gone? I wanted to tell you my grandmother was sick and we'd be flying to see her, but there wasn't time before the plane left.'

I stared at him with huge wistful eyes. 'How is your grandmother now?'

'Fine. She had a small stroke, but seemed to feel much better when we left.'

'That's nice,' I said in a choked way.

'What did I say wrong? Something, I can tell! Heaven, haven't we sworn to always be honest with one another? Why are you crying?'

My head bowed and then I was telling him about Granny, and he said all the right words to console me. I cried awhile on his shoulder, and with his arm still about my shoulder we headed up the trail toward home. 'And what about the baby your stepmother was expecting?' asked Logan, appearing happy that Tom and Fanny stayed out of sight with Our Jane and Keith.

'It was stillborn,' I answered stiffly. 'Granny died the same day . . . guess all of us went kind of numb, losing two, and on the same day.'

'Oh, Heaven, no wonder you looked so funny when I said my grandmother recovered. I'm sorry, so damned sorry. Someday, I hope, someone will tell me the right words to say at moments like this. Right now I feel inadequate . . . except I know I'd have loved your granny just as much as you did.'

Yes, Logan would have loved Granny, even if she would have embarrassed his parents. As Grandpa would still embarrass them, if ever . . .

The next day Miss Deale beckoned me to stay after class for a few minutes. 'You go for Our Jane and Keith,' I whispered to Tom before I stepped up to her desk. I was eager to meet with Logan, and anxious to avoid a teacher who could sometimes ask too many questions I didn't know if I should answer.

She looked at me for long moments first, as if she saw changes in my eyes as Logan had. I knew my eyes were shadowed underneath, knew I was losing weight, but what else could she be seeing? 'How are things going with you now?' she asked, staring directly into my eyes as if to keep me from lying.

'Fine, just fine.'

'Heaven, I heard about your grandmother, and I'm so very sorry you had to lose someone you loved so much. I see you in church often, so I know you have the same kind of faith your grandmother did, and you do believe we all have eternal souls.'

'I want to believe that . . . I do . . .'

'Everyone does,' she said softly, laying her hand on mine.

I sighed heavily and tried not to cry. And without meaning to be a tattletale and show lack of family loyalty, I had to speak when I didn't know what others might have already told her. 'Granny died, I guess, from heart failure,' I said before my tears came. 'Sarah had a baby that was stillborn and sexless, and Pa's gone, but other than that, we're all just fine.'

'Sexless. . . Heaven, all babies are one sex or the other.'

'I thought the same thing myself, until I helped deliver this one. Don't tell a soul, please, for it would hurt Sarah if others knew – but this last baby didn't have any genitals.'

She paled. 'Oh . . . I'm so sorry to have been so tactless. I did hear a few rumours, but I try never to listen to them. Of course nature sometimes creates oddities. Since all your father's children are so beautiful, I naturally presumed your mother would have another perfect child.'

'Miss Deale, it's a wonder you haven't heard about me. Sarah is not my mother. My father has been married twice. I am his first wife's child.'

'I know,' she whispered in a low voice. 'I've heard about your father's first wife, and how lovely she was, and how young when she died.' She blushed and looked uncomfortable, then began to pick invisible lint from her expensive knit suit. 'I presumed you love your stepmother very much, and like to pretend she is your mother.'

'Used to like doing that.' I smiled. 'I've got to run along now, or else Logan will be walking another girl home. Thank you, Miss Deale, for being a good friend; for growing with us in school; for making Tom and me feel good about ourselves. Why, Tom and I said just this morning, school would sure be a bore without our wonderful Miss Deale.'

Chuckling and tearfully smiling, she touched my hand and excused me with: 'You're prettier each time I see you, Heaven – but set your goals now. Don't give them up just to become another girl who rushes into marriage too soon.'

'Don't you worry that I'll not head for my goals!' I sang out, backing toward the door. 'It'll be a rare fine day when I'm thirty before I go into some man's kitchen to bake his biscuits and wash his dirty clothes – and have his babies once a year!' And out of the classroom I ran, hurrying to where I thought Logan would be waiting.

This particular day in the valley was sunny, mild, with fat white clouds heading for London, Paris, and Rome as I ran to where six or seven boys clustered in a tight gang yelling.

'Yer a sissy city boy!' one bully called Randy Mark yelled at a filthy, dirty boy whom I gasped to see was Logan! Oh, they'd finally got him – and he'd said they never would. There he was on the ground, wrestling with another boy his age. Already Logan's shirt sleeve was torn, his jaw red and puffy, and his hair fell over his forehead.

'Heaven Casteel is just another whore in the making like her sister – even if she won't let us, she lets you!'

'She does not!' roared Logan, red-faced and so angry he seemed to give off smoke even as he managed to snatch a good leg lock on Randy before he twisted that leg ruthlessly. 'You take back everything nasty you said about Heaven! She's the most honourable, decent girl I've met in my whole life!'

'Cause ya don't know rotten apples from good!' screamed another boy.

Who had started this, and what had been said? I glanced around to see one of the girls in my class who always laughed at my shabby clothes, and she was grinning slyly. I ran to where Tom crouched, ready to jump into the fight. 'Tom,' I cried, 'why don't you help Logan?'

'I would if it wouldn't convince all the others he didn't know how to fight. Heavenly, Logan's got to do this himself, or he'll never live it down that I had to help.'

'But hill boys don't fight fair, you know that!'

'Don't matter. He's got to do it their way, or forever be picked on.'

Fanny was jumping up and down, terribly excited, as if Logan were fighting for her honour, not mine. Keith pulled Our Jane over to the swings and began to push her back and forth so she wouldn't cry to see one of her friends hurt. How sensitive Keith was, I had time to think before I looked back at the pair on the ground.

It was awful to stand there and watch those boys take on Logan one after the other, not giving him time to catch his breath before a new boy jumped into the dirt ring they'd drawn and began throwing blows. By this time Logan was bloody, his face bruised and swollen, and his left eye was all closed. I clutched Tom, almost crying. 'Tom, you have to help him now!'

'No . . . hang on . . . he's doing fine.'

How could he say that when Logan looked ten times worse than any of the others? 'They're killing him, and you say he's doing fine!'

'They're not gonna kill him, silly. They're just testing to see if he's got what it takes.'

'What does it take?' I yelled, ready to pitch in myself and help, but Tom caught and held me.

'Don't you dare shame him by helping,' he whispered urgently. 'As long as he keeps slinging blows and fighting back, they'll respect him. Once you or I help, it's all over for him.'

As I stood there and watched, cringing every time Logan was hit, and yelling savagely every time he delivered a blow, he quickly glanced my way, dodged the next blow, and delivered a swift uppercut. I screamed encouragement, feeling as vicious as any girl there.

Now Logan was on top, and the boy underneath was screaming. 'Now apologise . . . take back what you said about my girl!' ordered Logan.

'Yer girl's a Casteel . . . ain't none of 'em good!'

'Take it back, what you said, or I'll break your arm.' Logan gave that arm a vicious twist.

The boy beneath him yelled for mercy. 'I take it back.'

'Apologise to her. While she's here and can hear.'

'Ya ain't like yer sister Fanny!' screamed the boy about to have his arm broken. 'But she's sure gonna be one damned whore, the whole town knows it!'

Fanny ran to give him several hard kicks while all the others laughed. Only then did Logan release the boy's arm, turning him over before he slammed his fist into the boy's jaw. Instantly everyone stopped yelling and stared down at the unconscious face as Logan stood up, brushed off his clothes, and glared at everyone there but Tom and me.

Funny how they all disappeared, leaving me, Tom, and Fanny standing together as Keith and Our Jane continued to use the swings and paid no attention to the fight. Tom ran to pound Logan on the back. 'Boy, buddy, you were great, really great! You threw that right hook just perfect. Timed your leg twist just right . . . couldn't have done it better myself.'

'Thanks for giving me the lessons,' murmured Logan, looking dazed and terribly exhausted. 'Now, if you don't mind, I'm going into school and wash up. If I went home looking like this, my mother would faint.' He smiled my way. 'Heaven, hang around, will you, until I'm back?'

'Sure.' I stared at all his bruises, and his black eye. 'Thanks for defending my honour . . .'

'Why, he defended all our honours, dummy!' shrieked Fanny. Then, so help me, she ran to throw her arms about Logan and kissed him squarely on his swollen, bleeding lips.

I should have done that.

Logan walked off toward the school as Tom grabbed Fanny's arm, called Our Jane and Keith, and all of them headed for our trail. All alone in the schoolyard I waited for Logan to come out of the boys'.

On the swing Our Jane had used I shoved myself higher and higher, hanging back and dangling so my hair would fan and almost sweep the ground. I hadn't felt so happy since before Granny died. I closed my eyes and flew even higher on the swing.

'Hey . . . you up there in the sky, come on down so I can walk you home before dark, and we can talk.'

Logan looked somewhat cleaner, somewhat less damaged, as I dragged my feet and brought the swing to a stop. 'You're not really hurt, are you?' I asked with concern.

'No, not really hurt.' His one eye peered at me. 'Do you really care if I am?'

'Of course I care.'

'Why?'

'Well . . . I don't know why, except, well, you did call me your girl. Am I your girl, Logan?'

'If I said so, then you must be. Unless you have some objections.'

I was up now, and he had my hand, gently urging me toward the mountain trail that spiraled steeply up, up, up.

Winnerrow had only one main street, and all the others branched off from that. Even placed in the middle of town the school backed up to the mountain range. There wasn't any way the town could escape the surrounding Willies. 'You haven't answered,' urged Logan when we'd strolled on for fifteen minutes without speaking, only holding hands and glancing often at one another.

'Where'd you go last weekend?'

'My parents wanted to see the college where I'll be going.

I wanted to call and tell you, but you have no telephone, and I didn't have time to walk to your place.'

There it was again. His parents didn't want him to see me, or he could have found time. I turned and put my arms about his waist and pressed my forehead against his dirty, torn shirt. 'I'm thrilled to be your girl, but I've got to warn you now, I don't intend to get married until I've had the chance to live and grow on my own, and to become somebody. I want my name to mean something after I'm dead.'

'Looking for immortality?' he teased, holding me closer and bowing his face into my hair.

'Something like that. You see, Logan, a psychiatrist came to our class one day and he said there are three kinds of people. One, those who serve others. Two, those who give to the world by producing those who serve others. Three, the last kind, those who can't be satisfied unless they achieve on their own, not by serving others but by their own merits and talents, producing, and not through their children, either. I'm the third kind. There's a niche in this world meant for me and what innate talents I have . . . and I won't find it if I marry young.'

He cleared his throat. 'Heaven, aren't you getting way ahead of this situation? I'm not asking you to be my wife, just my girl.'

I drew sharply away. 'Then you don't really want to marry me someday?'

His hand spread helplessly. 'Heaven, can we predict the future and who we'll want we're twenty, twenty-five, or thirty? Take what I offer now, and let the future take care of itself.'

'What are you offering now?' I asked suspiciously.

'Just me, my friendship. Just me, and the now-and-then right to kiss you, hold your hand, touch your hair, and take you to the movies, and listen to your dreams because you listen to mine, and be silly once in a while, build a past we'll enjoy remembering – that's all.'

That was enough.

Hand in hand we continued to stroll, and it was sweet to reach the cabin near twilight that flattered the tiny house nestled on the hillside. He had only one good eye anyway, and I knew he couldn't truly see the shoddiness of how we lived until he went inside.

I turned and cupped his face between my palms. 'Logan, would it be all right, and not too much like Fanny, if I kissed you just once for being so exactly what I want?'

'I think I could bear up.'

Slowly my arms slid up around his neck – how awful his eye looked now that we were inches apart – I closed my eyes and puckered my lips, and kissed that swollen eye, his cut cheek, and finally his lips. He was trembling by this time. So was I.

I was scared to say another word, so afraid realities would spoil the sweetness of what we had. 'Good night, Logan. See you tomorrow.'

'Good night, Heaven,' he whispered, as if he'd lost his voice. 'Sure has been a great day, sure has been . . .'

In that part of the day Granny used to call the gloaming I watched until Logan was out of sight, disappearing into darkness, before I turned away and entered the cabin that immediately depressed my soaring spirits. Sarah had stopped making any attempt to keep the cabin clean, or even tidy. Meals that had been adequate before had become haphazard affairs of bread and gravy without greens or vegetables, and seldom did we have chicken or ham anymore. Slab bacon was a memory food better not to think about. Our garden out back where Granny and I had spent so much time pulling weeds and planting seeds was neglected. Ripe vegetables were left to rot in or on the ground. No salt pork or ham was in the smokehouse to flavour our bean soup or greens, spinach, or turnips, now that Pa never came home. Our Jane was in a finicky mood, refusing to eat, or throwing up what she did, and Keith cried constantly because he never had enough to eat, and Fanny did nothing but complain.

'Somebody but me should do something!' I yelled, turning in circles. 'Fanny, you go to the well and fill the bucket, and bring it in with the water to the brim, not just a few cupfuls, which is your lazy way. Tom, go to the garden and pull up whatever is there we can eat. Our Jane, stop that wailing! Keith, entertain Our Jane so she'll stay quiet and I can think.'

'Don't ya give me orders!' screamed Fanny. 'I don't have to do nothing ya say! Just cause ya had a boy fight for ya don't mean yer queen of the hill!'

'Yes, you do have to obey Heaven,' backed Tom, who gave Fanny a shove toward the door. 'Go to the spring and bring back really good water.'

'But it's dark out there!' wailed Fanny. 'Ya know I'm scared of the dark!'

'Okay, I'll fetch the spring water, you pick the vegetables, and stop back-talking . . . or I'll be the king of the hill and give yer bottom ten solid wacks!'

'Heaven,' Tom whispered from where he lay on his floor pallet that night, looking at me with so much compassion, 'someday, I can feel in my bones, it's all gonna turn out fine for all of us. Ma will go back to how she was, and start cooking good meals again. She'll clean up the house and you won't have so much to do. Pa will come home cured, and nicer to us than before. We'll grow up, graduate from school, go to college, be so smart we'll make piles of dough, and we'll ride around in big cars, live in mansions, have servants, and we'll sit and laugh at how tough we thought we had it, never suspecting all this was good for us. Makes us determined, hardy, better kids than those who have it easy – that's what Miss Deale says, anyway. The best often comes out of the worst.'

'Don't feel sorry for me. I know it's going to be better, someday.' I brushed away weak tears.

He crawled over to cuddle in the pallet beside me, his strong young arms feeling good, warm, safe. 'I can hunt up Pa, and you talk to Ma.'

'Ma,' I said the very next evening, hoping to cheer her with casual talk before I got down to serious matters, 'only a few short hours ago I thought I had fallen in love.'

'Yer a damned fool if ya do,' muttered Sarah, glancing at my figure, which was definitely taking on a woman's shape. 'Ya get off this mountain – get far from here before ya let some man put his kid in ya,' she warned. 'Ya run fast and ya run far before ya become what I am.'

Distressed, I threw my arms about Sarah. 'Ma, don't say things like that. Pa'll come home soon, and he'll bring all the food we need. He always comes home before we're really hungry.'

'Yeah, sure he does.' Sarah's expression turned ugly. 'In the nick of time our dear Luke comes back from whoring and boozing, and he throws his bags on the table like he's bringing us solid gold. An that's all he does for us, ain't it?'

'Ma . . .'

'I ain't yer ma!' yelled Sarah, red-faced and looking ill. 'Never was! Where's all the brains ya think ya got? Can't ya see ya don't look like me?'

She stood with her bare feet braced wide, her long red hair in complete disarray, not washed since the baby was born dead, not combed or brushed either, nor had Sarah bathed in more than a month. 'I'm getting out of this hellhole, an if ya got any brains at all, ya'll run soon after.'

'Ma, please don't go!' I cried out in desperation, trying to catch hold of her hands. 'Even if you aren't my real ma, I love you, I do! I always have! Please don't go and leave us here alone! How can we go to school and leave Grandpa? He doesn't walk as well as he did when Granny was alive. He can't chop wood anymore. He can hardly do anything. Please, Ma.'

'Tom can chop the wood,' she said with a deadly calm, as if she'd decided to leave, no matter what happened to us.

'But Tom has to go to school, and it takes more than one to chop enough wood and kindling to last the entire winter, and Pa is gone.'

'Ya'll get by. Don't we always?'

'Ma, you can't just up and leave!'

'I can do anything I damn well please – will serve Luke right!'

Fanny heard and came running. 'Ma, take me with you, please, please!'

Sarah shoved Fanny away, backed off to stare at us all with calm indifference. Who was this dead-faced woman who didn't care? She wasn't the mother I'd always known. 'Good night,' she said at the curtain that was her bedroom door. 'Yer Pa'll come when ya need him. Don't he always?'

Maybe it was the fruit in the middle of the table that tickled my nostrils and made me come awake.

Why, look at all that food stacked there. Where had it come from, when last night our cupboard had been bare? I picked up an apple and bit it as I went to call Sarah and tell her that Pa had come home during the night and brought us food. In the doorway, holding back the flimsy curtain, I froze, my teeth deep into the red apple, my eyes wide and shocked . . . no Sarah. Just a rumpled bed with a note left on the mattress.

During the night while we slept, Sarah must have slipped out into the dark. leaving a note we were supposed to pass on to Pa when he returned – if ever he returned.

I shook Tom awake to show him the note. He sat up and rubbed at his eyes, and read it over three times before comprehension dawned. He choked, tried not to cry. He and I were both fourteen now. Birthdays came and went without parties or any kind of celebrations to mark our years.

'What y'all doing up so early?' grumbled Fanny, grouchy as she always was when she came out of sleep and found her bones stiff from hard floorboards and not enough padding between her skeleton and the floor. 'I don't smell no biscuits bakin, no bacon frying . . . see no gravy in the pan.'

'Ma's gone,' I said in a small voice.

'Ma wouldn't do that,' said Fanny, sitting up and looking

around. 'She's in the outhouse.'

'Ma don't leave notes to Pa when she does that,' Tom reasoned. 'All her things are gone – what little she had.'

'But the food, the food, I see food on the table!' screeched Fanny, jumping up and running to grab a banana. 'Bet ya Pa came back and brought all this here stuff . . . and he and Ma are out somewhere fighting.'

When I gave it more thought, it seemed very likely that Pa had slipped into the cabin at night, left the food, then drove off without a word to anyone; and perhaps finding the food there, and knowing Pa hadn't bothered to stay or even greet her, had given Sarah the final motivation to leave, thinking now we had food to provide for us until he came back again.

How oddly Our Jane and Keith took the absence of Sarah, as if they'd always lived on unstable ground and Sarah had never given either one enough loving attention to make any difference. Both came running to me, staring up into my face. 'Hev-lee,' cried Our Jane, 'ya ain't going nowhere, are ya?'

How fearful those big eyes. How beautiful the small doll face that looked up into mine. I tousled her reddish blonde hair. 'No, darling, I'm staying. Keith, come closer so I can give you a big hug. We're going to have fried apples and sausages for breakfast today, with our biscuits . . . and see, Pa brought us margarine. Someday we're going to eat real butter, aren't we, Tom?'

'Well, I sure hope so,' he said as he picked up the package of oleo. 'But I'm glad right now we have this. Hey, do you really think Pa came in the night, like Santa Claus, and left all this stuff?'

'Who else would?'

He agreed. As hateful and mean as Pa was, he did try to see that we were kept fed, and as warm as possible.

Now life got down to basics. Sarah had run out and Granny was dead.

Grandpa couldn't do anything but sit and stare, and whittle. I went to his rocker where he'd slept bent over and miserable-looking all night, took his hand, and helped him to stand. 'Tom, see that Grandpa visits the outhouse while I fix breakfast, and after he's eaten, give him more wood to whittle, for durn if I can stand seeing him doing nothing at all.'

I guess that breakfast on such a heartrending day, made it somewhat easier, when we had hot sausages to eat and fried apples and taters, and biscuits with what had to taste as good as butter.

'Wish we had a cow,' said Tom, who worried about none of us drinking enough milk. 'Wish Pa hadn't gambled away our last one.'

'Ya could steal one,' contributed Fanny, who knew all about stealing. 'Skeeter Burl's got the one that used to be ours. Pa don't have no right to gamble away our cow – so steal it back, Tom.'

I felt hollow inside, beset with worries far too heavy for my years; when I gave it more thought, I realized there was many a girl my age with a family of her own. Still, those girls didn't desire a college education as I did. They were happy to live out their lives being wives and mothers, and living in shacks, and if their men beat them once a week, they thought it their due.

'Heaven, aren't ya coming?' Tom asked as he readied himself for school.

I glanced again at Grandpa, at Our Jane who was feeling poorly. She'd barely tasted the best breakfast we'd had in weeks.

'You go on, Tom, with Fanny and Keith. I can't leave Our Jane when she's not feeling well. And I want to see that Grandpa doesn't just sit and rock and forget to walk around.'

'He's all right. He can take care of Our Jane.'

I knew, even as he said that, he didn't believe it; he blushed and bowed his head and looked miserable I felt like crying again. 'In a few days we'll adjust, Tom. Life will go on, you'll see.'

'I'll stay home,' Fanny volunteered. 'And I'll take care of Our Jane and Grandpa.'

'A perfect solution,' Tom agreed happily. 'Fanny's not ever going to finish school. She's old enough to do something simple.'

'Okay,' I said as a test. 'Fanny, first you'll have to give Our Jane a cool bath. You'll have to see that she drinks eight glasses of water a day, and make her eat a little food off and on, and walk Grandpa back and forth to the outhouse, and do what you can to clean up and keep this place tidy.'

'Going to school,' stated Fanny. 'I ain't no slave to Grandpa, ain't no mother to Our Jane. I'm going where the boys are.'

I might have known.

Reluctantly Tom backed toward the door. 'What should I tell Miss Deale?'

'Don't you tell her Sarah ran off and left us!' I flared hotly. 'You just say I'm staying to help out with all there is to do when Grandpa's feeling bad and Our Jane is sick. That's all you tell her, understand?'

'But she could help.'

'How?'

'I don't know how, but I'll bet she could think of something.'

'Thomas Luke, if you hope to reach your goals in life, you can't go around begging for help. You rise above all difficulties and find your own solutions. Together you and I will see this family through, and find ways to stay healthy. You say anything you have to say to keep Logan and Miss Deale unaware that Ma has walked out on us . . . for she might come back any minute, once she realizes what she did was wrong. We wouldn't want to shame her, would we?'

'No,' he breathed, appearing relieved. 'She could come back once she thinks more about how wrong it is to go.'

He took Keith's right hand, and Fanny took Keith's left hand, and off they set toward the school, leaving me standing on the porch with Our Jane in my arms. She wailed to see Keith trudging dutifully toward school, while I longed to be there with them.

First thing I did after bathing Our Jane and putting her into the big brass bed was to hand Grandpa his whittling knives and his pieces of prime wood. 'Whittle something Granny would like, say a doe with big sad eyes. Granny had a special liking for does – didn't she?'

He blinked once or twice, glanced at the empty rocking chair he refused to use even though it was the best one, and two fat tears slid down his wrinkled cheeks. 'Fer Annie,' he whispered when he picked up his favourite knife.

I turned my attention back to Our Jane, and dosed her fever as I thought Granny would have done, with herbal medicine, and then I set about doing all that Sarah used to do before she turned on us.

Tom seemed stricken when he came home from school to see if Ma had returned and found she hadn't. 'I guess it's up to me now to be the man in the family,' he said, as if overwhelmed by all he'd have to do. 'Won't be no money coming in if somebody doesn't go out and make it. Yard jobs are hard to find when ya don't have the right equipment. Stores don't give away food staples, and what we got won't last nearly long enough. And we sure could all use new shoes. Heavenly, ya can't go to school wearing shoes without toes.'

'I can't go to school, shoes or not,' I said tonelessly, wiggling my toes that stuck out of shoes much too small, so I'd had to cut them. 'You know I can't leave Grandpa alone, and Our Jane isn't well enough to take her to a doctor.'

'Doctors can't help what she's got,' mumbled Grandpa with his head bowed low. 'Something inside Our Jane don't work right, and ain't no doctor can give her what she needs.'

'But how do you know that, Grandpa?' I challenged.

'Annie had a young 'un once, same as Our Jane. Put him in a hospital, they did. Cost me an Annie all our savings . . . and didn't do one bit of good. Sweetest boy I ever had, up and died on Easter Sunday. Told myself he was like Christ on the cross, too good and too sweet for this mean, ole world.'

There went Grandpa talking just like Granny, when he'd never said much of anything when she lived. 'Grandpa, don't say things like that!'

'No, Grandpa,' put in Tom, holding fast to my hand. 'Doctors can save people from dying. Medicine gets better year by year. What killed your son doesn't have to kill Our Jane.'

Tom stared at me with wide, frightened eyes as we readied ourselves for bed after a meal of more fried taters, more sausage, and biscuits and gravy, and apples for dessert. All the energy drained from his eyes. 'What are we gonna do, Heavenly?'

'Don't you worry, Tom. You, Fanny, Keith, and Our Jane will go to school. I'll stay home and take care of Grandpa, and do the wash, and cook the meals. I know how,' I finished defiantly.

'But it's you who loves school, not Fanny.'

'Don't matter. Fanny's not responsible enough to stay home and run things.'

'She acts that way on purpose,' said Tom, tears in his eyes. 'Heavenly, no matter what you say, I am gonna tell Miss Deale. Maybe she can think of something that will help.'

'No! You can't do that. We've got our pride, Tom, if we don't have anything else. Let's save something we can cherish.'

Pride was important to both of us. Perhaps because it was something free, something that made us feel important. We, Tom and I, had to prove ourselves to the world, and also to ourselves. Fanny wasn't included in our pact. Fanny already had proven herself untrustworthy.

Seven

Coping

Tom hurried home each day to help me with the wash, with the floor scrubbing, with taking care of Our Jane; then he'd chop wood, always he had to chop wood. Sometimes we all ran about madly, trying to round up hogs and pigs that had escaped through our frail fence rails, our chickens which were one by one being killed off by bobcats or foxes, or stolen by vagabonds.

'Did Logan ask about me again today?' I asked when I'd missed three days of school.

'He sure did. Got me after school and wanted to know where you are. How you are. Why ya don't come. I told him Sarah is still sick, and Our Jane, too, and ya had to stay home and take care of everybody. Boy, you never saw anybody look so unhappy as he did.'

I was happy to know that Logan really cared, and at the same time I felt angry to be so mired in our troubles. With a pa who had syphillis. With a stepmother who ran out on her responsibilities. Oh, life wasn't fair!

I was angry at the world, at Pa most of all, for he'd started all of this. And what did I go and do but turn on the person I loved most. 'Stop saying *yer* instead of your – and *ya* instead of you!'

Tom grinned. 'I love *you*, Heavenly. Now, did I say that right? I appreciate what *you* do to make this a family . . . did I say that correctly? I'm glad *you are* what you are, different from Fanny.'

I sobbed, turned and fell into his arms, thinking he was the best thing in my life – and how could I tell him now that I wasn't wonderful, special, or anything but a cynical, hateful person who hated my life, and the man who'd made it what it was.

Two weeks after Sarah left I just happened to glance out a front window and there was Tom trekking home with more books, and beside him was Logan! Tom had broken his word and told Logan of our desperate situation!

Instantly I went on the defensive and ran to the door blocking both Tom's and Logan's entrance. 'Let us in, Heavenly,' ordered Tom, 'it's mighty cold out here for you to stand there in the way like a human wall.'

'Let them in!' shrieked Fanny. 'Yer letting out the heat!'

'You don't want to come in here,' I said hostilely to Logan. 'City boys like you would shiver with disgust.'

I saw his lips tighten with surprise, then came his voice of calm determination. 'Heaven, step aside. I am coming in. I am going to find out why you don't go to school anymore – and Tom's right, it is cold out here. My feet feel like ice.'

Still I wouldn't move. Behind Logan Tom signalled widly for me to stop acting like a fool, and let Logan in. 'Heavenly . . . you'll waste all our wood if you keep holding that door open.'

I started to push the door shut, but Logan forced me backward and entered with Tom close behind him. It took both of them to shove the door closed when the wind was so strong behind it. For a lock we had a board that dropped down and secured the door as a latch.

His face cold and red, Logan turned to me apologetically: 'I'm sorry I had to do that, but I no longer believe Tom when he says Our Jane is sick, and Sarah isn't feeling well. I want to know what's going on.'

He had on dark glasses. Why, on a dull grey winter day when the sunlight was frail and hardly existent? He wore a warm winter jacket that reached his hips, while poor Tom had only second-hand sweaters, worn in layers that at least kept his upper torso warm, if not his bottom half.

I stepped aside, resigned. "Come in, Sir Logan," said the maiden in distress, and enjoy what you see.'

He stepped closer, turned his head, seeming to peer around, while Tom hurried over to the stove and began to warm his hands, his feet, before he even bothered to take off a few sweaters. Fanny, crouched as close to the stove as possible was not about to give up her place or her bed pallet, though she did set about combing her hair in a big hurry, and she fluttered her long black lashes and smiled at Logan invitingly. 'Come here and sit with me, Logan.'

Tom ignored her, as did Logan. 'Well,' said Tom cheerfully, 'this is home to us, Logan.'

Obviously Logan didn't know what to say, so he said nothing.

'You really don't need sunglasses in here, Logan,' said I, moving to pick up Our Jane, then I sat to rock her back and forth in Granny's old rocker. The minute I did that, the squeaking of the floor encouraged Grandpa to reach for his whittling and begin another rabbit. His eyesight for near work was very good, but once you were six feet away, he couldn't see much. I suppose I must have looked to him like Granny when she was young, and holding a child on her lap. Keith ran to climb up on my lap as well, though he was getting too big and heavy for this kind of cuddling. Still, the three of us together warmed each other.

It was so embarrassing to have Logan here, at our poorest time. I busied myself wiping Our Jane's runny nose, and I tried to put her tousled hair in order. I didn't notice what Logan did until he was seated near the table, and he had his head turned my way. 'It's a long, cold walk up this mountain, Heaven. The least you could do is make me feel welcome.' he said with reproach in his voice. 'Where's Sarah? – I mean your mother.'

'We don't have an indoor bathroom,' I said harshly. 'She's out there.'

'Oooh . . .' his voice was weak, his face flushed from my frank information. 'Where's your pa?'

'Working, somewhere.'

'I wish I could have known your granny. And I'm still sorry.'

So was I.

So was Grandpa who stopped whittling and looked up, a fleeting shaft of sorrow wiping away the contentment he'd just found in some memory image. 'Tom, I've got my hands full. Would you please boil some water so we can serve Logan hot tea, or cocoa?'

Tom stared at me with astonishment and spread his hands wide. He knew we didn't have tea or cocoa.

Still he rummaged about in the cupboard, empty almost and came up with some of Granny's sassafras, giving Logan worried looks before he put the water on to boil.

'No, thank you, Tom, Heaven. I've got only a short time to stay, and it's a long trek back to Winnerrow. I want to get there before dark since I don't know my way like you do, being a city boy.' Logan smiled my way, then leaned forward. 'Heaven, tell me how you are? Surely your mother can look out for Our Jane when she's sick. And Fanny's stopped going to school, why?'

'Oh,' said Fanny, looking more alert, 'ya missed me, huh? Why ain't that sweet of ya. Who else misses me? Anybody been asking where I am?'

'Sure,' Logan said in an off-hand way, still staring at me, 'all of us wonder why the two prettiest girls in the school stay away.'

What could I say to embellish bleak lives of hunger and cold? All he had to do was look around to see how poorly we lived. Why did he just keep his head turned toward me, refusing to stare at a room with no creature comforts but those rolled up straw mattresses we put on the floor? 'Why are you wearing dark glasses, Logan?'

He stiffened. 'I guess I never told you I wear contacts. That last fight I had, well, a fist hit me in the eye, and the lens cut my iris, and now my opthalmologist wants me to keep strong light out of my eyes. When you favour one eye, you have to favour the other as well, or wear an eye patch. I prefer the shades.'

'Then you can hardly see a thing, can you?'

He flushed. 'Not much, to be honest. I see you as a dim

figure . . . and I think you've got Our Jane and Keith on your lap.'

'Logan, she's not Our Jane to ya . . . only to us,' spoke up Fanny. 'Ya can call her just Jane.'

'I want to call her what Heaven calls her.'

'Can ya see me?' Fanny asked, standing up, and when she did, she had on only her panties with several of Granny's old shawls about her shoulders . . . and beneath those shawls she was bare from the waist up. Her tiny breasts were just beginning to poke out like hard green apples. Fanny carelessly let the shawl fall open as she rose and sauntered about barefooted. Oh, the shame of her doing that, in front of Logan . . . and Tom!

'Go put on clothes,' ordered Tom, red faced. 'Ya ain't got enough of anything for anyone to notice anyway.'

'But I will have!' screamed Fanny. 'Have bigger and better than Heaven will!'

Logan stood to go. He waited for Tom as if he needed help finding the door – when it was right in front of him. 'If you can't talk to me when I walk all this way, Heaven, I'm not coming again. I thought you knew I am your friend. I came to prove that I care, and I worry when I don't see you for so long. Miss Deale worried. Just tell me this before I go . . . are you all right? Do you need anything?' He paused for my answer, and when I didn't give it, he asked: 'Do you have enough food? Wood? Coal?'

'We don't have enough of nothing!' yelled Fanny loud mouth.

Logan kept his eyes on me, not on Fanny who'd covered herself again, and was now covered up as if half asleep.

'What makes you think we wouldn't have enough to eat?' I asked, pride making my voice haughty.

'I just want to make sure.'

'We're fine, Logan, just fine. And of course we have wood and coal –'

'We do not!' cried Fanny. 'We've never had coal! Wish to God we did. Heard tell it turns hotter than wood!'

Quickly I spoke, 'As you know, Logan, Fanny is a greedy soul and out to get all she can, so ignore anything she says. We're fine, as you can plainly see. I do hope your damaged iris will heal soon and you can take off those dark glasses.'

Now he appeared offended and stayed close behind Tom who led the way out. 'Goodbye, Mr Casteel,' he said to Grandpa, 'See you later, Keith, Our Jane . . . and keep your clothes on, Fanny.' He turned one last time to me, reaching out as if to touch me, or perhaps it was a motion to draw me to him. I sat on, determined not to contaminate his life with Casteel troubles. 'I hope you'll be coming back to school soon, Heaven,' and he flicked his hand to include Fanny and Keith and Our Jane. 'If you ever you do need anything, or just want something, remember my dad has a store full of things, and what we don't have there, we can get elsewhere.'

'How nice for you,' was my sarcastic reply, showing no gratitude at all. 'Must make you feel grand and rich . . . why it's a wonder you'd even bother with a hillbilly girl like me.'

I pitied him as he stood there in the open door, staring at me, not knowing what to say. 'Goodbye, Heaven. I risked the good health of my eyesight coming to see you when the sun on the snow up here is not what I'm supposed to see – yet I came anyway. I'm sorry I did now. I wish you luck, but I'll not be coming again just to be insulted.'

Ooooh, don't go away feeling hurt, Logan . . . please . . . but I didn't say those words. I just rocked on and on and allowed him to slam out the door, with Tom chasing after, to see him through the woods where he might get lost, and down the safest trail to the valley, where he'd never lose himself, even wearing those damned glasses.

'Boy, were you hateful to Logan,' said Tom when he returned. 'Durn if I didn't feel sorry for him, trekking all this way up here, almost blind, to meet a hateful girl who snapped her eyes at him, and lied her crazy head off . . . ya know we don't have anything much. And he could help.'

'Tom, do you want everyone to know that Pa has . . . you know.'

'No . . . but do we have to tell him about Pa?'

'We'd have to give him some reason why he isn't here, wouldn't we? I guess Logan presumes he's still coming and going, and more or less providing.'

'Yeah, I guess yer right,' agreed Tom, sinking into dialect when he was discouraged and hungry. 'Back to the fishin lines, the traps, so keep yer fingers crossed.' And with briefly warmed hands and feet, he again left the cabin to search for food. Never could we keep our laying hens when our cooking pot called them to early deaths.

Life not only grew a thousand times more difficult after Sarah left, it also grew impossibly complicated. Pa didn't come home. That meant no money to buy what we needed to keep us going. Our kerosene was so low, we had to use candles.

Hours passed that seemed like bits of eternity, waiting for life to begin when Tom came home with Fanny and Keith, and sometimes Our Jane. I wanted to convince myself that Grandpa didn't matter, and I could go to school when Our Jane recovered, and he'd take care of himself just fine. But all I had to do was look at him and see how lost he was without Granny. 'Go on,' said Grandpa one day when I had the cabin tidy, but was wondering what we'd eat tonight. It was almost Thanksgiving, 'I don't need ya. Can do for myself.'

Maybe he could, but the next day Our Jane came down with another cold. 'Hungry . . .' she wailed, running to tug on my shiftlike garment. 'Wanna eat.'

'Sure, honey. You just go back to bed and rest, and in no time at all, supper will be ready.' How easily I said that, how lightly, when there wasn't anything in the house to eat but some stale biscuits left over from breakfast, and a half cupful of flour. Oh, why hadn't I rationed the food we'd had when Sarah left? Why was it I thought Pa would always show up, as if by magic, just when our supplies ran out? Where was he anyway?

'Tom, is it possible to fish after dark?' I asked.

He looked up from his reading, startled. 'You want

me to go out in the dark and fish?'

'You could also check your rabbit traps.'

'I already checked them before I came from school. Nothing. And at night, how could I find what I hide so well?'

'That's why you've got to fish now,' I said in a whisper near his ear, 'or there's nothing to eat but two biscuits, and I'll be lucky if I can scrape enough lard out of the can to make the gravy.' I was whispering for if Our Jane heard, or Keith did, there'd be such a clamour none of us could stand it. Our Jane's stomach had to be fed on time or it hurt. Hurting tummy made her wail, and when she was wailing, it was impossible to do anything.

Tom got up and took a rifle down from the wall. He checked it for buckshot. 'Deer season opened, so maybe I can draw a bead on something . . . doe or not.'

'Ya mean we ain't got nothing to eat if ya don't shoot a deer?' shouted Fanny. 'Jesus Christ, we'll starve to death if we have to depend on yer shooting!'

Tom stalked to the door, threw Fanny a hard, long look of disgust, then smiled at me. 'Go on, get your gravy ready – and in half an hour I'll be back with meat – if I'm lucky.'

'What if you're not?'

'I won't come home until I can bring something.'

'Well,' said Fanny, rolling over on her back and staring into a small cheap mirror, 'guess we won't ever see Tom again.'

Tom slammed the door and left.

Fishing and hunting were both part of our daily routine now. Part of my time during the day was spent out of doors, setting traps, baiting fish lines. Tom made the snares to catch rabbits or squirrels. We had already hunted for mushrooms that Granny had taught us how to distinguish from deadly toadstools. We had picked berries until our hands turned bloody from the briars, searched for wild bean and pea pods in the woods, dug for turnips that could be found near the edge of Winnerrow. We stole spinach, lettuce, collards, and other things from Winnerrow backyard gardens. When real cold winter came, the berry bushes stopped producing. The peas and beans dried up. The rabbits and squirrels disappeared in their hidden hibernation places, and weren't attracted to our snares and boxes now that we didn't have decent bait. And mushrooms didn't favour freezing cold nights any more than we did. That was why our larder of food had been reduced to almost nil.

'Heaven,' complained Fanny, 'cook what ya got. We can't sit around and wait all night for Tom to come with nothing. Ya got beans and apples hidden somewhere, I just know ya have.'

'Fanny, if just once in a while you'd do more to help, maybe I would have hidden a store of beans and peas . . . but I don't have anything but lard scrapings and two dry old biscuits.' All this said in a low voice that the keen ears of Our Jane and Keith couldn't hear.

For once Grandpa's ears perked up. He craned his neck and peered my way. 'Taters planted in the smokehouse floor.'

'Used all those last week, Grandpa.'

Our Jane let out a terrible shriek. 'Gotta eat!' she howled. Hurts! Tummy hurts so bad . . . Hev-lee, when we gonna eat?'

'Now,' I said, running to pick her up and sit her down at the table on a chair raised by two blocks of wood placed on the seat. I kissed the sweet place on the back of her slender neck and ruffled her soft hair. 'Come, Keith. You and Our Jane eat first tonight.'

'What ya mean, *they* can eat first – What about me?' cried Fanny. 'I'm a member of this family much as they are!'

'Fanny, you can wait until Tom gets back.'

'If he's gotta shoot something first, I'll be old and in my grave before he does!'

'Oh you of little faith,' said I, busy heating up the little lard I had, putting water and a little flour in a small bowl and mixing it until the lumps disappeared, before I added it to the hot lard, shaking into it salt and pepper, stirring and stirring so it wouldn't go lumpy. I tasted it, sprinkled in more salt, stirred some more, actually feeling the hungry eyes of Our Jane and Keith devouring it while it still heated in the pan. Grandpa rocked on and on, eyes glazed, thin hands clutched on the chair arms, not expecting to eat anything again today. If Our Jane and Keith suffered most, second most had to be Grandpa, who was losing weight so rapidly I could have cried for him.

'Annie could sure make the best blueberry pies,' Grandpa mumbled wistfully, his eyes closed, his thin lips quivering.

'Ya only got two biscuits for six of us?' asked Fanny. 'What ya gonna do, give us each a crumb?'

'Nope. Gonna give Keith and Our Jane each a half, and Grandpa gets the other half, and you, Tom, and me will split the last half into three portions.'

'A crumb! Just what I thought! Grandpa don't need a whole half for himself!'

Grandpa shook his head. 'Ain't hungry, Heaven chile. Ya give my half to Fanny.'

'No! I did that this morning. Fanny can eat her portion or forget about eating until tomorrow, or when Tom comes back with meat.'

'I'm not waiting for Tom!' stormed Fanny, throwing herself into a chair by the table. 'I'm eating now! I'm three times bigger than Our Jane. She don't need a whole half.'

I was doing everything as slowly as possible, not that there was much to do. Two cats had returned today, a black one and a white one, both perched high on a shelf near pots and pans, and both were staring down at me with hope in their hungry eyes, needing their food as much as we did. And there I was, staring up at them, wondering if anybody ever ate cats.

Then I was staring down at Pa's old hunting hounds that had returned with the cats. Oh, how awful to even contemplate eating pets we loved. Yet that's just what I was doing.

Suddenly Fanny was beside me, whispering and pointing

at old Snapper, the hound Pa loved best of all. Sixteen years old, and almost blind, and yet he could always forage for himself and come home looking fat and well fed. 'He's got meat on those ole bones,' Fanny said in an intense way. 'Sure would like to eat meat again. You can do it, Heaven, know you can. Slit his throat, like they do hogs. For Our Jane, for Keith – and Grandpa – why, we could all eat . . .'

At that point Snapper opened his sleepy hooded eyes and stared at me soulfully. I glanced at where Our Jane and Keith sat, each moaning.

'Better an old dog than us,' Fanny crooned more urgently. 'All ya gotta do is bash in his head.' She handed me the hatchet we used for chopping kindling for Ole Smokey. Even now it was belching out foul black smoke that stung our eyes.

'Go on. I know you can do it,' encouraged Fanny, shoving me toward Snapper. 'Take him out first – then give it to him.' Snapper suddenly jumped to his feet, as if sensing my intention, and ran for the door. Fanny let out a shriek of dismay and ran after. At that moment the door opened, and hell-bent to escape our murdering intentions, Snapper disappeared in the night.

Tom strode in, grinning at us, his rifle on his shoulder, and slung on the other a sack heavy with something in it.

His grin faded when he saw the hatchet in my hand, and my look of shame and guilt. 'You were going to kill Snapper?' Incredulity was in his voice. 'But I thought you loved that dog.'

'I do,' I sobbed.

'But ya didn't have faith, did ya?' he asked bitterly. 'I ran all the way there and back.'

He hurled his lumpy bag on the table. 'Two dead chickens inside. 'Course Race McGee is gonna wonder who shot into his henhouse, and if he ever finds out he'll kill me, but at least I'll die with a full stomach.'

We ate well that night, devouring an entire chicken, and saving the other for the next day. But the day after, when both chickens were eaten, we were again faced with the same problem. No food. Tom whispered not to worry; where there was a will there was also a way.

'It's time now to forget honour and honesty, and steal,' Tom figured. 'Didn't see a deer. Nary a coon in sight. I would have shot an owl, but they didn't hoot. Every night, along about twilight, when folks in Winnerrow are settling down at their tables to eat, you, me, an Fanny gonna sneak down to the valley and steal what we can.'

'What a wonderful idea!' cried Fanny, quite delighted. 'They don't hang shotguns on their walls down there, do they?'

'Don't know,' answered Tom, 'but we're gonna sure find out.'

It was a fearsome, scary thing what we set out to do the next twilight, while we still had chicken in our stomachs to give us courage. We wore dark clothes, soot on our faces, and trudged through all the cold until we came to a small, outlying farm where the meanest man alive lived. What was worse, he had five giant sons, and four huge daughters, and a wife who would have made even Sarah look weak and dainty.

Fanny, Tom, and I clung to the protection of dense scrubs and fir trees until we saw every member in that family settle down in the kitchen to make such a racket it would surely cover any noise we might make. They had a yard full of dogs, same as we used to have, and cats and kittens.

'Soothe the dogs,' ordered Tom in a hissy, scary whisper, 'so Fanny and I can raid the henhouse and not use my rifle.' He gestured to Fanny. 'You grab for the feet, two for each hand, and I'll grab my four. That should hold us for a while.'

'Do they peck ya?' asked Fanny, looking strange.

'Nah, ain't ya ever heard about being chicken-hearted? They don't put up much fight, just lots of squawking.'

Tom had assigned me the chore of diverting the most vicious-looking dogs I'd ever seen. I had a way with animals, and most of the time they trusted and liked me . . . but that great big dog looked half-English bull, and from the mean look in his eyes he hated me on sight. I had with me a tiny bag of chicken necks, and tail ends, and feet.

Inside, the McLeroys were eating and fussing, while I threw out a chicken foot and said softly, 'Nice doggy . . . you don't hate me, and I can't hurt you . . . so eat the chicken foot . . . go on, eat.'

He sniffed the dried yellow foot with disgust, then growled. That seemed to be a signal to all the other dogs. There must have been seven or eight of them left in the yard to protect the fenced in pigs, chickens, and other farm animals. All of a sudden all the dogs were coming my way! Snarling, barking, showing the sharpest-looking teeth I'd ever seen. 'Stop it this minute!' I ordered sharply. 'Stop! You hear?'

Inside the kitchen a woman was bellowing out almost the same words. The dogs stopped, seeming undecided. While they were, I tossed them the chicken necks and tails and the rest of the feet. They ran to gobble up what they could, not nearly enough, then came at me with tails wagging for more.

About that time a terrible squawking came from the henhouse, and the dogs took off, running toward the chicken coop.

'Stop!' I ordered. 'Fire!' One dog hesitated and looked back at me as I leaned over and set fire to a pile of dead leaves left for some lazy son or daughter to sweep up and put in a mulch pit.

'Ma!' bellowed a giant of a man in overalls. 'There's someone setting our yard on fire!'

I ran.

Never had I run so fast, with all the dogs at my heels. Perhaps I ran twenty feet before the swiftest hound was almost on me. I shinned as fast as possible up a tree, and sat on a thick limb staring down at dogs who had gone crazy now that I'd shown fear.

'Go away!' I ordered in a firm voice. 'I'm not afraid of you!'

Out of the darkness came old Snapper running to my defence, and into that pile of younger, stronger dogs he threw his strength just as Farmer McLeroy came on the run with a rifle!

Immediately he fired his gun over the head of the dogs. They scattered in all directions, leaving me to cringe up there, trying not to draw attention to myself.

Unfortunately, the moon was out. 'Ain't that ya, Heaven Casteel?' asked the giant farmer. He could have been one of Sarah's relatives, his hair was so red. 'You the one who's been stealing my chickens?'

'I'm the one your dogs chased up this tree, just because I went hunting for Pa's favourite hound. He's been missing for weeks, and just a few days he come home . . . now he's gone again.'

'Get down here!' he snapped.

I gingerly lowered myself to the ground, hoping and praying Fanny and Tom had stolen the chickens and were well on the way home.

'Where did you hide them?'

'Hide what?'

'My chickens.'

'Do you think I could shinny up that tree holding chickens? Mr McLeroy, I've only got two hands.'

Behind him loomed three huge sons, all with bushy heads of red hair. All had thick, coarse beards, and two had flashlights which they aimed at my face, and one travelled slowly down to my feet, then up again. 'Hey, look, Pa, she's done and grown up to look like her ma, the pretty city one.'

'She's a chicken thief!'

'Do you see any chickens on me?' I asked, bold as brass.

'Well, we ain't felt ya all over yet,' said a boy hardly older than Logan. 'Pa, I'll do the searching.'

'You will not!' I snapped. 'All I was doing was looking for my pa's dog, and that's not against the law!'

Boy, was I learning how to lie, giving Tom and Fanny time to run to safety in the hills.

Those giants let me go near the edge of the woods, convinced I wasn't a chicken thief – just a big liar.

Tom and Fanny had managed to get away with five chickens, and Tom had pocketed six eggs, though only three remained unbroken when he reached the cabin. 'We'll save two hens,' I said when I reached there, flushed and breathless, 'so they can lay eggs and Our Jane and Keith can have eggs every day.'

'Where were you all that time?'

'Up a tree, dogs underneath.'

We became pretty good at stealing, never robbing from the same place twice. We'd leave Grandpa in charge of our two youngest and set off each night, learning all kinds of sneaky ways to grab what we could. In the gloom of winter twilight, we waited for women to empty car boots of bags of groceries. Some of the women made four or five trips inside . . . and that gave us the chance to run fast, seize a bag, and leave quickly. It was stealing, out and out, yet we reasoned we were saving our lives, and one day we'd pay those women back.

One day each of us managed to grab a bag, barely escaping before a woman yelled out, 'Help, thieves!' And what I had in my bag was only paper towelling, waxed paper, and two bundles of toilet rolls. Fanny doubled over laughing. 'Dummy, ya gotta go for the heavy bags.'

For the first time in our lives we had real toilet paper, paper towelling, and waxed paper – whatever we could do with it? Didn't have anything to wrap up and save in a refrigerator.

Tom and I lay side by side on our floor pallets, thinking now that Grandpa should use the bed to comfort his old bones with softness for a change. 'It makes me feel bad,' Tom whispered. 'Stealing from people who work hard to earn money. I gotta get a job, even if I don't come home till midnight. And I can always do a little stealing from rich folk's gardens. They don't need extras anyway.'

Trouble was, valley folks didn't trust hill boys not to steal, and finding a job wasn't easy. In the end all of us had to sneak again and again to Winnerrow and steal. Then came the day when Tom stole a pie he saw cooling on a window ledge and ran all the way back to the cabin to share the pie with us. I'd never seen such a delicious-looking pie, with a crust fluted perfectly even all around the edges, and juice bubbling out of holes punched in a flower design on the top crust.

It was a tart apple pie that tasted so good I didn't really want to scold him for becoming an expert thief.

'Oh, it's all right,' laughed Tom with twinkling eyes. 'This pie we just finished off was made by your boyfriend's mother, and ya just know Logan would give up anything to make his Heaven's family happy.'

'Who's Logan?' mumbled Grandpa, while the taste of the pie still warmed my mouth and thrilled my taste buds.

'Yeah,' growled a familiar deep voice from the doorway, 'who's Logan? And where the hell is my wife? Why is this place such a pigsty?'

Pa!

He strode in, carrying over his shoulder a huge burlap bag with bulky things inside that had to be food supplies, and he hurled all that he'd brought onto the tabletop.

'Where the hell is Sarah?' he yelled again, glaring at each of us in turn.

Not one of us could find words to tell him. Pa stood tall and lean, his bronze face clean shaven and paler than usual, as if he'd undergone a great ordeal, and had lost at least ten pounds, and yet he looked fresher, cleaner, and in a way, healthier than when I'd seen him last. He appeared a dark-haired giant, reeking of whisky and that strange overpowering scent that was strictly male. I shivered to know he was back, at the same time, I was overcome with relief. As mean as he was, he'd save us from starvation, now that real winter was upon us, and every day snow would be falling, and the wind would be whistling around our frail cabin, finding all kinds of ways to get in and chill our bones.

'Ain't nobody here who knows how to talk?' he asked sarcastically. 'Thought I sent my kids to school. Don't they learn nothing? Not even how to greet their own pa, and say they're glad to see him home again?'

'We're glad,' said Tom, while I got up and turned again to the stove, ready to do my best to cook another meal, now that we had plenty from the looks of that bag. And I was, in my own way, trying to hurt Pa as he so often hurt me with his indifference.

'Where's my wife?' he bellowed again. 'Sarah!' he shouted, 'I'm back!' His yell could have been heard down in the valley . . . but it didn't bring Sarah.

He checked the bedroom, standing with his hands holding the curtains spread apart, his legs wide, as he looked in and didn't understand. 'In the outhouse?' he asked, turning again to Tom. 'Where is Ma?'

'I'll be only too happy to tell you,' I spoke up when Tom floundered.

He flashed his dark eyes my way. 'I asked Tom. Answer me, boy – where the hell is your mother?'

As if I'd been born for this moment, this chance to sting his pride – I was ready to pounce. I could tell from his expression he thought now Sarah might possibly be dead – as Granny died when he was absent – and for a moment I hesitated before I went on, speaking harshly.

'Your wife's left you, Pa,' I said, glaring at him. 'She couldn't stand any more grief and suffering after her baby was stillborn. Couldn't take this cabin and never having enough with a husband who had to have his fun, while she had none. So she's gone, and she left you a note.'

'I don't believe you!' he roared.

No one said anything, just stared at him, even Fanny.

Then it was Grandpa who found the strength to rise from his rocker and face his son. 'Ya ain't got no wife now, son.'

His voice seemed full of pity for this son who'd lost twice, and would no doubt lose all of his life, and it wouldn't be anybody's fault but his own. That was my mean thought on the night that Pa showed up after being gone almost a month.

'Your Sarah packed up her things and left in the night,'

Grandpa concluded with great difficulty, for easy words had long ago departed.

'Somebody fetch her note,' Pa whispered, as if he'd lost his strength now, and was suddenly as old as Grandpa.

Silently, with vicious pleasure, I stepped toward the highest shelf, where we placed our valuables that were so few, and from a chipped sugar bowl Granny had once told me Pa had bought new for his angel, I took out the brief note, folded four times into a tiny hard wad.

'Read it to me,' ordered Pa, gone numb and strange-looking.

> 'Dear husband (I read),
>
> Can't stay no longer with a man who just don't care enough about anything. Going where it's better. Good luck and good-bye.
>
> Much as I loved ya, hate ya now.
>
> Sarah'

'And that's all?' bellowed Pa, snatching the note from my hand and trying to read the scratchy, childish handwriting. 'She runs off and leaves me with five kids, and she wishes me good luck?' He balled up her note and hurled it into the open door of the stove. His long fingers raked through his dark mane of hair. 'Goddamn her to hell!' he said dully, before he jumped up and bellowed, shaking his fist at the cabin ceiling. 'When I find her I'm gonna wring her damned neck, or cut out her heart – if I can find it. To go when there's no woman here, to leave little children on their own – damn you, Sarah, I expected better, I did!'

In a flash he was out the door, leaving me to think he was going this very minute to hunt up Sarah and kill her, but in a minute or two he was back, hurling down on our table more supplies. He brought in two sacks of flour, salt, slab bacon, beans, dried peas, a huge tin of lard, bundles of tied spinach, apples, potatoes, orange yams, bags of rice, and lots more we'd never had before, such as boxes of crackers and cookies, and peanut butter and grape jelly.

Our tabletop was covered, seeming enough to last a year. And when he had it all spread out, he turned to all of us and spoke to no one in particular.

'I'm sorry your granny is dead. Sorrier your ma ran out on me, and that means all of you as well. I'm sure she's sorry to hurt you just to get to me.' He paused before he continued.

'I'm going this day and not coming back until I'm cured of what I've got. I'm almost well, and would like to stay and take care of ya, but staying would do more harm to ya than my leaving. And I've got a job that suits my condition. So you go easy on this food, for there won't be more coming from me until I get back.'

Aghast, I wanted to cry out and tell him not to leave, that we just couldn't survive the rest of this bitterly cold autumn, much less the winter, without him.

'Don't none of ya have any idea where she went?'

'Oh, Pa!' cried Fanny, trying to run into his arms, but he held up his hands to stay her.

'Don't touch me,' he warned. 'Don't understand much what I got, but it's a nasty thing to have. See how I had a man put everything in sacks? Burn all the sacks when I'm gone. I've got a friend who will try and find Sarah, and make her come back. Hold on till she does, or I do . . . hold on.'

As bad as he was, as evil and cruel as he could sometimes be, still he'd work long enough selling somebody's moonshine to buy us basic food supplies, a few treats, and enough clothes to keep us covered, if not well, at least warmly.

For I was staring at the used clothes that Fanny was pawing through and squealing over. Sweaters and skirts, blue jeans for Tom and Keith, and underwear for all of us, and five pairs of shoes, though he'd had to guess at our shoe sizes. Tears welled up in my eyes. No coats or boots or hats, and we needed those things. Still, I was grateful to see the heavy, ugly sweaters, gone nubby from others' wearing them.

'Pa!' yelled Tom, running after him. 'Ya can't leave us all alone! I'm doing what I can to help, but it ain't easy when nobody in Winnerrow trusts a Casteel, and already Heavenly can't go to school – and I've gotta go, Pa! Gotta go or stop breathing! Pa! Are ya listening? Hearing me?'

Pa strode on, closing his ears to the pitiful words of a son I knew he loved. The wails of Fanny crying surely must have followed him for many days. But a daughter named Heaven didn't plead or cry, or say a word. I just felt the cold, clammy hand of fate squeezing the blood out of my heart. Alone, just as in my nightmares.

Alone in the cabin. Without parents, without any way to support ourselves.

Alone when the wind blew, when the snow fell, when the trails to the valley disappeared beneath ice and snow.

We didn't have snowshoes, coats, skis, none of the things that would take us swiftly to the valley, to school, or to church. And that pile of food, as high as it looked now, would disappear soon enough. What then?

Pa stood near his truck, staring at us in turn, at all but me. It hurt that even now he couldn't bring himself to meet my eyes.

'Take care,' he said, and disappeared in the dark. We heard the roar of his old truck as it took off and sped down the dark trails to wherever it was that he went.

As Sarah would have done, I did, too. I set about putting things away, not a tear in my eye, my lips set in a thin grim line as I faced up to the responsibilities of running this cabin until Pa came home again.

Eight

Squalor and Splendour

For a brief and wonderful moment before Pa stalked out into the night, leaving us alone again, hope lit up all our hearts, lifted us high only to plunge us into even deeper despair once he was gone, and we were, again, left alone.

Trapped in our nightmare, we stood in a tight group and listened to the lonely night sounds when we could no longer hear his truck driving away. We had food on the table to show he'd cared a little, if not enough. I damned him for not staying, damned him for a thousand reasons.

I stared at the table covered with what he'd brought, and though it seemed a great deal – would it last until he came back again?

Out into our primitive wooden box on the porch that served us well enough as a refrigerator during the winters, we put what meat we wouldn't use today. In some ways it was a blessing this was winter and not summer when we'd have to gobble down everything before it spoiled in the heat. When Granny was alive, with Sarah and Pa there had been nine of us, and there was never enough left to spoil.

I didn't realize until later that Pa had come on Thanksgiving Day to bring us our Thanksgiving Day dinner.

Hunger dictated our menus. Only too soon all that Pa had brought to last until he came again dwindled down to nothing but beans, peas, and the eternal staple of our lives, biscuits and gravy.

The howling wind added nothing to our happiness, nor did the cold that kept us all huddled around Ole Smokey. Hours and hours Tom and I spent in the yard chopping wood, felling small trees, and searching to find dead branches broken off during the storms.

Life in the cabin flipped backward into that same familiar nightmare that even the brightest morning light couldn't dispel. I stopped hearing the early-morning birdsongs (those few brave birds that dared to stay), stopped watching the glory of winter sunsets. No time to linger out of doors when we might catch our deaths, and there'd be no one wise enough to make us well again. No time to linger near a window where it was drafty. Only too much time to crowd near the fire and think bitter thoughts.

Up at dawn every morning, I continued the daily struggle to do all the things that Sarah had once done. Not until my stepmother was gone did I realize how much I'd been spared, even when she was at her laziest. Tom tried, really tried to help, but I kept insisting that he continue with his schooling, though Fanny was only too happy to stay home.

Trouble was, Fanny stayed home not to help out with the work but to steal out and meet with the kind of boys who'd never go anywhere in this world but to jail, or to early graves – the ones who incessantly played hooky, were already hooked on booze, pool, gambling . . . and girls.

'Don't need no education,' Fanny flared scornfully, 'already got enough!' A zillion times she said that as she admired herself in that silver mirror that had been my mother's; unfortunately, Fanny had immediately seized it from my hand when foolishly I took it out of its hiding place, and she tried to claim it for her own. It was tarnished, and she didn't recognize it as valuable. Rather than battle her for it then and there, and allow biscuits to burn in the oven, I decided that later on, while she slept, I'd reclaim my mirror and hide it in a better place. At least she hadn't found the suitcase with the doll yet.

'Worst thing is, the school's warmer than here. Heaven, why do you have to have so much pride? Ya done stuck some of it on me, so the only time I can yell the truth is when yer near to say it's a lie, or I'd go yelling out to everybody we're hungry! Cold! Miserable and dying!'

Fanny cried real tears. 'There's gonna come a day when

I'm never gonna be hungry or cold again . . . ya wait and see!' she sobbed brokenly. 'Hate this place! All the things I have to do to keep from crying all the time. Hate crying! Hate not having what city girls have. Heaven, let go yer pride so I can let go of mine.'

I hadn't known she had any until this startling minute. 'It's all right, Fanny,' I said softly; 'go on and cry. I figure a good cry sets you free to have pride . . . and that will help us to be better people, stronger people. Granny always said that.'

The moon was riding high before Tom came home from school, the fierce wind blowing him in the door and slamming it behind him before he threw two squirrels on the table, tiny grey ones he quickly skinned while I hid Our Jane's eyes and Keith stared wide-eyed and teary to see his 'friends' stripped of their pretty fur. Soon I had the meat boiling to make a stew, adding the last of our carrots and potatoes. Keith crouched in a corner and said he wasn't hungry.

'You have to eat,' Tom said softly, going to pick him up and carry him to the table. He plopped Keith down beside Our Jane on her cushion. 'If you don't eat, then Our Jane won't eat, and she's already weak and too thin . . . so eat, Keith, show Our Jane you like Heavenly's stew.'

Day after day passed and Logan didn't come again, nor did Tom see him in the school hallways. Tom wasn't as old as Logan, so they weren't in the same classes.

Ten days after Logan's visit Tom told me, 'Logan's gone away with his parents somewhere.' He had made a real effort to find out what had happened to Logan Stonewall. 'His pa's got another pharmacist working in his store until they come home. Maybe somebody in the family died.'

I hoped not, yet I sighed in relief. My worst fear was that Logan would move away, forget about me, and even if he didn't, he'd stay so angry he'd never look my way again. Better to believe Logan was off on a vacation, or even attending a funeral or visiting a sick grandmother, than disappearing because he didn't like me anymore. Soon he'd be coming home again. Someday better than now he'd show up, we'd meet, I'd say I was sorry, he'd smile, say he understood, and everything would be fine between us.

There was mending and sewing to do. Once Sarah had picked up fabric at sales, ugly, cheap stuff that nobody else wanted; by ripping apart old dresses and using them for patterns she'd fashioned wearable clothes, even if they weren't fitted properly and looked hideous. I didn't know how to make dresses for Our Jane or Fanny, much less for myself. Tom's shirts grew ragged, and there was no money to buy him new ones. I sewed on patches; sewed up rips with clumsy large stitches that soon pulled out. I pulled together split seams, tried to weave threads so they filled tiny holes. I took apart old dresses I'd outgrown and tried to put together a new dress for Our Jane, who could be made very happy by something new and pretty. It was freezing cold in the cabin, and as much as I hated to, I went to the magical suitcase, hunted through all the beautiful summer clothes, and pulled out a soft pink sweater. It had three-quarter sleeves, and still was much too big for Our Jane to wear as a dress. But the moment she spied it, she wanted that sweater in the worst way. 'Now, hold on until I make it fit.'

And make it fit I did, by running thin elastic through the neckline to draw up the shoulders. Now Our Jane had a full-length pretty, warm pink sweater-dress.

'Where'd ya get that kind of fabric?' asked Fanny, coming in from the woods, immediately suspicious when she saw Our Jane skipping happily about in the cabin, showing off her new dress. 'I never saw that pink thing before . . . where'd ya get it, huh?'

'I found it blowing wild on the wind,' answered Tom, who had a terrific imagination for embroidering his own hunting tales. 'There I was, lying flat on my belly, buried deep in the snow, waitin for a wild turkey to poke up his head so we'd have a tasty Christmas meal. Had my beady dead eye on the bush it was hiding, my rifle cocked and aimed, my eye slotted and sure, and here comes this pink thing flying through the air. Almost shot it dead, I did, but it landed on a bush, and durn if it weren't a sweater-dress with Our Jane's name on the tag.'

'Yer lying,' proclaimed Fanny. 'Biggest, stupidest lie ya ever told – and ya done told a million.'

'Ya ought to know, having told your own ten zillion.'

'Grandpa, Tom's calling me a liar! Make him stop!'

'Stop, Tom,' Grandpa said dully. 'Ya shouldn't tease your sister Fanny.'

That's the way it went, Fanny and Tom fighting, Keith and Our Jane staying quiet, Grandpa whittling and staying off his feet which he constantly said were sore from corns, bunions, and other scaly things that I thought soap and water would cure. Grandpa didn't favour soap and water too much; even on Saturday night we had to force him to take a bath. Grandpa tried hard not to do anything but whittle.

Fanny used any excuse to keep from doing her share of the work even if she didn't go to school, so eventually I just gave up on Fanny and decided if being ignorant was her goal and her style, she already had a college-degree. It was Tom who had to finish his education, and to that we were both dedicated.

'All right,' he said to me with a touching sad smile, 'I'll go on, and really try to learn enough for two, so I can teach you when I'm home. But wouldn't it be better if I could tell Miss Deale, and then she could write assignments for you to complete – wouldn't it be, Heavenly?'

'If you make sure she doesn't know we are alone up here, suffering, hungry, cold, miserable. We don't want her to know that, do we?'

'Would it be so awful? Maybe she could help . . .' he said tentatively, as if afraid I'd blow.

'Look, Tom, Miss Deale earns what Logan calls a

pittance, and she'd spend it all on us, she's so generous. We can't let her do that. Besides, didn't she give all of us a lecture one day in class, saying poverty and hardships made for strong backbones and hearty characters? Boy, are we going to end up with iron spines and sturdy, unbreakable characters!'

He stared at me with great admiration. 'Boy, you sure got character right now, and an iron spine as well! If you had any more, we really might starve to death.'

Each and every day Tom trudged off to school, his homework completed to perfection. Nothing stopped him, not the cold drenching rains, the sleet, the wind, or the cold. Like the mail, he went, regardless. He walked to and fro, never having the appropriate clothing to wear. He needed a new winter jacket to keep him warm; no money for that. He needed new shoes and high boots to keep his feet dry, for the shoes Pa had brought didn't fit anybody. Sometimes, to escape the dreary sameness of the cabin, Fanny trailed behind Tom, sitting in class learning nothing, but it did give her time to flirt with the boys. Keith went to school when Our Jane was so sick she didn't scream to see him go.

We still took baths on Saturday nights, with the tin tub pulled close to the fire. Our hot water, drawn from the well, was heated on the stove so we could also wash our hair. We were getting ready for the only fun event we had left to enjoy: going to church.

Every Sunday morning when the weather was halfway decent, at dawn we set out, wearing our pitiful best.

Tom carried Our Jane half the way. I'd help her walk the rest, or pick her up myself. If she hadn't had visions of ice-cream cones in her head, I don't think she would have gone so willingly. Keith skipped and danced alongside whoever was in control of his most beloved possession, his sister. Fanny always raced on ahead. Way behind, the last of all, trudged Grandpa, slowing us down more than Our Jane did. Grandpa used a walking cane now, and often Tom had to drop back to help Grandpa over some fallen tree or boulder. The last thing we needed was for Grandpa to fall and break a bone.

It took one or two hours for Grandpa to make the descent into the valley, and that meant four of us were out in the cold that long just to keep him company. The fifth, Fanny, was snug inside the church long before we got there, hidden in some dark cubbyhole, enjoying forbidden adult delights. Tom hunted her up immediately, smacked the boy she was with, dragged Fanny away, made her straighten her skirt, and we all arrived late, usually the last to enter, and were the objects of the all-over scrutiny that told us again we were the worst of the hill folks, the scummiest of the scum, the Casteels.

But to go to that small white church with the high steeple gave us hope. It was born in us to believe, to have faith, to trust.

As arduous as these Sunday excursions were for all of us, going to church gave us not only pleasure but much to talk about during our long, lonely times. To sit in the back pew and look around and see all the prettily dressed people, to feel just a small part of the human race once a week, helped us to endure the tortures of the rest of the days.

I tried to avoid Miss Deale, who didn't always come to church, but this particular day she was there, turning to smile at us with relief in her pretty eyes, welcoming us with her gestures to sit next to her. And sharing the hymnbook with me, in glorious celebration of life Miss Deale raised her beautiful voice and sang. Our Jane lifted her small face and gazed at Miss Deale with such rapt adoration it made tears come to my eyes. 'How do you do that?' she whispered once we were seated and Reverend Wise was at the podium.

'We'll discuss singing after church,' whispered Miss Deale, leaning to lift Our Jane and hold her on her lap. From time to time I'd see her gazing down at Our Jane, touching her silky hair, tracing a delicate finger over Our Jane's sweet cheek.

To stand and hold the hymnbook and sing was the best part of all. The worst came when we had to sit still and listen to all those frightening sermons about deeds that were so sinful. Christmas was just around the corner, inspiring Reverend Wayland Wise to be his most fervent, which meant his fire-and-brimestone sermons that gave me nightmares as bad as being in hell.

'Which one of you hasn't sinned? Rise up and let us stare in awe, in admiration – and disbelief! We are all sinners! Born from sin! Born through sin! Born into sin! And we will die in sin!'

Sin was all around us, inside us, lurking in the corners, in the dark side of our natures, sure to catch us.

'Give and ye shall be saved!' yelled Reverend Wise, pounding his fist on the podium and making it shake. 'Give and ye shall be delivered from Satan's arms! Give to the poor, the needy, the beset and bereft . . . and from the river of your gold all goodness shall flow back into your own lives. Give, give, give!'

We had a little change that Tom had earned doing odd jobs for valley wives, but it sure was going to hurt giving up any of it in hopes of that river of gold flowing uphill to us.

Sitting on Miss Deale's lap, Our Jane coughed, sneezed, needing someone to help her blow her nose, to go to the bathroom. 'I'll do that,' I whispered, leading her out to where she could again be held in thrall by the pretty ladies' room with its row of pure white basins, its liquid soaps, its paper hand towels. She entered a tiny compartment where she could sit and not smell 'bad' odours, and then had the pleasure of flushing the toilet. She had a real compulsion to keep dropping in paper so she could watch it go down, flushing and flushing. When we returned, I refused to let her sit on Miss Deale again and wrinkle that pretty suit. Our Jane complained her feet hurt in shoes that were too small, and it was too cold in here, and why did that man up there yell and take so long to finish talking? And when did we stand to sing again? Our Jane loved to sing, though she couldn't carry a tune.

'Sssh,' I cautioned, lifting my sweetest little one up on my lap. 'It will soon be over, and we'll sing again, and then we can have ice cream in the store.'

For an ice-cream cone Our Jane would have walked on red-hot coals.

'Who's gonna pay for it?' Tom whispered worriedly. 'We can't let Miss Deale do it again. And we won't have any cash left if we drop our change into the collection plate.'

'Don't drop it in. Just pretend you do. We're the poor, the needy, the beset and bereft – and rivers don't flow upward, do they?'

Tom reluctantly agreed, though he would have been willing to gamble on God's generosity. We did have to keep what money we had left to buy Keith and Our Jane their ice cream, if nothing else. At least we could do that for them.

The collection plate was passed down our aisle. I'll pay for all of us,' whispered Miss Deale when Tom reached into his pocket. 'You keep what you have for yourselves' – and darn if she didn't drop in two whole dollars!

'Now,' I whispered when the last hymn was over and Miss Deale was standing and collecting her purse, pulling on her fine leather gloves, picking up her personal hymnbook and Bible, 'head fast for the door, and don't hesitate for anything!'

Our Jane resisted, dragging her feet. Quickly I swept her up, and she let out a howl. 'Ice cream! Hev-lee, ice cream!' And that gave Miss Deale the chance to catch up with us as we slipped by Reverend Wise and his grim wife.

'Stop, wait a minute!' called Miss Deale, hurrying after us, her high heels clicking on the slippery pavement.

'It's no use, Tom,' I whispered as he tried to support Grandpa and keep him from falling. 'Let's make up good excuses so she won't fall and break a leg.'

'Oh, thank goodness,' gasped Miss Deale when we turned to wait for her. 'What do you mean hurrying off when you know I promised Our Jane and Keith ice cream? Don't the rest of you still like treats?'

'We'll always adore ice cream!' Fanny declared fervently as Our Jane stretched her arms toward her ice-cream godmother. Like a burr, Our Jane clung to our teacher.

'Now let's all go where it's warm, and sit and relax, have some fun.' Miss Deale turned and led the way back toward Stonewall's Pharmacy, with Keith skipping along, clinging to her free hand, and Fanny was almost as childish-acting as Keith and Our Jane . . . and just a few minutes ago she'd been ready to seduce some pimply-faced valley boy if he'd give her some money.

'And how is your father?' called back Miss Deale, turning into the drugstore. 'I haven't seen him lately.'

'He'll come home one day,' I said in a forbidding way, hoping and praying she'd never hear about his disease.

'And your mother, Sarah, why didn't she come today?'

'She's home, not feeling so well, just resting.'

'Tom told me you've been ill; you look fine, though much thinner.'

'I'll be coming back to school, soon . . .'

'And Keith and Jane, when will they be coming back?' she persisted, her sky-blue eyes narrowing suspiciously.

'Both have been kind of sickly lately . . .'

'Heaven, I want your honesty. I'm your friend. A friend is someone you can depend on, always, who is there to help when you need it. A friend understands. I want to help, need to help, so if there's anything at all that I can do, I want you or Tom to tell me what you need. I'm not rich, but I'm not poor, either. My father left me a small inheritance when he died. My mother still lives in Baltimore, and isn't feeling too well lately. So, before I go home for the Christmas holidays,

I want you to tell me what I can do to help make your lives happy and more bearable.'

Here was my golden chance. Opportunity seldom knocked twice on any door – but pride tightened my throat and froze my tongue, and because I didn't speak out, neither did Tom, or Grandpa. Fanny the bold and shameless had, fortunately or unfortunately, wandered away to flip through pages of magazines.

And while I stood just inside the door, debating the wisdom of confessing everything, Miss Deale turned to stare at Grandpa sitting so dejectedly on a padded bench behind a small table. 'Poor dear man, he misses his wife, doesn't he?' she asked with so much compassion. 'And you must miss her just as much.' Then she was meeting my eyes and smiling warmly. 'I've just had the most marvellous idea – ice cream is fine, but not a real meal. I'm planning to have lunch in a restaurant. And I hate eating alone, it makes everyone stare – please do me the honour of joining me, and that will give you the time to tell me what's been going on in your lives.'

'We'd love to!' Fanny shouted eagerly. She had the nose of a bloodhound for a free meal. Suddenly she was there, her smile a yard wide.

'Thank you very much, but I'm afraid we can't accept,' I said briskly, caught in my own snare of devilish stubbornness, all the time wishing I could throw away my pride and be like Fanny. 'It was very nice of you to ask, more than kind, but we have to get home before dark.'

'Don't ya listen to her, Miss Deale,' yelled Fanny. 'We're hungry since Pa went away! Ma's gone, Granny's dead and it will take Grandpa the rest of this day to make the trip back. And when we get there we won't have nothing much to eat. And it will be dark before we reach there!'

'But Pa's coming back any day,' I hurriedly added. 'Isn't he, Tom?'

'Yeah, any day,' confirmed Tom, looking wistfully at the restaurant across the street. It was one we'd often stared into, wishing that just once we could sit at a round table with a crisp white tablecloth, with a crystal vase holding a single red rose, with waiters wearing black and white, and pretty chairs with red velvet seats; oh, how lovely the combination of white, red, and gold. How clean and fresh it must smell in there, not to mention how warm it had to be, and how delicious the food would surely be.

'And your mother is gone . . .?' questioned Miss Deale with a strange look on her pretty face. 'Now, I've heard rumours about town that say say she has gone for good. Is that true?'

'Don't know,' I answered shortly, 'She may change her mind and come back. She's like that.'

'She ain't like that!' yelled Fanny. 'She's never comin back! She left a note and said so. Pa read it and got madder'n hell! Then he ran out to get her . . . and we're suffering, Miss Deale, all of us . . . ain't got no ma, ain't got no pa, and not even got enough food to eat, or warm clothes to wear, and half the time no wood to burn – why, it's awful, downright awful!'

I could have shot Fanny dead on the spot. Fanny had screamed out our humiliating condition right in the drugstore where perhaps twenty pairs of ears heard every word she said.

I stood with my face flushed, wishing I could sink through the floor or go up in smoke, so embarrassed and ashamed to have all our secrets exposed. It was like being naked in public. I wanted to stop Fanny, who went on and on telling more about our lives and family secrets. Then I glanced over at Grandpa, and back at Keith and Our Jane, and sighed heavily. What was pride when compared to seeing huge eyes sunken in deep, hungry hollows? What kind of fool was I to reject the kindness of this wonderful, caring woman? An idiot, I decided. Fanny had ten times more sense.

'Come now, Heaven, if Fanny wants to eat in a restaurant, and Tom looks as if he would as well, and Jane and Keith are so thin, should you vote against the majority? You are outvoted, and it's decided. The Casteel family are my dinner guests this Sunday, and every Sunday until your father is back to take care of you all.'

Oh, I had to swallow to keep from crying. 'Only on the condition that you allow us to repay you someday when we can.'

'Why, of course, Heaven.'

Fate had stepped in, wearing an expensive suit with a mink collar – and when fate came dressed like that, who could resist?

Like Moses leading his starving horde, Miss Deale strode across the Main Street, with Our Jane clinging devotedly to her gloved hand. Prouder than one of those peacocks I'd never seen, she entered that fancy restaurant where men in black and white stared at us as if we were circus freaks they fervently hoped would vanish. Other diners stared, wrinkled their noses, and looked contemptuous, but Miss Deale smiled at everyone.

'Why, good afternoon, Mr and Mrs Holiday,' she greeted pleasantly, nodding to a handsome-looking couple dressed as finely as she was, 'how nice to see you again. Your son is doing marvellously in school. I know you're proud of him. It's so wonderful to have a family to dine with me.' She sailed like a ship knowing its home port, despite the ragged line behind her, heading toward the best table in the restaurant.

Once there, she arrogantly gestured to an astonished older man to seat us properly as she explained to us, 'This table has the best view of your mountain.'

I was overwhelmed, scared, embarrassed. In a fancy gold chair with crimson velvet covering the seat and back, I sat as if in a dream of royal riches. Our Jane's nose was running again. Tom quickly grabbed at Keith and asked directions to the nearest men's room. Fanny smiled at everyone as if she truly belonged here, no matter how shabby she looked. Before Fanny would even sit, as the waiter held her chair, she tugged off her three sweaters one by one. Every pair of eyes in the place watched with astonishment and dismay, no doubt thinking Fanny would strip to her skin – as did I. However, Fanny stopped at her shabby dress and smiled brilliantly at Miss Deale.

'Never felt so happy in my whole miserable life as I do right now.'

'Why, Fanny, that's sweet, and hearing you say that makes me feel just as happy.'

Keith was not as fond of flushing as was Our Jane, and he and Tom came rushing back as if afraid they'd miss something wonderful. Tom beamed at me happily. 'Some Christmas treat, right, Heavenly, right?'

Oooh, yes! Christmas was only five days away. I stared at the tall splendid tree in the corner, at the poinsettias placed around the room. 'Ain't it pretty, though, Heaven?' Fanny said much too loudly. 'When I'm rich and famous I'll lunch like this every day, every day in the year!'

Miss Deale beamed at all of us in turn. 'Now, isn't this nice? Much better than you going your way and me going mine. You can each tell me what you'd like most. We'll start with you, Mr Casteel.'

'I'll just have what the rest of you does,' muttered Grandpa, appearing overwhelmed and ill at ease. He kept trying to hide his mouth with his hand, afraid others would see his missing teeth, his watery eyes still downcast, as if still awed to be seated where he was.

'Miss Deale,' Fanny said without hesitation, 'ya pick out the best there is, what ya like most, and that's what we all want. And dessert. Just leave out the collards, the biscuits and gravy.'

Even after that Miss Deale managed to keep her compassionate expression.

'Yes, Fanny,' she concluded, 'a very good idea, I must say, for me to select what I like most for all of you. Now, is anyone here who doesn't like beef?'

Beef! We never had beef at home, and it would put colour in the cheeks of Our Jane and Keith.

'Love beef!' Fanny cried with loud, lusty passion. Grandpa nodded, Our Jane sat looking wide-eyed all around, and Keith had his eyes on his small sister, while Tom just glowed.

'Anything you like will suit us just fine,' I said humbly, everlastingly grateful to be here, and at the same time so afraid we'd shame her yet with our bad table manners.

Miss Deale lifted her napkin, which was folded like a flower, and shook it open, then slipped it over her lap. I quickly did the same, even as I kicked Fanny's shin under the table, and helped Keith with his napkin, as Miss Deale helped Our Jane with hers. Grandpa somehow managed to catch on and did the same; so did Tom. 'Now, for the first course we should have salad or soup. The main course will be the meat and vegetables. If you'd rather have seafood, lamb, pork, speak up now.'

'We'll have beef,' stated Fanny, almost drooling.

'Fine, everybody agreed?'

We all nodded, even Our Jane and Keith.

'Now . . . we'll have to decide if we want our beef roasted rare, medium, or well-done, – or would you rather have steak?'

Baffled again, Tom and I met eyes. 'Roast beef,' I whispered. In my favourite books all the really romantic men ate roast beef.

'Good, I adore roast beef myself, medium rare, I think, for all of us. And we'll have potatoes . . . and for vegetables –'

'Don't want none,' Fanny informed, quickly. 'Just give me the meat, the taters, and the dessert.'

'That's not a well-balanced meal,' Miss Deale went on without even glancing up from her menu as the waiter took ours away and delicately brushed them off. 'We'll all have a tossed salad, and green beans. We should enjoy that, don't you agree, Mr Casteel?'

Grandpa nodded dumbly, appearing so intimidated I

doubted he'd be able to eat anything. As far as I knew, Grandpa had ever eaten 'out.'

It wasn't a meal . . . it was a feast!

Huge plates of salad were put before us. We just stared for a few minutes before I lifted my eyes to watch which fork Miss Deale used, and then I picked up mine. Tom did the same, but Fanny just plucked out what she wanted with her fingers until I nudged her under the table again. Our Jane picked at hers, and Keith looked troubled as he did his best to swallow strange food without crying. Miss Deale buttered two hot rolls and handed one each to Our Jane and Keith. 'Try that with your salads; it helps a lot.'

To my dying day I'll remember that salad full of green leaves we'd never seen before, and tomatoes at this time of the year, and teeny ears of corn, and green peppers, and raw mushrooms, and so many other things I couldn't name. Tom, Fanny, and I devoured our salad in short order, reaching often to seize up hot bread from a covered basket, and three times it had to be replaced.

'Real butter,' I whispered to Tom, 'it has to be.'

Before Our Jane, Keith, and Grandpa could finish their salads, the *entree* arrived.

'Do ya eat like this every day?' asked Fanny, her dark eyes glowing with happiness. 'Why, it's a wonder ya don't weigh a ton.'

'No, I don't eat like this every day, Fanny. Sunday is my day to treat myself, and from now on, when I'm in town, it will be your day to enjoy with me.'

It was too good to believe. Why, we could live all week on what we ate today, and with great determination I decided I'd eat everything, even though it did appear an enormous amount. I think Fanny, Tom, and even Our Jane and Keith made the same decision. Only Grandpa had trouble with the beef since he had so few teeth.

I felt like crying I was so happy to see Our Jane eating with real enjoyment. In no time Keith cleaned his plate, even if he did overdo it when he leaned over to put his head in his plate so he could lick up the last bit of the dark sauce.

Miss Deale's hand on my arm restrained my scolding. 'Let him sop up his gravy with the roll, Heaven; it does my heart good to see all of you enjoy your meal.' She smiled radiantly.

When we'd all emptied our plates, leaving them so clean they sparkled, she said, 'And of course you'll be wanting dessert.'

We'd love dessert!' shouted Fanny, making other diners turn to stare at us again. 'I want that fancy chocolate cake,' she said, pointing to the dessert cart.

'And you, Mr Casteel?' asked Miss Deale in the softest of voices, her eyes looking so kind. 'What will you have for dessert?'

I could tell Grandpa was uncomfortable, no doubt suffering from gas when his stomach surely was not accustomed to so much food all at once, and chewing took him forever.

'Anything . . .' he mumbled.

'I think I'll have chocolate pie,' Miss Deale said. 'But I know Our Jane and Keith will love the kind of chocolate pudding they serve here, and Mr Casteel, Heaven, Tom, all of you select what you want, for it would really make Fanny and me feel miserable to be eating sweets if everyone doesn't join us.'

Pie, cake, chocolate pudding? Which one? I chose the pie because Miss Deale had to know best. Fanny's huge piece of cake topped with whipped cream and a cherry enchanted me even as I quickly devoured the pie. But Grandpa, Tom, Our Jane, and Keith were served the chocolate pudding in fancy footed dishes that made me wish I'd chosen differently.

As if paradise had finally found its way into her mouth, Our Jane spooned her chocolate pudding onto her tongue so fast she was finished before Keith. She beamed the broadest smile of her life on Miss Deale. 'That was good!' she said.

Several people seated near us smiled.

It had gone fairly well up until now, but for Keith licking his plate.

I should have know our luck couldn't hold out.

Abruptly, without the slightest warning, Our Jane gagged, turned greenish, then suddenly threw up, right on Miss Deale's wine-coloured skirt! Some splattered on the crisp tablecloth, some on me.

Our Janes eyes turned huge, dark, before she began to wail, loud, terrified cries. She tried to bury her face in my lap as I apologised and dabbed at the mess on Miss Deale's skirt with my huge white napkin.

'Oh, Heaven, don't look so distressed,' said Miss Deale calmly, not appearing disturbed in the least even as she mopped at her smelly skirt. 'I'll send this to the cleaners, and it will come back as good as new. Now, everybody stop looking worried, be calm, and I'll pay the bill while all of you put your warm clothes back on; then I'll drive you home.'

The other diners turned their eyes away, ignored the scene. Even the waiters didn't seem disturbed, as if they'd correctly presumed the moment we came in the door that we'd ultimately do something like this.

'I did a bad thing,' sobbed Our Jane as Miss Deale signed the bill. 'Didn't wanna, Hev-lee. Couldn't help it, Hev-lee.'

'Just tell Miss Deale you're sorry.'

But Our Jane was too shy to speak, and again she wailed.

'It's all right, Jane dear. I remember doing the same thing when I was your age. Things like that happen to all of us, don't they, Heaven?'

'Yes, yes,' I said eagerly, grasping at the straw. 'Especially when you have a tiny stomach not used to so much.'

'I never threw up on nobody,' proclaimed Fanny. 'My stomach knows how to behave.'

'Yer tongue don't,' threw in Tom.

I carried Our Jane out to Miss Deale's expensive black car.

Light snow began to drift down as Miss Deale drove higher and higher, up into the misty clouds where we lived. All the way home I fretted, fearful Our Jane's queasy stomach might let loose again and ruin the interior of the magnificent car; but Our Jane managed to keep what else she'd eaten down, and we arrived home without soiling anything else.

'I don't know how to thank you enough,' I said humbly, standing on the sagging porch, my sister still in my arms. 'I'm terribly sorry about your beautiful suit. I hope the stain comes out.'

'It will, I know it will.'

'Please ask us again next Sunday,' implored Fanny; then she opened the cabin door and disappeared inside, slamming it behind her. In a second the door popped open and she called out, 'And thanks a heap, Miss Deale. Ya sure know how to throw a party.'

Bang went the door.

'You're one in a million,' Tom said gruffly, leaning to kiss Miss Deale's cold cheek. 'Thanks for everything. If I live to be a hundred and ten, I'll never forget today, and you, and your meal, the best I've ever eaten, no disrespect to you, Heavenly.'

Of course, now was the time to invite Miss Deale inside and show our hospitality. But to let her in would give her too much information, and that I couldn't do. Though I could sense she was waiting for an invitation, and the chance to see how we really lived. The cabin as viewed from the outside was pitiful enough, but for her to see the inside would keep her sleepless

'Thanks again, Miss Deale, for all that you've done. And please forgive Fanny for being too aggressive, and Our Jane is terribly sorry, even if she can't say so. I'd ask you in, but I left the house in a terrible mess . . .' Boy, that was no lie.

'I understand. Maybe your father is inside, wondering where you are. If so, I'd like to speak with him.'

Fanny stuck her head out again. 'He ain't in here, Miss Deale. Pa's sick and –'

'He was sick,' I interrupted hastily. 'He's much better, and is due home tomorrow.'

'Oh, that's a relief to hear.' She smiled and hugged me close, and her perfume filled my nostrils as her soft hair tickled my face. 'You're so brave and so noble, but too young to endure so much. I'll be back tomorrow afternoon, shortly after school is over, to deliver your presents to put under your Christmas tree.'

I didn't tell her we didn't have a Christmas tree. 'We can't let you do that,' I protested weakly.

'Yes, you can; you must. Expect me tomorrow about four-thirty.'

Again Fanny put her head out the door; obviously she'd been listening through the flimsy door. 'We'll be waiting. Don't forget.'

Miss Deale smiled, started to speak, but seemed to change her mind before she touched my cheek gently. 'You're such a lovely girl, Heaven. I would hate to think you won't finish school, when you have such a gift for learning.'

Suddenly a small, frail voice spoke up, when I never expected to hear Keith volunteer anything. 'Yes,' whispered Keith, clinging to my skirt. 'Our Jane is sorry.'

'I know she is.' Miss Deale lightly touched Our Jane's round cheek, then ruffled Keith's pretty hair before she turned to leave.

In the cabin that was almost as cold as outside, Tom stuffed more wood into Ole Smokey. I sat down and rocked Our Jane, feeling the cold winds blowing in through the openings in the walls, seeping up through the floor cracks coming in through the ill-fitting window frames. For the first time this cabin seemed totally unreal, not home at all. I had the vision of the restaurant with its soft, white walls, its crimson carpet, its fancy furniture; that was the world I wanted for all of us. And to think the best meal of my life made me realize just how miserable we all were, so much I began to cry.

Tonight I was going to say my longest, most sincere prayer, down on my knees. I was going to stay there for hours and hours, and this time God would hear me and answer my prayer, and send Pa home again.

Yet I was up at dawn the next morning, singing as I began my day with cooking, with seeing Tom off to school, and right away I set in to make the cabin as clean and tidy as possible, enlisting Fanny's help.

'Ya can't make it pretty!' she complained. 'Ya can scrub, dust, sweep, and still it'll stink!'

'No, it won't. Not when you and I are finished; this place is gonna shine, really shine – so get busy, lazybones, and do your share, or no more treats for you!'

'She won't slight me, I know she won't!'

'Do you want her to sit in a dirty chair?'

That did it. Fanny made an effort to help, though it wasn't more than an hour before she fell down and rolled up to go back to sleep. 'Makes the time go faster,' she mumbled, and when I looked Grandpa was dozing in his rocker, also waiting for the miracle of Miss Deale who would come at four-thirty.

Four-thirty came and went without Miss Deale showing up.

It was almost dark when Tom came home with a note from Miss Deale.

> Dearest Heaven,
>
> When I returned home last night, there was a telegram under my door. My mother is in a hospital and seriously ill, so I'll be flying to be with her. If you need me for any reason whatsoever please call the number below, and reverse the charges.
>
> I am sending a delivery boy to your home with

everything I think you need. Please accept my gifts to children I love as my own.

Marianne Deale

She'd written a number with the area code, perhaps forgetting we didn't have a telephone. I sighed and looked up at Tom. 'Did she have anything else to say?'

'Lots. Wanted to know when Pa was coming home. Wanted to know what we needed, and what size clothes we all wore, and shoe sizes. She pleaded with me, Heavenly to let her know what we needed most. How could I tell her when the list would be a mile long? We need everything, most of all food. And ya know, I stood there like a jackass and wished to God I could be like Fanny, and shout it all out, and have no pride . . . and feel no humiliation, just take what I could – but I couldn't, and she's gone. The only friend we have, gone.'

'But she's sending gifts anyway.'

He laughed. 'Hey . . . where's all that pride?'

Three days passed, and that box of presents didn't arrive.

On the day before Christmas Eve Tom came home with bad news. 'Went to the store Miss Deale told me about, to ask where were the things she wanted them to deliver, and they said they didn't deliver in this county. I argued with them, but they insisted we'd have to wait until she was back again, and paid an extra fee. Heavenly, they must not have told her that, or she would have taken care of it. I know she would have.'

I shrugged, trying to appear indifferent. It was all right, we'd manage. But my heart went bleak.

Real winter mountain weather chose this day to attack with such ferocity we were left totally unprepared. We ran about stuffing rags in the cracks we could reach. We stuffed rags under the doors, in between the floorboards, around the rattling window glass. Our cabin looked like a loosely knitted, ragged scarf inside, giving fleas, roaches, and spiders good nesting places, even if they were cold. Sunsets were always fleeting in the mountains, and night always fell with alarming swiftness. With the night came the smothering cold to settle down on the montains like an ice blanket. Even when we rolled up mattresses used for bedding and slept in the middle of the roll, all of us failed to keep warm when the floor near the stove was so cold. Grandpa slept in the big brass bed when he could remember to leave his rocker, and that's where I wanted to keep his old, tired bones, off the floor where it was hard and cold.

'No,' Grandpa objected stubbornly. 'Ain't a right thing to do, when the young'uns need the bed more than me. No back talk now, Heaven girl, ya do as I say. Ya put Jane and Keith in the bed, and if the rest of ya crowd in ya'll should keep each other warm.'

It hurt to take the bed from Grandpa, but he could be stubborn about the oddest things. And always I'd believed him to be so selfish. 'The bed was for the young'uns,' he insisted, 'the frailest,' and of course that had to be Our Jane and Keith.

'Now, ya wait a minute!' bellowed Fanny, using her bull-moose voice. 'If young'uns deserve soft, warm beds, I'm next in line. Plenty of room for me, too.'

'If there's plenty of room for you, then there's plenty of room for Heavenly as well,' insisted Tom.

'And if there's room for me, Tom, there should be room for just one more,' I contributed.

'But there ain't enough room for Tom!' yowled Fanny.

There was.

Tom found room at the foot of the bed, his head on the portion where Our Jane and Keith lay, so he wouldn't have longer legs thrusting bare feet that close to his face – and cold feet at that.

Tom, before he could go to bed, had to chop more wood in order to get enough to build a hotter fire to melt the ice for water. Ole Smokey kept coughing out more evil-smelling smoke.

It was Tom who got up in the night to add more wood to the fire. Wood was running low. Every spare moment after school, until the night was dark, and all Saturday and Sunday found Tom outside chopping wood for an old stove that devoured wood the way elephants ate peanuts.

He'd chop with determined dedication until his arms and back ached so much he couldn't sleep without tossing and turning and crying out in pain. His muscles ached so badly, he slept lightly. I got up to rub his back with hot castor oil that Granny used to swear by, good for any ailment under the sun. Enough of it could cause an abortion, and that I didn't doubt. Enough caster oil inside, and all that was in would melt and flow away. However, it did help Tom's aching muscles.

When I wasn't hearing Tom groaning, I heard other things in the night: the wheezing rattle in Grandpa's chest, the small incessant coughs of Our Jane, the rumblings of hunger in Keith's tummy; but most of all I heard footsteps on the rickety porch.

Pa coming home?

Bears on the porch?

Wolves coming nearer and nearer to eat us all?

It was Tom's fervent belief that Pa would not abandon us to starve and freeze to death. 'No matter what ya think, he loves us, Heavenly, even you.' I was curled up on my side, with my feet on the small of Tom's back, but I had my head turned so I could stare up at the low ceiling, the unseen sky beyond, praying that Pa would come home again, healthy and strong, pleading for our understanding.

The next day was Christmas Eve. In our cupboard was only about half a cup of flour, a tablespoon or so of lard, and two dried apples. I woke that morning with a sense of doom that weighed me down so much I could hardly move about. I stood staring at what food I had left, tears streaking my face; Our Jane could eat all the gravy I made and still she wouldn't have enough. The floor squeaked behind me as Tom slipped his arms around my waist.

'Don't cry, Heavenly, please don't. Don't give up now. Something will turn up to save us. Maybe we can sell some of Grandpa's whittled animals in town, and if we can do that, we'll have money to buy lots of food.'

'When the snow is over,' I whispered hoarsely, my hunger pains a dull throb that never let up.

'Look,' he said, turning to the window and pointing at a bright streak in the leaden grey sky, 'it's brightening. I can almost see the sun breaking through. Heavenly, God hasn't forgotten about us. He's sending Pa home, I can feel it in my bones. Even Pa wouldn't leave us here to starve alone, you know that.'

I didn't know anything anymore.

Nine

Christmas Gift

It seemed Tom and I could have travelled a hundred miles on a sunny day in less time than it took us to creep to the smokehouse on Christmas Eve, holding one to the other, as the wind howled in our ears, blew snow in our faces to almost blind us. But when we headed back, we had in our pockets a dozen of Grandpa's best wooden carvings that he'd never miss, they'd been so long in the smokehouse.

The relief of feeling the porch beneath my feet allowed me to open my eyes for the first time and see how white our world was, not from new snow, but from the old snow the wind banked around our crouched cabin. Tom fought to open the door, and then he shoved me through and quickly followed.

Stumbling inside, at first I couldn't focus my eyes, they were so heavily lidded with snow caught on my lashes. Fanny was screaming, and there was so much other noise. Startled, I looked around – only to freeze in shock and then feel the instant flaring hope.

Pa! Come home for Christmas Day . . .? Our prayers answered, at last, at last!

He stood in the dim firelit room, gazing down at where Keith and Our Jane were huddled together for warmth. Even with Fanny dancing around and yelling her head off they slept on and on, as did Grandpa in his rocker.

Pa didn't seem to hear or see Tom and me as we quietly slipped into the room, keeping as far from him as possible. Something in his stance, in his manner as he gazed down at the two youngest, put me on guard.

'Pa,' Tom cried joyfully, 'you've come back to us!'

Pa turned, his expression blank, as if he didn't know that large, flame-haired boy. 'I've come to bring a Christmas gift,' he said dully, with no joy in his eyes.

'Pa, where ya been?' asked Tom, while I stood back and refused to greet him, just as he refused to look my way and acknowledge my presence.

'Nowhere ya'd care to hear about.'

That's all he'd say before he fell to the floor beside Grandpa's rocker, and now Grandpa woke up enough to smile weakly at his son, and only too soon both he and Pa were snoring.

Bags and sacks and boxes of food were on the table. We could eat again, yet it wasn't until I was in bed that night that I wondered what wonderful gift Pa had brought home, so huge he couldn't carry it in. Clothes? Toys? He never brought us toys, yet hopefully I longed for all of that.

Tomorrow was Christmas Day.

'Thank you, God,' I whispered full of gratitude when I got up to pray on my knees by the bed, 'you sent him in the nick of time, you truly did.'

On Christmas morning I was cooking mushrooms that Tom had found in a shallow woodsy ravine just yesterday, when Pa got up from the floor, went out briefly to use the outhouse, then strode back inside, unshaven and stale-looking, and plucked Our Jane and Keith from their warm, snug bed. He held them both easily in his strong arms, looking at each with affection, while they stared at him with wide, kind of frightened eyes, as if they no longer knew him. They were my children now, not his. He didn't love them as I did, or else he wouldn't leave them for so many days without enough food. Holding my tongue by sheer force of will, I kept on cooking the mushrooms.

For an extra treat today we'd have eggs, but I'd save the bacon until Pa went away again. I'd not waste even a thin slice on him.

'Hurry up with the meal, girl,' barked Pa. 'Got company coming.'

Company?

'Where's the Christmas gift?' asked Tom, striding in from an hour of chopping wood.

Pa ambled to the nearest window, not noticing it was sparkling clean, and stared out. 'Get these two dressed, and quick!' he ordered without meeting my eyes as he put Our Jane and Keith down on the floor.

Why did his eyes shine like that? Who was the company? Sarah? Could it be Sarah – was she our gift? How wonderful, absolutely wonderful!

Our Jane and Keith flew to me, as if I represented their mother, their security, their hopes and their dreams, and quickly enough I wiped both their faces. Soon I had them both dressed in their best, which was poor enough.

Life would get better now, I thought. I still possessed that childish optimism that refused to be dreary or depressed during the day. Steadfastly I held tight to hope, despite what I saw in Pa's eyes, sensed in the air, felt in my bones. Something – something bad. His cold, hard eyes glanced my way briefly before they lingered on Tom, Fanny, and, last of all, Keith and Our Jane.

Of all his five children he preferred Tom, and next Fanny. 'Hi there, darling,' he said to her with a sweet smile. 'Got another hug for yer pa?'

Fanny laughed. She had a smile and a hug for anyone who noticed she was alive. 'Pa, I prayed every night, every day, ya'd come back. Missed ya so much it hurt.' She pouted her full lower lip and asked where he'd been.

I heard a car drive up outside and pull to a stop. I moved to the window to see a car and in it a stout man and his wife waiting, it seemed, for Pa's signal. Glancing at Pa, I could tell he was having a difficult time making up his mind as he lifted Fanny onto his lap and stroked her long, black hair. 'Now, you kids gotta face some hard facts,' he began in a short, gruff way, with pain in his eyes. 'Yer ma ain't never coming back. Hill folks are like that. Once they make up their minds, put action behind it, ain't nothing short of death can make them undo a decision. Not ever. What's more, don't want to ever see her again. If she shows her face here

– I'll use my shotgun and blow it off.' He didn't smile to show he was only joking.

Not one of us spoke.

'Now, I've found nice, rich folks who can't have kids of their own, and they want one so much they're willing to pay good money for what they want. They want a young child. So it's gonna be either Keith or Our Jane. Now, don't none of ya yell out or say no, because it has to be done. If ya want to see them grow up healthy and strong, and have nice things I can't afford to give them, ya keep yer mouths shut, and let this couple make their choice.'

I went cold inside. All the hopes that had lit up were snuffed out in the harsh winds of knowing what Pa was going to do. Pa was Pa and would never, never change. A no-good, filthy, rotten, drunken Casteel! A man without a soul or heart, not even for his own.

'It's my way to give Keith and Our Jane the best kind of Christmas gift – and don't none of ya go yelling and crying and spoiling it. Ya think I don't love none of ya, but I do. Ya think I ain't been worried about what's going on in this cabin, but I've worried. Been sick inside, sick outside, trying to find a way to save ya all. And one dark night when I was sicker than any starving dog in a gutter, it came to me.'

He bestowed on Fanny a charming smile, gave another to Tom, Keith, and Our Jane, but he didn't even look at me. 'Already told yer grandpa. He thinks it's a good thing to do.'

Fanny slowly left Pa's lap and backed up to where I was holding Our Jane, and Tom had both hands on Keith's narrow, frail shoulders.

'Pa,' said Fanny, looking pale and concerned for once, 'what ya planning on doing?'

Again Pa smiled in his most winning way. (I thought he looked exceptionally cunning.) 'I got to thinking just how willing rich folks are to pay for what they want. Me, I got more kids than I can take care of. Some want kids and can't have any. There's lot of rich folks out there, wanting what I got plenty of – and so I'm selling.'

'Pa,' Tom said stoutly, beginning to tremble, 'yer just joking, ain't ya?'

'Shut up, boy,' warned Pa in a low, intense tone. 'I'm not joking. Dead serious. Got my mind set on this being the best thing. The only way out. At least one of ya will be saved from starving.'

This was our Christmas present? Selling Keith or Our Jane?

I felt sick. My arms clutched Our Jane tighter to my breasts as I buried my face in her soft, curling hair.

Pa moved to the door to let in that couple from the black car.

A fat lady wearing high-heeled shoes entered, followed by a fatter man. Both wore warm, heavy coats with fur collars, and gloves, and big, happy smiles on their faces that soon faded when they saw the hostility on our faces. Then they turned in a slow circle to stare with abject horror at all the poverty.

No Christmas tree here. No gifts, no trimmings, no packages spread around. Nothing at all to indicate this was anything but another day to suffer through.

And here was Pa planning on selling his own.

Beyond belief, those city folks' expressive, shocked eyes said. 'Oh, Lester,' cried the rather pretty, fat woman, getting down on her knees to try and cuddle Keith to her enormous bosom, 'did you hear what he said as we came up the steps? We can't let this dear, lovely child starve! Look at his eyes, so huge and pretty. Look at this fine, silky hair. And he's clean. Sweet-looking. And that dear little girl the older one is holding – isn't she just a darling, isn't she, Lester?'

Panic was all I could feel. Oh, why had I bathed and shampooed them yesterday? Why didn't they look dirty so she wouldn't want them? I sobbed and held Our Jane tighter as she clung to me with trembling fear. Maybe Our Jane or Keith would be better off – but would I, would I? They were mine, not hers. She hadn't stayed up with them all night, and walked the floors, or spoon-fed them taking hours and hours that could have been spent outdoors playing.

Go away, go away, I wanted to scream, but what did I say? This:

'Our Jane is only seven years old.' My voice was hoarse as I determined to save Our Jane from this woman, this man. 'Neither she nor Keith has ever been away from home. They can't be separated from each other; they'll cry and scream, be unhappy enough to die.'

'Seven,' murmured the woman, appearing shocked. 'I thought she was younger. I wanted a younger child. Lester, can you believe she's seven – and how old is the little boy?'

'Eight!' I cried. 'Too old to adopt! And Our Jane is sickly,' I went on with hope in my heart. 'Actually, she's never been what anyone could call healthy. She throws up often, has every disease that rolls around, colds all the time and high fevers . . .' and on and on I would have gone trying to ruin Our Jane's chances, because I couldn't bear to see her go, for her own good or not – but Pa scowled and ordered me to shut up.

'Then we'll take the little boy,' spoke up the fat man called Lester, pulling out his bulging leather wallet. 'I always wanted a son, and that boy there is a good-looking young man, and well worth the price you're asking, Mr Casteel. Five hundred, right?'

Our Jane began to scream.

'No! No! No!' she yelled right in my ear.

She wriggled free from my tight embrace and ran to join Keith, throwing her arms about him and continued to scream, terrible screams expressing the kind of anguish a child should never know. Keith saw her pain, joined in, and clung to his sister.

More desperate words from me: 'Keith is not what you'd want in a son. He's very quiet, uneasy in the dark, scared most of the time – can't bear to be without his sister. You don't want to go, do you Keith?'

'Don't wanna go!' cried Keith.

'No! No! No!' wailed Our Jane.

'Oh, Lester . . . isn't this heartbreaking, just heartbreaking? We can't separate such two little dears. Lester, why not take both? We can afford both, and then they won't cry or miss their family so much, if they have each other. And you'll have your son, and I'll have my daughter, and we'll all be so happy, our family of four.'

Oh, God! In trying to save each of them, I'd lost both!

But there was hope, for Lester was hesitant, however insistent his wife. If only Pa would keep quiet, but he said in a sad, caring way: 'Now, that's what I call real quality, a woman with a heart of gold, willing to give to two instead of one,' and that's all it took for Lester to make his decision, and then he was pulling out papers and was adding another line or two before he signed, and Pa bent over to painstakingly form his own signature.

As difficult as Pa made writing seem, and as painfully slow as he was, I knew when he was finished there would be a signature as beautiful as any. Like many ignorant people, to Pa appearances meant more than content.

During all of this, I'd backed to the stove and picked up the heavy, iron poker. Once I had it in both my hands, I raised it high and had the courage to actually hiss when I yelled at Pa. 'Ssstop thisss! I won't let you do this! Pa, the authorities will come and put you in jail if you sell your own flesh and blood! Keith and Our Jane are not hogs or chickens for sale, they're your own children!'

Pa moved like lightning, even as Tom hurried to protect me. With one painful twist of my arm, I had to release the poker or have my arm broken. The poker fell to the floor with a clatter.

The stout woman looked my way, alarmed. 'Mr Casteel, you did say you'd talked this over with the other children. They agreed, didn't they?'

'Yes, of course they agreed,' lied Pa. His charm, his sincerity, created some mesmerizing aura of integrity that convinced that married pair easily enough. 'Ya know how younger ones are, agreeing one moment, squabbling the next. Soon as they enjoy what this money buys, all left here in this cabin will know I did the right thing.'

No! No! No! my mind was screaming. Don't believe him, he's a liar! But I was speechless, caught up in the horror of knowing I might never again see my little brother and sister.

Before it could even be absorbed, Keith and Our Jane were sold, like hogs at the market, and that man named Lester said to Pa: 'We hope you realize, Mr Casteel, that this sale is legally binding, and you can never seek to recover your two children once we leave. I'm an attorney, and I've written a contract that says you are fully cognizant of what you're doing, and the consequences of this act, and this contract that states firmly that you did willingly, without altercation or argument or persuasion, without force, agree to sell your two youngest children to me and to my wife, and you do irrevocably give up all rights to see them again, or contact them in any way in the future.'

I cried out. Pa might not even know what *irrevocably* meant!

No one heeded me, but Tom moved to my side and pulled me into his arms. 'It's not going to happen, Heavenly,' he whispered. 'After hearing all that, Pa surely won't go through with it.'

'And,' the lawyer went on, 'you hereby grant to us' – pointing to his name, and where his wife had signed – 'the right to make all decisions considering the future of your two children, named Keith Mark Casteel and Jane Ellen Casteel, and if you seek to legally or illegally take them from me and from my wife, there will be a suit for which you will have to pay all court and lawyers' fees, and all the expenses accrued by the children while they are in our care, and of course there will be various other expenses, such as medical and dental ones, for we intend to take both children as soon as possible to doctors for physicals and dental checkups, and we will be sending them to school, and buying them new clothes, and books, and toys, and the proper furniture for their rooms. And there will be various other items I'm forgetting about now . . .'

Oh, my God.

Pa would never have enough money to buy them back! Not in a thousand years!

'I understand completely,' said Pa, appearing not in the least troubled. 'That's one of the reasons I'm doing what I am. Our Jane needs medical attention, and perhaps Keith does as well. So even if my eldest girl is emotional, she did speak truthfully, so you know exactly what you are getting.'

'A dear, a sweet little dear who will turn out just fine,' crooned the fat lady, who held fast to Our Jane's frail arm to prevent her from pulling away and running back to me. 'A wonderful little boy,' she added, patting Keith on the head, for he stood as always, as close to Our Jane as possible, his hand holding hers. If she didn't escape, he wouldn't either.

I was crying now. I was losing the brother and sister I'd helped raise. All the memories of how they'd looked and behaved as babies and little toddlers came flooding back, filling me with fresh tears. Visions flashed behind my eyes: All of us on the hills teaching Our Jane to walk, and how sweet she'd looked on her bowed legs and baby toes, her arms out for balance. Tom and I guiding Keith's first toddling steps as well. My voice instructing them how to speak clearly, correctly, and Fanny always so jealous because they loved me best, and Tom second best.

I'd gone numb now, held frozen by the forbidding glance Pa threw my way, warning me not to speak again as he pocketed more money than he'd ever had before in his life.

One thousand dollars.

Excitement made his dark eyes glow like hot coals.

'Fanny, it's beginning to rain,' said Pa, showing concern for those two in their rich, warm clothes when he'd shown none for us. 'Fetch that ole umbrella we got somewhere so the lady won't ruin her nice hairdo.'

Pa scooped up Keith and Our Jane and ordered them to stop screaming, and I ran for a quilt to wrap them with.

I dashed back, carrying the best quilt we had, hand-sewn years ago by Granny. 'They don't have coats, hats, boots, or anything,' I said to the lady urgently. 'Please be good to them – give them lots of orange juice and other fruit. And meat, especially red meat. We've never had enough meat, even chicken and pork. Our Jane loves fruit and won't each much of anything else. But Keith has a good appetite, even if he does catch cold often, and they both have nightmares, so leave on a little light so the dark won't frighten them . . .'

'Shut up,' hissed Pa again.

'Why, child, I'll be good to your brother and sister,' the lady said kindly, touching my cheek lightly and appearing sorry for me. 'Aren't you a dear one, just like a little mother. Now, don't you worry yourself about these two. I'm not a cruel woman, nor is my husband a cruel man. We're going to be kind, give them all new clothes, and Christmas morning is waiting for them at our house, everything their hearts can desire. We didn't know if we'd take the boy or the girl, so we bought things both sexes can use . . . a rocking horse, a tricycle, a dollhouse, lots of lorries, cars, and clothes . . . not enough for two, but they can share until we go shopping again. We'll do that tomorrow, buy everything they can possibly need. So you feel good about this, honey. Don't cry. Don't worry. We'll do our best to make wonderful parents, won't we, Lester?'

'Yes,' Lester said shortly, eager to leave. 'Let's get a move on, dear. It's growing late, and we have a long drive ahead.'

Now Pa handed the woman Our Jane, and the man carried Keith who had given up fighting and was now only screaming, as was Our Jane.

'Hev-lee . . . Hev-lee!' sobbed Our Jane, stretching out her slender arms toward me. 'Don't wanna go, don't wanna . . .'

'Hurry, Lester. I can't bear to see this child cry.' Out the door in a hurry went the two, carrying the screaming children, with Pa running in servile attendance, holding the torn old umbrella over the head of the lady and Our Jane.

I sank to the floor and sobbed.

Tom ran to a window, and despite my will not to look, I jumped up and hurried to stand beside him, and then Fanny was crouched down on her knees, staring out and saying: 'Wish they'd chosen me. Oh, holy Jesus on the cross, I wish I could have all that stuff on Christmas morning! Why didn't they want me instead of Our Jane, who cries all the time? And Keith ain't much better, and he wets the bed. Why didn't ya tell them that, Heaven, why didn't ya?'

I wiped away tears and tried to gain control of my emotions. I tried to tell myself it wasn't so bad, not really, to lose Our Jane and Keith if they were to have so many fine things – oranges to eat, and toys to play with – and a doctor to make Our Jane well.

Then I was flying toward the door and the porch so I could call out breathlessly, just as the black car prepared to drive off, 'And be sure to send them both to good schools – please!'

The lady rolled down a window and waved. ' Please don't worry, darling,' she called. 'I'll write you from time to time and let you know how they are, but there won't be a return address. And I'll send you photographs.' And up went the window again, smothering Our Jane's loud, anguished wails, and those of Keith.

Pa didn't even bother to enter the cabin again to find out what his children thought about the 'Christmas gift' he'd just given.

He ran, as if from me and my accusing eyes; me and all the angry words I had ready to scream in his face. He jumped into his old truck and drove off, leaving me to think he'd soon throw away his thousand dollars on whores, booze, and gambling. And in bed tonight he wouldn't give one single thought to Our Jane, to Keith, to any of us.

Like a flock of chickens paralyzed by strange events beyond our understanding, we huddled, with Grandpa sitting quietly and whittling as if nothing untoward had happened, and then we met eyes. Soon Fanny began to cry. She wrapped her arms about me and sobbed. 'They'll be all right, won't thcy? People do love all little children, even those not their own, don't they?'

'Yes, of course they do,' I said, trying to choke back fresh tears and save my anguish for later, when I was alone. 'And we'll see them again. If the lady writes long letters we'll hear how they are, and one day Our Jane and Keith can write themselves, and won't that be wonderful . . . won't it be . . . wonderful.' I broke anew, tears flooding down my face before I could manage to ask a very important question. 'Tom, did you notice their licence plates?'

'Sure did,' he answered in a gruff, hoarse voice. 'Maryland. But I didn't have time to catch the last three numbers. First were nine-seven-two. Remember that.' Tom always noticed things like that. I never did.

Now the little ones I'd worried about were gone. No wailing in the night and in the morning. No wet beds and quilts, not so much washing to do, plenty of room in the brass bed now.

How empty the small cabin, how sad all the hours, minutes, and seconds after Our Jane and Keith went away. And maybe in the long run they would be better off – especially since those people appeared so rich – but what about us? Love, wasn't that worth anything? Wasn't blood the tie that bound us, not money?

'Grandpa,' I said in my constantly hoarse voice, 'we got room for you in the bed now.'

'Not proper or healthy to put the old in with the young,' Grandpa mumbled again and again, his gnarled hands quivering as if with some ancient ague. His faded old eyes pleaded with me to understand. 'Luke's a good boy, chile, he is. He meant well. Though ya don't know it. He wanted to help, that's all. Now, don't ya go thinking bad about yer pa, when he did all he knew what to do.'

'Grandpa, you'd say good things about him no matter what he did, because he's your son, the only one you've got left. But from this day forward, he's not my father! I'm not calling him Pa from now on. He's Luke Casteel, an ugly, mean liar, and someday he's going to pay for all the suffering he's put us all through! I hate him, Grandpa, hate his guts! Hate him so much I feel sick inside!'

His poor old withered face went dead white, when already it was pale and sickly, crosshatched with a million wrinkles, and he really wasn't that old. 'The Good Book says to honour thy mother and thy father . . . ya remember that, Heaven girl.'

'Why doesn't the Good Book say honour thy children, Grandpa, why doesn't it?'

Another storm blew in, and turned into a blizzard. Snow banked as high as the top of our windows, covering the porch. Ice sheeting prevented us from looking through the cheap glass even when Tom went out to shovel some of the snow away. Luckily, Pa had brought enough food to see us through another few days.

Heartbreak ruled the cabin without the cheerful chirping of Our Jane and the sweet quiet of Keith. I forgot all about the trouble Our Jane had been, forgot the plaintive wails, the tempestuous stomach that was so difficult to please. I remembered only the tender, young body, the sweetness of the back of her neck where her curls turned damp when she slept. Two angels they'd appeared when they cuddled in the bed and closed their eyes; I remember Keith and how he liked to be rocked to sleep, wanting to hear bedtime stories I'd read a thosand times or more. I remembered his sweet good-night kisses, his strong legs; I heard his small voice saying his prayers, saw him next to Our Jane, both on their knees, their small feet bare, pink toes curled; they never had the proper kind of nightclothes. I sobbed, felt sicker, meaner, angrier, and everything I remembered formed steel bullets that sooner or later would gun down the man who'd taken so much from me.

Poor Grandpa forgot how to talk. Now he was as silent as he'd been when Granny was alive, and he didn't whittle, didn't fiddle, only stared into space and rocked to, fro, to, fro. Once in a great while he'd mumble some prayer that was never answered.

We all said prayers that were never answered.

In my sleep I dreamed of Our Jane and Keith waking up to a fantasy of what I believed the merriest of all Christmas mornings. I saw them in pretty, red flannel nightclothes playing in an elegant living room where a magnificent Christmas tree spread over all the new toys and new clothes underneath. Laughing with the silent merriment of dreams, my youngest brother and sister raced about ripping open all their gifts, riding in miniature cars, Our Jane small enough to crawl inside the dolls' house; and long colourful stockings that were full of oranges, apples, sweets and chewing gum, and boxes of biscuits; and finally came a meal served on a long table with a white tablecloth, sparkling with crystal and gleaming with silver. A huge golden-brown turkey arrived on a silver platter, surrounded by all the things we'd eaten that time in the restaurant, and there was pumpkin pie straight from one of the glossy magazines I'd seen. Oh, the things my dreams gave to Our Jane and Keith.

Without Keith and Our Jane to distract me, I heard more from Fanny, who continually grouched about not being the child chosen to go with those rich people in their fine clothes and long car.

'It could have been me and not Our Jane that rich lady wanted,' she said for the hundredth time, 'if I'd have had time to wash my hair and take a bath. You used all the hot water on them, Heaven! Selfish, ya are! Them rich folks didn't like me because I looked messy – why didn't Pa tell us to get ready?'

'Fanny!' I exclaimed, quite out of patience. 'What's wrong

with you? To go away with strangers you don't even know. Why, only God above knows what will happen to –' And then I broke and started to cry.

Tom came to comfort me 'It's gonna be all right. They truly did look rich and nice. A lawyer has to be intelligent. And think of this, wouldn't it have been terrible if Pa had sold them to folks as poor as we are?'

As was to be expected, Grandpa took his son's side, 'Luke only does what he thinks is best – and ya hold yer tongue, girl, when next ya see him, or he might do something awful to ya. This ain't no fitting place for kids nohow. They'll be better off. Stop crying and accept what can't be changed. That's what life is about, standing firm against the wind.'

I should have known that Grandpa, like Granny, wouldn't be any help when it came to Pa. She'd always had excuses to explain her son's brutal behaviour. A good man – at heart. Underneath all that cruelty, a frustrated gentleman who couldn't find the right way.

A monster only a parent could love, was my opinion.

I stood as far as I could from the old man, who disappointed me in so many ways. Why couldn't Grandpa be stronger and stand up for all our rights? Why didn't he open his silent mouth and put his tongue to good use? Why did all his thoughts come out in the form of charming, little wooden figures? He could have told his son he couldn't sell his children. But he hadn't said a word, not a word.

How bitter I felt to think my grandfather went to church every Sunday he could, to sing and stand up and say prayers with bowed head, and then he came back to a home where small children were whipped, starved, brutalized, and then sold.

'We'll run away,' I whispered to Tom when Fanny was asleep and Grandpa was in his pallet. 'When the snow melts, before Pa comes back again, we'll put on all our clothes and run to Miss Deale. She must be back from Baltimore by now. She has to be. She'll tell us what to do, and how to get back Our Jane and Keith.'

Yes, Miss Deale would know, if anyone did, just how to thwart Pa and keep him from selling us to strangers. Miss Deale knew a thousand things that Pa would never know; she had connections.

It snowed for three days without letup.

Then suddenly, dramatically, the sun broke out from behind clouds. The bright light pouring in almost blinded us when Tom threw open the front door to stare out.

'It's over,' Grandpa murmured weakly. 'That's the way of our Lord, to save his own just when we think we can't live on another hour.'

How were we saved? Not saved at all by sunlight, only warmed a bit. I turned again to the old, chipped and rickety cupboard that held our pitiful store of food. Again, nothing to eat but a few of the nuts harvested in the fall.

'But I like nuts,' Tom said cheerfully, setting down to munching on his two. 'And when the snow has melted enough, we can put on our warmest clothes and escape. Wouldn't it be nice to head west, into the sun? End up in California, living on dates and oranges, drinking coconut milk. Sleeping on the golden grass, staring up at the golden mountains . . .'

'Do they have golden streets in Hollywood?' asked Fanny.

''Spect everything is golden in Hollywood,' mused Tom, still standing and looking outside. 'Or else silver.'

Grandpa said nothing.

We lived in a capricious country. Spring could come as quickly as a lightning bolt and do just as much damage. Springlike days would warm up the earth in December, January, and February, trick the flowers into blooming ahead of time, fool the trees into leaf; then winter would come back and freeze the flowers, kill off the new baby leaves, and when real spring came, those flowers and trees wouldn't repeat their performance since they'd been deceived once, wouldn't be deceived again, or at least not this season.

Now the sun turned the mounds of heaped snow into slushy mush that soon melted and flooded the streams, causing bridges to be swept away . . . and trails were lost in the woods. There was no way to escape now that the bridge was gone. Exhausted and exceedingly tired from his long quest to find a way out, Tom came home to report the loss of the nearest bridge.

'The current is running fast and strong, or else we could swim across. Tomorrow will be a better day.'

I put down *Jane Eyre* which I was reading again, and drifted over to stand beside Tom, both of us silent until Fanny ran to join us. 'Let's swear a solemn vow now,' Tom whispered so Grandpa wouldn't hear, 'to run the first chance we get. To stay together through thick and thin, one for all and all for one . . . Heavenly, we've said this to each other before. Now we have to add Fanny. Fanny, put your hands on top of mine. But first cross your heart and hope to die if ever you let us be split apart.'

Fanny seemed to hesitate, and then with rare sisterly camaraderie her hand covered mine, which rested on top of Tom's. 'We do solemnly swear . . .'

'We do solemnly swear . . .' repeated Fanny and I.

'To always stay together, to care for one another through joys and suffering . . .'

Again Fanny hesitated. 'Why do ya have to mention suffering? Yer making this sound like a wedding, Tom.'

'All right, through thick and thin, through good and bad, until we have Our Jane and Keith with us again – is that good enough for you two?'

'It's fine, Tom,' I said as I repeated his vows.

Even Fanny was impressed, and more like a real sister than she'd ever been as she snuggled up beside me, and we talked about our futures out in the big world we knew nothing about. Fanny even helped Tom and me search the woods for berries as we waited for the swollen river to go down and the bridge to be restored.

'Hey,' Tom said suddenly, hours later, 'just remembered. There's another bridge twenty miles away, and we can reach it if we're determined enough. Heavenly, if we all have to hike twenty miles or more, we're gonna need more than one hazelnut apiece, I can tell ya that right now.'

'Think we can make it on two nuts apiece?' asked I, who'd been holding back just for an emergency like this.

'Why, with all that energy, we could probably walk to Florida,' Tom said with a laugh, 'which might almost be as good as California.'

We dressed in our best, put on everything we owned. I tried not to think of leaving Grandpa all alone. Fanny was eager to escape a cabin where only sadness and old age and hopelessness had come to stay. Guilty, with reluctant determination, we kissed Grandpa good-bye. He stood up feebly, smiled at us, nodding as if life never held any surprises for him.

In my hand I held my mother's suitcase that finally Fanny had seen, though her excitement had been lessened by the knowledge we were leaving . . . for somewhere.

'Good-bye,' called all three of us in unison, but I hung back when Tom and Fanny raced outside. 'Grandpa,' I said in an embarrased voice, really hurting inside, 'I'm sorry to be doing this to you. I know it's not right to leave you alone, but we have to do it or be sold like Keith and Our Jane. Please understand.'

He looked straight ahead, one hand holding a knife, the other his bit of wood to shave, his thin hair trembling in the drafts. 'We'll come back one day when we're grown-up and too old for Pa to sell.'

'It's all right, chile,' whispered Grandpa, his head bowed low so I couldn't see his tears. 'Ya just take care.'

'I love you, Grandpa. Maybe I've never said that before, don't know why now that I didn't, because I always have.'

I stepped closer to hug and kiss him. He smelled old, sour, and felt brittle in my arms. 'We wouldn't leave you if there was any other way, but we have to go and try and find a better place.'

Again he smiled through tears, nodded as if he believed, and continued to rock. 'Luke will come back soon with food – so don't ya worry none. Forgive me for saying nasty things I didn't mean.'

'What nasty things did ya say?' bellowed a rough voice from the open doorway.

Ten

Too Many Farewells

Pa towered in the open doorway, glowering at us. He was wearing a thick red jacket that reached his hips. Brand new. His boots were better than any I'd ever seen him wear, as were his trousers; his hat and a furry band across the top that ended in earmuffs. With him he had more boxes of food. 'I'm back,' he said casually, as if he'd just left yesterday. 'Brought food with me.' And then he turned to leave, or so I thought.

Trip after trip he made to his truck to bring things in. What was the use of our trying to run now, when his long legs could catch up and swiftly bring us back again – if he didn't chase us in his truck?

More than anything, now Fanny didn't want to escape. 'Pa!' she cried, happy and excited, dancing around him and trying to find a way to hug and kiss him before he had all the supplies in from the truck.

Many times she tried to throw herself into his arms, and then succeeded. 'Oh, Pa! Ya've come to save us again! Knew ya would, knew ya loved me! Now we don't have to run away! We were hungry and cold and going to find food or steal it, and waiting for the snow to melt and the bridges to come back, and I'm so durn happy we don't have to do none of that!'

'Running away to find food, huh?' asked Pa with his lips tight, his eyes narrow. 'Can't run nowhere I can't find ya. Now sit and eat, and get ready for the company that's coming.'

It was going to happen again!

Fanny's face lit up as if an electric switch had been pushed. 'Oh, Pa, it's me this time, ain't it? Ain't it? Just let it be me!'

'Get yourself ready, Fanny,' Pa ordered as he fell into a chair and almost tipped it over backward. 'Found ya a new ma and pa, just like ya asked me to do, and as rich as the ones who took Jane and Keith.'

This information made her squeal in delight. She hurried to heat a pot of water on the stove. While that was warming, she pulled out the old aluminium basin we all used for a bathtub.

'Oh, I need better clothes!' Fanny bewailed as the water began to boil. 'Heaven, can't ya do something with a dress of yours so it'll look good on me?'

'I'm not doing anything to help you leave,' I said, my voice so cold it chilled my throat, while I felt hot tears in my eyes. Fanny cared so little about leaving us and breaking her vow.

'Tom, run fetch me more water,' she called in her sweetest voice, 'enough to fill up the tub and rinse my hair!' And Tom obeyed, though reluctantly.

Maybe Pa read my thoughts. He glanced my way, caught my full, hard glare, and perhaps saw for the first time why he hated me, who was so different from his angel. You bet I was different. I would have had better sense than to fall for an ignorant mountain man who lived in a shack and ran bootleg moonshine. He seemed to read my mind as his lip pulled back in a sneer that showed one side of his upper teeth so he no longer looked handsome.

'Yer gonna do something now, little gal? Go on. Do it. I'm waiting.'

Unconsciously I'd picked up the poker again.

Tom came in, quickly set down the pail of water, then sprang forward to keep me from using the poker. 'He'll kill you if you do,' he whispered urgently, pulling me back from harm's way.

'Got ya a real champion, haven't ya?' Pa asked, looking at Tom with scorn. Casually he stood up, yawned, as if nothing at all had happened to make either one of us hate him. 'They'll be coming any minute. Hurry up there, Fanny girl. Ya'll soon know just how yer pa loves ya when ya see who's gonna take ya in and treat ya better than gold.'

Hardly were the words out of his mouth when a car pulled

into our dirt yard. Only this was not a strange car, it was a car we knew very well having seen it many times on the streets of Winnerrow. It was a long, black, shiny Cadillac that belonged to the wealthiest man in Winnerrow, the Reverend Wayland Wise.

At last, at last! Miss Deale had found a way to save us!

Squealing more, Fanny hugged her arms over her small breasts and shot me a smug, delighted look. 'Me! They want me!'

In a moment she was dressed in what used to be my best.

Pa flung open the door and cordially invited inside the Reverend and his thin-faced wife, who didn't smile, didn't speak, only looked sour and unhappy. She didn't stare at what must have been a shock to someone so affluent, but then I reckoned she must have expected to see such living conditions. As for the handsome Reverend, he didn't waste one moment.

I was wrong to have presumed that Miss Deale had sent him to save us, much less that God was going to work one of his miracles. Fanny knew much more about reality than I. God's man already knew which one of Pa's remaining three he wanted. Though, when the Reverend looked us over up close, his eyes lingered long and lusting on me.

I backed away, terribly frightened by the holy man. I shot an angry glance at Pa, to see him shaking his head, as if he didn't want me living too near his home.

That was confirmed when Pa said: 'My eldest is a troublemaker, quick to answer back, stubborn, hard headed, and mean, Reverend Wise, Mrs Wise. Take my word for it, this younger girl, Fanny, is far the better choice. Fanny is easygoing, beautiful, and sweet. Why, I call her my dove, my doe, my lovely, loving Fanny.'

What a lie! He never called any of us by pet names.

This time there would be no caterwauling, no fighting, no holding back. Fanny couldn't have been happier. Her smile was dazzling she was so happy. The Reverend handed out boxes of chocolates to all three of us, and also gave Fanny a beautiful red coat just her size, with a black fur collar. Fanny was won over. That's all it took!

She didn't even wait to hear about the beautiful room of her own they said they'd have decorated to suit her fancy, or other things they planned to give her, like dancing and music lessons.

'I'll be what ya want!' cried Fanny, her dark eyes shining. 'Be anything ya want! I'm ready, willing, eager to go! And thank ya for coming, for wanting me, thank ya, thank ya.'

Fanny ran and threw her arms about the Reverend. 'Blessed are ya – blessed am I! Two million times I say, thank ya! I'll never be hungry or cold again. Already I love ya, I do, I do – for choosin me and not Heaven.'

Fanny! Fanny! I silently screamed. Have you forgotten already our pledge to stick together through thick and thin? God didn't plan it this way, for families to be split and given one to this person and one to that. *Fanny, you've been like my own.*

'Ya see, ya see,' Pa exclaimed proudly. 'Best choice, this one. A loving, sweet girl ya'll never be ashamed of.'

He threw me another of those sneering looks as I stared straight ahead, ashamed of Fanny, fearful for Fanny. What did a thirteen-year-old know about anything? Tom stood beside me, holding my hand, his face pale, his eyes dark with his own frightened pain.

Five little Indians we were playing.

All disappearing one by one. Two left.

Who'd it be next time, Tom or me?

'I'm so proud they chose me,' Fanny pronounced happily again as if she couldn't get over the wonder of it. When she was wearing her new red coat, she whispered in a breathless, touching way, 'I'm gonna live in a big rich house, and ya can come to see me.' She sniffed once or twice, enough to show at least a little regret, before she threw several beseeching looks at me and Tom. Then she picked up her two-pound box of chocolates and smiled before she turned and led the way out to the big car. 'See ya in town,' she called without looking back, not even at Pa.

Paperwork finished, the Reverend paid his five hundred in cash, accepted Pa's carefully written receipt, and turned to follow Fanny, with his wife a step or two behind him. And, like a true gentleman, the Reverend helped both Fanny and his wife into his car. All sat on the front seat, Fanny in the middle.

Bang! went the heavy car door.

The sharp pain came again, not as bad as it had been for Our Jane and Keith. Fanny wanted to leave, and hadn't screamed and howled and kicked her legs and flailed her arms – the little ones had wanted to stay. Who could say which decision was right?

And Fanny was only going to Winnerrow. Our Jane and Keith were way off in Maryland, and Tom could remember only three of the licence-plate numbers. Would that be enough to lead us to them . . . someday?

Now it was my time to miss Fanny, my tormentor, my now-and-then friend and sister. Fanny, also my shame when I was in school and heard her giggles coming from the cloakroom. Fanny with her sexy ways, her uninhibited inheritance from the hills.

This time Pa didn't go after Fanny left. As if the information Fanny gushed when first he came in had put him on guard, and he'd not leave to find Tom and me gone when he came back again. Both Tom and I were anxious to see him go so we could escape before we too were sold. We waited without speaking, sitting side by side on the floor not far from the stove. We sat so close I felt his heat, as he must have felt mine. I heard his hard breathing, as surely he heard mine.

In no way was Pa going to give us a chance to run. He ensconced himself in a hard chair on the other side of the stove, tipping it backward before he half lowered his lids, and seemed to be waiting. I tried to convince myself days would pass before someone else came. Time for us to escape. Plenty of time . . .

No such luck.

A muddy maroon-coloured pickup truck just as old and beat up as Pa's pulled to an abrupt stop in our yard, putting panic in my heart that was echoed in Tom's eyes. He reached again for my hand, squeezed it hard, as we both backed to the wall. Fanny'd only been gone two hours, and here was another buyer.

Footfalls on the porch steps. Heavy feet crossing the porch. Three loud raps, then another three. Pa's eyes opened; he jumped up, sprang to the door, threw it open. Now we could see a burly, short man who stepped inside, looked over the cabin with a frown on his grizzly, bearded face. He saw Tom, who was already a head taller than he was.

'Don't cry, Heavenly, please don't,' pleaded Tom. 'I won't be able to stand it if you do.' He squeezed my fingers again, touched my tears with his free hand, then lightly kissed me. 'Ain't nothing we can do, is there? Not when people like Reverend Wise and his wife don't see nothing wrong in buying kids. It's been done before, ya know it and I know it. Ain't gonna be the last time it happens either, ya know that.'

I threw myself into his arms, held tight. I was not going to cry, not going to let it hurt so bad this time. Best thing to do, really it was. Nobody could be more heartless than Pa, nobody more shiftless and rotten. Everybody would be better off. Sure we would. Nicer houses, more and better food to eat. It was going to be wonderful to know we were all eating three meals a day like everybody else in this free land called the United States.

That's when I broke and began to bawl.

'Tom, run! Do something!'

Pa moved to block any chance of Tom's escaping, though he didn't try. We had only one door, and the windows were too high and too small.

Pa didn't see my tears, refused to see the anguish on Tom's face before he hurried over to shake the hand of the burly man wearing worn, dirty overalls. His face was heavyset, what could be seen of it. His dense, grizzly beard hid everything but his bulbous nose and his small, squinty eyes. His thick salt-and-pepper hair made his head seem to sit atop his broad shoulders without a neck; then came his bulging chest, his huge, swollen beer belly – all half concealed beneath those loose-fitting overalls.

'I come to get him,' he said without preliminaries, looking straight at Tom, not even glancing at me. He was about three feet away, and between him and us and Pa. 'If he's what ya said he is, that is.'

'Take a look at him,' said Pa, not smiling this time. He was all business with this farmer. 'Tom is fourteen years old and already he's almost six feet tall. Look at those shoulders, those hands and feet; that's how you judge what kind of a man a boy's gonna make. Feel his muscles, made strong from swinging an axe, and he can pitch hay as good as any full-grown man.'

Sick, it was cruel and sick treating Tom like a prize calf to be sold.

That farmer with the red face yanked Tom closer, held him as he looked into Tom's mouth, checked over his teeth, felt his muscles, his thighs and calves, asked him intimate questions. Pa answered when Tom refused to reply. As if Pa could possibly know, or even care, whether or not Tom had headaches or early-morning lusts.

'He's a healthy boy; he must be sexually aware. I was at his age, eager and ready to do my damndest for the girls.'

What did he want with Tom anyway, stud services?

The burly farmer stated his occupation; he was a dairy farmer named Buck Henry. Needed help, he did. Needed someone young and strong and eager to earn good wages. 'Don't want nobody weak, shiftless, or lazy, or unable to take orders.'

Pa took umbrage at that. 'Why, my Tom has never had a lazy day in his life.' He looked proudly at Tom, while Tom scowled and seemed miserable, and tried to stay at my side.

'Good, strong-looking boy,' Buck Henry said with

approval. He handed Pa the five hundred in cash, signed the papers Pa had ready, accepted his receipt, seized Tom by the arms, pulled him toward the door. Tom tried to drag his feet, but Pa was behind him shoving him on, and kicking his shins when he moved too slowly. Grandpa rocked on and on, whittling.

At the door Tom broke. 'I don't want to go!' he yelled, fighting to free himself.

Pa moved quickly to position himself directly behind me; though I tried to escape, I moved too late. Pa caught me by the hair. His large hands moved downward to rest lightly on my shoulders, his fingers spread in such a way all he had to do was move them slightly and he'd have a choking grip on my neck and throat.

It seemed to chill Tom to see me held like a chicken about to have its neck wrung.

'Pa!' he yelled. 'Don't you hurt her! If you sell Heavenly like the rest of us – you find her the best parents! If you don't, I'll come back one day and make you regret you ever had a child!' His wild eyes met mine. 'I'll come back, Heavenly!' he cried. 'I promise I won't forget our pledge. I love what you've tried to do for me, and for all of us. I'll write often, keep you so much in touch you won't even miss me – and I'll get to where ever you are! I make this solemn vow never to be broken.'

My eyes felt strained, swollen, as if I had two discoloured, dreary suns behind the blackest of all moons. 'Tom . . . write, please, please. We'll see each other again – I know we will. Mr Henry, where do you live?'

'Don't tell her,' warned Pa, tightening his fingers about my throat. 'This one means nothing but trouble, and don't let Tom write. At least not to this one named Heaven. She should have been called Hell.'

'Pa!' screamed Tom. 'She's the best you got, and you don't know it.'

Tom was outside now and the door had been left open. I managed to call out, my voice hoarse, 'There's always a bridge up ahead, Thomas Luke, you keep remembering that. And you'll achieve your dream, I know!'

Turning, he heard and understood, waved, smiled, then got in the truck and kept his head out of the window, yelling back to me. 'No matter where you go or who tries to keep us apart, I'll find you, Heavenly! I'll never forget you! Together we'll find Keith and Our Jane, just like we planned to do!'

The dirty old truck drove off, headed toward the rough road, and disappeared, and I was alone with Pa and Grandpa. Feeling numb, in a state of despairing shock I sank to the floor when Pa released me.

Already I sensed just what lay ahead for Tom.

No more education for Tom, no more fun hunting and fishing for Tom, or baseball playing, or fooling around with his buddies, just work, work, and more work.

Tom with his brilliant mind, his dreams and aspirations, would be buried out in the middle of cow pastures, living a farmer's life, the kind he'd often said he'd never put up with.

But what lay ahead for me frightened me just as much.

Eleven

My Choice

Tom was gone.

I was without a soul to love me. Who would ever call me Heavenly again?

Tom took with all the laughter, all the excitement, brightness, courage, encouragement, and good humour he'd given to a grim, struggling household. The fun side of myself disappeared in that pickup truck with licence plates so covered with mud I couldn't read them. And I'd tried so hard. I'd thought before, foolishly, that I'd been alone after Keith and Our Jane left. Now I was truly the only one left, and I was the one Pa hated.

I tried to comfort myself by believing I was also the only one who did anything useful in the cabin, like cooking and cleaning, and caring for Grandpa – certainly Pa wouldn't want to leave Grandpa here alone . . . .

I willed Pa to go, to slam out the door, jump into his truck, and drive for Winnerrow, or wherever he went now that he had to stay out of Shirley's Place.

He didn't go.

He positioned himself near the only door to our shack like a guard dog, to keep me imprisoned until he had me sold, too.

He didn't speak, just sat sullen and quiet, and when night fell, he moved his chair closer to the stove, his large feet propped up, his eyes half closed, a look of misery on his face.

All through the remainder of the week after Tom left with Buck Henry I tried to find the strength to run off alone if ever I had the chance – that meant when I had to use the outhouse.

Without Tom, Keith, Our Jane, I had no heart, no spirit, no will to run anywhere to save myself from what had to be my certain fate. If only I could send a message to Miss Deale.

Was she back yet? I prayed each night for Miss Deale or Logan to come to my rescue.

No one came.

I was the one Pa hated, and I would be the one he'd turn over to the very worst kind of people. No rich folks for me. Not even anyone as good as Buck Henry. Very likely he'd sell me to that madam who ran Shirley's Place.

The more my thoughts dwelled on my fate, the angrier I grew. He couldn't do this to me! I wasn't a dumb animal to be sold off and forgotten. I was a human being with an eternal soul, with the inalienable right to life, liberty, and the pursuit of happiness. Miss Deale had said that so often it was imprinted on my brain. Then, to myself, I had to grin bitterly, for in that class of hers there dwelled a spirit that reached out to me, telling me to hold on, she was coming to the rescue. It was almost as if I heard Miss Deale calling out encouragement, her voice coming closer and closer over the hills.

Hurry, Miss Deale, I wanted to yell across the mountains. This is my needing time, Miss Deale! All pride gone now, vanished, conquered! Without shame I'll take from you! Come, come fast to save me, for it won't be long now!

I prayed, then got up from my knees, moved to the kitchen cabinet, and peered inside. Life went on despite everything, and meals had to be prepared.

Hope was in Grandpa's reddened, watery eyes when he came back from his necessity trip with more tree branches. He carefully seated himself in his rocker. He didn't pick up his whittling knife, only fixed his eyes on me. Don't leave me, his eyes were pleading. Stay, they begged silently, even as he motioned me close and whispered, 'I'm all right chile. I know what yer thinking. Ya want to run. So go when ya get the chance – steal out when Luke's sleeping.'

I loved him for saying that. Loved him so much I forgave him for keeping quiet when the others were sold, knowing even as I thought this that I had to love somebody or curl up and die. 'You won't hate me if I leave you here alone? You'll understand?'

'Nope, won't understand. Just want ya to have what ya want. In my heart I know yer pa's doing what he thinks is best. In yer heart ya think he's doing what's worst.'

It seemed Pa had slept his last sleep in some distant unknown place. He didn't doze, didn't even close his eyes all the way. His cold, dark eyes never left me. Not that he met my challenging glares; he only gazed with hooded eyes at some part of me, my hair, my hands, my feet, my middle, anywhere but my face.

Seven days passed, and Pa stayed on and on.

Then one day Logan came to our door, come like a prince to save me!

I opened it expecting to see Grandpa coming from the outhouse. 'Hi,' Logan said, smiling broadly and then flushing. 'Been thinking a lot about you lately, wondering why you, Tom, and the others don't come to school now that the weather's not so bad. Why are all of you staying away? What you been up to?'

He hadn't seen Fanny – why not?

I yanked him in the door when once I would have shoved him out, or thought of a million reasons why he couldn't come in. 'Pa's chopping wood out in the back,' I whispered frantically, 'and Grandpa's in the outhouse, so I won't have much time. Pa comes in to check on me every few minutes. Logan, I'm in trouble, big trouble! Pa is selling us off, one by one. Our Jane and Keith first then Fanny, next Tom . . . and soon it'll be me.'

'Who ya talking to, girl?' bellowed Pa from the door. I shrank inside my skin as Logan turned to face the powerful brute who was my father.

'My name is Logan Stonewall, sir,' said Logan in a polite yet firm way. 'My father is Grant Stonewall, and he owns Stonewall Pharmacy, and Heaven and I have been good friends ever since we came to Winnerrow to live. It's been troubling me why Heaven, Tom, Fanny, Keith, and Our Jane don't go to school anymore, so I came to check on all of them.'

'Why they go or don't go is none of yer damned business,' snapped Pa. 'Now take yerself out of here. We don't need nosy people checking on what we do or don't do.'

Logan turned again to me. 'I guess I should go home before the sun goes down. Please take care of yourself. By the way, my teacher said that Miss Deale will be back next week.' He gave Pa a long, significant look, making my heart thrill. He did believe me, he did!

'You tell that teacher to stay away and mind her own goddamn business,' roared Pa, moving towards Logan in a threatening manner. 'Now you've had your say, so git.'

Calmly Logan swept his eyes around the cabin, drinking in all the poverty that was only too plain to see. I knew he was trying to keep pity and shock from showing in his eyes, but I saw it there, nevertheless. Logan's dark blue eyes met mine, giving me some silent message I didn't know quite how to intepret. 'I hope to see you again in a few days, Heaven. I'll tell Miss Deale you're not sick. Now tell me where Tom is, and Fanny, Our Jane, and Keith.'

'They've gone to visit relatives,' said Pa, throwing open the door, standing aside, and motioning for Logan to go or to be thrown out.

Logan glared at Pa. 'You take good care of Heaven, Mr Casteel.'

'Get out,' Pa said with disgust, and slammed the door behind Logan.

'Why'd that boy come?' he asked when I turned back to the stove, and Grandpa came stumbling in from the other room. 'Did ya send for him in some way, did ya?'

'He came because he cares, and Miss Deale cares, and the whole world is going to care when they know what you've done, Luke Casteel!'

'Thanks for warning me,' he said with a sneer. 'I'm scared real scared.'

He was worse after that, even more vigilant.

I kept hoping and praying Logan would run into Fanny,

and she'd tell him what was going on, and Logan would do something before it was too late. Yet, at the same time, I suspected Pa might have warned the Reverend to keep Fanny close until he had a chance to get rid of me.

I'd read in the newspapers about adopted children selling for ten thousand dollars, and Pa was stupid enough not to ask for that much. But five times five hundred meant he'd have more money than he'd ever had in his entire life; a fortune to any hillbilly in the Willies who couldn't think as high as a thousand.

'Pa,' I said on the tenth day after Tom had gone, 'how can you go to church every Sunday for most of your life, and do what you've done?'

'Shut up,' he said, his eyes hard as flat river stones.

'I don't want to shut up!' I flared. 'I want my brothers and sisters back! You don't have to take care of us. Tom and I found a way to support ourselves.'

'Shut up!'

Oh, I hate you! my wild inner voice raged, even as my instinct warned me to keep quiet or be severely punished.

'Others sell their kids,' he said suddenly, taking me off guard, that he would speak – to me – as if trying to explain himself, when I'd thought he'd never do such a thing. 'I'm not the first, won't be the last. Nobody talks about it, but it happens all the time. Poor people like us have more kids than the rich ones who can afford kids, and we who can't afford them, most of us don't know how to keep from having them. When there's nothing else better to do on a cold winter's night but go to bed and take what pleasure ya can with yer woman – we make our own gold mines, our kids, our pretty young'uns. So why not take advantage of the laws of nature's balance?'

It was more than he'd said to me in my entire life. And he was well now, his cheeks were flushed with healthy colour, no longer gaunt. Strong, high cheekbones – damned handsome face! If he died, would I feel sorry? No, I told myself over and over, not in a million years.

Late one night I overheard him talking to Grandpa, saying all sorts of melancholy things about his life going to pot, kids holding him back, keeping him from reaching the goal he'd set for himself. 'When I get all the money, Pa, it won't be too late. I'm going to do what I always wanted, and would have done but for *her* . . . and *them* . . .'

I stopped crying that night. Tears didn't do any good.

I stopped praying for God to send back my brothers and sisters, stopped thinking Logan would be able to save me. I stopped betting on Miss Deale, and fate that had killed her mother, and lawyers who were holding her in Baltimore. I had to plan my own escape.

On Sunday the sun came out. Pa ordered me to dress in my best, if I had any best. My heart jumped, thinking he'd found a buyer. His hard eyes mocked me. 'It's Sunday, girl, churchgoing time,' he said, as if several Sundays hadn't come and gone without any Casteel showing up.

Hearing the word 'church,' Grandpa immediately brightened. With stiff joints and many grunts and groans he managed to pull on his only fairly decent clothes, and soon we were ready for our trip into Winnerrow and church.

The church bell chimed clear, resonant tones, giving me a certain false serenity, the sense that God was in his heaven and all was right with the world; as long as the church stood, the bell kept ringing, the people kept coming, kept singing, kept believing.

Pa parked our truck far from the church (others had taken all the close parking places), and we walked the rest of the way, with him holding my arm in a vicelike grip.

Those already in the church were singing when we entered.

> 'Bringing in the sheaves,
> Bringing in the sheaves,
> We shall go rejoicing
> Bringing in the sheaves . . .'

Sing, sing, sing. Make the day brighter, make it less cold, less forbidding. I closed my eyes, saw Our Jane's sweet small face. Kept them closed, heard Miss Deale's soaring soprano. Still keeping my eyes closed, I felt my hand clasped in Tom's felt Keith tugging on my skirt, and then came that loud, commanding voice. I opened my eyes and stared up at him, wondering how he could buy a child and then call her his own.

'Ladies, gentleman, will you please stand and turn to page one hundred and forty-seven in your hymnbooks, then all together sing our most beloved hymn of all,' instructed Reverend Wayland Wise.

> 'And we walk with him,
> And we talk with him,
> And he tells us we are his own,
> And the voice we hear singing
> In our ears,
> No other has ever known . . .'

Singing made my heart lighter, happier, until I caught sight of Fanny sitting in the front pew next to Rosalynn Wise. Fanny didn't even glance around to see if any member of her 'former' family was seated in a back pew. Maybe she hoped we wouldn't be there.

I sucked in my breath when she turned her head in profile. Oh, how beautiful she looked in that white fur coat, with a hat to match, and a fur muff to stuff her hands into; even though the church was stifling hot, still Fanny kept on all that fur and made sure that everyone behind glimpsed the muff at least once. She managed this by standing up from time to time, and excusing herself for one reason or another; then off to the right she'd stroll to a small hidden chamber, and in there she did something or other that took a few minutes, then slowly, slowly, she sauntered back to her pew, to primly take her place beside her new 'mother.'

Of course this gave everyone a good view of all the new

clothes Fanny wore. Including white boots with fur trim at the top.

When the services were over, Fanny stood with Reverend Wise and his tall wife to shake hands with all the congregation, who considered themselves deprived, if they didn't have the chance to shake the hand of the Reverend or his wife before they left somehow to endure six entire days of solid sinful living, only to come again to be forgiven. For it seemed the more you sinned during the week, the more the Lord above loved you for giving him so much to forgive.

If the Lord loved sinners so much, he must really be thrilled to have Luke Casteel in his church. Why, if I were truly lucky he might glue Pa's feet to the floor and never let him go.

Inch by slow inch we followed in the wake of everyone else. No one spoke to us, though a few mountain folk nodded. The cold wind whistled inside each time someone passed through the wide double doors. Everyone but me wanted to touch the hand of the spokesman of God here on earth, the handsome, smooth-talking Reverend Wise, and if not him, his wife . . . or his newly adopted daughter.

Like a lovely princess was Fanny in her costly white fur and bright, green velvet dress, displayed every time Fanny put one leg or another forward, shuffling like an idiot dancer just to show off. For one brief moment I forgot my loss, my predicament, and enjoyed Fanny's gain.

But lo, when Fanny's own family showed up, she turned away, whispered something into the ear of Rosalynn Wise, and disappeared in the crowd.

Pa sailed right on by, heading straight for the door without even pausing to turn his eyes on the Reverend or his wife. He had me by the arm, holding it with steely fingers. Nobody looked at the Casteels, or what was left of us.

Grandpa followed Pa's lead obediently, his grey, almost bald head bowed and subservient, until I tore my arm away from Pa and dashed back to deliberately hold up the line as I fixed my most penetrating glare on Rosalynn Wise.

'Will you kindly tell Fanny when you see her next that I asked about her?'

'I will.' Her voice was cold and flat, as if wishing I had followed Pa's example and ignored her as he had. 'And you tell yer father not to come to this church, and we would all greatly appreciate if no Casteel ever came to services again.'

Shocked, I stared at the woman whose husband had just given his sermon about the Lord loving sinners and welcoming them into his home. 'You have a Casteel living in your home, don't you?'

'If you are referring to our daughter, her name has been legally changed to Wise. Louisa Wise is her name now.'

'Louisa is Fanny's middle name!' I cried. 'You can't just change her names when her father is still living.'

Someone shoved me from behind.

Suddenly I was forced by many hands out to the wooden steps. Alarmed and angry, I spun around to yell out something or other about hypocrites, when I saw Logan Stonewall directly in front of me. But for him I would have confronted Reverend Wise himself, shouted out the whole truth to everyone here – but Logan was staring at me, through me. He didn't speak. He didn't smile either.

It was as if he didn't want to see me! And I, who thought nothing could hurt me more after losing Sarah, Granny, Our Jane, Keith, and Tom, felt my heart plunge into a deep well of darkness. Of hopelessness.

What had happened between the time he came to see me and now?

Logan, Logan, I wanted to cry out, but pride reared its head, and I didn't say a word, just lifted my chin and strode on past the Stonewall family, who stood in a separate little group of three.

Pa seized hold of my arm again and dragged me away.

That night, lying on the floor close to belching Ole Smokey, I heard the creak of the old, pine floorboards as Pa got out of the brass bed and paced the small space of the other room.

He stole as quietly as one of his Indian ancestors to where I lay very still. With my eyes half lidded, I could just see his bare feet, his bare legs. Pretending to turn in my sleep, I rolled over on my side, presenting him with my back, and curled up tighter in the old stained quilt.

Did he kneel on the floor by the stove just so he could touch my hair? I felt something moving lightly over my head. He'd never touched me before. I froze, almost stopped breathing. My heart beat wildly; my eyes, unable to stay closed, popped wide and staring. Why was he touching me?

'Soft,' I heard him murmur, 'like hers . . . silky, like hers . . .'

Then his hand was on my shoulder that had somehow worked its way free of the covering; that hand that had always battered me cruelly slid tenderly down my upper arm, and then back up, lingering where my shoulder joined my neck. For long, long moments I felt scared, holding my breath and waiting, waiting for something horrible to happen.

'Luke . . . what ya doing?' Grandpa asked in an odd voice.

Pa snatched his hand away.

Pa hadn't hit me! Hadn't hurt me! I kept thinking as I lay there marvelling at the kindness of that hand on my shoulder and arm. Why, after all these years, had he touched me lovingly – why?

Grandpa's frail voice woke me near dawn. He was at the stove, heating water, giving me a few extra moments of sleep. I'd overslept, perhaps from worrying so late into the night.

'I saw ya, Luke! I won't have it. I won't! Ya leave that chile be. There's a whole town of women to take once ya know it's safe, but right now ya don't need a woman, or a girl.'

'She's mine!' Pa raged. 'And I'm well now!' His face was red when I dared to take a peek. 'Born of my seed . . . and I'll do what I damn well like with her. She's old enough, plenty old enough. Why, her ma wasn't but a little older when she married up with me.'

Grandpa's voice turned to a thin wind from the north. 'I

remember a night when all the world went dark for ya, and it'll go even darker if ya touch that girl. Get her away from here, out of temptation's reach. She's no more for ya than the other one was.'

Monday night Pa disappeared while I slept. He came back near dawn. I felt drugged when I woke up, heavy-hearted, dull-spirited, yet I got up to do what I always did, opening the iron stove door, shoving in more wood, putting on water to boil. Pa watched me closely, seeming to weigh my mood, or judge what I might do. When I looked again, Pa seemed reflective, as if trying to pull himself together, before he said in a strange, tight kind of voice, with better pronunciation than usual:

'You, my sweet young thing, are going to have a choice. A choice not many of us have.' He moved so I had to look at him or be trapped in a corner. 'Down in the valley are two childless couples who have seen you from time to time, and it seems they both admire you, so when I approached them, saying you needed new parents, both couples were eager to have you. Soon they'll be coming. I could sell you to the highest bidder, but I won't.'

My eyes clashed with his defiantly, yet I could find nothing to say that would prevent him from doing what he wanted to do.

'This time, I'm allowing you to choose just which set of parents you want.'

A certain kind of indifference fell like a cloak over me. Over and over again Grandpa's words echoed in my mind: 'Get her away from here . . .' Even Grandpa didn't want me. As Fanny had shouted out, anyone, any place, would be better than here.

Any house!

Any parents!

Grandpa wanted me to go. There he sat whittling on a figure, as if a thousand grandchildren could be sold away, and still he'd just sit and whittle.

Thoughts of Logan Stonewall flitted like doomed moths

to the candle of my burning despair. He wouldn't even meet my eyes. Wouldn't even turn his head to stare after me, as I'd hoped he would do. And even if his parents beside him had made him shy or embarrassed, still he could have managed a secret signal, but he hadn't made any. Why not? He'd trudged all the way up the mountainside. Had seeing inside the cabin shocked him to such an extent his feelings for me had changed?

I don't care, I said to myself over and over. Why should I care? He wouldn't believe me when I told the truth.

For the first time I truthfully believed maybe life would be better living with decent folks. And when I was safely away from this place I'd find a way to search for those I loved.

'You'd better get dressed,' Pa said after I'd wiped the table clean and put away the floor bed pallets. 'They'll be coming soon.'

I sucked in my breath, tried to meet his eyes, and failed. Better so, I told myself, better so. Without zest I looked through the boxes to find the best of what clothes I had. Before I put them on, I swept the cabin floor – and not once did Pa move his eyes from me.

I made the bed, just as if this were another ordinary day. Pa didn't move his eyes from whatever I did. He made me self-consious. Made me nervous. Made me clumsy and slow when usually I felt graceful and swift. Made me feel so many emotions I grew confused, reeling with my long-lived hatred for him.

Two shiny, new cars crawled into our dirt yard and parked one behind the other. A white car, a black car. The black one was long and luxurious-looking, the white one smaller, snazzier, with red seats.

I was wearing the only dress Fanny hadn't taken, a simple, shiftlike garment that had once been blue and was now grey from years of washings. Underneath I had on one of the two pair of underpants I owned. I needed to wear a bra now, but I didn't own one. Quickly I brushed my hair; then I remembered the suitcase. I had to take that suitcase with me!

Soon I had, retrieved the cherished suitcase that held the treasures of my mother, and around it I wrapped several of Granny's handmade shawls.

Pa's dark eyes narrowed when he saw me with the suitcase that had been hers. Still, he didn't say a word to stop me from taking my mother's belongings. I would have died to save them from his destruction. Maybe he guessed that.

Twice Pa seemed to rip away his eyes from staring at my mouth. Was he seeing how much I looked like her, his dead angel? Inwardly I shivered. My own mother's lips, the same lips on the doll – a doll in a wedding gown – a doll who looked no older than I did now.

Deep in my thoughts, I didn't hear the raps on the door. Didn't glimpse the two couples who came in until they were there, in the middle of our largest room. Ole Smokey coughed and spat out smoke. Pa shook hands, smiling, acting like a genial host. I looked around, trying to see something I'd forgotten. In the suitcase I'd stuffed Keith's childish portrait of Our Jane.

Then came the silence. The long, awful silence as four sets of eyes turned on me, the item up for sale. Eyes that swept over me from head to feet, took my measurements, studied my face, hands, body, while I was caught in a web of darkness so intense I could hardly see them at all.

Now I knew how Tom must have felt. Tom – I could feel him beside me, giving me strength, whispering his encouraging words. *It'll be all right, Heavenly . . . don't it all work out in the end, don't it?*

Pa spoke loud and sharp, making my eyes focus on an older couple who stood slightly in front of a younger one, who held back considerately for the middle-aged couple to have the first chance at the sale merchandise. I edged backward toward a corner not so far from where Grandpa sat whittling.

Look at me, Grandpa, see what your good-hearted son is doing! Stealing from you the only one you have left that loves you! Say something to stop him, Toby Casteel . . . say it, say it, say it!

He said nothing, only whittled.

The grey-haired man and woman before me were tall and very distinguished, both wearing grey coats with suits underneath, as if they came from a foreign world, with education and intelligence an aura all around them. They didn't stare around the way the younger man and woman did at the shocking poverty and the pitifulness of Grandpa whittling and acting as if no one had come to call.

Their bearing was arrogant, regal, their eyes kind as they looked at me pressed back against the wall, with panic in my face and heart. What my eyes must have shown flicked a shimmer of pity in the man's blue eyes, but the woman refused to show anything. She could have been thinking about the weather. I sighed again, swallowed the lump in my throat, or tried to, feeling trapped. I wished time would speed up, and it would be two years from now. But right at this moment my heart was thudding madly, drumming out a tune of fright in the cage of my ribs, making me feel weak in the knees and queasy in the stomach. I wanted Grandpa to glance upward and meet my eyes and do something to stop this, but I'd never succeeded in forcing Grandpa to do anything when Pa was around.

They don't like me, don't like me, I kept thinking about the older couple, who refused to smile encouragement my way that would make me feel right about choosing them. With the kind of desperate hope that had been Fanny's, I darted a quick glance at the younger pair.

The man was tall and good-looking, with dark brown, straight hair and light brown eyes. Beside him stood his wife, almost as tall as he was. Six feet, or very near it, she had to be, even without those high heels. Her hair was a huge mass of auburn red, darker and richer than Sarah's hair had been. Sarah had never been to a beauty parlour, and only too obviously this woman's hair couldn't survive without one. Hair teased to such exaggerated fullness it seemed quite solid. Her eyes were a strange pale, colour, so light they seemed not to have any colour at all, only huge pupils swimming in a colourless sea. She had that porcelain-white skin that often came with naturally red hair, flawless and made up to perfection. A pretty face? Yes. Very pretty.

She had the look of the hill people . . . something there . . .

Unlike the older couple who wore those heavy grey tailored coats, she wore a hot-pink suit, so tight it appeared painted on. She sashayed about, staring at everything, even leaning to peer into the oven that she opened. Why did she do that? Straightening up, she smiled at everyone and at no one in particular, turning about to stare brazenly at the old brass bed that I had just made, staring up at the baskets on the ceiling, gaping at the pitiful attempts to give the cabin comforts and coziness. Her face wore myriad expressions, changing fleetingly, as if all struggled to survive new impressions that wiped out former gasps, shocks, shudders, . . . and other unspoken surprises. With two long-nailed lacquered fingers she picked up the cloth I had used to wipe off the table, held it gingerly two seconds, then dropped it to the floor as if she'd touched a loathsome disease. Her bright, pink lips froze in the smile she tried to maintain.

And all the time the good-looking, young husband kept his eyes glued on me. He smiled as if to reassure me, and that smile of his lit up his eyes. For some reason that made me feel better – he, at least, approved of what he saw.

'Well,' said Pa, planting his big feet wide apart, his huge fists on his hips, 'it's up to ya, girl, up to ya . . .'

I stared from one couple to the other. How could I know from appearances? What was I supposed to look for? The auburn-haired woman in the bright, pink knit smiled winningly, and that made her even prettier. I admired her long, painted nails, her earrings big as half-dollars; admired her lips, her clothes, her hair. The older, grey-haired woman met my eyes without blinking and she didn't smile. Her earrings were tiny pearls and not impressive at all.

I thought I saw something hostile in her eyes that made me

draw back and look at her husband – and he wouldn't meet my gaze. How could I tell if there was no eye contact? The soul was read through the eyes – deceiving eyes if they didn't meet yours squarely.

Again I turned to the younger couple, who wore the 'in' kind of clothes and not the tailored expensive type of the older couple the kind of clothes that would never go out of style. Stuffy, dowdy clothes, Fanny would say. At that time I knew nothing at all about comparing real wealth with tacky nouveau rich.

And all this only made me feel less than human in my shapeless garment, drooping low on one shoulder because the neckline was much too large, with its jagged hemline that I was always meaning to fix but never had time to tend to. Even as I stood there, I felt wispy wild hair tickling my forehead, so automatically I reached up to brush it away. This drew everyone's attention to my reddened, chapped hands with short broken fingernails. I tried to hide my hands that scrubbed clothes every day of my life and did all the dishwashing. Who'd want me when I was such a mess?

Neither pair would.

Fanny had been chosen quickly, eagerly. Fanny hadn't ruined her hands, and Fanny's long straight hair was heavy enough to stay in place. I was too ordinary, too ugly, and too pathetic – who could ever want me – if Logan couldn't bear to meet my eyes anymore? How could I have dared to think that perhaps one day he might even love me?

'Well, girl,' Pa said again, frowning and showing his disapproval because I was taking so long. 'I said ya'd have yer pick, and if ya don't make it soon, I'll do it for ya.'

Troubled, sensing something of an undercurrent and not understanding what it was, I tried to guess what was behind the older pair's withdrawn, cold attitude, their eyes resting on me but apparently not wanting to really see me. That made me see them as dull, staid, perhaps cold, and all the time the auburn-haired woman with the colourless eyes was smiling, smiling, and Sarah had been red-haired and so loving – at least until the babies started dying.

Yes, the younger couple would be exciting and less strict. And that was how I made my hasty decision.

'Them,' I said, indicating the redhead and her handsome husband. The wife seemed a bit older, but that was all right, she was still young enough, and the longer I stared the prettier she became.

Those colourless sea eyes with round black fish swimming took on a glistening glow – of happiness? She hurried to me, gathered me in her embrace, smothered my face against her voluptuous bosom. 'Ya'll never regret it, never,' she said, half laughing, glancing triumphantly at Pa, then at her husband. 'I'm going to make ya the best mother there is, the very best there is . . .'

Then, as if she'd touched red-hot coals, she dropped her arms and stepped back from me, glancing down to see if I'd dirtied her hot-pink suit before she brushed it off vigorously.

She wasn't really so pretty on close inspection. Her darkly fringed, pale eyes were set a bit too close together, and her ears were small and lay close to her head, making them almost not there. And yet, when you didn't pick her apart bit by bit, altogether she made a woman marvellous to behold.

Truthfully, I'd never seen a woman with so much exaggerated femininity, radiating sexuality with her heavy bosom, her full buttocks, her tiny waist that must have stuggled to support all it had to. Her knit top was strained so much it appeared thin over the stress areas. Her pants emphasized the wide V of her crotch – making Pa stare at her with a queer smile, not of admiration but of contempt.

Why was he smiling like that? How could he feel contmptuous of a woman he didn't know – did he know her? Of course, he'd have seen her before to set this thing up.

Again, fearfully alarmed, I looked at the older couple, too late. Already they had turned and were heading for the door. I felt a sinking sensation.

'Thank you, Mr Casteel,' said the older gentleman,

stepping outside, assisting his wife over the doorstep, and, as if with relief, they both headed for their long, black car. Pa hastened after them, leaving the door open behind him, said a few words in a low tone, and then hurried back.

No sooner was Pa in the door than he grinned at me in the most mocking way.

Had I chosen wrong? Panicky butterflies were on the wing again, battering my brain with doubts, buffeting my heart with indecision that came too late.

'My name is Calhoun Dennison,' said the good-looking husband, stepping forward and taking my trembling hand firmly between both of his, 'and this is my wife, Kitty Dennison. Thank you for choosing us, Heaven.'

His voice was soft, barely above a whisper. I'd never heard a man with such a soft voice before. Was his an educated voice? It had to be, since all the uneducated roared and shouted, yelled and bellowed.

'Oh, Cal, ain't she just darling, just darling?' asked Kitty Dennison in a voice slightly on the shrill side. 'Ain't it gonna be fun dressing her up and making her look pretty, ain't it, though?'

I was breathing hard. Beside me Grandpa was quietly crying. *Grandpa, Grandpa, you could have said something before – why wait until it's too late to show you care?*

'And weren't it easy, Cal?' laughed Kitty, hugging and kissing him, making Pa turn away as if revolted by her display. 'Thought she might want them in their big, rich car and heavy expensive coats, but it were easy, so easy.'

Again I felt panic.

'Honey,' Kitty Dennison said to me when she had finished playing with her man, 'ya run along and put on yer coat, but don't ya bother to pack any of yer clothes. Going to buy ya everything new, brand-new. Don't want to carry no filthy germs into my clean home . . .' She gave the cabin another look, this time clearly showing her repugnance. 'Can't wait to get ya out of here.'

With lead in my legs, I pulled my old coat from the nail

in the bedroom, put it on, and, daring her disapproval, picked up the suitcase I'd swathed about with Granny's old shawls. I wasn't going to leave my mother's things here to rot, especially not that beautiful bride doll.

'Ya remember now,' called Kitty Dennison, 'just bring yourself, nothing else.'

I strolled out of what we called the bedroom into full view, wearing my shabby old coat, lugging my unsightly bundle, and stared defiantly at Kitty Dennison. Her pale eyes glittered strangely. 'Didn't I tell ya not to bring anything,' shrilled Kitty Dennison, irritation on her face. 'Can't take that filthy stuff into my clean house, ya can't.'

'I can't leave here without what I hold dearest in the world,' I said with determination. 'My granny made these shawls, and they're clean. I just washed them.'

'Ya'll have to wash them again, then,' said Kitty, somewhat placated but still looking angry.

I paused beside Grandpa, leaning to kiss the top of his balding head. 'Take care, Grandpa. Don't fall and break your bones. I'll write often, and somebody can always . . .' And here I hesitated, not wanting those strangers to guess that Grandpa couldn't read or write. 'Well, I'll write.'

'Ya done been a good girl, the best. Couldn't have wanted anyone better.' He sobbed, dabbed at his tears with a handful of his shirt-tail, and continued brokenly, 'Ya go and ya be happy, ya hear?'

'Yes, I hear, and please do take care of yourself, Grandpa.'

'Ya be good now, ya hear.'

'I'll be good,' I swore. I blinked back my own tears. 'Good-bye, Grandpa.'

'Bye . . .' said Grandpa. Then he picked up a new stick and began to shave off the bark.

When, if ever, has he really looked at me? I was going to cry, and I didn't want Pa to see me cry. I stared him straight in the eyes, and for a change his dark eyes locked with mine in silent combat. *Hate you, Pa. Not saying good-bye to you and take care. I'm going and I don't care.* Nobody needs me here.

Nobody has ever needed me but Tom, Keith, and Our Jane . . . not Fanny, not Granny, not really, and certainly not Grandpa, who has his whittling.

'Now, don't ya cry, girl,' Kitty said in a strong voice. 'Ya've seen me before, and just didn't know it. I've seen ya in church when I come to visit my ma and pa who live in Winnerrow. There ya sits with all yer kinfolks, looking like an angel, truly like an angel.'

Pa's head jerked upward. His hard, dark eyes clashed with Kitty's. He didn't say a word, not a word, leaving me floundering again in uncertainty. There was something unspoken between them, something that hinted that they knew each other more than just casually. It terrified me that she was the kind of woman Pa went after – different from my real mother.

'Really did envy that red-haired ma of yers,' Kitty gushed on, as if Pa didn't matter a hoot to her – and that made me even more suspicious. 'Since ya were knee-high to a grasshopper, I've been watchin yer ma lugging all her brood to church and back. Envied her then, really did. Wanted kids so bad, because they were all so pretty.' Her loud, shrill voice turned dull and cold.

'Can't have none of my own.' Her strange eyes filled with bitterness and fixed on Pa in a hard, accusing way. Oh, oh, oh . . . she did know him!

'There's some who might say that's my good luck, not to have no kids of my own . . . but I got me one now . . . and she's an angel, a real live angel; even if she don't have silvery-blonde hair, she's still got the angel face and the angel-blue eyes . . . ain't that right, Cal?'

'Yeah,' agreed Cal. 'She's sure got the look of innocence, if that's what you mean.'

I didn't know what either one was talking about. I feared the battle of unspoken recognition between Pa and Kitty. I'd never seen this woman before, and she wasn't the kind anyone would easily overlook. I glanced again at her husband, who was staring around the cabin. His pity showed when he looked at Grandpa sitting like a limp rag doll in his rocker. Eyes blank, his hands idle now. What was he thinking, if anything? Had Granny and Grandpa ever thought? Did minds close off as age came on? Did old ears go deaf just so they wouldn't have to hear what might make them miserable?

'First name is Kitty. Not a nickname. Wouldn't want to be no Katherine, or Katie, or Kate, or Kit. And, honey, you can call him Cal, like I does. Now, when you're living with us, you're going to enjoy all the big colour TV sets we got. Ten of them.' She flashed her eyes again at Pa, as if to show him just what kind of rich man she'd captured. Pa seemed indifferent.

Ten TV sets? I stared at her disbelievingly. Ten? Why have ten when one would be enough?

Shrilly Kitty laughed. She hadn't even heard my silent question. 'Knew that would give ya a jolt. Cal here runs his own TV repair and sale shop, and some dummies turn in their old sets for nothing or almost nothing, so he can bring them home and fix them up good as new, and he sells them as new to poor folks who don't know no different. Got me a smart man, a handsome, clever man, best kind of man to have. Turns a tidy profit, too, don't ya, Cal?'

Cal looked embarrassed.

Kitty laughed again.

'Now ya hurry up and say all yer good-byes, Heaven,' said Kitty, assuming an air of authority and looking with distaste at the contents of the cabin again, as if to make sure Pa saw how little she thought of his home and his money-making abilities. 'Say good-bye to yer father, and we'll set off. Got to get home soon as possible.'

I could only stand there, not looking at Pa, not wanting to look at Pa.

It was Kitty who was holding up our leave-taking. Kitty who addressed Pa, not me. 'I keep my house spick and span, everything in its place. And everything's got its place, believe-you-me. Not like this shack of yours.'

Pa leaned back against a wall, pulled out a cigarette, and lit it. Kitty turned to me. 'Can't stand dirt and messiness. And yer pa done said ya know how to cook. I pray to God he didn't tell us no lie.'

'I can cook,' I answered in a small voice. 'But I've never made anything complicated.' An edge of panic was in my voice as I realized this woman might expect fancy meals when all I really knew how to make well were fluffy biscuits and tasty lard gravy.

Pa wore an odd look, half sad, half full of satisfaction, as he looked from me back to Kitty and Cal Dennison. 'Ya done made the right choice,' he said solemnly, then turned to smother either a sob or laughter.

That it could be laughter put fears in me I hadn't felt before. I sobbed, my tears beginning to flow fast. I sailed right on past Pa, saying nothing. Nor did he speak to me.

At the door I turned and looked back. Something sweet and sour was in my throat; it hurt me to leave this shabby house that had known my first steps, and Tom's and Fanny's, and it hurt too much to think of Keith and Our Jane.

'Oh Lord, give me my day in the future,' I whispered before I turned and headed for the steps.

The late-winter sun shone hot on my head as I strode towards the nice-looking, white car with the red seats. Pa drifted out to the porch, his hunting hounds back again, as if he'd rented them out and reclaimed them so they could crowd about his legs. Cats and kittens perched on the roof, on lidded rain barrels, peered out from under the porch, and the pigs were rooting with snorts and grunts. Chickens roamed at will, a cock chasing a hen with obvious intent on reproducing himself. I stared in amazment. Where had they come from? Were they really there? Was I seeing them only in my imagination? I rubbed my eyes that were smeary with tears. It had been so long since I saw the hounds, the cats, the pigs and chickens. Had Pa brought them all here in his pickup truck – planning to stay a while and take care of his father?

The sky was full of those stringy long clouds slowly forming into fat billowing ones that painted pictures of happiness and fulfilment up ahead.

Cal and Kitty Dennison got into their car, using the front seat, and telling me I could have the back one all for myself. Stiff, anxious, I twisted about to stare back at what I knew so well, and once believed I'd want to forget as quickly as possible.

Say good-bye to poverty and growling stomachs that were never really satisfied.

Say good-bye to the old smelly outhouse, the belching kitchen stove, the worn and tattered bed pallets on the floor.

Say good-bye to all the miseries, as well as all the beauty of the hills: the wild berries, the flaming leaves of autumn, the babbling brooks and freshwater streams where trout jumped, and fishing with Tom and Logan.

Say good-bye to memories of Keith and Our Jane and Tom and Fanny.

Say good-bye to all the laughter and all the tears. Going to a better place, a richer place, a happier place.

No reason to cry – why was I crying?

Up there on the porch Pa wasn't crying, just staring off into space with that blank look still on his face.

Cal turned the key and gunned the motor, and away we sped, causing Kitty to squeal and fall backward on the seat. 'Slow down, ya damn fool!' she cried. 'I know it were horrible and the stink will cling to us for weeks, but we got us a daughter, and that's what we came for.'

A shiver rippled down my spine.

It was all right. All right.

Going away to a better life, a better place, I kept repeating.

Yet all I thought about was what Pa had done. Sold his children for five hundred dollars apiece. I hadn't seen the papers signed in this last transaction, or heard the sale price. Pa's soul would rot in hell. Not for one moment did I doubt that.

From what I'd heard between Kitty and her husband, they were heading for Winnerrow, where I'd always wanted to live in some pretty painted house not so far from Stonewall Pharmacy. There I would finish school, go on to college. And I'd see Fanny often, see Grandpa when we went to church.

But what was this?

Why was Cal taking the right turn and heading his car past Winnerrow? I swallowed over another of those burning throat lumps.

'Didn't Pa say you were from the valley?' I asked in a low, scared voice.

'Sure, kid,' said Kitty, twisting about in the front seat and smiling back at me. 'I was born and raised in that crummy town of Winnerrow,' she went on in a voice turned more country, her dialect all hillbilly and slurry. 'Couldn't wait to get away from there. Ran off one day when I was thirteen with a truck driver, we wed up, and then I found out he was already married, but not until years later. Made me sick, made me hate men, most men; then I met up with sweet Cal. Loved him on first sight. We've been married five years, and wouldn't have been down this way at all except we had to get away from all the stink of having our house redecorated inside and out. Fresh paint makes me sick. Get so sick of bad odours, perm lotions and such. Gonna have white wall-to-wall in every room. All white-on-white wallpaper, gonna be so pretty, so clean-looking. Cal, now, he done said it's gonna be sterile, like a hospital, but it won't be, ya just wait and see. Gonna pretty it up with all my things. Won't it be pretty when all my beautiful things are put in there for colour contrast, ain't it gonna be, Cal?'

'Sure.'

'Sure what?'

'Sure it will be pretty.'

She patted his cheek, then leaned to kiss him.

'Now that we're away from yer old man,' intoned Kitty, her sharp chin again resting on her folded arms, 'I can be more honest. Knew yer ma, your *real* ma. Not that Sarah woman. Now, your real ma was some looker. Not just pretty, but beautiful – and I hated her guts.'

'Oh,' I breathed, feeling sick, unreal. 'Why did you hate her?'

'Thought she had a real catch in Luke Casteel. Thought Luke Casteel should have been mine when I was a kid and didn't know no better. What a damned idiot I was then, thinking a handsome face and a strong, beautiful body was all there was to it. Now I hate him – hate his guts!'

This should make me feel good, yet it didn't. Why would Kitty want the daughter of the man she hated?

I'd been right, she had known Pa a long time. Her dialect was just as bad as his, and all the others in our area.

'Yeah,' continued Kitty in a strange, soft voice like a cat's purr. 'Saw yer real ma every time she came to Winnerrow. Every hotshot man in town had the hots for Luke's angel. Nobody could understand how she would marry the likes of Luke. Love made her blind, was my thinking. Some women are like that.'

'Shut up, Kitty.' Cal's voice, full of warning.

Kitty ignored him. 'And there I was with the hots for yer big, handsome pa. Oh, every girl in town wanting and waiting for him to get into her pants.'

'Kitty, you've said enough.'

The warning in his voice was more intense. Kitty threw him an impatient look, jerked around, and swithced on the car radio. She fiddled with the dial until she found country music. Loud, twangy guitar music filled the car.

Now we couldn't talk.

Miles and miles and miles slid by like a long ribbon picture postcard that has no end. Out of the hills, down into the flatlands.

Soon the mountains became distant shadows. Miles and miles later, afternoon light faded away. Sun going down, turning twilight time. Where had all the hours gone? Had I fallen asleep without knowing it? Farther away than I'd ever been before. Little farms, big farms, small villages, petrol stations, long stretches of barren land with patches of red dirt.

Deep twilight came to smear the sky rosy with violet and orange, with bright gold edging all those heavenly colours. Same sky I'd seen in the hills, but the country look that I was accustomed to was left behind. Petrol stations by the dozens rose up, and quick-food places with colourful neon lights, imitating the sky, or trying to and failing.

'Ain't it something,' said Kitty, staring out her window, 'the way the sky lights up? Like driving when it's twilight time. Heard say it's the most dangerous time of all, makes people feel unreal, caught up in dreams . . . always had me a dream of having lots of kids, all pretty.'

'Please don't, Kitty,' pleaded her husband.

She shut up, left me to my own thoughts. I'd seen twilight skies many a time, but I'd never seen a city at night. Fatigue forgotten, I stared at everything, feeling a true hillbilly for the first time in my life. This was no Winnerrow, but the biggest city I'd ever seen.

Then came the golden arches, and the car slowed, as if drawn there magnetically without discussion between husband and wife. Soon we were inside, seated at a tiny table. 'What ya mean, ya ain't never ate at McDonald's before?' asked Kitty, amused and disgusted at the same time. 'Why, I bet ya ain't even had Kentucky Fried.'

'What's that?'

'Cal, this girl is ignorant. Really ig-nor-ant. And her pa told us she was smart.'

Pa had said that? It made me feel funny to hear he had. But he'd say anything to gain another five hundred dollars.

'Eating in joints like this doesn't make anybody smart, Kitty. Just less hungry.'

'Why, I bet ya ain't never been to a moving-picture show, have ya?'

'Yes I have,' I answered quickly. 'Once.'

'Once! Did ya hear that, Cal? This smart girl has been to a movie *once*. Now, that is something, really something. What else ya done that's smart?'

How to answer that when it was asked in such a mocking, sarcastic tone?

Suddenly I was homesick for Grandpa, for the miserable cabin and its familiar space. Again those unwanted, sad pictures flashed behind my eyes. Our Jane and Keith saying, 'Hev-lee.' I blinked once or twice, glad I had the wonderful doll with me. When Kitty saw her, she'd be impressed, really impressed.

'Now . . . say what ya think of the burger,' asked Kitty, dispatching hers in mere seconds, and applying hot-pink lipstick to lips that wore a perpetual stain. She handled the tube expertly despite her inch-long nails, shiny with polish that matched her pink clothes exactly.

'It was very good.'

'Then why didn't ya eat all of it? Food costs good money. When we buy ya food we expect ya to eat it all.'

'Kitty, you talk too loud. Leave the girl alone.'

'I don't like yer name, either,' Kitty flared, as if annoyed at Cal's defence. 'It's a stupid name. Heaven's a place, not a name. What's yer middle name – something just as dumb?'

'Leigh,' I answered in a tone of ice. 'My mother's Christian name.'

Kitty winced. 'Damn!' she swore, slamming her fist one into the other. 'Hate that name!' She swung her seawater eyes to her husband and met his mild look with fierce anger. 'That was *her* name, that Boston bitch who took Luke! Goddam if I ever want to hear it said aloud again, ya hear?'

'I hear . . .'

Kitty's mood swung in a different direction, from anger to thoughtfulness, as Cal got up and headed for the men's room. 'Always wanted a girl I could call Linda. Always wanted to be named Linda myself. There's something sweet and pure about Linda that sounds so right.'

Again I shivered, seeing those huge, glittery rings on Kitty's large, strong hands. Were they real diamonds, rubies, emeralds – or fakes?

It was a relief to be in the car again, on the road speeding toward some distant home. A relief, that is, until Kitty told Cal she was changing my name. 'Gonna call her Linda,' she said matter-of-factly. 'Like that name, really I do.'

Immediately he barked, 'No! Heaven suits her best. She's lost her home and her family; for God's sake, don't force her to lose her name as well. Leave well alone.'

There was some forceful quality in his voice this time that stilled Kitty's incessant chatter for a peaceful five minutes, and, best of all, Cal reached to turn off the radio.

In the back seat I curled up and tried to stay awake by reading the road signs. By this time I'd noticed that Cal was following all the signs that directed us toward Atlanta. Overpasses and underpasses, through cloverleafs and down expressways, under train bridges, over bridges crossing rivers, through cities large, small, and medium, going onward towards Atlanta.

I gasped to see the skyscrapers rearing up black in the night, glittering with lit windows, wearing clouds like wispy scarfs. I gasped at store windows on Peachtree Street, stared at policemen standing right in the middle of everything and not afraid, and some were on horseback. Pedestrians were strolling the avenues as if it was midday and not long after nine. Back home I'd be on the floor sound asleep by this time. Even now I had to rub my eyes, gritty with sleep. Maybe I did sleep.

All of a sudden a loud voice was singing. Kitty had the radio on again and was snuggled up close to Cal, doing something that made him plead for her to stop. 'Kitty, there's a time and a place for everything – and the time and place isn't right for this. Now take your hand away.'

What was Kitty doing? I rubbed my eyes, then leaned forward to find out. Just in time to see Cal pull up his fly. Oh – was that nice? Fanny would think so. Quickly I slid backward, alarmed that Kitty might have seen me peek at what was, really, none of my business. Again I stared out the window. The big city with all its majestic skyscrapers had disappeared. Now we were driving down streets not so wide or so busy.

'We live in the suburbs,' Cal explained briskly. 'Subdivision called Candlewick. The houses are split-levels and almost alike, six different styles, you take your pick. And then they build them for you. You can be an individual only with the way you decorate outside and in. We hope you will enjoy living here, Heaven. We want to do our best by you and give you the kind of life we'd give our own, if we could have children. The school you'll be attending is within walking distance.'

Snorting, Kitty mumbled, 'Mind. Mind. What the hell difference does it make? She's going to school if she has to crawl there. Damned if I want some ignorant kid spoiling my reputation.'

I sat up straighter, tried to keep sleep from stealing my first view of my new home, and with interest I studied the houses that were, as Cal had said, almost alike, but not quite. Nice houses. No doubt everyone had at least one bathroom, maybe more. And all those wonderful electrical conveniences city folks couldn't live without.

Then the car pulled into a driveway, and a garage door was sliding magically upward, and then we were inside the garage, and Kitty was yelling for me to wake up. 'We're home, kid, home.'

Home.

I quickly opened the car door and left the garage to stand and stare at the house in the pale moonlight. Two storeys. How sweet it looked snuggled in the midst of lush shrubbery, mostly evergreens. Red brick with white blinds. A palace in comparison to the shack in the hills I'd just left. A pretty house with a white front door.

'Cal, ya put her dirty things in the basement where they belong, if they belong.' Sadly I watched my mother's wonderful suitcase, much better than any bag Kitty owned, disappear . . . though of course Kitty couldn't know what was under all those dark knitted shawls.

'C'mon,' Kitty called impatiently. 'It's going on eleven. And I'm really pooped. Ya got yer whole life long to stare at the outside, ya hear?'

How final she made that sound.

PART TWO

Candlewick Life

Twelve

A New Home

Kitty flicked a switch near the door, and the entire house lit up. What I saw made me gasp.

It was so wonderful, this clean and modern house. It thrilled me to know I was going to live here. The whiteness – all this pure snowy cleanliness! – and elegance! I shivered again, seeing cleansing snow that would never melt with sunlight, wouldn't be turned into slush by tramping feet. Deep inside me, all along, I'd know there had to be a better place for me than the cabin with all its dirt and unhappiness.

From the first second I thought of this as Kitty's house. The authoritative air she took on, the way she ordered Cal to take my 'nasty things to the basement,' told me clearly that this was her house, not his. There was not one thing to indicate a man lived in all this feminine prettiness, nothing masculine at all here, also gave me the notion that Kitty was the boss in this house.

While Cal followed her instructions, Kitty went around switching on other lamps, as if dim corners terrified her. I soon knew my judgement was wrong. Kitty was looking for flaws in the new paint job.

'Well, now, it sure is better than yer shack in the hills, ain't it, kid? Better by heck than anything in Winnerrow . . . hick town. Couldn't wait to escape it. Don't know why I keep going back.' A frown of displeasure darkened her pretty face. Soon she began complaining that workmen left on their own, had done a great many 'wrong' things. She saw her home differently than I did – to her it was not wonderful at all.

'Would you just look and see where they put my chairs? And my lamps? Nothing's right! I told them where I wanted everything, I did! Ya can bet your life they're going to hear about this –'

I tried to see what she saw, but I thought everything looked perfect.

Kitty glanced at me, saw my awed expression, and smiled with tolerant indulgence. 'Well, c'mon, tell me what ya think.'

Her living room was larger than our entire cabin – but the most surprising thing about this room was the colourful zoo it contained. Everywhere, on the windowsills, in corner cabinets, on the tables, lining the white carpet up the stairs, sat animals made into fancy stands to hold plants; animal faces and forms made picture frames, lamps, baskets, candy dishes, footstools.

Live plants sprouted from the backs of giant, green, ceramic frogs with bulging yellow eyes and scarlet tongues. There were huge, golden fish with gaping mouths and frightened, sea-blue eyes bearing more plants. There were blue geese, white and yellow ducks, purple and pink polka-dotted hens, brown and tan rabbits, pink squirrels, hot-pink, fat pigs with cute curly tails. 'C'mon,' said Kitty, grabbing my hand and pulling me into the centre of that domestic zoo, 'you have got to see them up close to appreciate all the talent it takes to make em.'

I was speechless.

'C'mon, say something!' she demanded.

'It's beautiful,' I breathed, impressed with all this white, the wallpaper that looked like white silk tree rings, the white lounging chairs, the white sofa, the white lampshades over huge fat, white, shiny bases. No wonder Kitty had been so appalled by the cabin with all its generations of filth. Here there was a fireplace with a carved, white wooden mantel and frame, and a white marble hearth, and tables of a rich-looking dark wood I was to find out later was rosewood, and glass and brass tables, too. Not a speck of dust anywhere. No fingerprints. Not a thing out of place.

She stood beside me, as if to see her glorious living room

through my naive country eyes, while I was afraid to step on that white carpet that had to dirty more quicker than a dog could wag his tail. I glanced down at my clumsy, ugly old shoes, and right away pulled them off.

My feet sank into the pile as I drifted dreamlike from one object to the other, marvelling. Fat cats, skinny cats, slinky, sneaky, slithering cats. Dogs sitting, standing, sleeping: elephants and tigers, lions and leopards, peacocks, pheasants, parakeets, and owls. A mind-boggling array of animals.

'Ain't they something though, my creations? Made them, I did, with my own hands. Baked them in my huge kiln. Gotta little one upstairs. I hold classes every Saturday. Charge each student thirty dollars, and got thirty who come regular. None of my students is as good as I am, of course, and that's a good thing, keeps then coming back, hoping to outmaster the master. Did ya notice all the fancy decorations, the flower garlands I put on them? Ain't they something, ain't they?'

Still overwhelmed, I could only nod in agreement. Oh, yes, I had to be impressed that Kitty could create such wonders as those carousel horses galloping around a white lamp base. I said again, my voice full of admiration, 'So beautiful, all of them.'

'Knew ya'd think so.' Proudly she picked up and displayed what I might have overlooked. 'Teaching makes for lots of cash; won't take no cheques, then there's no taxes to pay. Could teach ten times as many if I'd give up my beauty-salon business, but I just can't see myself doing that when I earns so much when the celebrities come to town and wants their hair done . Do everything from bleach and tint jobs to perms and pedicures, my eight girls do. Save myself for special customers, and in my shop I sell thousands of what ya see all around ya. Clients love them, just love them.'

She stood back and crossed her strong arms over her high-rise bosom and beamed at me. 'Ya think ya could do as well, do ya, do ya?'

'No. I wouldn't know where to begin,' I confessed.

Cal came in from a back door and stood back and looked at Kitty with a certain kind of disgust – as if he didn't admire her 'creations' or didn't like all the hours she spent teaching.

'Would ya say I'm an artist, would ya?'

'Yes, Kitty, a real artist . . . did you go to school and study art?'

Kitty scowled. 'There's some things ya just know how to do, born knowing, that's all. I'm just gifted that way – ain't I, honey?'

'Yes, Kitty, you are gifted that way.' Cal strolled towards the stairs.

'Hey!' yelled Kitty. 'Yer forgetting this kid has to have new clothes. Can't let her sleep in our new-painted house in those old rags she's got on. She stinks, can't ya smell her? Cal, ya get yerself back in that car and drive to the supermarket that stays open all night, and get this chile some decent clothes – specially nightgowns – and ya make sure they're all too large. Don't want her grown out of stuff before they're worn out.'

'It's almost eleven,' he said in that cold, distant voice that I had heard before in the car, and was already beginning to recognize as his disapproving voice.

'I know that! Ya think I can't tell the time? But no kid is sleeping in my clean house without a bath, without a shampoo, without a delousing, and most specially, without new clothes – ya hear!'

Cal heard. He whirled about, grumbling under his breath, and disappeared. Pa would never let a woman tell him what to do and where to do it, much less when. What kind of leash did Kitty have about Cal's neck that he would obey, even grudgingly?

'Now, ya come along with me, and I'll show ya everything, just everything, and yer gonna love it all, ya will, know ya will.' She smiled and patted my cheek. 'Knew yer pa. Guess ya know that by now. Knew he couldn't do nothing for ya, not like I'm gonna do. Gonna give ya all the things I wanted when I was a kid like ya. Advantages I never had are going to be yours. It's your good luck to have picked me, and my Cal . . . and yer Pa's bad luck. Serves him right, too, to lose everything . . . everyone of his kids.' Again she smiled her strange smile. 'Now, tell me what ya like to do most.'

'Oh . . . I love to read!' I answered quickly. 'My teacher, Miss Deale, used to give Tom and me lots of books to bring home, and for birthdays and such she'd give us our very own books – brand-new ones. I brought a few with me, my favourite ones – and they're not dirty, Kitty, really they're not. Tom and I taught Keith and Our Jane to love books and respect them as friends.'

'Books . . .?' she asked, distaste on her face. 'Ya mean that's what you would rather have, more than anything? Ya must be crazy.' And with that she spun on her heel and seemed eager to lead me into the dining room, though my vision was smeary with fatigue, my impressions becoming vague from too many changes all at once.

Yet I had to view the dining room with its large, oval glass-top table, sitting on top of a fancy gold-coloured pedestal formed by three golden dolphins that obligingly fanned their tails to support the thick, heavy glass. I was swaying on my feet, exhausted. I tried desperately to listen to Kitty, to see all the objects that Kitty kept pointing out.

Next we visited the spanking-white kitchen. Even the white floor tiles shone. 'Expensive vinyl,' she explained. 'the best money can buy.' I nodded, not knowing the best from the worst. Through sleepy eyes I beheld the modern-day wonders I'd dreamed about all my life: the dishwasher, the double porcelain sinks, the gleaming chrome fixtures, the large kitchen range with two ovens, all the white cabinets, the long countertops, the round table and four chairs. Everywhere possible, to keep all the white from being monotonous, were more of Kitty's works.

She'd taken animal forms and made them into different

kinds of containers. Ceramic baskets were really flour, sugar, tea, and coffee canisters: a pink pig held utensils too large to fit inside a drawer; and a magenta horse was sitting down as a human would, holding pink paper napkins.

'Now what ya think, really think?' demanded Kitty.

'It's pretty, so clean, colourful, and pretty,' I whispered, my voice gone hoarse.

We returned to the front hall, where Kitty again checked over the living room and then narrowed her eyes. 'They done put them in the wrong places!' she shrieked. 'Would ya look where they put my elephant end tables? And I just noticed! In the corners – in the damned corners – where ya can't even see them! Heaven, right now we got to put this place into order.'

It took an hour to move everything to where Kitty wanted it to be. The large ceramic pieces were surprisingly heavy. I was tired enough to drop. Kitty stared at my face, seized hold of my hand, and pulled me toward the stairs. 'Give ya a better tour tomorrow. You're going to love it. Right now we have got to get you ready for bed.'

All the way up the stairs Kitty rambled on about her famous movie-star clients, all stars who insisted only she could do their hair right. 'They come to perform in shows, and always they ask for me. Why, I've even seen things ya wouldn't believe – Lord, haven't I? Secrets, I've got them by the million – won't tell a soul, not a single soul. Closemouthed, I am.' Kitty paused, turned me around, and stared deep into my eyes. 'What's wrong with ya? Can't you hear? Aren't you listening?'

She was a blurred image. So exhausted I could sleep on my feet, I made an effort to be more enthusiastic about Kitty's rich clients, and also an honest excuse about it being a long day, and I wasn't hearing or seeing too well.

'Why ya talk like that?'

I winced. All my life I'd fought not to talk the way she did, as hill folks talked, slurring their conjunctions so they ran into nouns, verbs, whatever, and she was criticising me.

'Miss Deale always insisted we should not slur our words and contractions.'

'Who the hell is Miss Deale?'

'My teacher.'

Kitty snorted. 'Never had no use for school or teachers. Nobody uses yer kind of Yankee talk. Ya'll make enemies, ya will, with that accent. Ya learn to talk like the rest of us, or suffer the consequences.'

What consequences?

'Yes, Kitty.'

We'd reached the top of the stairs. Walls were wavering before my eyes. Suddenly Kitty turned to seize me by the shoulders; then she began to bang my head against the nearest wall. 'Wake up!' yelled Kitty. 'Ya wake up and hear this – I'm not Kitty to ya! Yer to call me *Mother!* Not Momma, not Mommy, not Mom and, least of all, not Ma! But Mother, understand?'

I was dizzy, my head hurt. She was amazingly strong. 'Yes, Mother.'

'Good, that's a nice girl, good girl now let's take that bath.'

Oh, I must never become too tired again, and risk the wrath of a woman who could turn on me in a second, and for no apparent reason.

Down a short hall toward an open door that revealed shiny black wallpaper with gold designs Kitty led me. 'Now, here's the master bathroom,' informed Kitty, stepping inside first and dragging me along by the arm. 'That thing over there is called a commode by fancy folks, but I'm not fancy – it's a toilet. You lift the lid before ya sit down, and you flush every time you use it – and don't ya fill it with paper or it'll stop up and flood over, and it'll be yer goddamn job to clean it up. In fact, this whole house is yers to keep clean. I'll explain how to keep my plants alive, watered and fed, dusted, my planters shiny, all my stuff dusted, clean, vacuumed, and ya'll do the laundry, but first the bath.'

Here I was, my most fervent wish come true, an indoor

bathroom, with hot and cold running water, a bathtub, a basin, mirrors on two walls – now I was too tired to enjoy any of it.

'Are ya listening, girl – are ya?' came Kitty's shrill voice through my ever-thicker fog of fatigue. 'All this paint, wallpaper, and carpet is brand-new, as ya can plainly see. I want it to stay that way. It's yer duty to see it stays this way, brand-new – ya hear?'

Blindly I nodded.

'And ya might as well know from the beginning, I expect ya to work out the expense of staying here, and the cost of what ya eat, by doing the chores I assign. I'm sure ya don't know the least thing about housework, and that's going to waste a good deal of my valuable time, but ya'll learn fast if ya hope to live here.' She paused again and stared deep into my eyes.

'Ya do like it here, don't ya?'

Why did she keep asking, when I hadn't had time to do more than glance around? And the way she talked was already putting me on guard, stealing my hope that this would be a home rather than a jail.

'Yes,' I said, trying to show more enthusiasm. 'Everything is beautiful.'

'Yeah, ain't it?' Kitty smiled softly. 'Got another bathroom on the first level. Just as pretty – save it for guests. Like to keep it spotless, shining. That'll be yer job.'

All the time Kitty was reaching for bottles and jars hidden behind mirrored doors that slid open, and soon she had quite a collection on the counter shelf that was pink marble, to match the oval bathtub. Black and pink and gold, everything in the 'master bath.' More rainbowed fish swimming on the black and gold walls . . .

'Now,' continued Kitty, all business, 'the first thing we got to to is scrub all that filth from yer skin. Wash that dirty, buggy hair. Kill the lice yer bound to have. Kill all the nasty germs. That pa of yers has got to have everything, and ya've been wallowing in his filth since the day ya were conceived.

Why, the tales they tell about Luke Casteel in Winnerrow would curl hair better than perms. But he's paying the price for all that fun now . . . paying a heavy price,' She seemed glad, smiling her scary, secret smile.

How did she know about Pa's disease? I started to say he was well now, but I was too tired to speak.

'Oh, forgive me, honey. Yer feelings hurt? But ya gotta understand I just don't like yer pa.'

That confirmed my choice. Anyone who didn't like Pa had to have good judgement. I sighed, then smiled at Kitty.

'Grew up in Winnerrow, parents still live there,' she continued; 'in fact, they wouldn't live nowhere else. People get like that when they never go nowhere. Scared living, that's what I call it. Afraid if they leaves home no big city is gonna know they exist. In Atlanta, where I work, they'd be just nobody important. Don't know how to do nothing like I do. Don't have no talents like mine. Now, we don't live in Atlanta, like we said before, but in this subdivision twenty miles away; both Cal and I work, and there we have to fight the world. That's what it is, ya know, a daily battle out there, me and him against the world. He's mine and I love him. I'd kill to keep him.' She paused, eyeing me thoughtfully with hard, narrowed eyes.

'My shop is in a big, fancy hotel that draws all the rich folks. Can't buy a house here in Candlewick unless ya make more than thirty thousand a year, and with both Cal and me working, we double that some years. Why, honey, yer gonna love it, just love it. Ya'll go to school in a three-storied building where they have an indoor swimming pool, an auditorium where they show movies, and of course ya'll be much happier there than in that lil old second-rate school . . . and just think, yer right in time to start the new term.'

It made me hurt to think of my old school, and to remember Miss Deale. It was there I'd learned about the rest of the world, the better world, the different world that cared about education, books, paintings, architecture, science . . . not just existing from day to day. And I hadn't even been able to say good-bye to Miss Deale. I should have been nicer, more grateful for her caring. I should have thrown away my pride. I tried to stifle a sob. Then there was Logan, who might not have spoken because his parents were there that last time at church. Or some other reason. Now not only my beloved teacher but Logan too seemed unreal, like dreams I'd never have again. Even the cabin had gone fuzzy in my mind, and I'd left only hours ago.

Grandpa would be sound asleep by this time. And here the stores were still open and people were still shopping. Like Cal, off somewhere buying me new clothes that would be too large. I sighed heavily; some things never changed.

With leaden legs, I waited for Kitty to finish filling the fancy, pink tub with water.

Steamy vapour clouded all the mirrors, filled my lungs, misted the air so Kitty seemed miles and miles away, and into fantasy land Kitty and I had drifted, up in the clouds near the moon – black, foggy night full of golden fish drifting with us. I felt drunk from lack of energy, swaying on my feet, and heard, as if truly from the moon, Kitty ordering me to undress and drop everything into the trash can she'd lined with a plastic bag, and everything I had on would go out into the garbage, in the city dump and eventually be burned.

Clumsily I began to undress.

'Yer gonna have everything new. Spending a fortune on ya, girl, so ya think of that whenever ya feel homesick for that pigsty cabin ya called home. Now strip down, instantly! Ya gotta learn to move when I speak! not just stand there like ya don't hear or understand – understand?'

With fingers made awkward from fear and fatigue, I began to work on the buttons of my old dress. Why weren't my fingers working better, faster? Somehow I managed to unfasten two, and even as I did this, Kitty pulled from a cabinet drawer a plastic apron. 'Stand on this and drop yer clothes down around yer feet. Don't let anything ya wear touch my clean carpet or my marble countertops.'

Naked, I stood on the plastic apron, with Kitty eyeing me

up and down. 'Why, bless my soul, yer not a little girl after all. How old are ya anyway?'

'Fourteen,' I answered. My tongue felt thick, my thoughts thicker, my eyes so sleepy they had grit in them, and even as I tried to obey Kitty, I blinked, yawned, and swayed.

'When will ya be fifteen?'

'February twenty-second.'

'Ya had yer first monthly bloody time yet?'

'Yes, started when I was almost thirteen.'

'Well, now, never would have guessed. When I was yer age I had boobs, big ones. Made the boys hot just to look my way, but all of us can't be that lucky, can we?'

Nodding, I wished Kitty would leave me alone to take my first bath in a real porcelain tub. Apparently Kitty had no intentions of getting out, or giving me a moment to use the bathroom alone.

I sighed again and moved toward the pink toilet seat, realizing that she didn't intend to leave.

'No! First ya have to cover the seat with paper.' And even that body function had to wait for Kitty to spread tissues all over the seat, and then she turned her back. What good did that do when she could still hear, and there were mirrors everywhere to reflect everything even if they were cloudy from steam?

Then Kitty sprang into action. She squatted down near the tub and informed me as she tested the water temperature, 'Hot water is what ya have to sit in. Gotta scrub ya with a brush, put sulphur and tar soap on that hair of yers to kill all those nits ya must have.'

I tried to speak and tell Kitty I bathed more often than most hill people did, and once a week I washed my hair (only this morning), but I was without energy, without will to speak and defend myself. All kinds of confused emotions were churning within me, making me more tired and weak.

Funny how sick I felt. Silent screams stuck in my throat, tears froze behind my eyes, and, as Fanny often did, I wanted to yell and scream and throw some kind of tantrum, kick out and hurt somebody just so I wouldn't hurt so much inside; but I did nothing but wait for the tub to fill.

And fill it did. With scalding water.

All that was pink in the small room suddenly seemed red – and in that hellish misty red I saw Kitty taking off her pink knit top and pants. Underneath she wore a pink bikini bra and panties so small they hardly covered what they should.

Warily I edged away, watching Kitty move to pour something from a brown bottle into the tub. The stench of Lysol.

I knew the smell from school, when I'd stayed late to help Miss Deale, and the cleaning ladies and men had used Lysol in the rest rooms. I'd never heard of anyone taking a bath in Lysol.

Somehow a pink towel had found its way into my hand, a towel so large and thick I felt I could hide safely behind it. Not that anyone in the cabin had ever cared much about modesty, but I was ashamed to let Kitty see how thin I was.

'Put down the towel! Ya shouldn't touch my clean towel. All the pink ones belong to me, and only I use them, ya hear?'

'Yes, ma'am.'

'Yes, *Mother,*' she corrected. 'Never call me anything but Mother . . . say it like that.'

I said it like that, still clutching the towel and dreading the feel of that hot water.

'Black velvet towels belong to Cal, not ya, remember that. When my pink ones fade almost white, I'll turn them over to ya. Right now ya can use some old ones I brought home from my salon.'

I nodded, my eyes riveted on the steam coming from the tubful of water.

'Now I've got everything ready.' She flashed me a smile of assurance. 'Now, slide yer feet along on the plastic apron, and make it move with ya, so when yer near enough ya can step into the tub.'

'The water's too hot.'

'Of course it's hot.'

'It will burn me.'

'How the hell ya think ya can come out clean without scalding the filth from yer skin? How? Huh? Now, get in!'

'It's too hot.'

'It . . . is . . . not . . . too . . . hot.'

'Yes, it is. It's steaming hot. I'm not used to hot water, only barely warm.'

'I knows that . . . that's why I gotta scrub ya off with hot real hot.'

Kitty closed in.

The dense fog of steam almost hid the long-handled pink brush in her right hand. She smacked the palm of her left hand with that brush. The threat was unmistakable.

'Another thing. When I tell ya to do something – *anything* – ya'll do it without question. We have paid out good money to buy ya, and now yer our property to do with as we will. I took ya in because once I was idiot enough to love yer pa so much I let him break my heart. Made me pregnant, he did, made me think he loved me, and he didn't. Told him I'd kill myself if he didn't marry me . . . and he laughed and said, 'Go ahead' then walked out. Took off for Atlanta, where he met up with yer ma and married her . . . her! And me, I'm stuck with a baby, so I gave myself an abortion, and now I can't have a baby. But I got her baby . . . even if ya aren't a baby now, yer still his. But don't ya go thinking cause I was sweet on yer pa once, I'm gonna let ya run my life. There are laws in this state that would put ya away if they found out yer so bad yer own pa had to sell ya.'

'But . . . but . . . I'm not bad. Pa didn't have to sell me.'

'Don't stand there an argue with me! Get in the tub!'

I neared the tub gingerly, obeying Kitty by slipping my bare feet in such a way the plastic apron slid with me. I was doing everything I could to give that water time to cool off. First I closed my eyes and balanced on one leg as I tentatively extended my foot over heat-shimmering water. It was like dangling my foot over hell. Uttering a small cry, I jerked back my foot and turned to Kitty, pleading with my eyes, even as she snatched the pink towel away and hurled it toward the dirty-clothes hamper.

'Mother, it really is too hot.'

'It *is not too hot*. I always bathe in hot water, and if I can stand it, so can ya.'

'Kitty . . .'

'Mother – say it.'

'Mother, why does the water have to be so hot?'

Perhaps Kitty liked the submissive tone in my voice, for she changed almost as if a magician had pushed a switch.

'Oh, honey,' she crooned, 'it's truly for yer own good, really it is. The hot water will kill all the germs. I wouldn't make ya do anything that would hurt ya.' Her seawater eyes turned soft, her tone as well; she appeared kind, motherly, persuading me I'd been mistaken. Kitty was a good woman needing a daughter to love. And I so wanted a mother to love me.

'See,' Kitty said, testing the water by putting in her hand and arm up to her elbow, 'it's not as hot as ya think. Now, step in like a good girl, and sit down, and let Mother scrub yer skin cleaner than it's ever been in yer whole life.'

'Are you sure your bathwater is this hot?'

'Not lying, honey baby. I do take baths in hot water like that all the time.' Kitty shoved me closer. 'Once yer in and the shock is over, it feels good, really good; makes ya relax and feel sleepy. See, I'll pour in some pretty pink bubble bath. Ya'll like that. Ya'll come out smelling like a rose, looking like one, too.'

Kitty had to let out some water in order to put in the bubble bath so she could again let the hot water gush and make the pink crystal foam – and this, unfortunately, took away water that might have cooled down a bit from all I'd done to hesitate.

There it was before me, one of the dreams I'd prayed someday to enjoy, a perfumed bubble bath in a pink tub with mirrors all around . . . and I wasn't going to enjoy it.

I just knew it was going to burn.

'It'll be all right, sweetheart, really it will be. Would I ask ya to do something that would hurt ya? Would I? I was a girl like ya once, and I never had the chance to enjoy what-all I'm gonna do for ya. One day in the future ya'll go down on yer knees and give thanks to the Lord for saving ya from the depths of hell. Think of the hot water as holy water. That's how I do it. Think of cold things like ice, tons of crushed ice, sitting in ice and sipping cola drinks, think of that. It won't hurt. Never hurt me, and I've got baby-soft skin.'

Kitty moved suddenly. She caught me off balance, and in a flash, instead of hovering above the water to test it again, I was face down in the water!

The scalding water seared me like liquid hot coals from Ole Smokey. I shoved upward blindly, pulled up my knees, balancing on my hands, trying blindly to fight my way out of the tub; but Kitty held me down, grasped my shoulders with strong hands, and twisted me over so I was sitting in the water. Now I could scream!

Time and time again I let go, howling, flailing my arms as Our Jane would, as Fanny would, yelling, 'Let me go, let me go!'

Wham!

Kitty's hand slapped me!

'Shut up! Damn ya! Shut up! Don't ya be yelling when my Cal comes in, and make him think I'm being mean. I ain't, I ain't! I'm doing what I have to do, that's all.'

Where was Cal . . . why didn't he come back and save me?

It was terrible, so terrible I couldn't find another scream, not when I was gasping, choking, crying, struggling to push Kitty away, to stop that brutal brush from taking off all my red, seared skin. I was stinging all over – and inside as well. The Lysol water was seeping into my most private parts. My eyes pleaded with Kitty to have mercy, but Kitty grimly set about scrubbing off the germs, the contamination, the Casteel filth.

It seemed I could hear Reverend Wayland Wise preaching, chanting me into paradise as I lingered on the verge of unconsciousness. Shock had taken over. My mouth was open, my eyes as well, and Kitty's face above me was a pale, mean moon, bent on destruction.

On and on the bath lasted, until at last the water began to cool, and Kitty poured dark-looking shampoo from an orange bottle onto my hair. If my scalp hadn't already been burned, perhaps it wouldn't have stung so much, but it hurt, really hurt! I found strength to struggle and nearly pulled Kitty into the tub.

'Stop it!' yelled Kitty, slapping me hard. 'Yer acting like a damned fool! It's not that hot!' And there she went and put in her arms, thrusting her face close to mine. 'See, it's not hot. I'm not screaming.'

Oh, oh, oh . . . it was hot.

It was the worst experience of my life to flip and turn, kick and struggle, and never get away from Kitty, who managed to lather up every strand of my hair with that dreadful-smelling soap that was almost black. That was the worst thing anyone could do to my hair. It was long and fine, and screwing it around like that would mat it so badly it would never untangle. I tried to tell Kitty that.

'Shut up, damn ya! Ya think I don't know what hair is, and how to wash it? I'm a professional! A professional! Been doing this all my adult life. People pay to have me wash their hair, and yer complaining. One more yelp out of ya, and I'm turning on the hot water again, and I'll hold ya down and take the skin from yer face.'

I tried to stay still while I allowed Kitty to do what she would.

After my hair was lathered, it had to set to kill whatever was hidden in its depths, and during that time Kitty picked up the long-handled brush again and scrubbed my already tortured skin. Whimpering, I managed to stay in the water that gradually cooled more, and now I didn't have to wiggle or whimper, not that any of what I'd done had prevented Kitty from completing a through scrubdown and inspection of all my crevices that might conceal running sores.

'I don't have sores, Mother . . . I really don't, not ever . . .'

Kitty didn't care. She was intent on what she felt she had to do, even if it killed me.

Dream of hell, that's what this was – steaming vapours of hellfires, looming, pale, white face that wasn't pretty now that her hair was in damp strings, hanging all around that hateful moon that had a red slash that kept crooning about how babyish I was acting.

Oh, my God, oh, my God, oh, my God, I whispered, though I didn't hear any words coming from my throat. I felt as if I'd been cooked for dinner, a chicken in the pot, now being scrubbed with a brush and making skin already red and tender sting like fire.

I turned into Our Jane and began to cry, helplessly, uncontrollably. The Lysol in the water crept into my eyes, burned them. Reaching blindly, I found the cold-water spigot and turned it on, threw a handful of water in my face, relieving the pain in my eyes.

Strangely, Kitty didn't object. She seemed intent on finishing her inspection of the cleft between my buttocks. On hands and knees, I kept throwing cold water on my face, chest, shoulders, back.

'Now I'm gonna rinse off all the suds,' Kitty crooned tenderly, patting my raw bottom as if I were a baby. 'Germs all gone now, all gone. Clean baby, clean, sweet, nice, obedient baby. Turn over, let Mother rinse ya off.'

Deep in my private hell, I turned to sprawl helplessly in the tub, my feet lifted and hanging over the side to lend some relief and coolness to the rest of me.

'I'm gonna be real careful not to get any of this in yer eyes, but yer gonna have to do yer part by holding still. Stuff done killed yer lice, if ya had any. Yer a new person, almost. Ya want that, don't ya? Ya want us to do nice things for ya, don't ya? Want Cal and me to love ya, don't ya? We can't if ya don't cooperate, can we? It's yer duty to be clean, to do what we want. Stop crying. Don't tell dear Cal it hurt, that'll make him cry. He's weak, and tender hearted, ya know. All men are. Babies more than they're lil' boys. Ya can't tell them that, makes them mad, but that's the truth. Scared of women, all of them are, every last man in this old mean world, terrified of mommy, of wifey, of daughter, of sister, of auntie, of granny, of lovey-dovey girlfriend. Got pride, they have. Too much of it. Feared of rejection, like we don't get it all the time. They want ya, can't leave ya alone, but when they got ya, they wish they didn't have ya, or, worse than anything, wish they didn't need ya. So they go around thinking they can find another woman who's different.

'Ain't none of us different. So be sweet to him, make him think he's got ya sold on how big, strong, and wonderful he is, and ya'll be doing me a big favour, so then I can do ya a big favour.'

Kitty kneaded deeper and deeper into my mass of matted hair. 'I saw the shack ya lived in. I know what ya are underneath that sweet, innocent face. Same look yer ma had. Hated her then. Ya make sure I don't end up hating ya.'

Now the water was cold, soothing my burning skin, my sore scalp, and Kitty was smiling. Smiling, and fanning away the steam.

By the time I was out and standing on a plain white mat that Kitty pulled from the linen closet, I was trembling with relief to be alive. Every bit of me stung, every bit was red, even the whites of my eyes when I glanced in the long mirrors. But I was alive – and I was clean. Cleaner than I'd ever been in my entire life – about that Kitty was right.

'Ya see, ya see,' soothed Kitty, hugging and kissing me. 'It's all over, all over, and yer better than new. Look new, ya do. Look spick and span and sweet. And honey, now I'm gonna smooth on some nice, pink lotion that will help take the burn from yer poor red skin. Didn't mean to scare ya. Didn't know yer skin was so tender, but ya gotta realize I had to do something drastic to remove all the years of accumulated filth. The stink of those hockeypots and outhouses was ground into yer skin, clinging to yer hair; even if ya couldn't smell it, I could. Now yer cleaner than a newborn babe.'

Smiling, she picked up a big pink bottle with a gold label and gently smoothed on lotion that felt cooling.

Somehow I managed to smile gratefully. Kitty wasn't so bad, not really. She was like Reverend Wayland Wise, shouting and putting the fear of God's retaliation into everyone to make them better. God and hot water, about the same thing.

'Don't ya feel wonderful, better than ever before? Haven't I saved ya from the gutter, haven't I? Don't ya feel reborn, fresh, brand-new? Ready now to face the world that would condemn ya but for me?'

'Yes . . '

'Yes what?'

'Yes, Mother.'

'Ya see,' said Kitty, towel-drying my hair, wrapping it in a clean faded pink towel before she used another towel to dry my almost raw body, 'ya survived. If yer skin is a little red, It's still there. Yer hurting, but all medicine meant to heal is nasty. Ya have to suffer to be cleansed and made whole and decent.'

Kitty's hypnotic voice in the fading mists lulled me into a sense of security as the pain eased. Then she began to comb my still-damp hair.

Ouch!

It hurt!

My hair was matted in thick wads to my scalp – wads that Kitty was determined to untangle even if she had to pull out every strand.

'Let me do it,' I cried, snatching the comb from her hands. 'I know how.'

'Ya know how? Have ya spent years and years of yer life standing on yer feet until they ache up to yer waist? Have ya studied hair? Have ya – have ya?'

'No,' I whispered, really trying to work out the tangles with my fingers before I attempted to use the comb, 'but I know my own hair. When it's washed you have to be careful not to bunch it up and screw it around, like you just did.'

'Are ya trying to tell me my own business?'

At that moment a door slammed downstairs. Cal's soft voice called out. 'Honey, where are you?'

'Up here, darling love. Helping this poor chile rid herself of filth. Soon as I've finished with her, I'm coming to take care of ya.' She hissed in my ear. 'Now, don't ya go complaining to him, sister. What we do when we're alone is none of his damned business . . . understand?'

Nodding, I clutched at my body towel and backed off.

'Darling,' Cal called from the other side of the locked bathroom door, 'I've bought new clothes for Heaven, including a couple of nightgowns. Didn't know her size, so I just guessed. Now I'm going downstairs again to make up the sofa bed.'

'She's not going to sleep downstairs,' Kitty called in that strange, flat way.

His voice sounded shocked. 'What do you mean? Where else can she sleep? That second bedroom is jam-packed with all your ceramic junk that should be in your workshop. You knew she was coming. You could have had it all moved out, but no, you wouldn't do that. You wanted to put the kid on the sofa – and now you don't. What's with you, Kitty?'

Kitty smiled at me as if her lips were stiff. Silently she moved to the door, holding my fearful gaze with her commanding eyes. 'Not a word, darling dear, not a word, ya hear, not a single word to him . . .'

Throwing back her red hair, she managed to look seductive when she unlocked and opened the door just a crack. 'She's a terribly modest little thing, sweetheart love. Just hand me one of those nightgowns and we'll be seeing ya.'

Bang!

She slammed the door and tossed me a thin nightgown with a dainty print.

I'd never owned a nightgown before, but I'd always anticipated this momentous step of drawing a sleeping garment over my head. The height of luxury to have special clothes just to sleep in, when nobody saw you once you went to bed. But as soon as I had it on, the thrill was over.

The stiffness of the new fabric chafed my raw skin. The lace ruffling about the neck and sleeves felt like sandpaper.

'Ya remember, now. All yer towels, washcloths, and toothbrushes will be white – or near white. Mine are the hot-pink ones. Cal has black – and don't ya ever forget.' She smiled, opened the door, led me down the hall a short way, then showed me the very fancy large bedroom beside the bath.

Cal was in there, just beginning to unzipper his pants. Quickly he zippered again and blushed as we came in. I bowed my head low to hide my embarrassment.

'Really, Kitty,' he began with a sharp edge to his voice, 'haven't you learned about knocking first? And where do you plan to put her in here – in our bed?'

'Yeah,' quipped Kitty without hesitating. I glanced up in time to see her expression – odd, so odd. 'She's gonna sleep in the middle. Me on one side, ya on the other. Ya know how wild and obscene these hill girls are, and this is one I'm gonna have to tame by seeing she is never left alone when she's lying down.'

'Good God in heaven!' stormed Cal. 'Have you gone crazy?'

'I'm the only one here with good sense.'

What a fearful thing to hear.

'Kitty, I just won't have it! She sleeps downstairs, or we take her back!'

He was standing up to her – hooray!

'What do ya know about it? Ya were raised in a big city, and this girl here has no morals, unless we give them to her. And starting tonight, our lessons are beginning. When I have her straightened out, she can use the sofa downstairs – but not until then.'

That's when he caught a glimpse of my face, though I'd tried to keep myself hidden behind Kitty. 'My God, what have you done to her face?'

'Washed it.'

He shook his head disbelievingly. 'You've taken off her skin! Kitty, goddamn you for doing that! You should be ashamed.'

He turned kind eyes on me and held out his arms. 'Come, let me see if I can't find some medication to put on all that raw red skin.'

'Ya leave her alone!' yelled Kitty. 'I've done what I had to do, and ya know I'd never hurt anything. She was dirty, smelly; now she's cleansed, and in our bed she's going to sleep till I can trust her to be alone at night.'

What did Kitty think I was going to do?

Cal looked cold, seeming to retreat, as if anger made him ice instead of fire, like Pa. Striding out to the bathroom, slamming the door hard, leaving Kitty to hurry in there and say whatever she had to as I sighed, gave in to necessity and crawled into the big bed. I no sooner lay down than I was asleep.

Cal's loud voice woke me up. An innate sense of timing told me I'd been asleep only a few minutes. Keeping my eyes closed, I heard them arguing.

'Why the hell did you put on that black lace nothing nightgown? Isn't that kind of gown your way of letting me know what you want? Kitty, I can't perform with a child in the bed and between us.'

'Why, of course I don't expect ya to.'

'Then why the hell the black lace nightgown?'

I opened my eyes a crack and took a peek. There was Kitty stuffed into tight black mist of gown that barely shaded her nudity. Cal stood there in his jockey shorts, a huge bulge in the crotch that made me hastily close my eyes again.

Please, God, I prayed, don't let them do it in the bed – not with me here, please, please.

'This is my way to teach you some self-control,' Kitty replied primly, and crawled into bed beside me. 'Ya don't have any, ya know. It's all ya want from me, and ya ain't gonna have any till I got this girl trained the way I want her to be.'

I listened, amazed that he took what she dished out. Pa never would have. What kind of man was Kitty's husband? Wasn't a man always the boss in his family? I felt a bit sick that he didn't fight back and stand up to her.

Cal slipped into the bed on the opposite side of me. I stiffened when I felt the brush of his bristly skin against my arm. I felt angry that he hadn't gone downstairs and made up the sofa himself, overriden her desires and staked his own bed for his own reasons; yet, for some reason, I pitied him.

I knew already who was the real man in this family.

His low voice rolled over me. 'Don't push me too far, Kitty,' Cal warned before he turned on his side and tucked his arm under his head.

'I love ya, sweetheart darling, I do. And the sooner this girl learns her lessons, the sooner ya and me can have this bed all for ourselves.'

'Jesus Christ,' was the last thing he said.

It was awful to sleep between a man and his wife, and know he was resenting my presence. Now he'd never learn to like me, and I'd been depending on his favour. Without it, how could I manage to endure Kitty and her strange behaviour and swings of mood? Maybe this was Kitty's way to see that he never liked me. What a hatefully mean thing to do.

Mother, Mother, I lay sobbing, desperately wanting that long-dead mother, who was buried on the mountain side where the wolves cried at the moon and the wind sang in the leaves. Oh, to be home again, back with Granny alive, with Sarah cutting out biscuits, with Grandpa whittling, and Tom, Fanny, Keith, and Our Jane running in the meadows.

I was suspecting already . . . paradise lived in Winnerrow. Hell was up ahead.

No, didn't have to be that way. Not if I could make Kitty like and trust me.

Not if I could somehow convince Kitty I wouldn't do anything dangerous or wicked when I slept alone downstairs on the sofa bed. I closed out the pain of my raw skin and again fell into deep, merciful sleep.

Thirteen

Fevered Dreamer

As if I still lived in the cabin in the Willies, my mental cock crowed.

I woke up stiff and aching; it hurt every time I moved. Visions of the night before and the hot bath made me think I'd had a nightmare, but my burning skin was proof I hadn't dreamed that scalding bath.

Five o'clock, my body clock said. I thought of Tom, and how he would be outside chopping wood or hunting now; seldom did I awake to find Tom sleeping – back in the Willies where my heart ached to be. Disoriented, I blindly reached to find the soft sweetness of Our Jane, and touched a strong arm bristly with hair. I bolted more wide awake, stared around, reluctant to look at Kitty or her husband sprawled asleep on the wide bed. Frail morning light poured in through the open curtains.

Moving stiffly, I carefully crawled over Cal, thinking him the better choice to risk awakening. I slipped out of bed and looked around, admiring so much of what I saw, while some things left me bothered, such as the careless way Kitty had dropped all her clothes on the floor and just left them there. Why, we didn't do that in the cabin. All the fine ladies I'd read about in novels had never dropped their clothes on the floor. And Kitty had made such a fuss about everything being neat and clean! Then, I reasoned, Kitty had no worries about finding roaches and other vermin in her floor-scattered clothes, which had always been on my mind when I hung a garment on a nail. Still . . . she shouldn't do that. I picked up her clothes and hung them neatly in her closet, amazed at all the other clothes I saw there.

Quietly leaving the bedroom, I eased the door behind me, breathed a sigh of relief. Oh, I couldn't keep sleeping between husband and wife . . . it just wasn't right.

How silent this house was. I stepped down the hall and into the bathroom, and saw myself in the long wall-length mirror. Oh, my poor face! It was red and swollen, and when I touched it, it felt soft in some places, hard and irritated in others. The rash of small red dots burned like fire. Some of the larger patches were even bloody, as if I'd scratched them in the night. Helpless tears coursed down my face . . . would I ever be pretty again?

What had Granny always said? 'Ya takes what ya gets and makes the most of it . . .'

Well, I would have to accept what couldn't be helped now. Though it hurt to pull off my brand-new nightgown, hurt to raise my arms, hurt to move my legs. In fact, every move I made hurt my skin. How had I managed to sleep so soundly? Fatigue so deep even pain didn't reach me? But the night had delivered not so much rest as seething bad dreams about Tom, Keith, and Our Jane, leaving unpleasant impressions to trouble my mind as first I used that pink seat, and hesitated before flushing it. Next I set about frantically trying to untangle the impossible mess of my hair.

Through the thin walls that separated the bath from the bedroom drifted Kitty's grunts and groans, as if the new day gave Kitty immediate problems. 'Where the hell are my bedroom slippers? Where the hell is that dumb kid? She'd better not use all the hot water – she'd better not!'

Cal's calm, soft voice consoled Kitty as if she were a small child and had to be indulged. 'You go easy on her, Kitty,' he cautioned. 'You're the one who wanted her, you keep remembering that. Though why you insist on her sleeping in our bed is beyond comprehension. A girl her age needs her own room, to decorate, to dream in, to keep her secrets.'

'Ain't gonna be no secrets!' fired Kitty.

He continued as if she hadn't spoken, and my hopes rallied. 'I was against this from the first. Still, I feel sorry for her. Especially after what you did last night. And when I think of that pitiful cabin, all those attempts to make it cozy,

I realize how blessed we are to have what we do. Kitty, even if you don't want to move out your pottery wheel and all the other junk, we could manage to put a twin bed in our second bedroom, and a nice dresser. A bedside table and a lamp, and maybe a desk where she could do her homework. C'mon, Kitty . . . what do you say?'

'I say no!'

'Honey, she appears to be a nice girl, very sweet.'

He was trying to persuade her, maybe with kisses and hugs. Why from the noises they made, I could almost see what he was doing.

A slap! A hard hand striking soft flesh! 'Ya think she's pretty, don't ya? Yer noticing already, huh? But ya can't have her, ya keep remembering that! I got patience, and I got tolerance, but don't ya go fooling around with no kid who's gonna be our daughter.'

How loud she yelled.

'Don't you ever slap me again, Kitty,' Cal said in a hard, cold voice. 'I put up with a lot from you, but I draw the line at physical violence. If you can't touch me with love and tenderness, don't touch me at all.'

'Honey, it didn't hurt, did it?'

'That's not the issue, whether or not it hurt. The issue is, I don't like violent women, or ones that shout and raise their voices. And the walls are paper-thin. I'm sure Heaven thinks you treat her fine, just like a mother always treats a daughter she loves. Putting her to bed with her parents. She's a teenager, Kitty, not an infant.'

'Ya just don't understand, do ya?' Kitty sounded more than grouchy. 'I know how hill gals are; ya don't. Ya can't begin to know the evil stuff they do – and they don't need no man to be there, neither. And if ya want peace in this house, ya'll let me do it my way.'

Not a word from Cal to defend me. Not a word about the boiling bath and all the damage it had done – why not? Why was he timid around Kitty when she was in the house, when he'd stood up to her in the car?

The bedroom door opened. The slip-slop of Kitty's feathered slippers sounded on the hall floor, coming this way. I panicked. Quickly I seized one of the faded old towels and swathed it about my sore body.

Kitty came in without knocking, threw me a hard glance, then without a word whipped off her flimsy black nightgown, kicked off her pink slippers, and sat down naked on the toilet. I started to leave, but she ordered me back. 'Do somethin for yer head . . . it looks awful!' she said flatly.

I bowed my head, trying not to see or hear anything Diligently I worked with as much careful speed as my tangled hair would allow.

Soon Kitty was in the shower, singing country tunes in a loud voice. All the time I kept trying to unsnarl my hair.

Kitty came out of the shower, drying her body with a lush pink towel, scowling my way. 'Never wanta come in here again and see what I just saw in that toilet – ya hear?'

'I'm sorry. But I was afraid if I flushed it, it would waken you and your husband. Tomorrow morning I'll use the downstairs bath.'

'Ya better,' mumbled Kitty. 'Now ya hurry up and finish, then put on one of the nice dresses Cal bought for ya to wear. This afternoon, Cal and me's gonna show ya around, go to Atlanta, let ya see my shop, how pretty it is, how much my girls love me. Tomorrow we'll go to church, and Monday ya'll start school with all the other kids yer age. Sacrificing my ceramic classes for yer sake, ya keep that in mind. Could make plenty today, but won't, just to get ya started right.'

I again set diligently to work on my hair as Kitty made up her face and dressed all in pink. She picked at her bush of auburn hair with a funny-looking wire thing, then turned to beam at me. 'What d'you say?'

'You look beautiful,' I answered truthfully. 'I never saw anyone so beautiful.'

Kitty's pale eyes glistened. Her smile spread to show large, even white teeth. 'Never guess, would ya, that I'm thirty-five?'

'No,' I breathed. Older than Sarah, imagine that, and Kitty looked so much younger.

'Cal's only twenty-five, and that worries me some, being ten years older than my own husband. Caught me a fine man, I did, a real fine man, even if he is younger – but don't ya tell nobody my age, ya hear?'

'They wouldn't believe me if I did.'

'Why, ain't that sweet of ya,' Kitty said in a new softer voice. She stepped closer to give me a quick hug, a swift kiss on my raw cheek. 'Didn't really want to make yer skin look so red and raw. Does it really hurt?'

I nodded, and then Kitty was finding ointment to touch lightly on my face with great kindness. 'Guess sometimes I overdo things. Don't want ya to hate me. Want more than anything for ya to love me like ya would yer own mother. Honey, I'm sorry – but ya gotta admit, we done killed all the bad stuff ya had clinging to ya like moss on a rotten tree.'

She said everything I had been secretly been praying to hear, and impulsively I hugged Kitty back, kissed her cheek very carefully so as not to spoil that perfect makeup job. 'And you smell so good,' I whispered tearfully, overcome with relief.

'Ya and me are gonna get along fine, just fine, we are, we are,' enthused Kitty smiling happily. Then, to show she meant right, she took the comb from my hand and began to work on my tangled hair. With gentleness and great adroitness she soon had my hair a smooth-flowing cascade. Next she picked up a brush she said I could use from now on, and she brushed and brushed, using if in mysterious ways. Dipping it in water, shaking off most, curling hair over her fingers . . . and when I again looked into the mirror, I saw a beautiful head of shining, dark, curling hair around a white patchwork face and two huge blue eyes.

'Thank you,' I whispered gratefully, loving Kitty for being kind, and more than willing to forget the torture of last night.

'Okay. Now let's head for the kitchen and the tour I

promised ya. Gotta be quick about all of this. Got so much to do.'

Together we descended the stairs. Cal was already in the kitchen. 'I've got the coffee water boiling, and I'm fixing breakfast today,' Cal said in a cheerful voice. He was busy frying bacon and eggs in separate skillets, so he couldn't turn his head. 'Good morning, Heaven,' he greeted, laying the bacon carefully on paper towelling, spooning hot grease over the sunny-side ups. 'Do you like toast best, or English muffins? I'm an English muffin fan, especially with currant jelly or orange marmalade.'

It wasn't until we all sat down at the pretty round table to eat that he really saw me again. His eyes widened with pity to see my face, not even noticing how lovely my hair looked. 'Good Lord in heaven, Kitty, it's an awful shame to take a pretty face and make it look like a clown. What the hell is that white stuff smeared all over her?'

'Why, honey, it's the same stuff ya would have used.'

He appeared thwarted, disgusted, and turned to pick up the newspaper. 'Please refrain from washing her face again, Kitty. Let her do it herself,' he said from behind the newspaper, as if so angry he couldn't bear to look at Kitty.

'She'll be all right again, give her time,' stated Kitty matter-of-factly, sitting down and picking up a section of the paper he'd laid aside. 'Okay, Heaven, eat up. Got a lot to do today, all of us. Gonna show ya the time of yer life, ain't we, honey?'

'Yeah,' he said gruffly, 'but it would have been nicer for Heaven if she didn't have to be seen as she is.'

Despite my face, once I had the ointment wiped off I did have a wonderful time seeing Atlanta and the hotel where Kitty had her beauty salon, all decorated in pink, black, and gold, where rich ladies sat under slick white hoods banded in pink and gold, where eight pretty girls worked, and everyone there was a blonde.

'Ain't they pretty, though, ain't they?' asked Kitty, looking so proud. 'Just love bright golden hair that looks sunny and cheerful . . . not dull silvery-blonde hair that's hardly no colour at all.'

I winced, knowing she was referring to my mother's hair.

She introduced me to everyone, while Cal stayed out in the hotel lobby, as if Kitty didn't want him in here with all these girls.

Then they took me shopping again. Already I was wearing a pretty new blue coat that Cal had chosen, and it fitted perfectly. Unhappily, all that Kitty selected for me – skirts, blouses, sweaters, underwear – she bought a size too large, and I hated the heavy, clumsy white saddle shoes she thought I should wear. Even the valley girls in Winnerrow wore better than those. I tried to tell Kitty this, but she had her own memories of what kind of shoes she'd worn. 'Don't ya say another word! Kids don't wear fancy shoes to school – they don't!'

Yet, when we were again back in the car, I had to feel happy with so many new clothes, more than I'd had in all my life. Three pairs of shoes. Nicer ones to wear tomorrow when we went to church.

We ate again in a fast-food place that seemed to disgust Cal. 'Really, Kitty, you know I hate this kind of greasy junk.'

'Ya like to throw good money around just to show off. Me, I don't care what I eat if it's cheap enough.'

Cal didn't reply, only frowned and turned very quiet, letting Kitty do all the talking as he drove and she explained the sights. 'This is the school where ya'll be goin,' she said as Cal drove slowly past a huge red-brick building that was surrounded by several acres of lawn and playing fields. 'Ya can ride the yellow buses on rainy days, but walk on sunny ones – Cal, darling honey, did we buy her all she needs for school?' she shouted.

'Yes.'

'Why ya mad at me?'

'I'm not deaf. You don't have to shout.'

She snuggled closer to him as I leaned back and tried not to see how she kissed him even as he drove through traffic.

'Honey sweetheart, love ya, I do. Love ya so much it hurts.'

He cleared his throat. 'Where is Heaven sleeping tonight?'

'With us, honey – ain't I done told ya how it is with hill girls?'

'Yes . . . ya done told me,' he said with sarcasm, and then said no more, not even when we settled down that night so I could watch my first colour television show. It was so thrilling it took my breath away. How beautiful all those colourful dancing girls, how little they wore, and then the scary movie came on, and Cal disappeared.

I hadn't even noticed when he left. 'That's what he does when he's mad,' said Kitty, getting up to switch off the TV. 'Goes to hide in the basement, and pretends to work. We're going up now. Ya'll take another bath, wash yer hair yerself, and I won't enter while yer in there.' She paused and looked thoughtful. 'Right now I gotta go down and do some sweet-talking to my man.' She giggled, and headed toward the kitchen, leaving me to enjoy my bath in the pink tub.

I hated to sleep again between Kitty and Cal. Hated the way she teased and tormented him, giving me the impression she didn't really love him half as much as he loved her. Did Kitty really hate men?

Sunday I was up first again. On bare feet I padded down the stairs, hurried through the kithcen, hunted for the door to the basement, and found it in a small back hall. Once I was down there in the dimness, I searched and searched among all the clutter that Kitty didn't keep neat and clean, until I found my suitcase put high on a shelf over a workbench. Granny's shawls were neatly folded in a pile beside it. I climbed up on the bench to pull down the suitcase, wondering if Cal had opened it.

Everything inside was exactly as I'd left it. I'd stuffed in six favourite books given to me by Miss Deale . . . even a nursery-rhyme book that Keith and Our Jane had loved for me to read at bedtime. Tears filled my eyes just to see that book . . . 'Tell us a story, Hev-lee. Read it again, Hev-lee.'

I sat down at the workbench, pulled out a notepad, and

began a letter to Logan. Quickly, with a high sense of peril all around, I scribbled out my desperate situation, how I needed to find Tom, Keith, and Our Jane, would he please do what he could to find out where Buck Henry lived? I gave him the Maryland licence plate's first three numbers. When I finished the letter I gathered up a few other things, then hurried to the front door to see the address. I had to dash down to the corner to find the street name. When I was back in the door I'd left open, I felt a fool, for there were magazines neatly stacked with Kitty's name, and the address and zip-code number. I rifled through a small desk to find an envelope and stamps.

Now all I had to do was find an opportunity to mail my first letter. Down in the basement my beautiful bride doll slept peacefully, awaiting that wonderful day when she and I, with Tom, Keith, and Our Jane, would head for Boston, leaving Fanny to enjoy herself in Winnerrow.

I tiptoed up the stairs, then on toward the bathroom, my letter stashed under the corner of the hall rug. I closed the bathroom door behind me and breathed a sigh of relief. The letter to Logan was my highway to freedom.

'Why, look there, Cal, our lil' gal is all dressed, ready for church. So let's be on time for a change.'

'You look very pretty this morning,' said Cal, sweeping his eyes over my new dress, and my face that had lost its redness, and most of the swelling had gone down.

'She'd look better if she'd let me trim and shape that hair,' said Kitty, eyeing me critically.

'No, leave her hair alone. I hate hair so placed and perfect. She's like a wildflower.'

Kitty scowled and stared long and hard at Cal before she entered the kitchen and whipped breakfast together so fast I couldn't believe it would taste so good. Omelettes. Why, I'd never known eggs could be so light and fluffy. Orange juice . . . oh, I prayed Our Jane, Keith, and Tom were drinking orange juice now too.

'Ya like my omelettes?'

'It's delicious, Mother. You really know how to cook.'

'I just hope ya do,' she said flatly.

The church we attended was like nothing I'd seen before, a stone cathedral, tall, splendid, dark inside. 'Is it Catholic?' I whispered to Cal as we were entering and Kitty was talking to a woman she knew.

'Yes, but she's a Baptist,' he whispered back. 'Kitty is trying hard to find God and tries all religions at least once. Right now she's pretending to be Catholic. Next week we may be Jewish, or Methodist, and once we even went to a ceremony worshipping Allah. Don't say anything to make her feel foolish. The fact that she goes to church at all surprises me.'

I loved the dark interior of that cathedral with all its candles burning, with its niches and holy statues, and the priest up there in his long robes saying words I couldn't understand, and I imagined he spoke of God's love for mankind, not his desire to punish them. The songs they sang I'd never heard before, yet I tried to sing along, while Kitty just moved her lips and I heard not a sound. Cal did as I did.

Before we could leave, Kitty had to visit the ladies' room, and that was when I ran to mail my letter to Logan. Cal watched me with a sad look. 'Writing home already?' he asked when I returned. 'I thought you liked it here.'

'I do. But I have to find out where Tom is, and Our Jane and Keith. Fanny will be okay with Reverend Wise, but I have to keep in touch with my family or else we'll grow apart, so it's better to start now. People move about . . . I might never find them if I let too much time pass.'

Gently he tilted my face up toward his. 'Would it be so awful if you just forgot your old family and accepted your new one?'

Stinging tears filled my eyes. I blinked them away, or tried to. 'Cal, I think you've been wonderful . . . and Kitty – I mean Mother – is trying . . . but I love Tom, Our Jane, and Keith . . . even Fanny. We're blood kin, and have suffered through so much together, and that ties us together in ways happiness doesn't.'

Compassion flickered through his light brown eyes. 'Would you like me to help you find your brothers and sisters?'

'Would you?'

'I'll be happy to do what I can. You give me what information you have, and I'll do my best.'

'Do yer best what?' asked Kitty, looking hard at both of us. 'What ya two whispering about, huh?'

'Doing my best to see that Heaven always stays happy in her new home, that's all,' he said easily.

She kept her frown as she strode toward their white car, and we again headed for a place to eat, more fast food that didn't waste good money. Now Cal wanted to see a movie, but Kitty didn't like movies. 'Can't stand sitting in the dark with so many strangers,' she complained. 'And the kid's gotta get up early so she can start school tomorrow.'

Just the word school made me happy. A big-city school – what was that going to be like?

More television watching that night, and for the third time I was put in the middle of their bed. This time Kitty put on a red nightgown edged with black lace. Cal didn't even glance her way. He slipped into the bed, snuggled up close to me. His strong embraced arms me tightly as he nestled his face in my hair. I felt terribly frightened. And surprised.

'Get out of the bed!' yelled Kitty. 'Won't have no kid seducing my man! Cal – take yer arm off her!'

I thought I heard him chuckle as I headed downstairs, to open up the sofa that Cal had shown me how to use. In my arms I had sheets, blankets, and a wonderfully soft goosedown pillow. For the first time in my life – a bed all my own. A room all my own, filled to overflowing with such a colourful zoo it's a wonder I was able to sleep at all.

The moment my eyes opened I thought of that new school, where there'd be hundreds or even thousands of new kids and I wouldn't know even one. Although my clothes were so much better than they used to be, I'd already seen enough in Atlanta to know the clothes I had now weren't what most girls my age wore. They were cheap copies of better dresses, skirts, blouses, and sweaters. Lord, don't let them laugh at me in my too-large clothes, I prayed silently as I took a quick bath and pulled on the best of what Kitty had selected.

Something must have happened in Kitty's bedroom that night, something that made her grouchier than usual in the morning. In the kitchen her pale eyes raked over me from head to feet. 'Been easy on ya so far – but today begins yer real life. I expect ya to be up early, and cooking evey morning from now on, not fiddling in the bathroom with yer hair for hours on end.'

'But, Mother, I don't know how to use a stove like that.'

'Didn't I show ya how yesterday – the day before?'

From the range to the dishwasher to the garbage disposal to the refrigerator she showed me again how to do everything. Then once more she led me down to the basement, where there was a pink washer and dryer set in a little alcove all its own, with shelves to hold more of Kitty's animal collection, and cabinets for boxes and plastic bottles of soap and detergents, softeners, bleaches, waxes, polishers, cleansers, window cleaners, toilet cleaners, brass and copper polish, silver polish – why it went on forever. I wondered how they had any money left for food.

Food had been the main objectives in our lives and back home in the hills; none of these cleaning products had even been imagined, or considered in the least necessary. Only lye soap for everything from shampoos to baths to scrubbing filthy clothes on the washboard. No wonder Kitty considered me a heathen.

'And over there,' said Kitty, pointing to a large space full of technical-looking equipment, 'is where Cal has his home workshop. Likes to fiddle away his time down here, he does. Now, don't ya bother none of his stuff. Some of it could be dangerous. Like that electric saw and all those carpentry tools. For gals like ya, not used to the stuff like that there all, only thing ya can do is stay away. Keep that in mind, ya hear?'

'Yes.'

'Yes what?'

'Yes, Mother.'

'Now back to business. Ya think ya can wash and dry our clothes without tearing them up or burning them?'

'Yes, Mother.'

'Ya better mean it.'

Back in the kitchen we found Cal had put on water for the coffee, and he was now sitting down to peruse the morning newspaper. He put it aside and smiled when we joined him. 'Good morning, Heaven. You're looking very fresh and pretty for your first day at a new school.'

Kitty whipped around. 'Didn't I tell ya she'd look all right soon enough?' she quibbled, sitting down, snatching up a section of the morning paper. 'Gotta see what celebrity is coming to town . . .' she mumbled.

I stood in the middle of the kitchen, not knowing quite what to do. Kitty looked up, her eyes hard, cold, ruthless. 'Okay, girl, cook.'

Cook. I burned the thinly, sliced bacon I'd never fried before. Our kind came in thick slabs, not done up in narrow slices and wrapped in fancy packages.

Kitty's eyes narrowed as she watched without comment.

I burned the toast, not knowing I'd moved the lever to dark when I'd wiped away fingerprints with the sponge Kitty had given me earlier, telling me I had to keep all chrome appliances free of spots and fingerprints.

The sunny-side ups that Cal wanted I fried too long. He barely ate his rubbery eggs. The coffee was the final straw. In a flash Kitty was up and across the slick, kitchen floor, delivering to my face a stunning slap!

'Any damn fool can toast bread!' she screamed. 'An idiot fool can fry bacon! I should have known, should have!' She dragged me to the table and shoved me down. 'I'll do it today, but tomorrow, it's you from then on – and if ya do what ya did today, I'll boil ya in water next time! Cal, ya take yerself off to work, buy another breakfast somewhere. I'll have to stay home from work another hour to enroll this kid in school.'

Cal put a kiss on Kitty's rouged cheek. Not a long, passionate one, only a dutiful peck. 'Take it easy on the girl, Kitty. You're expecting an awful lot when you know she's not accustomed to modern gadgets. Give her time and she'll do just fine. I can tell by her eyes that she's intelligent.'

'Can't tell by her cooking, can ya?'

He left.

Alone with Kitty I felt a fresh wave of anxiety. Gone was the considerate woman who'd brushed my hair and curled it over her fingers. I'd already learned to fear the irrational, tempestous swings of Kitty's moods, learned enough not to be fooled by her attempts at caring. Yet, with surprising patience, Kitty taught me all over again how to operate the kitchen range, the dishwasher, the garbage disposal; and then she was instructing me on just how I had to stack the dishes, precisely stack them.

'Don't ever want to look in these cabinets and see one thing out of place, ya understand?'

I nodded. She patted my cheek, hard. 'Now run along and finish dressing for it's school time.'

The brick building had looked huge from the outside. Inside, I feared I'd be lost. Hundreds of adolescent children swarmed, all wearing wonderful clothes. Mine didn't fit at all. Not another girl had on the ugly kind of saddle shoes I wore, with white socks. The principal, Mr Meeks, smiled at Kitty as if overwhelmed to see such a voluptuous woman in his office. He beamed at her bosom, which was on his eye level, and darn if he could raise his eyes long enough to see she had a pretty face as well.

'Why, of course, Mrs Dennison I'll take good care of your daughter, of course, why, of course . . .'

'Gonna go now,' said Kitty at the door that would take her out into the hall. 'Do what teachers tell ya to do, and walk home. I've left ya list of what to do when I'm not there. Ya'll find the cards on the kitchen table. Hope to come home to a cleaner, better house – understand?'

'Yes, Mother.'

She beamed at the principal, then sashayed down the hall, and darn if he didn't follow out to the hall to watch her departure. I realized from the way he stared after her that Kitty was the woman of many men's fantasies, all her feminine differences exaggerated.

It was hard that first day. I don't know if I imagined the hostility, or if it was real. I felt self-conscious with my long, wild hair, my cheap, ill-fitting clothes (better than any I'd owned before, and yet I wasn't happy), my obvious distress at not knowing where to go or how to find the girls' room. A pretty-looking girl with brown hair took pity on me and showed me around between classes.

I was given tests to see which class my country education had prepared me for. I smiled to read the questions. Why, Miss Deale had covered all this a long time ago. And then I was thinking of Tom, and tears slipped from my eyes. I was placed in the ninth grade.

Somehow I found my way around the school, and managed to get through a day that was exceptionally long and tiring, and slowly, slowly, I walked home. It wasn't nearly as cold here as it had been in the mountains, nor was it as pretty. No white water, bubbling over rocks, and no rabbits, squirrels, and raccoons. Just a cold winter's day, a bleak, grey sky, and strange faces to tell me I was an alien in this city world.

I reached Eastwood Street, turned in at 210, used the key Kitty had given me, took off my new blue coat, hung it carefully in the hall cupboard, then hurried into the kitchen to stare at the five-by-eight cards on the kitchen table. I could almost hear Kitty saying, 'Read those over. List of instructions. Read them and learn yer duties.'

'Yes.'

'Yes what?'

'Yes, Mother.'

I shook my head to clear it, then sat to read the cards in the sunless kitchen that didn't look so cheerful without all the lights on. I'd been warned to use the lights as little as possible when I was home alone, and never was I to look at TV unless either Kitty or Cal was looking too.

The lists of what to do and not to do filled four cards.

Do's

1. Every day, after every meal, wipe the countertops, scrub the sinks.
2. After every meal, use another sponge to wipe off the refrigerator door, and keep everything inside neat and tidy, and check the meat and vegetable compartments to see nothing is rotten, or needing to be thrown out. It's up to you to see everything is used before it goes bad.
3. Use the dishwasher.
4. Grind up the soft garbage in the disposal, and never forget to turn on the cold water when it's running.
5. Washed dishes are to be removed immediately, put in cupboards in exact placement. Never stack cups one inside the other.
6. Silverware is to be neatly arranged in trays for forks, knives, spoons, not tossed in the drawer in a heap.
7. Clothes have to be sorted before washing. All whites with whites. Darks with darks. My lingerie goes in a mesh bag – use gentle cycle. My washable clothes, use cold water, and cold water soap. Wash Cal's socks by themselves. Wash sheets, pillowcases, and towels by themselves. Your clothes wash last, by themselves.
8. Dry clothes as instructed on the dryer I showed you how to use.
9. Hang clothes in cupboards. Mine in mine, Cal's in his. Yours in the broom cupboard. Fold underwear and put in correct drawers. Fold sheets and cases like what you find in the linen cupboard. Keep everything neat.

10. Every day wipe kitchen and baths with warm water containing disinfectant.
11. Once a week, scrub kitchen floor with liquid cleanser I showed you, and once a month remove buildup of wax, then reapply wax. Once a week, scrub bathroom floors, clean grout in shower stall. Scrub out tub after every bath you take, I take, and Cal takes.
12. Every other day run the vacuum over all the carpets in the house. Move the furniture aside once a week and sweep under everything. Check under chairs and tables for spiders and webs.
13. Dust everything, every day. Pick things up.
14. First thing after Cal and me are gone, clean up the kitchen. Make the bed with clean linens, change towels in bathrooms.

The cards fell from my hand. I sat on, stunned. Kitty didn't want a daughter, she wanted a slave! And I'd been so ready to do anything to please her if only she'd love me like a mother. It wasn't fair for fate to always rob me of a mother just when I thought I had one.

Hot, bitter tears coursed down my cheeks as I realized the futility of my dream of winning Kitty's love. How could I live here or anywhere without someone who loved me? I brushed at my tears, tried to stop them, but they came, like a river undamned. Just to have someone who needed me, who really loved me enough to be caring, was that too much to ask? If Kitty could only be a real mother, gladly I'd do everything on her list, and more – but she was making demands, issuing orders, making me feel used without consideration. Never saying please, or would you? – even Sarah had been more considerate than that.

So I sat on, doing nothing, feeling more betrayed by the moment. Pa must have known what Kitty was, and he'd sold me to her, without heart, without kindness, forever punishing me for what I couldn't help or undo.

Bitterness dried my tears. I'd stay only until I could run,

and Kitty'd rue the day she took me in to do more work in one day than Sarah had done in a month!

Ten times more work here than in the cabin, despite all the cleaning equipment. Feeling strange, weak, I stared at the cards lying on the table, forgetting to read the last one, and when I tried to find it later on, I couldn't.

I'd ask Cal, who seemed to like me, what Kitty could have written on that last card. For if I didn't know what not to do, ten to one I'd be sure to do it, and Kitty would somehow know.

For a while I just sat on in the kitchen, everything clean and bright around me, while my heart ached for an old rickety cabin, dim and dirty, for familiar smells and all the beauty of the outside world. No friendly cats here to rub against my legs, or big dogs that wagged furious tails to show how mean they were. Only ceramic animals of unnatural colours holding kitchen utensils, cat faces grinning from the wall, pink ducks parading toward an unseen pool. Dizzy, that's how I felt from seeing so many colours against all the white.

When next I glanced at a clock, I jumped up. Where had the time gone? I began to race around – how to finish before Kitty was home again? Those panicky butterflies were on wing again, battering my self-confidence. I'd never be able to please Kitty, not in a million years. There was something dark and treacherous in Kitty, something slippery and ugly hidden beneath all those wide smiles, lurking in those seawater eyes.

Thoughts of my life as it had been came like ghosts to haunt me – Logan, Tom, Keith, Our Jane . . . and Fanny – are they treating you like this, are they?

I vacuumed, dusted, went carefully from plant to plant and felt the dirt, all damp. I returned to the kitchen to try and begin the evening meal, which Kitty said should be called *dinner* because Cal insisted the main meal of the day was dinner and not supper.

About six Cal came in, looking fresh enough to make me

wonder if he did anything all day, and then he was smiling broadly. 'Why are you looking at me like that?'

How could I tell him that he was the one I instinctively trusted, that without him here I couldn't stay on another minute? I couldn't say that during our first time alone together. 'I don't know,' I whispered, trying to smile. 'I guess I expected you to look . . . well, dirty.'

'I always shower before I come home,' he explained with a small, odd smile. 'It's one of Kitty's rules – no dirty husband in her house. I keep a change of clothes to put on after I'm finished for the day. Then, too, I am the boss, and I have six employees, but I often like to pitch in and do the trouble-shooting on an old set.'

Feeling shy with him, I gestured to the array of cookbooks. 'I don't know how to plan a meal for you and Kitty.'

'I'll help,' he said instantly. 'First of all, you've got to stay away from starches. Kitty adores spaghetti, but it makes her gain weight, and if she gains a pound, she'll think it's your fault.'

We worked together, preparing a casserole that Cal said Kitty would like. He helped me slice the vegetables for the salad as he began to talk. 'It's nice having you here, Heaven. Otherwise I'd be doing this by myself, as before. Kitty hates to cook, though she's pretty good at it. She thinks I don't earn my way, for I owe her thousands of dollars and I am in hock up to my neck, and she holds the purse strings. I was just a kid when I married her. I thought she was wise, beautiful, and wonderful; she seemed to want to help me so much.'

'How'd you meet her?' I asked, watching how he tore the lettuce and sliced everything thin and on an angle. He showed me how to make the salad dressing, and it was as if his busy hands set free his tongue, almost as if he were talking more to himself than to me as he chopped and sliced. 'You trap yourself sometimes, by thinking desire and need is love. Remember that, Heaven. I was lonely in a big city, twenty years old, heading for Florida during spring break. I met Kitty quite by accident, in a bar my first night here in Atlanta. I thought she was absolutely the most beautiful woman I'd ever seen.' He laughed hard and bitterly. 'I was naive and young, Heaven. I had come for the summer from my home in New England while I was still going to university, had two more years to go before I graduated. Alone in Atlanta I felt lost. Kitty was lost too, and we found we had a lot in common. After a while, we married. She set me up in business. I'd always planned to be a history professor, can you imagine? Instead I married Kitty. Haven't been on a university campus since. I've never been home again, either. I don't even write to my parents anymore. Kitty doesn't want me to contact them. She's ashamed, afraid they might find out she didn't finish school. And I owe her at least twenty-five thousand dollars.'

How'd she make so much money?' I asked, half forgetting what I was doing.

'Kitty goes through men like castor oil, leaving them weak emotionally and drained financially. She told you she married first when she was thirteen? Well, she's had three other husbands, and each has provided her very well – in order to get out of a marriage each must have found abominable after a while. Then, to give her credit, her beauty salon is the best in Atlanta.'

'Oh,' I said, with my head bowed low. His confession was not what I'd expected. Yet it felt so good to have someone talk to me as if I were an adult. I didn't know if I should ask what I did. 'Don't you love Kitty?'

'Yes, I love her,' he admitted gruffly. 'When I understand what makes her what she is, how can I not love her? There's one thing, though, I want to say now, while I have a chance. There are times when Kitty can be very violent. I know she put you into hot water on your first night here, but I didn't say anything since you weren't permanently harmed. If I'd said something then, she would be worse the next time she has you alone. Just be careful to do everything she wants.

Flatter her, say she looks younger than I do . . . and obey, obey, and be meek.'

'But I don't understand!' I cried. 'Why does she want me, execpt to be her slave?'

He looked up, appearing surprised. 'Why, Heaven, haven't you guessed? You represent to her the child she lost when she aborted your father's baby and ruined herself so she can never have another child. She loves you because you are part of him, and hates you for the same reason. Through you, she hopes one day to get to him.'

'To hurt him through me?' I asked.

'Something like that.'

I laughed bitterly. 'Poor Kitty. Of all his five children, I am the one he despises. She should have taken Fanny or Tom – Pa loves them.'

He turned to put his arms about me, and tenderly he held me, the way I'd always wanted to be held by Pa. I choked up and clung to this man who was almost a stranger; my need to be loved was so great I grasped greedily, then felt ashamed and so shy I almost cried. He cleared his throat and let me go. 'Heaven, above all, never let Kitty know what you just told me. As long as you arc valuable to your father, you have value for Kitty. Understand?'

He cared. I could see it in his eyes, and with trust that he'd always keep confidences to himself, I had the courage to tell him about the suitcase in the basement and what it contained. He listened as Miss Deale would have listened, with compassion and understanding.

'Someday I'm going back there, Cal, to Boston, to see my mother's family. And I'll have the doll with me, so they'll know who I am. But I can't go unless I have found –'

'I know,' he said with a small laugh, his eyes sparkling at last. 'You must take with you Tom, Keith, and Our Jane. Why on earth do you call your little sister Our Jane?'

He laughed again when I told him. 'Your sister Fanny sounds like a real character. Will I ever meet Fanny?'

'Why, I sure hope so,' I said with a worried frown. 'She's

living now with Reverend Wise and his wife, and they call her Louisa, which is her middle name.'

'Aaah, the good Reverend,' he said in a solemn, slow way, looking thoughtful, 'the richest, most successful man in Winnerrow.'

'You don't like him?'

'I am always suspicious of any man that successful – and that religious.'

It was good to be with Cal in the kitchen, working alongside him and learning just by watching what he did. I'd never in a million years have believed a week ago that I could feel so comfortable with a man I hardly knew. I was shy, yet so eager to have him for my friend, for a substitute father, for a confidant. Every smile he gave me told me he'd be all of that.

Our casserole baked in the oven, the timer went off, and my biscuits were ready, and Kitty didn't come home, nor did she call to explain why she was late. I saw Cal glance at his watch several times, a deep frown putting a pucker of worry between his eyes. Why didn't he call and check?

Kitty didn't return home until eleven, and Cal and I were in the living room watching TV. The remainder of the casserole had long ago dried out, so it couldn't taste nearly as good to her as it had to us. Still, she ate it with relish, as if lukewarm food gone dry didn't matter. 'Ya cooked this all yerself?' she asked several times.

'Yes, Mother.'

'Cal didn't help ya none?'

'Yes, Mother, he told me not to prepare starchy foods, and he helped me with the salad.'

'Ya washed yer hands in Lysol water first?'

'Yes, Mother.'

'Okay.' She studied Cal's expressionless face. 'Well, clean up, girl; then let's all go to bed after our baths.'

'She's sleeping down here from now on,' Cal said, steel in his voice as he turned cold eyes her way. 'Next week we are going shopping and we are going to buy new furniture and replace all that clutter in our second bedroom. We will leave the potter's wheel and what you have locked in the cabinets, but we're adding a twin bed, a chair, a desk, and a dresser.'

It scared me the way she looked at him, at me, it really did.

Still, she agreed. I really was going to have a room of my own, a real bedroom – as Fanny had with Reverend Wise.

Days of school and hard work followed. Up early, late to bed, I had to clean up after Kitty's dinner, even if she came home at midnight. I found out that Cal liked me by his side when he watched television. Every evening he and I prepared dinner, and ate it together if Kitty wasn't there. I was adjusting to the busy school schedule, and making a few friends in school who didn't think I talked strange, though they never said what they thought of my too-large, cheap clothes, or my horrible clunky shoes.

Finally it was Saturday, and I could sleep late, and Kitty had given her permission for Cal and me to shop for furniture that would be mine alone to use.

And because of this shopping trip that loomed up bright and promising, I rushed about all the early hours of Saturday to finish the housework. Cal had half the day off and would be home by noon, expecting to eat lunch. What did city folks eat for lunch when they ate at home? So far I'd eaten lunch only in school. Poor Miss Deale had tried so many times to share the contents of her lunch bag with an entire class of underfed children. I had never eaten a sandwich before she forced one upon me. The ham, lettuce, and tomato was my favourite, though Tom and Keith had liked peanut butter and jelly well enough – and, more than any other kind, tuna fish.

I almost could hear Tom saying: 'That's why she brings six, you know. How could a petite lady like Miss Deale eat six sandwiches? So we really do help her out, don't we, when we eat up?'

I sighed, sad to think I'd left without saying thank you to Miss Deale, and sighed again when I though of Logan, who had not yet answered my first letter.

Thoughts of yesterdays slowed me down, so I had to rush about to check over downstairs, the living and dining rooms again, before I finished upstairs. I kept hoping to find shelves of books, or books put away in cupboards, but I didn't find even one book. There wasn't even a Bible. There were plenty of magazines, confession stories that Kitty had hid in table drawers, and pretty house magazines she put on top of the coffee table in a neat stack. But not one book.

In the small room Kitty had converted into a home ceramic hobby room, the one that was going to be mine, shelves lined the wall, and on those shelves were tiny animals and miniature people, all small enough to fit inside her little kiln. There were also cabinets lining one entire wall, all locked. I stared at those locked doors, wondering what secrets they held.

Downstairs again, I carefully stacked the dirty dishes in the dishwasher, filled the compartments with detergent, then stood back and fearfully waited for the thing to blow up, or discharge the dishes like bullets. But the darn thing still worked after almost a week of hill-scum handling. I felt strangely exhilarated, as if in learning to push the right buttons I had gained control over city living.

Scrubbing the floor was nothing new, except this one had to be waxed, and that required more reading of directions on the bottle. I watered the many live green plants, and found that some of Kitty's plants were silk, not real at all. Lord God above, don't let her see I watered a few before I knew they weren't real.

Noon came before I'd finished doing even one quarter of what was listed on those cards. It took so much time to figure out how to operate all the machines, and wrap the cords back like they'd been, and put the attachments on, and take them off, and put them away in neat order. At home all this had been done with one old broom.

I was tangled up in vacuum cord when the door from the garage banged and Cal appeared in the back hall, staring at me in a strange, intense way, as if trying to see what I was really feeling. 'Hey, kid,' he said after his survey, his eyes sort of unhappy, 'there's no need to work like a slave. She's not here to see. Slow down.'

'But I haven't cleaned the windows yet, and I haven't washed the bric-a-brac, and I haven't . . .'

'Sit down. Take a breather. Let me fix our lunch, and then we'll go shopping for the furniture you need – and how about a film for a treat? Now, tell me what you want for lunch.'

'Anything will suit me fine,' I said guiltily. 'But I should finish the housework . . .'

He smiled bitterly, still eyeing me in that odd way. 'She won't be home until ten or eleven tonight, and there is a special film I think you need see. Do you good to have some fun for a change. I presume you haven't had much. All life in mountain country isn't unpleasant, Heaven. Some mountains can deliver beauty, graceful living, peace, and even wonderful music . . .'

Why, I knew that.

It hadn't all been bad. We'd had our fun, running and laughing, swimming in the river, playing games we made up, chasing each other. Bad times when Pa was home. Or when hunger took over.

I shook my head again to clear it of memories that could make me sad. I couldn't believe he'd want to take me to the cinema, not when . . . 'But you have *ten* TV sets, two and three in some rooms.'

Again he smiled. He was twice as handsome when he smiled, though his smiles never lasted long enough to make him seem truly happy. 'They don't all work. They're just used as pedestals to hold Kitty's works of art.' He grinned ironically when he said that, as if he didn't admire his wife's artistic endeavours nearly as much as he should. 'Anyway, a television is not like a cinema, where the screen is huge, and the sound is better, and there are real people there to share your pleasure.'

My eyes locked with his a moment, then lowered. Why

was he challenging me with his eyes? 'Cal, I've never been to a film, not even once.'

He reached to caress my cheek, his eyes soft and warm. 'Then it's time you did go, so run on up and get ready, and I'll throw together a couple of sandwiches. Wear that pretty blue dress I bought for you – the one that's going to fit.'

It did fit.

I stared in a mirror that had known only Kitty's kind of beauty, and felt so pretty now that my face had healed and there were no scars. And my hair shone as it never had before. Cal was kind and good to me. Cal liked me, and that proved there were men who could like me, even if Pa didn't. Cal was going to help me find Tom, Keith, Our Jane. Hope . . . I had hope . . . a soaring kind of hope.

In the long run, it would all work out for the best. I was going to have my own bedroom with brand-new furniture, new blankets, real pillows – oh, glory day, who'd ever have dreamed Cal could be like a real father! Why, I could even see Tom smiling as I ran down the stairs, to see the first film of my life

My own father had refused to take me, but that didn't hurt so much now that I had a new and better father.

Fourteen

When There's Music

Cal's ham, lettuce, and tomato sandwiches were delicious. And when he held the new blue coat for my arms to slip into, I said, 'I can keep my head low so people won't notice I'm not really your daughter.'

He shook his head sadly and didn't laugh. 'No. You hold your head high, feel proud. You have nothing to be ashamed of, and I'm proud to escort you to your first film.' His hands rested lightly on my shoulders. 'I hope to God Kitty will never do anything to spoil your face.'

There was so much he left unsaid as we both just stood there, caught in the mire of what Kitty was, and what Kitty could do. He sighed heavily, caught hold of my arm, and guided me toward the garage. 'Heaven, if ever Kitty is unnecessarily hard on you, I want you to tell me. I love her very much, but I don't want her to harm you, physically or emotionally. I have to admit she can do both. Never be afraid to come to me for help when you need it.'

He made me feel good, made me feel that at last I had the right kind of father. I turned around and smiled; he flushed and quickly looked away. Why would my smile make him embarrassed?

All the way to the furniture shop I sat proudly beside him, filled with happy anticipation to have so much pleasure in one day, new furniture and a film. All of a sudden Cal changed from sad to lighthearted, guiding me by my elbow when we entered the shop full of so many different types of bedroom suites I couldn't decide. The salesman looked from me to Cal, pondering, so it seemed, our relationship. 'My daughter,' Cal said proudly. 'She'll choose what she likes.' The trouble was, I liked it all, and in the end it was Cal who chose what he considered appropriate for me. 'This bed, that dressing table, and that desk,' he ordered, 'the ones that aren't too girlish and will see you through to your twenties and beyond.'

A small flutter of panic stirred in my chest – I wouldn't be with him and Kitty when I was in my twenties, I'd be with my brothers and my sisters, in Boston. I tried to whisper this when the salesman stepped away. 'No,' Cal denied, 'we have to plan for the future as if we know what it is; to do otherwise cancels out the present and makes it meaningless.'

I didn't understand what he meant by that, except I liked the feeling that he wanted me permanently in his life.

Just thinking of how pretty my room was going to look must have put stars in my eyes. 'You look so pretty – like someone just plugged in your cord of happiness.'

'I'm thinking of Fanny in Reverend Wise's house. Now I'll have a room as nice as hers must be.'

Just for saying that he bought a bedside table and a lamp with a fat blue base. 'And two drawers in the table that lock, in case you have secrets . . .'

Strange how close this shopping expedition made us, as if creating a pretty room together gave us a special bond. 'What film are we going to see?' I asked when we were back in the car.

Again he was staring at me with that quizzical, self-mocking look fleeting through his golden-brown eyes. 'If I were you, I shouldn't think it would matter.'

'Not to me, but it must to you.'

'You'll see.' He'd say nothing more.

It was exciting driving to the cinema, seeing all the crowds on the street. So much better than it had been with Kitty to spoil the fun with the tension she caused. I'd never been inside a cinema before. I was trembling with excitement, seeing so many people all in one place, all spending money as if they had barrels of it. Cal bought popcorn, cola drinks, two bars of chocolate, and only then did we settle down side by side in the near dark. I'd never thought it would be this dark in a cinema.

My eyes widened when the colourful picture began with the woman on the mountaintop singing. *The Sound of Music!* Why, this was a film that Logan had wanted to see with me. I couldn't feel unhappy about that, not when Cal was sharing the single big box of buttery, salty popcorn. It was hot, and I couldn't eat enough. Occasionally we'd both reach into the box at the same time. To sit there, and drink and feast my eyes on the beauty of the film, filled me with so much delight I felt as if I were living in a picture book with sound, movement, dancing, and singing. Oh, truly this had to be the most exhilarating day of my entire life.

On and on I sat spellbound, my heart bursting with happiness, a kind of magic enveloping me so I felt I was in that film. The children were Tom, Fanny, Keith, and Our Jane . . . and me. That's the way we should have been, and I wouldn't have cared at all if Pa had blown a whistle, and hired a nun to tutor us. Oh, if only my brothers and sisters could be here with us!

After the film, Cal drove me to an elegant restaurant called the Midnight Sun. A waiter pulled out my chair and waited for me to sit, and all the time Cal was smiling at me. I didn't know what to do when the waiter handed me a menu, except to stare at him in a helpless way. All of a sudden I was inundated with need for Tom, for Our Jane, for Keith and Grandpa, so much so I was near tears . . . but he wasn't seeing that. Cal was seeing something beautiful written on my face, as if my very youth and inexperience made him feel ten times more a man than Kitty did. 'If you'll trust me, I'll order for both of us. But first tell me which you like most. Veal, beef, seafood, lamb, chicken, duck, what?'

Images of Miss Deale came again, she in her pretty magenta suit, smiling, appearing so proud to have us . . . when nobody else wanted to know we existed. I thought of her gifts – had they ever arrived? Were they back there on the porch of the cabin, with no one there to wear the clothes? eat the food?

'Heaven, what meat do you want?'

Oh, my God . . . how did I know? I frowned, concentrating on the complicated menu. I'd had roast beef when Miss Deale took us to a restaurant not nearly as fine as this one.

'Try something you've always wanted to eat and never have,' Cal softly prompted.

'Well,' I mused aloud, 'I've had fish caught in the river near the cabin – had pork – eaten many a chicken – and had roast beef once, and it was really good, but I guess I'll have something brand-new – you choose it.'

He laughed and ordered salad and veal cordon bleu for two. 'Children in France grow up on wine, but I guess we'll wait a few years before you try that.' He'd encouraged me to order escargots, and only after I had finished my six did he explain that they were snails in hot garlic butter, and the bit of French bread I was using to sop up the delicious sauce hesitated in my hand that was suddenly trembling.

'Snails?' I asked, feeling queasy, sure he was teasing me. 'Nobody, even the dumbest hill folks, eats things as nasty as snails.'

'Heaven,' he said with a warm smile in his eyes, 'it's going to be fun teaching you about the world. Just don't say anything about this to my wife. She's stingy about restaurants, thinks they charge too much. Do you realize that since the day I married her we have not once eaten out except in fast-food joints? Kitty just doesn't appreciate gourmet cooking, and doesn't really understand what it is. She thinks she does. If she spends half an hour preparing a meal, she thinks that's gourmet food. Haven't you noticed how fast she puts a meal together? That's because she refuses to tackle anything complicated. Warm-up food, I call what she cooks.'

'But you said Kitty was a wonderful cook before!'

'I know, and she is, if you like her breakfast menu . . . that's what she cooks best, and country food that I don't like.'

That very day that I began to fall in love with city life and city ways that were far, far different from mountain ways, or even valley life.

We were barely in the door when Kitty came home from her evening ceramic class, irritable as she stared at us. 'What ya two do all day?'

'We went shopping for the new furniture,' Cal said casually.

She narrowed her eyes. 'What shop?'

He told her, and her scowl came. 'How much?'

When he named a figure, she clasped her long-nailed hand to her forehead, seeming appalled. 'Cal, ya damn fool – ya should buy her only cheap stuff! She don't know good from bad! Now, ya send that all back if it comes when I'm gone. If I'm here, I'll send it back!'

My heart sank.

'You will not send it back, Kitty,' he said, turning to head for the stairs, 'even if you are here. And you might as well know I ordered the best mattress, the best pillows and bed linens, and even a pretty cover with a dust ruffle to match the curtains.'

Kitty screamed: 'Yer ten times a damned fool!'

'All right, I'm a damned fool who will pay for everything with my own money, not yours. Good night, Heaven. Come, Kitty, you sound tired – after all, it was your idea that we drive to Winnerrow and find ourselves a daughter. Did you think she'd sleep on the floor?'

I could hardly contain myself when the furniture arrived two days later. Cal was there to direct where things should go. He expressed a desire to have the room wallpapered. 'I hate so much white, but she never asks me what colour I'd like.'

'It's fine, Cal. I love the furniture.' Together, when the deliverymen had gone, he and I made the bed with the pretty new flowered sheets, and then we spread on the blankets, and topped everything off with the pretty quilted cover.

'You do like blue?' he asked. 'I get so damned tired of hot pink.'

'I love blue.'

'Cornflower blue, like your eyes.' He stood in the middle

of my small room, now prettier than I could have imagined, and seemed too big and too masculine for all the dainty things he'd chosen. I turned in circles and stared at accessories I hadn't known he'd ordered. A set of heavy brass duck bookends for the books I'd stuffed in the broom cupboard with my clothes. A desk blotter, pencil cup, and a pen and pencil set, and a small desk lamp and framed pictures for the wall. Tears came to my eyes, he'd bought so much.

I sobbed, 'Thank you,' and that's all I could manage before I lost my voice and cried all the tears I'd saved up through the years, flat on my face on that narrow twin bed that was so pretty, and Cal sat awkwardly on the side of the bed and waited for me to finish. He cleared his throat. 'I've got to get back to work, Heaven, but before I go, I have another surprise. I'll lie it here on your desk, and you can enjoy it after I'm gone.'

The sound of his feet departing made me turn over and sit up, and once more I called out, 'Thank you for everything.' I heard his car drive off, and I was still sitting on the bed . . . and only then did I look at the desk.

A letter lay on the dark blue of the desk blotter . . . a single letter.

I don't even remember how I got there and when I sat, except I did sit, and I stared for the longest time at my name written on that envelope. Miss Heaven Leigh Casteel. In the upper left-hand corner was Logan's name and address. Logan!

He hadn't forgotten me! He did care enough to write! For the first time I used a letter opener. What nice handwriting Logan had, not as scrawly as the way Tom wrote, or as precisely perfect as Pa's small script.

Dear Heaven,

You just can't know how much I've worried about you. Thank God you wrote, so now I can go to sleep knowing you're all right.

I miss you so much it hurts. When the sky is bright

and blue, I can almost see your eyes, but that only makes me miss you more.

To be honest, my mother tried to keep your letter hidden so I'd never read it, but one day I found it in her desk when I was hunting for stamps, and for the first time in my life, I was really disappointed in my own mother. We fought, and I made her admit she'd hidden your letter from me. Now she admits she was wrong, and has asked me, and you, to forgive her.

I see Fanny often, and she's fine, looking great. She's a terrible showoff, and to be honest again, I think that Reverend Wise may have his hands fuller than he thought.

Fanny says she wasn't sold! She says your father gave all his children away to save them from starving. I hate not to believe either one of you, yet you've never lied to me before, and it's you I do believe. I haven't seen your father – but I have seen Tom. He came into the store and asked if I had your address so he can write. Your grandfather is living in a rest home in Winnerrow.

I have no idea how to help you find Keith and Our Jane. Keep on writing, please I still haven't met anyone I like nearly as much as I do Heaven Leigh Casteel.

And until I see you again, I'm not even going to look.

My love as always,
Logan

I cried again I was so happy.

Shortly after Logan's letter came I turned fifteen. I knew better now than to call attention to myself and didn't say a word to Kitty or Cal, but somehow Cal knew and gave me an incredible gift – a brand-new typewriter!

'It will help with your homework.' His smile was wide, so pleased with my overwhelmed response. 'Take typing in school. It never hurts to know how to type.'

That typewriter, as much as I loved it, wasn't the biggest thrill of my fifteenth birthday. Oh, no. It was the huge card that came in the mail, bright with pretty flowers, sweet with a verse, and thick with a silk scarf and a letter from Logan.

Still, I longed to hear from Tom. He had my address now; why wasn't he writing?

In a whole school of girls I managed to make two good friends who repeatedly invited me to visit their homes. Neither one understood why I always had to refuse. Then, to my dismay, discouraged or put off, they began, bit by bit, to drift away. How could I tell anyone that Kitty flatly denied me friends who might take time away from the housework I had to do every day? The boys who asked me for dates I had to reject too, though not altogether for the same reasons. It was Logan I wanted to date, not them. Logan I was saving myself for, and not once did I question that he was doing the same thing.

The house I slaved to keep clean and tidy never stayed that way when Kitty could come in to devastate ten hours of work with her careless habits. The plants I watered and dusted and fertilized withered from too much care, and then Kitty yelled at me for being stupid. 'Any damn fool can keep a plant living . . . any damn fool!'

She found her water-spotted silk plants and slapped me for being an idiot hill-scum girl who didn't have brains. 'Yer thinking about boys, can see it in yer eyes!' she yelled when she caught me idling one afternoon when she came home unexpectedly. 'Don't ya sit in the living room when we ain't home! TV is off limits for ya when yer alone! Ya stay busy, ya hear?'

I was up early every day to prepare breakfast for Kitty and Cal. She seldom came home for the evening meal before seven or eight o'clock, and by that time Cal and I had eaten. For some reason this didn't annoy her. Almost with relief she fell into a kitchen chair and broodingly stared at her plate until I dished up the food which she wolfed down in mere seconds, without appreciation for all the trouble I took to learn her favourite dishes.

Before I could go to bed I had to put the kitchen in order,

check all the rooms to see that everything was in its proper places and no magazines or newspapers cluttered the tabletops or lay on the floor. In the morning I hurried to make my bed before Kitty came in to check, then rushed downstairs to begin breakfast. Before I left for school, I washed clothes while I made the beds, put the dirty dishes in the dishwasher, wiped off all fingerprints, smudges, spills, and such, and only when I had the door locked behind me did I begin to feel free.

Now I was well fed and my clothes were warm and adequate, and yet there were times when I thought longingly of home and forgot the hunger, the awful cold, the deprivations that should have scarred me forever. I missed Tom so much it hurt. I ached for Our Jane and Keith, for Grandpa and even Fanny. Logan's letters helped me not to miss him so much.

I was riding in the school bus now that it was raining every day and Kitty didn't want to buy me a raincoat or boots. 'Soon it'll be summer,' she said, as if there'd be no spring to mention, and that made me homesick again. Spring was a season of miracles in the mountains, when life got better and the wildflowers came out to coat the hills with beauty Candlewick would never know. In school I studied with much more determination than other students, on a mad, hurried schedule to get back home and dig into housework.

The many TVs were a constant temptation calling to me. It was lonely in the empty house, and despite Kitty's warning never to turn on a TV when I was alone, I soon was a soap-opera addict. I dreamed about the characters at night. Why, they had even more problems than the Casteels, though none were financial, and all of ours had been related to money problems – or so it seemed now.

Day after day I checked the letter box waiting for Logan's letters that came regularly, always anticipating that long-awaited letter from Tom that didn't show up. One day, out of pure frustration from not hearing from Tom, I wrote to Miss Deale, explaining how we'd been sold and pleading with her to help me find my brothers and sisters.

The weeks passed, and still no letter came from Tom. The letter I'd written to Miss Deale came back stamped Addressee Unknown.

Then Logan stopped writing! My first thought was he had another girl. Sick at heart, I stopped writing to him. Every day that passed without hearing from Logan made me think that nobody loved me enough to do me any good, except Cal. Cal was my saviour, the only friend I had in the world, and more and more I depended on him. The quiet house came alive when he came in the door and the television was snapped on and housework could be forgotten. I began to long for him as the hour of six drew near and my dinner was almost ready to serve. I took pains to set the table prettily, to plan menus I knew he'd enjoy. I spent hours and hours preparing his favourite dishes, not caring anymore if Kitty grew fat from the pasta dishes he preferred and I liked, too. When the clock on the mantel struck six, my ears listened for the sound of his car in the drive. I ran to take his coat when he came in the back door, loving the ceremony of his greeting that was the same each day:

'Hi there, Heaven. What's new?'

His smiles brightened my life; his small jokes gave me laughter. I began to see him as bigger than life, and forgot all his weaknesses when it came to Kitty. Best of all, he listened, really listened, when I talked to him. I saw him as the kind of father I'd always wanted, always needed, the one who not only loved me, but also appreciated what I was. He understood, never criticized, and always, no matter what, he was on my side. Though with Kitty that never helped much.

'I write and write, and Fanny never answers, Cal. Five letters I've written to her since I've been here, and not even a postcard in return. Would you treat your sister like that?'

'No,' he said with a sad smile, 'but then, my family never write to me, so I don't write to them – not since I married Kitty, who doesn't want any competition for my affection.'

'And Tom doesn't write, even though Logan gave him this address.'

'Maybe Buck Henry doesn't give him the time to write letters, or prevents him from mailing the ones he might write.'

'But surely he could find a way.'

'Hold on. One day you'll see a letter in our box from Tom, I'm sure of it.'

I loved him for saying that; loved him for making me feel pretty, for saying I was a good cook, for appreciating all I did to keep the house clean. Kitty never saw anything I did unless it was wrong.

Weeks passed during which Cal and I became closer and closer, like a true father and daughter. (Often Kitty didn't come home until ten or eleven at night.) I knew that Cal was the best thing in my Candlewick life, and for him I was going to do something special. He had a yen for all kinds of fancy egg dishes, so for the first time in my life I was going to prepare what he often asked Kitty to make – a cheese soufflé. An amusing lady on TV was teaching me all about gourmet cooking.

The perfect time was Saturday, before our trip into Atlanta to see a film.

I fully expected it to fail, as most of my experiments did – and then I was drawing it from the oven, amazed to see it looked right. Golden brown, high and light! I'd done it right! If I could have patted myself on the back, I would have done so. I ran to the china cabinet, wanting to serve it on the royal dishes it deserved. Then I stepped halfway down the basement stairs, leaned over, and called in my most demure voice, 'Lunch is served, Mr Dennison.'

'Coming right up, Miss Casteel,' he called back. We sat in the dining room, where he stared with admiration at my high and wonderful cheese soufflé. 'Why, it's beautiful, Heaven,' said Cal, tasting it, 'and delicious,' closing his eyes to savour it. 'My mother used to make cheese soufflés just for me – but you shouldn't have gone to so much trouble.'

Why did he look uneasy sitting in his own dining room,

– as if he'd never eaten in here before? I looked around, feeling very uneasy. 'Now you'll have lots of dishes to clean up before we head for town and fun . . .'

Oh, that was all.

No one moved more swiftly than I did that afternoon. I stacked the pretty china in the dishwasher; while it washed, I ran up stairs to bathe and dress. Cal was ready and waiting, smiling at me, seeming relieved to have the dining room restored to a museum piece. I was ready to step out the door before I remembered. 'One moment, and I'll be back. Wouldn't want Kitty to come home and find her china not put back exactly in place.'

As I finished doing this and that, he decided to go back to the basement to put his own tools away – that's when the doorbell rang. We so seldom had guests the sound of the bell startled me, and I quickly went to the door. The postman smiled at me.

'A registered letter for Miss Heaven Leigh Casteel,' he said cheerfully.

'Yes,' I said eagerly, staring at the pack of letters in his hand, so many.

He extended a clipboard with a paper. My hand trembled when I made my crooked signature.

Once I had the door closed, I sank down onto the floor. The sun through the fancy diamond windows near the door fell on the envelope of a letter I was sure was from Tom – but it wasn't. Strange handwriting.

Dearest Heaven,

I hope you don't mind my familiarity. I'm sure you will forgive me this when you hear my good news. You don't know my name, and I can't sign this letter. I am the woman who came with her husband to become the mother of your darling little sister and brother.

If you recall, I promised to write and keep you in touch. I remember your great love and concern for your brother and sister, and I have to admire and respect you for that. Both children are very well, and have, I believe, adapted to this family, and stopped missing their mountain family so much.

Your father didn't want to give me your address; however, I persisted, believing I should keep my promise.

Our Jane, as you used to call her, has recovered from an operation to correct a diaphragmatic hernia. You can look this up in a medical encyclopedia, and find out exactly what it was that made that dear child so frail. You'll be happy to know she is now healthy and gaining weight and has a good appetite. She is as healthy and normal as any seven-and-a-half year-old girl. Every day she and Keith have all the fruit juice they want. And I do leave night-lights on in both of their rooms. They attend a good, private school, and are driven there each day, and picked up when school is over. They have so many friends.

Keith shows great artistic talent, and dear Jane loves to sing and listen to music. She is taking music lessons, and Keith has his own easel, and equipment for drawing and painting. He is especially good at drawing animals.

I hope I have answered all questions, and given you enough information to keep you from worrying. Both my husband and I love these two children as if they were our own. And I believe they love us as much in return.

Your father says he has found good homes for all of his children, and I pray this it true.

Under separate cover I am sending you photographs of your brother and sister.

My best wishes to you.

R.

That's the way she signed her letter, with just an initial, no address to give me a clue. My heart thudded madly as I stared at the envelope again, trying to read fingerprints, hidden numbers and street names. It had been postmarked in Washington, D. C. What did that mean? Had they moved from Maryland? Oh, thank God the doctors had found out what was wrong with Our Jane and had cured her!

For the longest time I just sat there, thinking about Keith and Our Jane – and the kind lady who'd been thoughtful enough to write. Again and again I read the letter. I brushed tears from my eyes as I read it through. Oh, it was wonderful to hear that Our Jane was well and happy, and she and Keith had everything – but it wasn't good to hear they'd forgotten me and Tom, not good at all.

'Heaven,' said Cal from a few feet away, 'would you rather sit on the floor and read letters all day than go to the cinema?'

In a moment I was up, showing him the letter, eagerly telling him the contents even as he read them for himself. He appeared as delighted as I felt. Then he began to look through his own mail. 'Why, here's another envelope for Miss Heaven Leigh Casteel,' he said with a broad grin, handing a heavy brown envelope to me.

A dozen snapshots were inside, and three photographs taken at a professional portrait shop.

Oh, dear God – snapshots of Keith and Our Jane playing on the grass in a garden behing a huge, beautiful house. 'Polaroid shots,' said Cal, looking over my shoulder. 'What beautiful children.'

I stared at the lovely children in expensive-looking clothes, both sitting in a sandbox with a bright awning overhead. Behind them was a swimming pool, the chairs and tables placed on flagstone borders. The same man and wife were there, wearing swimsuits, smiling lovingly at Keith and Our Jane. It was summer where they were! Summer! Did that mean Florida? California? Arizona? I studied the other snapshots that showed Our Jane laughing as Keith pushed her on a swing. Others were taken in her pretty bedroom with all the dolls and toys: Our Jane sleeping in a fancy little bed, all ruffled, with a pink canopy overhead: Keith in his blue room full of all kinds of toys and picture books. Then I opened an large elaborate, cardboard folder to see Our Jane really dressed up, in pink organdy with ruffles, her hair curled, looking as if she belonged in the films, smiling at who ever was snapping her picture; and there was another of Keith dressed in a smart blue suit, wearing a small tie, and a third portrait showing them together.

'It cost money to take portraits like those,' Cal said from over my shoulder. 'See how they're dressed. Heaven, they are very beloved children, well cared for and happy. Why, look at the shine in their eyes. Unhappy children couldn't fake smiles like that – smiles that light up their faces. Why, in some ways you should thank God your father did sell them.'

I didn't realize how much I was crying until Cal blotted my tears by holding me against his chest. 'There, there . . .' he crooned, cuddling me in his arms, giving me his handkerchief to blow my nose. 'Now you can sleep at night without crying and calling out for them. Once you hear from Tom, your whole world will brighten. You know, Heaven, there are very few Kittys in this world. I'm just sorry you had to be the one to suffer at her hands . . . but I'm here. I'll do what I can to protect you from her.' He held me close, closer, so I felt every curve of my body pressed against his.

Alarm filled me. Was this right? Should I pull away to let him know he shouldn't? But it had to be right, or he wouldn't be doing it. Still, I felt uneasy enough to push him away, though I smiled tearfully into his face, and turned so we could leave, but not before I carefully hid the letter and the photographs. For some reason I didn't want Kitty to see how lovely Pa's other two children were.

That Saturday was even more special than the others had been. Now I could really enjoy myself, knowing Our Jane and Keith weren't really suffering . . . and someday I'd know about Tom, too.

It was ten-thirty when Cal and I drove back from Atlanta, both of us rather tired from trying to do too much: see a three-hour film, eat in a restaurant, and do some shopping. Clothes for me that Cal didn't want Kitty to see. 'I hate those saddle shoes as much as you do. However, don't let her see these new ones,' he warned before we drove into the garage. 'Sneakers are fine for gym, and the shoes she bought for church are just too young for you now. I'll keep these locked in one of my workshop cabinets, and give you a duplicate key. And if I were you, I'd never let my wife see that doll or anything that once belonged to your mother. I'm ashamed to say that Kitty has an abnormal hatred for a poor, dead girl who couldn't have known she was taking from Kitty the one man she could truly love.'

That hurt, really hurt. I turned big sad eyes his way. 'Cal, she loves you. I know she does.'

'No, she doesn't, Heaven. She needs me once in a while, to show off as her 'prize catch' – a college man – "her man" as she so often puts it. But she doesn't love me. Underneath all those exaggerated feminine curves is hidden a small, cold soul that hates men . . . all men. Maybe your father made her that way, I don't know. I pity her, though. I've tried for years and years to help her overcome her traumatic childhood. She was beaten by her father, by her mother, and forced to sit in hot water to kill her sins, and handcuffed to her bed so she wouldn't run off with some boy. Then, the moment she was set free, she ran off with the first man she met. Now I've given up. I'm just hanging around until one day I can't take it anymore – then I'll go.'

'But you said you loved her!' I cried out. Didn't you stay when you loved? Could pity be the same as love?

'Let's go in,' he said gruffly. 'There's Kitty's car. She's home, and there will be hell to pay. Don't say anything. Let me do the talking.'

Kitty was in the kitchen pacing the floor. 'Well!' she shouted when we came in the back way. 'Where ya been? Why ya look so guilty? What ya been doing?'

'We went to the cinema,' said Cal, stalking by Kitty and heading for the stairs. 'We ate dinner in the kind of restaurant you seem to hate. Now we're going to bed. I suggest you say good-night to Heaven, who must be as tired as I am, after cleaning this house from top to bottom before noon.'

'She ain't done one damn thing on my lists!' snapped Kitty. 'She went off with ya and left this house a mess!'

She was right. I hadn't really done much cleaning, since nothing ever seemed to get messy and dirty, and Kitty seldom bothered to check.

I tried to follow where Cal led, but Kitty reached out and seized my arm. Cal didn't look back.

'Ya damned stupid kid,' she hissed. 'Ya put my best china in the dishwasher, didn't ya? Don't ya know I never use my Royal Doulton and Lenox unless there's company? It's not for every day! Ya done chipped my plates, two of them! Ya done stacked my cups, broke a handle! Cracked another! Didn't I tell ya never to stack my cups, but to hang them up?'

'No, you never told me that. You just said don't stack them.'

'I did tell ya! I warned ya! Ya don't do what I say not to do!'

Slap slap slap.

'How many times do I have to tell ya?'

Slap slap slap.

'Didn't ya see the hooks under the shelves – didn't ya?'

Sure, I'd seen the hooks, and hadn't known what they were for. She hadn't had the cups hung from the hooks. I tried to explain, to apologize, promising to pay for the plates. Her eyes grew scornful. 'How ya gonna do that, dummy? Those dishes cost eighty-five dollars a place setting – ya got that kind of dough?'

I was shocked. Eighty-five dollars! How could I know the fancy dishes in the dining-room cabinet were only for looking at, never for using?

'Yer a damned fool – that's my best – took me forever paying for all those cups, saucers, plates, and things – now ya gone and ruined my things – goddamn Jesus Christ idiot hill-scum trash!'

Her pinching grasp hurt my arm. I tried to tug free. 'I won't do it again, Mother. I swear I won't!'

'Yer damned right ya won't do it again!' Wham! She punched my face, once, twice, three times!

I staggered backward, off balance, feeling my eye beginning to swell as my nose began to bleed from blows she threw like a boxer. 'Now ya get upstairs and stay in that room all day tomorrow – with the door locked. No church and no food until ya can come down and make me believe yer really sorry to have ruined my best things that should be hand-washed.'

Sobbing, I ran for the stairs, for the little room with the furniture Cal and I had chosen, hearing Kitty swearing behind me, saying such awful things about hill-scum trash I felt those words would be forever engraved on my brain. In the hall I collided with Cal. 'What's wrong?' he asked with alarm, then caught me and forced me to hold still so he could see my face. 'Oh, God,' he groaned when he saw my face. 'Why?'

'I chipped her best plates . . . broke a handle off a cup . . . put her wooden-handled knives in the dish-washer . . .'

He strode off, descended the stairs, and down there I heard him raise his voice for the first time. 'Kitty, because you were abused as a child is no reason for you to abuse a girl who tries to do her best.'

'Ya don't love me,' she sobbed.

'Of course I do.'

'No ya don't! Ya think I'm crazy! Ya'll leave me when I'm old and ugly. Ya'll marry some other woman, younger than me.'

'Please, Kitty, let's not go through this again.'

'Cal . . . didn't mean to do it. Never meant to hurt her. Or hurt ya. I know she's not really bad . . . it's just something about her . . . something about me, don't understand it . . . Cal, I got me yearnings tonight.'

Oh, God, what went on beyond their bedroom wall had

taught me only too well why he stayed on and on, despite all the ways she had of castrating him.

In that bedroom with the door shut and locked, he was putty in her hands. She didn't blacken his eyes, or make his nose bloody. What she did for him made him smile in the morning, made his eyes bright, his steps light.

The next morning was Sunday, and Kitty forgave me for chipping her china, forgave me for breaking a cup handle and ruining an expensive knife . . . now that she had Cal under her thumb again. Yet when Cal and I were in the car, waiting for her to finish checking to see what I'd failed to do, he said without looking my way, 'I promise to do all I can to help you find Tom. And when you're ready to go to Boston to see your mother's parents, I'll do some detective work myself, or hire others to find your mother's family. They must have been very wealthy, for I hear a Tatterton Toy Portrait Doll costs several thousand dollars. Heaven, you must show that doll to me one day – the day you fully trust me.'

To prove how much I did trust him, while Kitty rested upstairs that very afternoon Cal and I entered the basement. First I had to put in a load of Kitty's clothes, and while the washer spun I opened my precious suitcase of dreams and lovingly lifted out the doll. 'Turn your back,' I ordered, 'so I can straighten her gown, put her hair in order . . . and then look, and tell me what you think.'

He seemed stunned to see the bride doll with her long silver-gold hair. For long moments he couldn't speak. 'Why, that's you with blonde hair,' he said. 'How beautiful your mother must have been. But you are just as lovely . . .'

Hurriedly I wrapped the doll again, tucked her away. For some reason I felt deeply disturbed. After seeing the doll, why did Cal look at me as if he'd never seen me before?

There was so much I didn't know. So much to keep me awake at night in the small room with so much space still taken up by all the things Kitty refused to move out. Again Kitty and Cal were arguing, over me.

'Stop telling me no!' said Cal in a low but intense voice.

'Last night you said you wanted me every day, every night. Now you shove me away. I'm your husband.'

'Can't let ya. She's right next door. Where ya wanted her.'

'You put her in our bed! But for me she'd still be here between us!'

'I went in there – walls ain't thick enough. Makes me self-conscious to know she can hear.'

'That's why we have to get rid of all your stuff. Then we could put her bed on the other wall, much farther away. You do have a huge kiln in your classroom. And all the other junk should go as well.'

'It's not junk! Ya stop calling my things junk!'

'All right. They're not junk.'

'The only time I can get a rise out of ya is when ya defend her –'

'Why, Kitty, I didn't know you wanted a rise out of me.'

'Yer mocking me. Yer always mocking me by saying that, when ya knows what I mean . . .'

'No, I wish to God I knew what you really are up to. I wish I knew who and what you are, what thoughts go on beneath all that red hair –'

'Ain't red! Auburn! Titian . . .' she flared hotly.

'All right, call it whatever if you want. But I know this: If ever you hit Heaven again, and I come home to see her nose bleeding, her face bruised, her eyes black . . . I'll leave you.'

'Cal! don't say things like that—! I love ya, I do! Don't make me cry . . . can't live without ya now. I won't hit her, promise I won't. Don't want to anyway . . .'

'Then why?'

'Don't know. She's pretty, young – and I'm getting old. Soon I'll be thirty-six, and that's not far from forty. Cal, life ain't gonna be good after forty.'

'Of course it will.' His voice sounded softer, more understanding. 'You're a beautiful woman, Kitty, getting better each year. You don't look a day over thirty.'

She yelled: 'I want to look twenty!'

'Good-night, Kitty,' he said with disgust in his voice. 'I

won't see twenty again, either, but I'm not grieving about it. What did you have when you were twenty but insecurity? You know who and what you are now; isn't that a relief?'

No, apparently knowing who and what she was was the horror of being Kitty.

However, to celebrate Kitty's traumatic thirty-sixth birthday, that summer Cal reserved rooms in a fine hotel near a beach, and in August, the month of the lion, all three of us were under a beach umbrella. Kitty was the sensation of the beach in her skimpy, pink bikini. She refused to leave the shade of an umbrella bright with red stripes. 'Skin's delicate, burns easy . . . but ya go, Heaven, Cal. Don't mind me. I'll just sit and suffer while ya two have fun.'

'Why didn't you tell me you didn't want to come to the shore?'

'Ya didn't ask.'

'But I thought you liked to swim and sunbathe.'

'That's how much ya know about me – nothing.'

Nobody had any fun when Kitty didn't.

It was a flop of a holiday, when it could have been so much fun if Kitty had only shared the water with us, but Kitty made her birthday holiday a torture.

The day we returned from our holiday, Kitty sat me down at the kitchen table with her large box of manicuring equipment and began to give me my first manicure. I felt ashamed of my short, broken fingernails as I admired her long, perfectly groomed ones, with all the cuticle pushed back, and never a chip – never! My ears perked up when she began her lecture on how to have nails as nice as hers. 'Ya got to stop chewing on yers, and learn how to be a woman. Don't come naturally to hill girls, all the gracious ways a woman has to have. Why, it takes time and training to be a woman, takes a lot of patience with men.'

The air-conditioning made a soft, hypnotic sound as she continued.

'They're all the same, ya know, even the sweet-talking ones. Like Cal. All want one thing, and being a hill girl, ya know what it is. All is dying to slam their bangers into yer whammer, and after they done it, if ya start a baby, they won't want it. They'll say it's not theirs, even if it is. If they gives ya a disease, they don't care. Now, ya heed my advice, and don't listen to no sweet-talking boy – or man – including mine.'

Kitty finished painting my nails bright rose. 'There. They do look better now that yer not scrubbing on washboards no more and using lye soap. Knuckles done lost all the redness. Face done healed – and are ya harmed, are ya?'

'No.'

'No what?'

'No, Mother.'

'Ya love me, don't ya?'

'Yes, Mother.'

'Ya wouldn't take nothing from me that was mine, would ya?'

'No, Mother.'

Kitty rose to leave. 'Got another hard day of being on my feet. Slaving to make others look pretty.' She sighed heavily and looked down at her five-inch heels. She had remarkably small feet for such a tall woman; like her waist, they appeared to belong to someone petite and frail.

'Mother, why don't you wear low-heeled shoes to work? It seems a pity to make yourself suffer in high heels like that.'

Kitty stared with disdain at my bare feet. I tried to tuck them under the full skirt that fell to the floor when I was sitting.

'Shoes ya wear tell people what yer made of – and I'm made of the right stuff; steel. Can take the pain, the suffering – and ya can't.'

Hers was a crazy way of thinking. I vowed never again to mention her miserable, too-small shoes that curled her toes so they could never straighten out. Let her feet hurt . . . why should I care?

Summer days were full of work and cooking, and Saturday

treats. Soon there were signs of autumn, and school supplies showed up in shop windows, with sweaters and skirts, coats and boots. I'd been here eight months, and although Logan had begun writing to me again, still there was no word from Tom. It hurt so much I began to think it was better to stop hoping I'd never hear from him . . . and then, there it was, in the letter box! Just one letter.

Oh, Thomas Luke, it's so good to see your handwriting, so good, please let me find only happy things inside.

With his letter in my hand, it was almost as if I had Tom beside me. I hurried to sit and carefully open his letter so as not to tear his return address. He wrote with his flavour of the hills, but something new had been added . . . something that took me quite by surprise, and despite myself, I felt jealous.

Dear Heavenly,

Boy, I sure do hope you get this letter. Been writing my fool head off to you, and you never answer! I see Logan from time to time and he nags at me to write to you. I do, but I don't know what happens to my letters, so I'll keep trying. Heavenly, first of all I want you to know that I'm all right. Mr Henry is not cruel, not as mean as you no doubt think, but he can sure drive you to do your very best.

I live in his farmhouse which has twelve rooms. One of them is mine. It's a nice room, clean and kind of pretty in a plain way. He has two daughters, one named Laurie, age thirteen, and one named Thalia, age sixteen. Both are pretty, and so nice I don't really know which one I like best. Laurie is more fun; Thalia is serious, and gives everything more thought. I've told them both about you, and they say they're dying to meet you one day soon.

Logan told me about Our Jane's operation, and how well she's doing, and that Keith is happy and well. You know that's a load off my mind. Trouble is, according to Logan, you say little about yourself. Please write and tell me all that has happened since last you and I were together. I miss you so bad it hurts. I dream about you. I miss the hills, the woods, the fun things we used to do. I miss our talks about our dreams, miss so many things. One thing I don't miss is being hungry, cold, and miserable. I have lots of warm, good clothes, too much to eat, especially milk to drink (imagine) – and cheese and more cheese.

I'd write a letter two thousand pages long if I didn't have so many chores to finish before bedtime. But don't worry, please don't. I'm fine, and we will meet again someday soon. I love you,

Your brother,
Tom

I sat thinking about Tom long after I finished the letter. I hid his letter with those from Logan. Had Kitty somehow kept Tom's letters from me? That wasn't really possible since I was home every day while she worked, and I brought in the mail almost every day. I stared around my cluttered room, knowing Kitty had been in here and moved things about. It wasn't really my room as long as Kitty kept her 'things' locked behind those cabinet doors, and obviously she checked over all my belongings. Her huge pottery wheel was shoved into a corner, and she had shelves everywhere filled with little knick knacks where my books would have fitted nicely. Kitty had no use for books on her shelves. I sat down at my small desk and began to answer Tom's letter. All the lies I'd told Logan would also convince Tom that Kitty was an angelic mother, the best ever . . . but I didn't have to tell lies about Cal, who was the best father possible.

He's truly wonderful, Tom. Every time I look at him, I think to myself, that's how Pa should have been. It feels so good to know that at last I have a real father I can love, who loves me. So stop worrying about me.

And don't forget one day you're going to be president – and not of a dairy firm either.

Now that I'd heard from Tom, and knew Our Jane and Keith were happy, and Logan wrote that Fanny was having the time of her life – so what did I have to worry about? Nothing. Nothing at all . . .

Fifteen

Heartthrobs

Early-morning light in the city found me awake about six, when once I'd risen at dawn to begin my day. Downstairs in the second bath I took a quick shower, put on clean clothes, and began breakfast. I was looking forward to returning to school and renewing my neglected friendships. Unknown to Kitty, I had a brand-new outfiit that fit perfectly. Cal had paid far too much for it, but I wore it with so much pride. I saw the boys staring at me with ten times more interest now that my figure wasn't hidden by loose fabric. For the first time in my life I began to feel some of the power that women had over the opposite sex, just from being female, and pretty.

I could lose myself in class listening to the teacher talk about monumental people who left their marks on history. Did historians skip over character faults, just to inspire students like me to always strive harder? Would I leave my mark? Would Tom? Why did I feel so driven to prove myself? Miss Deale had always made the people in the past seem human, fallible, and that had given both Tom and me hope.

I made new friends who didn't understand, as my old friends hadn't, why I couldn't invite them home. 'What's she like, that mother? Boy, she sure is stacked. And your father – wow! What a man!'

'Isn't he wonderful?' I said with pride. Funny the way they looked at me. The teachers treated me with special consideration, as if Kitty had told them I was a dimwit hill girl who couldn't have much sense. I studied like crazy to prove her wrong, and soon enough I earned the teacher's respect. I was especially good at typing. I spent hours and hours typing letters – when Kitty wasn't home. When she was, the clickety-clack of the typewriter made her head ache. Everything made Kitty's head ache.

Cal saw to it that I had dozens of pretty dresses, skirts and blouses, trousers, shorts, swimsuits, clothes that Cal and I selected when we went shopping in Atlanta, clothes that he kept locked in one of his basement lockers that Kitty thought held only dangerous tools. Kitty feared his electronic equipment almost as much as she feared insects. In a small hall cupboard meant for storing cleaning equipment, my too-large ugly dresses, selected by Kitty, hung with the vacuum cleaner, the mops, brooms, pails, and other clutter. There was a wardrobe in my bedroom, but that was kept locked.

Even though I had the clothes, I still had to decline the invitations that came my way, knowing I had to scurry home and finish cleaning that white house that needed so much everlasting care. Housework was robbing me of my youth. I resented the hundreds of houseplants that needed so much attention; resented the ornate elephant tables with their silly fake jewels that had to be carefully washed and polished. If there was only one tabletop which wasn't cluttered, I could have made one clean swipe with my dustcloth, but I had to lift and move, shift and be careful not to scratch the wood; then run to fold Kitty's underwear, hang her dresses, blouses, put the towels in the linen cupboard and be sure only the folded ends showed in front. A thousand rules Kitty had to keep her house a display piece. And only her 'girls' ever came to admire it.

Saturday afternoons more than made up for all the abuses Kitty felt were my due. The hard, brutal slaps that came so readily over any trifling mistake, the cruel words meant to destroy my self-confidence, were more than paid for by the films, by delicious restaurant meals, by trips to amusement parks when the days weren't rainy or cold. In the park Cal and I threw peanuts to the elephants, and scattered corn to the wild ducks, swans, and geese that came running up from the zoo lake. I'd always had a way with animals, and Cal was charmed with my ability to 'talk' to chickens, ducks, geese, even elephants.

'What's your secret?' he teased when I had a wild-looking zebra nuzzling in my cupped palm looking for treats. 'They don't come running to me as they run to you.'

'I don't know,' I answered with a small, wistful smile, for Tom used to ask the same thing. 'I like them, and maybe they can tell in some mysterious way.' Then I told him about the days of stealing, when certain farmer's dogs hadn't been charmed with my abilities.

Real autumn came with brisk cold winds to blow away the leaves, and wistful thoughts of the hills and Grandpa kept coming back. A letter from Logan had given me the address of where Pa had put him, and that was enough for me to write Grandpa. He couldn't read, but I thought someone might read my letter to him. I wondered if Fanny ever visited him, if Pa went to Winnerrow now and then to visit her and his father. I wondered so many things I sometimes walked around in a daze, as if the best part of me were still in the Willies.

I planted tulips, daffodils, iris, crocus, all with Cal's help, as Kitty sat in the shade supervising. 'Do it right. Don't ya mess up my six hundred dollars' worth of Dutch bulbs. Don't ya dare, hill scum.'

'Kitty, if you call her that again, I'll dump all these worms we've dug up in your lap,' Cal threatened.

Instantly she was on her feet and running into the house, making both Cal and me laugh as our eyes met. With his gloved hand, he reached out and touched my face. 'Why aren't you afraid of worms, roaches, spiders? Do you speak their language, too?'

'Nope. I hate all those things as much as Kitty does, but they don't scare me nearly as much as she does.'

'Do I have your promise you will call me at work if things get rough here? Don't you allow her to do one more thing to you – do I have that promise?'

I nodded, and for a brief moment he held me tight against him, and I could hear the loud thumping of his heart. Then I glanced up and saw Kitty at the window staring out at us.

Pulling away, I tried to pretend he'd only been comforting my wounded hand . . . .

'She's watching us, Cal.'

'I don't care.'

'I do. I can call you, but it takes time for you to drive home, and by that time she could peel the skin from my back.'

For the longest time he stared at me, as if all along he'd not believed she was capable of that, and now he did. The shock was still in his eyes when we put our gardening tools away and entered the house to find Kitty asleep in a chair.

Then came the nights. Eventually I didn't have to try not to listen, for eventually Cal stopped making any attempts to reason with Kitty, and stopped kissing her passionately, only gave her pecks on her cheek, as if he no longer desired her. I felt his inner rage and frustration building, too. Along with mine.

On Thanksgiving Day, I roasted my first shop-bought turkey so Kitty could invite all her 'girls' and brag about her cooking. 'Weren't nothing to it,' she said over and over again when they praised all her housekeeping and cooking skills. ' – and I've got so little time, too. Heaven helps some,' she admitted generously as I waited on the table, 'but ya know how young gals are . . . lazy, and interested in nothing but boys.'

Christmas came with stingy gifts from Kitty, and expensive secret gifts from Cal. He and Kitty attended many a party, leaving me home to watch TV. It was only then that I learned that Kitty had a drinking problem. One drink started off a chain reaction so she'd have to drink more, more, more, and many a time Cal had to carry her in the door, undress her, and put her to bed, sometimes with my help.

It felt odd to undress a helpless woman with the help of her husband, an intimacy that left me feeling uneasy. Still, an unspoken but strong bond united Cal and me. Cal's eyes would meet mine . . . mine would meet his. He loved me, I knew he loved me . . . and at night when I snuggled down in my bed, I felt his protective presence guarding my sleep.

One fine Saturday in late February, he and I celebrated my sixteenth birthday. For one year and more than one month I'd been living with him and Kitty. I knew Cal wasn't quite like a real father, nor quite like an uncle, nor quite like any man I'd ever known. He was someone who needed a friend and family to love as badly as I did, and he was settling for the closest, the most available female. He never scolded or criticized me, never spoke harshly to me as Kitty usually did.

We were friends, Cal and I. I knew I loved him. He gave me what I'd never had before, a man who loved me, who needed me, who understood me, and for him I would gladly have died.

He bought me nylons and high-heeled shoes for birthday gifts, and when Kitty wasn't home. I practised wearing them. It was like learning to walk all over again on longer, newer legs. With nylons on, and high heels, I was very conscious of my legs, thinking they looked great, and unconsciously I'd stick them out so everyone could admire them. It made Cal laugh. Of course, I had to hide the shoes and nylons along with all my other new clothes down in the basement where Kitty never went alone.

Spring came quickly to Atlanta. Because of all the effort Cal and I had put into the yard, we had the most spectacular garden in Candlewick. A garden that Kitty couldn't enjoy because honeybees hovered over the flowers, and ants crawled on the ground, and inchworms swung from fine gossamer threads to catch in your hair. Once Kitty almost broke her neck brushing one from her shoulder, screaming all the while.

Kitty was afraid of dim places where spiders or cockroaches might hide. Ants on the ground sent her into panic; ants in the kitchen almost gave her heart attacks. A fly on her arm made her scream, and if a mosquito was in the bedroom she didn't sleep a wink, only kept us all up, complaining about the buzzing of that 'damned thing!'

Afraid of the dark, was Kitty. Afraid of worms, dirt, dust, germs, diseases, a thousand things that I never gave a thought to.

When Kitty grew too overbearing with her demands, I escaped to my room, threw myself down, and reached for a book brought home from the school library . . . and lost myself in the world of *Jane Eyre*, or *Wuthering Heights*. Over and over I read those two books before I went to the library and hunted up a biography of the Brontë sisters.

Bit by bit I was edging back Kitty's parade of tiny ceramics with my treasured collection of books. I'd brought the doll up from the basement, and every day I took her out of the bottom dresser drawer and stared into her pretty face, determined one day to find my mother's parents.

Once in a while I even wore a few of my mother's clothes, but they were old, frail, and I decided it was better to leave them stretched out as flat as possible, and save them for the day when I went to Boston.

Tom wrote long letters, and Logan wrote now and then, hardly telling me anything. Still I kept writing to Fanny, even if she didn't respond. My world was so tight, so restricted, I began to feel strangely out of touch with everyone . . . everyone but Cal.

Yet in many ways my life had become easier. Housework that had terrified me once with all its complexities of instructions was no longer so overwhelming. I could have been born with a blender in one hand and a vacuum in the other. Electricity was part of my life now, and honestly, it seemed it always had been. Every day Cal seemed more and more my saviour, my friend, my companion, and my confidant. He was my tutor, my father, my date to the cinema and restaurants; he had to be now that the boys in the school had stopped asking me to dances and movies. How could I leave him alone when once he had said: 'Heaven, if you have cinema dates who will I go with? Kitty hates films, and I enjoy them, and she hates the kind of restaurants I like. Please don't abandon me in favour of kids who won't appreciate you as I do . . . allow me to take you to the cinema. You don't need them, do you?'

How guilty that question made me feel, as if I were betraying him even to think about having a date. I tried many a time to think that Logan was faithful to me, as I was to him . . . and yet I couldn't help but wonder – was he? After a while I just stopped looking at boys, knowing better than to encourage them and perhaps alienate the only truly dependable friend I had.

To please Cal, I did as he wanted, went where he wanted, wore what he wanted, styled my hair to please him. And all the time my resentment against Kitty grew and grew. Because of her he was turning to me. He was wonderful, and yet it made me feel strange, guilty, especially when that odd burning look came into his eyes, as if he liked me so much – perhaps too much.

My school chums began to look at me in odd ways. Did they know Cal took me out? 'You got a boyfriend on the outside?' asked Florence, my best chum. 'Tell me about him – do you let him, you know, go all the way?'

'No!' I stormed. 'Besides, there isn't anyone.'

'There is too! I can tell from your blush!'

Had I blushed?

I went home to dust and vacuum to water the hundreds of plants, to do endless chores, and all the time I thought about why I'd blushed. There was something exciting going on in my body, waking it up, sending unexpected thrills to my groin at the most unexpected moments. Once I glimpsed my-self in the bathroom mirror, wearing nothing but a bikini bra and panties, and that alone sent a sexual thrill through me. It scared me and made me feel unwholesome that I could be thrilled just to see myself scantily clad. I'd never have the enormous bosom Kitty was so proud of, but what I had seemed more than adequate. My waist had slimmed down to a mere twenty-two inches, though it seemed I'd never grow any taller than five feet six and a half. Tall enough, I told my-self. Plenty tall enough. I didn't want to be a giant like Kitty.

Months ahead of her dreaded thirty-seventh birthday, Kitty started staring at calendars, seeming so cursed by the onset of middle age that she sank into a state of deep depression. When Kitty was depressed, Cal and I had to mirror her feelings, or be accused of being insensitive and uncaring. He was wild with frustration from wanting her all the time, as she provoked and teased him and then yelled, 'No, no, no! another time . . . tomorrow night . . .'

'Why don't you tell me never, for that's what you mean!' he shouted. He stalked off, down to the basement to whirr his electrical saw, to do damage to something instead of to her.

I followed Kitty into her bathroom, hoping I could talk as one woman to another, but she was preoccupied with staring into the mirror. 'Hate getting old,' she moaned, peering closer into a hand mirror, while the theatrical lights all around showed every tiny line she considered very noticeable.

'I don't see any crows-feet, Mother,' I said quite honestly, liking her much better now that she was acting more or less like a normal human being. If sometimes I slipped up and called her Kitty, she didn't demand that I correct myself. Still, I was warily suspicious, wondering why she didn't demand my respect as she had before.

'Got to go home soon,' she murmered, staring more intensely into the mirror. 'Ain't right to Cal what I'm doing.' She grinned broadly to see all her teeth, checking for yellow, for bad gums, going over her hair carefully looking for grey. 'Gotta put my feet on home ground – let them all back there see me again while I still look good. Looks don't last forever like I used to think they would. When I was your age, I thought I'd never grow old. Didn't worry about wrinkles back then; now all I do is think about them, look to find em.'

'You look too closely,' I said, feeling sorry for her. I also felt edgy, as I always felt when I was shut up in a room alone with her. 'I think you look ten years younger than your actual age.'

'But that don't make me look younger than Cal, do it?' she shouted with bitterness. 'Compared to me, he looks like a kid.'

It was true. Cal did look younger than Kitty.

Later that same day, when we were eating in the kitchen, Kitty again spoke mournfully about her age. 'When I was younger, used to be the best-looking gal in town. I was, wasn't I, Cal?'

'Yes,' he agreed, forking into the apple pie with a great deal of enthusiasm. I'd studied cookbooks for months just to make him his favourite dessert. 'You certainly were the best-looking girl in town.'

How did he know? He hadn't known her then.

'Saw a grey hair in my eyebrow this morning,' Kitty moaned. 'Don't feel good about myself no more, don't.'

'You look great, Kitty, absolutely great,' he said, not even looking at her.

How terrible she was making middle age seem even before she got there. Truthfully, when Kitty was all dressed up, with her makeup, she was a magnificent-looking woman. If only she could act as pretty as she could look.

I'd been with Kitty and Cal for two years and two months when she informed me: 'Soon as ya finish school this June we'll be heading back to Winnerrow.'

It thrilled me to think of going back where I happily anticipated seeing Grandpa again, and Fanny. And the prospect of meeting the strange, cruel parents of Kitty intrigued me. She hated them. They had made her what she was (according to Cal), and yet she was going back to stay in their home.

In April Kitty came from a shopping trip bearing gifts for me – dresses that fitted this time, expensive dresses from an exclusive shop, and this time she allowed me to select really pretty new shoes, pink, blue, and white, a pair to match each dress.

'Don't want my folks thinking I don't treat ya right.

Buying them early, for the best is all picked over. Shops rush summer at ya in winter, shove winter at ya in summer; ya got to move quick or be left out altogether.'

For some reason her words took the thrill away from the beautiful clothes that were bought only to prove something to parents Kitty said she hated.

Days later, Kitty took me to her beauty salon in the big hotel for the second time, and introduced me to her new 'girls' as her daughter. She seemed very proud of me. The shop was larger, more elaborate, with crystal chandeliers, and hidden lights to make everything sparkle. She had European ladies who gave facials in tiny cubicles, using magnifying optical glasses through which the specialists could peer and find even the smallest flaws in her clients' complexions.

Kitty put me in a pink leather chair that raised and lowered, tilted back, and swivelled, and for the first time in my life I had a professional shampoo, trim, and set. I sat there with the plastic apron about my neck and shoulders, staring into the wide mirror, scared to death when Kitty came in to inspect me that she'd say I looked horrible, and pick up the shears and make my hair even shorter. I sat tense and ready to jump from the chair if she chopped off too much. All eight of her 'girls' stood around to admire Kitty's artistry with hair. She didn't hack it up. She carefully layered, snipped, and when she was done, she stood back and smiled at all her 'girls.'

'Didn't I tell ya my daughter is a beauty? Ain't I done improved on nature? Hey, ya, Barbsie, ya saw her when she first came – ain't she done improved? Can't ya tell she's been fed right, treated good? She's my own kid, and mothers like me shouldn't brag about their own, but just can't help it when she's so beautiful – and mine, all mine.'

'Kitty,' said the oldest of her girls, a woman about forty, 'I didn't know you had a child.'

'Didn't want any of ya to disrespect me for marrying so young.' Kitty said with the sincerity of truth. 'She's not

Cal's, but don't she look like him, though, don't she?'

No, I didn't look like him. I took offence, and added another block to my tower of resentments that was bound to topple one day.

I could tell from all the faces of her girls they didn't believe her, yet she went on insisting I was hers, even when she'd told them differently before. Later, when I had the chance, I told Cal about that. He frowned and looked unhappy.

'She's slipping, Heaven. Living a fantasy life. Pretending you are the baby she destroyed. That baby would have been only a little older if she hadn't aborted it. Be careful to do nothing to set her off . . . for Lord knows she's unpredictable.'

Like a time bomb with a long fuse . . .

Waiting for my match.

However, when Kitty improved my looks, I was childishly overwhelmed with gratitude, as I was for the least kind thing she did for me. I took all her small deeds and treasured them as if I had precious jewels to keep me forever safe. For each kindness, I took off a heavy block of hostility, and yet the very next word she said could make my tower even higher.

I woke up with what I thought was a brilliant idea. I would do something wonderful for Kitty – perhaps just to hide the resentment I felt growing day by day. Now that she wasn't awful, I feared her even more. There was something in her eyes, those pale, more than strange eyes.

Cal called early the morning we planned to surprise Kitty with a spring party. 'Isn't it too much work? We can't really keep in a surprise,' he added with some exasperation. 'She doesn't like surprises. I'll have to tell her. If she comes home with a hair out of place, or chipped fingernail polish, she'd never forgive me, or you. She'll want to look perfect, and wear her best dress, and have her hair done – so have the house spotless, and maybe then she'll feel pleased to show off.'

He made out the guest list, including all Kitty's girls and their husbands, and her ceramic students (which included both sexes) and their spouses. He'd even given me one hundred dollars so I could buy Kitty a gift I choose myself. A hot pink leather handbag that cost sixty-five dollars had been my choice. With the money left I purchased party decorations . . . wasting money, Kitty would say later on, but I dared her wrath anyway.

Cal called the afternoon of the party, which we thought could be a kind of graduation party for her students. 'Look, Heaven, don't bother making a cake. I can buy one at the bakery, and it won't be so much trouble.

'Oh, no,' I said quickly. 'Bakery cakes aren't nearly as tasty as a cake made from scratch, and you know how she's always talking about her mother's cakes, and how difficult cakes are to make right. She mocks my cooking, and baking a cake will have to prove something, won't it? Besides, I've already baked one. You won't believe your eyes when you see all the sweet pink roses and little green leaves I put on the top and sides. If I say so myself, it's the most beautiful-looking cake I've ever seen – and also the first one I've seen that I can eat.' I sighed because I'd never had a party of my own, with guests; none of us had, back in the Willies. Even our birthdays had been celebrated by staring in Winnerrow shop windows at cakes probably made of cardboard. I sighed as I admired the lovely cake. 'I just hope it'll taste as wonderful as it looks.'

He laughed, assured me it would be delicious, and we both hung up.

The party was to begin at eight. Cal would eat in town, as would Kitty, who would then rush home to dress for her 'surprise' party.

In my own room I took out my mother's bride doll, sat her on my bed so she could watch as I began to undress, pulling over my head a wonderful dress of cornflower-blue georgette. To me the doll represented my mother, and through those glassy eyes the soul of my mother was looking at me with admiration, love, and understanding. I found myself talking to the doll as I brushed my hair and arranged it in a new style which was more adult. Along with pretty new shoes and stockings, the dress had been a gift from Cal on my seventeenth birthday.

By six o'clock I was ready for the party. I felt silly to be ready so early, like a child who just couldn't wait to dress up. Once more I checked over the house. I'd strung gay paper ribbons from the dining-room chandelier, and Cal had hung balloons after Kitty had left this morning. How festive the house looked; yet I grew tired when there was nothing left to do but sit and wait for guests to arrive. In my room again I stared out the window. The early evening grew darker exceptionally quickly as strorm clouds gathered overhead, blackening the sunset. Soon a light rain was falling. Rainy days always made me sleepy. I carefully lay on my bed, spreading my skirt so it wouldn't wrinkle, and then cuddled my bride doll in my arms, and I easily slid into sweet dreams of my mother.

She and I were running in the hills, she with her shining pale hair, me with my long dark hair – then I had her colour of hair and she had mine, and I didn't know who I was. We laughed in the silent way of dreams . . . and froze in a time frame . . . froze, froze . . .

I bolted wide awake. Seeing first the bulging yellow eyes of another green frog planter. What had awakened me? I rolled my eyes without turning my head. That golden fish? That elephant table that wasn't as perfect as some downstairs? All the junk went into my room, those ceramics not fit to be seen or sold. Why did everything have its glassy stare fixed on me?

A loud roll of thunder rumbled overhead. Almost immediately a bolt of lightning zigzagged through the room. I hugged my doll closer.

Abruptly the sky opened. It wasn't a pleasant summer drizzle that fell. I sat up and peered out of the blurry window to see the street below was flooded, the houses across the street out of focus and distant-appearing, as if they were in another world. Again I curled up on my bed, forgetful of my beautiful georgette dress. With my 'mother' doll in my arms, I drifted off again.

The rain was a loud, drumming sound, shutting out all other noise. The thunder overhead rumbled like those fabled giant bowlingballs heard by Rip Van Winkle, all rolling at once, colliding in thundering crashes, creating fierce electrical bolts that lit up the darkness every few seconds. Like a magic movie director I fitted all nature's noises into my dream scenes . . .

In the misty dream more beautiful than reality, Logan and I were dancing in a forest green and shadowy. He was older, so was I . . . something was building between us, some electrical excitement that made my heart beat faster, louder . . .

Out of the dark loomed a figure, not in misty white like a ghost, but in hot pink. Kitty!

I sat up, rubbed my eyes.

'Well . . .' drawled Kitty's deadliest flat voice when the thunder stilled momentarily, 'looky what hill-scum crud is doing now. All dressed up and on the bed.'

What was I doing so terrible that Kitty would look like the wrath of God come to end the world?

'Do ya hear me, idiot?'

This time I jerked as if slapped. How could she treat me like this when I'd slaved all day to make a party for her? Enough! I'd had enough! I was tired, at last, of being called so many ugly names, sick and tired and fed up. This time I wasn't going to be cowed, or weak. No! I wasn't hill-scum crud!

My rebellion rose lie a giant fire – maybe because she glared at me so hard, and that reminded me of all the times she'd slapped without cause. 'Yeah, I hear you, big mouth!'

'What's that ya said?'

'I said, big mouth, I hear you!'

'What?' Louder now, more demanding.

'Kitty big mouth. Kitty loud mouth. Kitty who yells *No* every night to her husband so I have to hear it. What's wrong with you, Kitty? Have you lost your sexual appetite now that you're growing old?'

She didn't hear me. She was distracted by what I held in my arms. 'What the hell ya got there? Caught ya, didn't I? Lying there on yer side, like I ain't done told ya one million times not to do nasty stuff like that!'

She snatched the doll from my arms, quickly turned on all the lights in my room, and stared down at the doll. I jumped up to rescue my doll.

'It's her! HER!' she screamed, hurling my irreplaceable heirloom doll at the wall. 'Luke's *damned angel!*'

I scurried to pick up the doll, almost tripping because I forgot I was wearing high-heeled sandals. Oh, thank God she wasn't broken, only her bridal veil had fallen off.

'Give me that thing!' ordered Kitty, striding to take the doll from me. She was again distracted by my dress, her eyes raking down my length to see my nylons, my silver sandals. 'Where ya get that dress, them shoes?'

'I decorate cakes and sell them to neighbours for twenty dollars apiece!' I lied with flair, so angry that she would sling my doll at the wall and try to ruin the most precious thing I owned.

'Don't ya lie to me, and say stupid things like that! And give me that doll.'

'No! I will not give you this doll.'

She glared at me, dumbfounded that I would answer her back, and in her own tough tone of voice she said, 'Ya can't say no to me, hill scum, and hope to get by with it.'

'I just said no, Kitty, and I am getting by with it. You can't buffalo me anymore. I'm not afraid of you now. I'm older, bigger, stronger – and tougher. I'm not weak from lack of nourishing strength, so I do have that to thank you for, but don't you ever dare lay a hand on this doll again.'

'What would ya do if I did?' she asked in a low, dangerous voice.

The cruelty in her eyes stunned me so much I was speechless. She hadn't changed. All this time when I'd lived apparently in peace, she'd been brewing some kind of hatred inside her. Now it was out, spewing forth from her pale gimlet eyes.

'What's the matter, hill scum, can't ya hear?'

'Yeah, I hear you.'

'What did ya say?'

'I said, Kitty, yeah, I hear you.'

'What?' Louder now, more demanding.

Aggressively, no longer willing to play humble and helpless, I held my head high and proud, flaring back: 'You're not my mother, Kitty Setterton Dennison! I don't have to call you Mother. Kitty is good enough. I've tried hard to love you, and forget all the awful things you've done to me, but I'm not trying anymore. You can't be human and nice for but a little while, can you? And I was stupid enough to plan a party, just to please you, and give you a reason for having all that china and crystal . . . but the storm is on, and so are you, because you just don't know how to act like a mother. Now it's ugly, mean time again. I can see it in your watery eyes that glow in the darkness of this room. No wonder God didn't allow you to have children, Kitty Dennison. *God knew better*.'

A lightning flash lit up Kitty's pale face which had gone dead white as the lights flickered on and off. She spoke in short gasps. 'I come home to fix myself up for the party – and what do I find but a lying, tricky, nasty-minded bit of hill scum filth who don't appreciate anything I've done?'

'I do appreciate all the good things that you've done, that's what this party is all about, but you take away my good feelings when you hit out at me. You try to destroy what belongs to me, while I do all I can to protect what belongs to you. You've done enough harm to me to last a lifetime, Kitty Dennison! I haven't done anything to deserve your punishment. Everybody sleeps on their sides, on their stomachs – and no one thinks it is sinful but you. Who told you the right and wrong positions for sleeping? God?'

'Ya don't talk to me like that when yer in my house!' Kitty

screamed, livid with rage. 'Saw ya, I did. Breaking my rules, ya were. Ya knows ya ain't supposed to sleep on yer side hugging anything . . . and ya went and done it anyway. Ya did!'

'And what is so bad about sleeping on my side? Tell me! I'm dying to know! It must be tied up somehow to your childhood, and what was done to you!' My tone was as hard as hers, aggressive too.

'Smartmouth, ain't ya?' she fired back. 'Think yer better than me, because ya gets A's in school. Spend my good money dressing ya up, and what for? What ya planning on doing? Ya ain't got no talents. Can't half cook. Don't know nothing about cleaning house, keeping things looking pretty – but ya think yer better than me because I didn't go no higher than the fifth class. Cal done told ya all about me, ain't he?'

'Cal's told me nothing of the kind, and if you didn't finish school I'm sure it was because you couldn't wait to sleep with some man, and run off with the first one who asked you to marry him – like *all* hill scum girls do. Even if you did grow up in Winnerrow, you're not one whit better than any scumbag hill-crud girl.'

It was Kitty's fault, not mine, that Cal was beginning to look at me in ways that made me uneasy, forgetting he was supposed to be my father, my champion. Kitty's fault. My rage grew by leaps and bounds that she would steal from me the one man who'd given me what I needed most – a real father. Yet it was she who found her voice first.

'He told ya! I know he did, didn't he?' she screamed, high and shrill. 'Ya done talked about me to my own husband, told him lies, made him so he don't love me like he used to!'

'We don't talk about you. That's too boring. We try to pretend you don't exist, that's all.'

Then I threw on more fuel, thinking that I'd already started the blaze, so I might as well heap on all the rotten wood I had been saving since the day I came. Not one harsh word she'd said had been forgotten or forgiven, not one slap, one bloody nose or black eye . . . all had been stored to explode now.

'Kitty, I'm never going to call you Mother again, because you never were and never will be my mother. You're Kitty the hairdresser. Kitty the fake ceramic teacher.' I spun around on the heel of one silver slipper and pointed at the line of wall cabinets. And I laughed, really laughed, as if I enjoyed this, but I wasn't enjoying myself, only putting on a false front of bravado.

'Behind those locked cupboard doors you've got professional moulds, Kitty, thousands of *bought* moulds! With shipping labels still on the boxes they came in. You don't create any of these animals! You buy the moulds, pour in the clay slip – and you display them and label them as one of a kind, and that's fraud. You could be sued.'

Kitty grew unnaturally quiet.

That should have warned me to shut up, but I had years of frustrated rage locked up within, and so I spewed it out, as if Kitty were a combination of Pa and everything else that had managed to spoil by life.

'Cal told ya that,' came Kitty's deadly flat statement. '*Cal . . . betrayed . . . me.*'

'Nope.' I reached for a drawer in my desk and pulled out a tiny brass key. 'I found this one day when I was cleaning in here, and just couldn't help opening the cabinets you always keep locked.'

Kitty smiled. Her smile couldn't have been sweeter.

'What do ya know about art, hill scum? I made the moulds. I sell the moulds to good customers – like myself. I keep them locked up so sneaks like ya won't steal my ideas.'

I didn't care.

Let the sky fall, let the rain swell the ocean, and wash over Candlewick, carry it to the bottom of the sea, to sleep forever next to lost Atlantis . . . what did I care? I could leave now that the weather was hot. I could hitchhike – who'd care? I'd live. I was tough. Somehow or other I'd make my way back to Winnerrow, and when I was there I'd tear Fanny away from Reverend Wise, find Tom, save Keith and Our Jane . . . for I'd thought of a way we could all survive.

To prove my strength, my determination, I turned and stuffed my doll far under the bed, then deliberately fell on the bed and curled up on my side, reaching for a pillow that I hugged tight against me. It hit me then – the thing I'd not thought of before – just what was the evil thing Kitty presumed I did. The girls in school talked about it sometimes, how they pleasured themselves, and foolishly I threw my leg over the pillow and began to rub against it.

I didn't do that more than two seconds.

Strong hands seized me under my armpits, and I was yanked from the bed. I screamed and tried to fight Kitty off, tried to twist around so my hands could rake Kitty's face or do some other damage that would force her to let me go. It was as if I were a struggling kitten in the jaws of a powerful tiger. I was carried and dragged down the stairs, into the dining room I'd made pretty with party decorations – she picked me up, plunked me down on the hard glass-top dining-room table.

'You're putting fingerprints on your clean tabletop,' I said sarcastically, idiotically dauntless in the face of the worst enemy I was ever likely to hve. 'I'm finished with shining your glass tabletops. Finished with cooking your meals. Finished with cleaning your stupid house that has too many gaudy animals in it.'

'Shut up!'

'I don't want to shut up! I'm going to have my say for once. I hate you, Kitty Dennison! And I could have loved you if you'd given me half a chance. I hate you for all you've done to me! You don't give anyone half a chance, not even your own husband. Once you have anybody loving you, you do something ugly so that person has to turn on you and see you for what you are – *insane!*'

'Shut up.' How calmly she said that this time. 'Don't ya move from that table. Ya sit there. Ya be there when I come back.'

Kitty disappeared.

I could run now. Flee out the door, say good-bye to this Candlewick house. On the motorway I could find a ride. But this morning's papers had spewed ugly photos on the front page. Two girls found raped and murdered alongside the freeway.

Swallowing, I sat frozen, snared by indecision, regretting, too late, all the things I'd said. Still . . . I wasn't going to be a coward and run. I was going to sit here, show her I wasn't afraid of anything she did – and what worse thing could she do?

Kitty came back, not carrying a whip, or a stick, or a can of Lysol to spray in my face. She carried only a thin long box of fireplace matches.

'Going home, back to Winnerrow for a visit,' said Kitty in her most fearsome monotone. 'Going so ya can see yer sister Fanny, and yer grandpa. So I can see my sister, Maisie, my brother, Danny. Goin' back to touch my roots again, renew my vows to never get like them. Gonna show ya off. Don't want ya looking ugly, like I might neglect ya. Ya've grown up prettier than I thought. Hill-scum boys will try and get ya. So I'm gonna save ya from yer worst self in a way that won't show. But ya'll know from this day on not to disobey me. Never again. And if ya ever want to find out where yer lil' sister Our Jane is, and what happened to that little boy named Keith, ya'll do as I say. I knows where they are, and who has them.'

'You know where they are, you really do?' I asked excitedly, forgetting all I'd said to anger Kitty.

'Does the sky know where the sun is? Does a tree know where to plant its roots? Of course I know. Ain't no secrets in Winnerrow, not when yer one of em . . . and they thinks I am.'

'Kitty, where are they, please tell me! I've got to find them before Our Jane and Keith forget who I am. Tell me! Please! I know I was ugly a moment ago, but you were, too. Please, Kitty.'

'Please what?'
Oh, my God!
I didn't want to say it. I wiggled about on the slippery tabletop, gripping the edge so hard that if it hadn't been bevelled the glass would have sliced off my fingers.
'You're not my mother.'
'Say it.'
'My real mother is dead, and Sarah was my stepmother for years and years . . .'
'Say it.'
'I'm sorry . . . Mother.'
'And what else?'
'You will tell me what you know about Keith and Our Jane?'
'Say it.'
'I'm sorry I said so many ugly things . . . Mother.'
'Saying sorry ain't enough.'
'What else can I say?'
'Ain't nothing ya can say. Not now. I seen ya doing it. I heard what ya said to me. Called me a fake. Called me a hill scumbag. Knew ya'd turn against me sooner or later, the minute I had my back turned ya'd do something nasty. Had to lay on yer side, wiggle round and round, and pleasure yerself, didn't ya? Then ya had to tell me off . . . and now I gotta do what I can to rid ya of evil.'
'And then you'll tell me where Keith and Our Jane are?'
'When I finish. When yer saved. Then . . . maybe.'
'Mother . . . why are you lighting the match? The lights have come back on. We don't need candles before it's really dark.'
'Go and get the doll.'
'Why?' I cried, desperate now.
'Don't ask why – just do as I say.'
'You'll tell me what you know about Keith and Our Jane?'
'Tell ya everything. Everything I know.'
She had one of the long matches lit now. 'Before it burns my fingers, fetch the doll.'

I ran, crying as I fell to my knees and reached under the bed and dragged out the doll that represented my dead mother, my young mother whose face I'd inherited. 'I'm sorry, Mother,' I cried, lavishing her hard face with kisses, and then I ran again. Two steps from the bottom I tripped and fell. I got up to limp as fast as I could toward Kitty, the pain in my ankle so terrible I felt like screaming.

Kitty stood near the living-room fireplace. 'Put her in there,' she ordered coldly, pointing to the andirons that held the iron gate. Logs were stacked there, kindling laid by Cal just for looks, for Kitty didn't like wood smoke dirtying and 'stinking up' her clean house.

'Please don't burn her, Ki – Mother . . .'

'Too late to make up for the harm ya done.'

'Please, Mother. I'm sorry. Don't hurt the doll. I don't have a photograph of my mother. I've never seen her. This is all I have.'

'Liar!'

'Mother . . . *she* couldn't help what my pa did. She's dead – you're still alive. You won in the end. You married Cal, and he's ten times the man my father is, or ever could be.'

'Put that nasty thing in there!' she commanded.

I stepped backward, causing her to step threateningly forward. 'If ya ever want to know where Keith and Our Jane is . . . ya have to give that hateful doll to me of yer own free will. Don't ya make me snatch it from ya – or ya'll never find yer lil' brother and sister.'

My own free will.

For Keith.

For Our Jane.

I handed her the doll.

I watched Kitty toss my beloved bride doll onto the grate. Tears streaked my face as I fell to my knees and bowed my head and said a silent prayer . . . as if my mother herself lay on her funeral pyre.

With horror I watched the fine lace dress with pearls and crystal beads burst into instant flame, the silvery-gold hair catching fire; the wonderfully alive-looking skin seemed to melt; two small licks of flames consumed the long, dark curling lashes.

'Now ya listen, scumbag,' said Kitty when it was over, and my irreplaceable portrait doll lay in ashes. 'Don't ya go telling Cal what I did. Ya smile, ya act happy when my guests show up. Stop that crying! It were only a doll! Only a doll!'

But that heap of ashes in the fireplace represented my mother, my claim to the future that should have been hers. How could I prove who I was, how, how?

Unable to refrain, I reached into the hot ashes and plucked from them a crystal bead that had rolled free from the hearth. It sparkled in my palm like a teardrop. My mother's tear. 'Oh, I hate you, Kitty, for doing this!' I sobbed. 'It wasn't necessary! I hate you so much I wish it had been you in the fire!'

She struck! Hard, brutally, over and over again until I was on the floor, and still she was slapping my face, slamming her fists into my stomach . . . and I blacked out.

Mercifully blacked out.

Sixteen

My Saviour, My Father

Shortly after the party was over and all Kitty's friends had gone, Cal found me lying face down on the floor in the room where I slept; no longer could I think of it as my room. He stood in the doorway silhouetted by the hall light behind him. I felt too sore and raw to move. My beautiful new dress was torn and dirty. And even though he was there I continued to lie in a crumpled heap and cry. It seemed I was always crying for what I'd had once and lost. My pride, my brothers and sisters, my mother – and her doll.

'What's wrong?' Cal asked, stepping into the room and falling down on his knees beside me. 'Where have you been? What's the matter?'

I cried on and on.

'Heaven darling, you've got to tell me! I tried to slip away from the party earlier, but Kitty clung to my arm like a burr. She kept saying you didn't feel well, that you were having cramps. Why are you on the floor? Where were you during the party?' He turned me over gently and gazed lovingly into my swollen and discoloured face before he stared at my torn dress and nylons full of runs. An expression of such rage flashed through his eyes it frightened me. 'Oh, my God,' he cried out, clenching his fists. 'I should have known! She's hurt you again, and I didn't save you from her! And that's why she treated me so possessively tonight! Tell me what happened,' he demanded again, reaching to cradle me in his arms.

'Go way,' I sobbed. 'Leave me alone. It's going to be all right. I'm not really hurt . . .'

I sought for the right words to soothe his anxiety and my own misery, which by this time I was thinking I'd brought on myself. Maybe I *was* hill-scum filth, and *did* deserve everything Kitty had done. My own fault. Pa couldn't love me. If your own father couldn't love you, who could? *Nobody* could love me. I was lost, all alone . . . and never would anybody love me, never love me enough.

'No, I won't go away.' He lightly touched my hair, his lips travelling all over my sore, puffy face. Perhaps he thought it was that way only from crying, not from a battering. There were no lights on for him to see well. Did he think his small kisses could ease the pain? Yet they did, a little. 'Does it hurt that much?' he asked with pity in his voice. He looked so sad, so loving.

His fingertips on my swollen eye were so tender. 'You look so beautiful lying here in my arms, with the moonlight on your face. You seem half a child, half a woman, older than sixteen, but still so young, so vulnerable and untouched.'

'Cal . . . do you still love her?'

'Who?'

'Kitty.'

He seemed dazed. 'Kitty? I don't want to talk about Kitty. I want to talk about you. About me.'

'Where's Kitty?'

'Her girlfriends,' he began in a mocking, sarcastic voice, 'decided that Kitty really needed a special gift.' He paused and smiled ironically. 'They've all gone to watch male strippers, and I was left here to sit with you.'

'As if I'm a baby . . . ?'

I stared at him with tears wetting my face. His smile grew tighter, more cynical. 'I'd rather be right where I am, with you, than any other place in the world. Tonight, with all those other people, drinking and eating, laughing over silly jokes, I realized something for the first time. I felt all alone because you weren't there.' His voice deepened. 'You came into my life, and truthfully I didn't want you. I didn't want to take on the role of father, even if Kitty did feel she had to be a mother. But now I'm so damned scared Kitty will hurt you in some horrible way. I've tried to be here as much as possible. And yet I haven't saved you from anything. Tell me what she did today.'

I could tell him. I could make him hate her. But I was scared, not only of Kitty but of him, a grown man who appeared at this very minute totally infatuated with a kid of sixteen. Limply I lay in his arms, completely exhausted, listening to his heart pound.

'Heaven, she slapped you, didn't she? She saw you wearing an expensive new dress and tried to tear it off, didn't she?' he asked in a voice thick with emotion. Deep in my own thoughts I didn't even notice that he'd raised my hand to press it against his heart. Beneath his shirt I could feel the steady heartbearts, thumping, making it seem I was already part of him. I wanted to speak and tell him I was almost his daughter, and he shouldn't be looking at me the way he was. But no one had ever looked at me with love before – love I had needed for so long. Why was it making me afraid of him?

He both comforted me and frightened me, made me feel good and made me feel guilty. I owed him so much, perhaps too much, and I didn't know what to do. A funny glazed look came into his eyes, as if I had unknowingly pushed some switch, perhaps because I lay so submissively in his embrace. Much to my surprise, his lips were making a trail all around my throat, savouring the taste and feel of my flesh. I shivered again, wanting to tell him to stop, afraid if I did he wouldn't love me. If I drove him away I wouldn't have anyone to protect me from Kitty, or to care any longer what happened to me . . . and so I didn't say stop.

I had journeyed away from tears into unknown territory, were I lay trapped, not knowing what to do, or what to feel . . . It wasn't wrong, was it, this sweet tenderness he showed when he brushed his lips over mine, gentle touching me as if afraid he'd frighten me with too bold an approach – and then I saw his face.

He was crying! 'I wish you weren't just a beautiful child. I wish you were older.'

Those tears glistening in his eyes filled my heart with pity for him. He was as trapped as I was, in debt to Kitty up to his hairline; he couldn't just walk out on all the effort and years of learning electronics. I couldn't pull away and slap his face when he'd given me the only kindness I'd ever had from a man, and saved me from a life that could have been so much worse here in Candlewick.

Still, I whispered, 'No,' but it didn't stop him from kissing where he wanted to kiss, or fondling where he wanted to fondle. I quivered all over, as if God above were looking down and condemning me to eternal hell, as Reverend Wise had said he would, and where Kitty reminded me every day that I was sure to go. It surprised me that he would want to nuzzle his face against my breasts while his tears poured like hot rain and he sobbed in my arms.

What had I done or said to make him think what he had to be thinking? Guilt and shame washed over me. Was I truly innately wicked, as Kitty was always saying? Why had I brought this on myself?

I wanted to cry out and tell him what Kitty had done, burned my mother's doll – but perhaps he'd think that a trivial, silly sorrow, to see a doll burned. And what were a few slaps when I'd endured so much more?

Save me, save me! I wanted to scream.

Don't do anything else to take away my pride, please, please! My body betrayed me. It felt good, what he was doing. It felt good to be held, rocked, cuddled and caressed. A precious thing he made me feel one second, an evil wicked thing the next. All my life long I'd been starved for hands that touched kindly, lovingly. All my life yearning for a father to love me.

'I love you,' he whispered, kissing my lips again, and I didn't ask how he loved me, as a daughter or as something more. I didn't want to know. Not now, when for the first time in my life I felt valuable, worthy enough for a fine man like him to love and desire . . . even if something deep within me was alarmed.

'How sweet and soft you are,' he murmured when he kissed my bared breasts.

I closed my eyes, tried to not think about what I was allowing him to do. Now he'd never leave me alone with Kitty. Now he'd find ways to keep me forever, and force Kitty to tell him wher Keith and Our Jane were.

Thank God caressing my thighs and abdomen and buttocks under my torn dress seemed to satisfy him enough. Perhaps because I began to talk, to make him remember who I was. In a burst of words I gushed it all out, about the doll, the burning, how Kitty had forced me by saying she knew where Keith and Our Jane were. 'Do you really think she does know?' I asked.

'I don't know what she knows,' he said shortly, bitterly, coming back to himself as the dazed look in his eyes went away. 'I don't know if she knows anything but how to be cruel.' He met my wide, frightened eyes. 'I'm sorry. I shouldn't be doing this. Forgive me for forgetting who you are, Heaven.'

I nodded, my heart pounding as I watched him take from his shirt pocket a tiny box wrapped in silver and tied with blue satin ribbon. He put it in my hand. 'I have a gift to congratulate you for being such a good student, and making me so proud of you, Heaven Leigh Casteel.' He opened the box and lifted the lid on the smaller black velvet box inside, which revealed a dainty gold watch. His eyes met mine, pleadingly. 'I know you're living for the day when you can escape this house, and Kitty, and me. So I give you a calendar watch, to count the days, hours, minutes, and seconds until you can find your brother and little sister. And I swear I'll do all I can to find out what Kitty knows. Please don't run from me.'

Truth was in his eyes. Love for me was there as well. I stared and stared, until finally I had to accept, and I held out my arm and allowed him to fasten the watch about my wrist.

'Naturally,' he said bitterly, 'you can't let Kitty see this watch.'

He leaned to kiss my forehead tenderly, cupping my face between his palms before he said, 'Forgive me for trespassing where I should never go. Sometimes I need someone so badly, and you're so sweet, so young and understanding, and as starved for affection as I am.'

He didn't notice that I'd sprained my ankle, since I took great pains to see that I didn't walk until he had left the room and my bedroom door was closed. I couldn't fall asleep. Cal was so close, dangerously close , and we were alone in the house. He was in the other room, a few feet away. Right through the walls I could almost sense his need for me, and my terrible fear that need would override his sense of decency made me get up, pull a robe over my nightgown, and painfully make my way down the stairs and into the living room, where I lay on the white sofa and waited for Kitty to come home.

All night long the rain was a steady drumming, slashing against the windowpanes, pelting the roof; rolling thunder and far-off flashes kept me always on edge. However, I had a purpose in mind. I meant to confront Kitty, and this time come out the winner. Somehow or other I had to force her to tell me where Keith and Our Jane were. I clutched in my hand a tiny crystal bead with a few threads of charred white lace I'd found in the fireplace. Yet as I sat there on her sofa, in her sparkling-clean white house, with her rainbowed creatures all around me, I felt outnumbered, overwhelmed. I fell into sleep and missed Kitty's stumbling steps when she came home, dead drunk.

Her loud voice coming from the bedroom woke me up.

'Done had me a good time!' Kitty bellowed. 'Best damned birthday ever! Gonna do it every year from now on – and ya can't stop me!'

'You may do as you damn well please,' answered Cal as I drifted nearer and nearer the stairs. 'I don't care anymore what you do, or what you say.'

'Then yer leaving me . . . are ya, are ya?'

'Yes, Kitty. I am leaving you,' he said, to my surprise and joy.

'Ya can't, ya know. Yer stuck with me. Once ya go, ya ain't got nothing. I'll take yer shop, and all these years ya done been married up to me go down the drain, and yer will be penniless again . . . unless ya go home to Mommy and Daddy and tell them what a damn fool ya are.'

'You do have a sweet and convincing way with words, Kitty.'

'I love ya. Ain't that all that counts?' Kitty said, her voice sounding suddenly vulnerable.

I stared upward, wondering what was happening. Was he stripping off her clothes, full of desire just because this time she was going to let him?

When I heard Cal in the downstairs bath the next morning, I got up and started breakfast. Cal was whistling. Was he happy now?

Kitty came from upstairs apparently a changed woman, smiling at me as if she hadn't burned my most beloved possession and punched me in the face. She didn't look to see the results of her fists, or see that I still limped.

'Why, honey baby,' she crooned, 'why'd ya stay upstairs during the party ya gave me, huh, why did ya? Missed ya, I did. Wanted ya there to show ya off to all my friends. Why, all the girls were dying to see ya, and ya were shy and didn't show up and let them see my pretty daughter who gets better looking every day. Really, honey doll, ya do gotta get used to monthly cramps, and forget all about them – or else yer never gonna enjoy being a woman.'

'You tell me where Keith and Our Jane are!' I shouted. 'You promised to tell me!'

'Why, honey, what ya talking about? How would *I* know?' She smiled, so help me, she smiled as if she'd competely forgotten all she'd done. Was she pretending? Oh, she had to be! She wasn't that crazy! Then came the more dreadful thought – maybe she really was insane!

Cal strode in and threw Kitty a look of disgust, though he didn't say anything. Behind her back his eyes met mine, sending me a silent warning. *Do nothing. Say nothing.* Let Kitty play her pretend game, and we'd play ours. A knot formed in the pit of my stomach. How could I live through day after day of this? My eyes lowered to watch the eggs sizzling in the pan.

It was May now, and the hustle and bustle of preparing for exams was in the air. I studied for hours on end so I'd gain good marks. Very late in the month, a weird kind of northeaster blew in and chased away spring warmth, and suddenly it was unseasonably cold. Furnaces that had been shut down in March were started up again. Sweaters put in mothballs came out with woollen skirts. On the coldest Friday in May I'd ever known, I stayed late for a conference with Mr Taylor, my biology teacher. He asked me if I'd please take our class hamster Chuckles, home for the weekend.

The dilemma I faced showed up clearly in my troubled expression as I stood by the hamster's large wire cage, wanting to shout out the truth about Kitty and her diabolical hatred of all living animals, when under any other circumstances I would have been delighted to be in charge of the pregnant hamster that was the biology-class pet.

'Oh, no,' I said quickly when he persisted. 'I've told you, Mr Taylor, my mother doesn't approve of pets in her house. They're messy, smelly, and she's always sniffing the air for odours she doesn't recognize.'

'Oh, come now, Heaven,' said Mr Taylor, 'you're exaggerating, I know you are. Your mother is a lovely, gracious woman, I can tell from the way she smiles at you.'

Yeah, how sweet and kind were the smiles of Kitty

Dennison. How dumb men could be, really. Even book-smart ones like Mr Taylor.

My teacher's voice took on a persuading tone while the wild northeast winds whipped around the school building, making me shiver even with heat on. On and on he wheedled: 'The city orders us to turn off the heat at weekends, and all the other students are gone. Do you want the poor little expectant mother to stay in a freezing room so we'll find her dead on Monday? Come, dear, share the responsibility of loving a pet . . . that's what love is all about, you know, responsibilities and caring.'

'But my mother hates animals,' I said in a weak voice, really wanting to have Chuckles for an entire weekend.

He must have seen some yearning in my expression, for he went on cajoling. 'Gets mighty cold in here,' he said, watching my face in a calculating way. 'Even if Chuckles has food and water, mighty cold for a wee, caged expectant mother.'

'But . . . but . . .'

'No buts. It's your duty. Your obligation. I'm leaving this weekend with my family or else I'd take Chuckles home with me. I could leave her in my home alone with plenty of food in her cage, and her bottle of water . . . but she might give birth any day. And I want you there with the movie camera I taught you how to use to show the class the miracle of birth, in case it happens while she's with you.'

And so I was persuaded against my better judgement, and in Kitty's spick-and-span white-and-pink house, among all the brilliant ceramic critters, tan-and-white Chuckles was established in the basement, a place Kitty never went now that she had a slave to do the clothes washing and drying.

However, Kitty was not in the least predictable. Her mood swings were startling, dramatic, and, most of all, dangerous. With much trepidation I bustled about making a clear and clean place, out of draughts, for the big cage. Under a sunny high window seemed to me just perfect. I found an old standing screen with its black lacquer peeling off, and I set it up. Now Chuckles would be protected not only from draughts but from Kitty's cruel, seawater eyes if ever she dared to enter the basement. There was absolutely no reason for her to come to where I had Chuckles cozily established against a distant wall. I felt only a small apprehension for Chuckles' safety.

'Now, you take it easy down here, Chuckles,' I warned the small animal, who sat up on her haunches and nibbled daintily on the slice of apple I gave her. 'Try not to use your treadmill so much. In your condition, you might overdo it.'

The darn wheel squeaked and squealed, and even after I took the wheel out and oiled the moving parts, it still made a certain amount of noise when I spun it with my fingers. Chuckles ran madly about in her cage, wanting her exercise wheel back. Once I put it back in the cage, Chuckles instantly jumped in and began to run in the wheel – it still squealed, but not very much.

Upstairs in the back hall I pressed my ear against the closed basement door. All was silent down there. I opened the door and listened. Still I couldn't hear anything. Good. I descended the stairs, five, six, then seven of them, paused to listen. Only then could I hear a faint sound . . . but it was all right. Kitty would never enter the basement alone, and she couldn't do anything if Cal was at his workbench. I had finished with the laundry, so why should she check?

In another few minutes I had a few old chairs put one on each side of the screen, so it wouldn't topple over and fall on the cage. I tested it, found it stable enough, and once more told Chuckles to be a good girl, '. . . and please don't have your babies before I have the camera set up and ready.'

Chuckles went right on spinning in the treadmill.

It was another of those strange evenings, with Kitty not working overtime as she used to do. There was a distraught look in her pale eyes. 'Got another migraine,' she complained in a whiny tone. 'Going to bed early,' she announced after an early supper. 'Don't want to hear the dishwasher going, ya hear? Makes the house vibrate. I'm gonna swallow some pills and sleep and sleep and sleep.'

Wonderful!

Saturday began like any other Saturday. Kitty got up grouchy, tired, rubbing at her puffy, reddened eyes, complaining of feeling drugged. 'Don't know if I can make it to my classes,' she mumbled at the breakfast table, while I dutifully tended to the sausages, browning them just right, with a bit of water added to keep them moist. 'All the time tired, I am. Life ain't good no more. Can't understand it.'

'Take the day off,' suggested Cal, unfolding the morning paper and beginning to read the headlines. 'Go back to bed and sleep until you can get up and not feel tired.'

'But I should go to my classes. Got my students waiting . . .'

'Kitty, you should go to a doctor.'

'Ya know I hate doctors!'

'Yes, I know, but when you have constant headaches that indicates trouble, or the need for eyeglasses.'

'Ya know I'm not gonna wear any damn spectacles and make myself look like an old lady!'

'You could wear contacts,' he said as if disgusted, and he glanced at me. 'I'll be working all day, until at least six. I just hired two new men who need training.' He was telling me not to expect too much in the way of entertainment tonight.

Kitty rubbed at her eyes again, staring at the plate I put before her as if she didn't recognize her favourite morning meal of sausages, fried eggs, and grits. 'Don't have no appetite for nothing . . .' She stood up, turned, saying she was going back to bed and sleep until she woke up without head pains. 'And ya can call and make my excuses.'

All morning I cleaned and scrubbed, and didn't hear or see Kitty. I ate lunch alone. In the afternoon I dusted, vacuumed downstairs, quickly saw to the needs of Chuckles, who very obviously didn't want me to go and leave her alone. She indicated this in playful, touching ways, sitting up and begging, acting up whenever I turned to leave. Oh, but for Kitty I'd bring Chuckles home every night, keep her in my room. 'It's all right, darling,' I said, scratching her soft, furry head, and that made her make soft sounds of contentment in her throat. 'You play as much as you want to. The demon in the house has drugged herself with Valium, and that keeps you safe, safe.'

Cal didn't take me to the cinema that Saturday; he and I watched television, neither one of us talking very much.

Sunday.

Kitty's loud singing woke me early.

'Feel good,' she shouted to Cal as I got up and quickly strode down the hall toward the stairs and the downstairs bath. 'Feel like going to church. Heaven,' she bellowed as she heard me pass her open door, 'get yer lazy butt down in the kitchen fast, and fix breakfast. We're going to church. All of us. Gonna sing praises to the Lord for chasing away my headaches . . .'

Why, she sounded just like her old self!

Feeling tired myself, burdened with too much to do, I dashed about trying to do everything before Kitty came down. I started for the bathroom to take a quick shower before I began breakfast. No, better to put the water on for the coffee first, and shower while it heated. After the shower, I'd check on Chuckles as the bacon fried slowly.

But someone had already put the water in the kettle, and it was hot and steaming. I headed for the bath, presuming Cal had been downstairs and was eager for his two cups of morning coffee.

My robe and nightgown I hung on a hook on back of the bathroom door, before I turned to step into the tub.

That's when I saw Chuckles!

Chuckles – in the tub – all bloody! A long string of

intestines spewed out of her mouth; her tiny babies strung out from the other end! I fell to my knees sobbing, heaving up the contents of an almost empty stomach so it splashed into the tub to blend with the blood and other sickening contents.

Behind me the door opened.

'Making a mess again, are ya?' asked a harsh voice from the doorway. 'Screaming and yelling like yer seeing something ya didn't expect. Now go on, take yer bath. Not gonna let no dirty hill-scum gal go into my church without a bath.'

Wide-eyed with horror, with hate, I stared at Kitty. '*You killed Chuckles!*'

'Are ya losing yer mind? I ain't killed no Chuckles. Don't even know what yer talking about.'

'Look in the tub!' I yelled.

'Don't see nothing,' said Kitty, staring directly at the pitiful dead animal and all the bloody mess there. 'Just use the plug and fill up while I watch. Ain't gonna take no hill filth into my church!'

'Cal,' I screamed as loud as possible. 'Help me!'

'Cal's in the shower,' said Kitty pleasantly, 'doing what he can to cleanse away his sins. Now ya do the same – cleanse yers!'

'You're crazy, really crazy!' I screamed.

Calmly Kitty began to fill the tub. I leaped to my feet and snatched for a towel to shield my nudity. And in reaching, I took eyes off of Kitty for one brief second.

Enough time. Like a baseball bat Kitty slung her stiffened arm so it struck and hurled me toward the tub. I stumbled, staggered off balance, and again Kitty moved, but this time I managed to dodge, and, screaming, I headed for the stairs, calling Cal's name as loudly as I could.

'Ya come back her and take yer bath!' shrieked Kitty.

I pounded on the door of the upstairs bath, screaming for Cal to hear me, but he was in there with the water going full blast, singing at the top of his voice, and he didn't hear. Any minute I expected Kitty to climb the stairs and force me to sit in that tub of filth and death. Daring embarrassment, I turned the knob on the door. Cal had locked it! Oh, damn, damn!

Sliding to the floor, I waited for him to come out. The minute he turned off the water I was up and calling again. Tentatively he cracked open the door, still dripping water from his hair, with a towel swathed about his hips. 'What's wrong?' he asked with great concern, drawing me into his arms and bowing his damp face into my hair as I clung to him for dear life. 'Why are you acting so frightened?'

I gushed it all out, Chuckles in the basement, how Kitty had used something to wrap about her middle and squeeze the life out of a harmless, helpless little creature.

His face turned grim as he released me and reached for his robe, and, with me in tow, headed for the downstairs bathroom. In the doorway I waited, unable to look at poor Chuckles again. Kitty had disappeared. 'There's nothing in the tub, Heaven,' he said, coming back to me. 'Clean as a whistle . . .'

I looked myself. It was true. The dead hamster and her young were gone. Sparkling-clean tub. Still wearing nothing but a towel, I tagged behind Cal to visit the basement. Empty cage with a wide-open door.

'What ya two doing down there?' called Kitty from above. 'Heaven, now ya take her shower, and hurry up. Don't wanna be late for church.'

'What did you do with Chuckles?' I shrieked when I was in the back hall.

'Ya mean that rat I killed? I threw it away. Did ya want to save it? Cal,' she said, turning to him and looking sweeter than sugar, 'she's mad because I killed a nasty old rat in the tub. And ya know I can't put up with filth like rats in my house.' Her deadly cold eyes riveted on me with warning.

'Go on, Heaven,' urged Cal. 'I'll talk to Kitty.'

I didn't want to go. I wanted to stay and fight it out, make Cal see Kitty for what she was, a psycho who should be locked up. Yet I felt too weak and sick to do more than obey. I showered, shampooed, even fixed breakfast, as Kitty protested over and over again, growing more and more vehement, that she'd never seen a hamster, didn't even know what one looked like, would never go alone into the basement no time, no how.

Her pale eyes swung to me. 'Hate ya for trying to turn my man against me! I'll go to the school authorities and tell them what ya did to that poor lil' critter – and trying to put the blame on me. It were yers, weren't it? I'd never do nothing so mean . . . ya did it just to blame me! Ya can stay here until ya finish school – then get out! Ya can go to hell for all I care.'

'Chuckles was pregnant, Kitty! Maybe that made her more than you could stand!'

'Cal, would ya hear this girl lie? I never saw no hamster – did ya?'

Could Cal believe I could do anything so horrible? No, no, his eyes kept saying. Let it pass this time, please, please.

Why didn't he look for evidence in the dustbin? Why didn't he come right out and accuse Kitty? Why, Cal, why?

The nightmare continued in the church.

Amazing grace . . .
How sweet the sound . . .

Everybody was singing reverently. How spaced out I felt standing beside Kitty, dressed in my best new clothes. We looked so fine, so respectably Christian and God-fearing, and all the time the memory of a dear, little, dead hamster was in my head. Who would believe me if I told?

Kitty dropped her tithe in the passed plate; so did Cal. I stared at the plate, then at the bland face of the deacon who passed it. I refused to put in one penny. 'Ya do it,' whispered

Kitty, giving me a sharp elbow nudge. 'Ain't gonna have no friends of mine thinking yer a heathen, an ungrateful for all yer blessings.'

I stood up and walked out of the church, hearing behind me all sorts of murmurs. Kitty's insanity was colouring everything, making me stare at people and wonder what they were really like inside.

Down the street I started walking fast, leaving Kitty and Cal still in the church. I hadn't gone two blocks before Cal's car was pulling up behind me, with Kitty leaning out to call, 'C'mon, kid, don't be silly. Ya can't go nowhere when ya ain't got more than two bucks – and that belongs to the Lord. Get in. Feeling better, I am. Mind's clear as a bell, though all night and all morning early it near gave me a fit.'

Was she trying to tell me she hadn't known what she was doing when she murdered Chuckles?

Reluctantly I got into the car. Where could I go with only two dollars in my purse?

All the way home from church I thought about what to do. She had felt she had to kill Chuckles. Only crazy people did sadistic things like that. And how was I ever going to find a reasonable excuse for Chuckles' death when next I saw Mr Taylor?

'You can't tell him,' said Cal when we had the chance to be alone, while Kitty was again sleeping to rid herself of a fresh assault of 'cluster headaches'. 'You've got to make it seem that Chuckles died in childbirth . . .'

'You're protecting her!' I cried angrily.

'I believe you, but I also want you to finish high school. Can you do that if we go now to the authorities and try to have her committed? She'll fight us. We'll have to prove her insane, and you know as well as I do that Kitty shows her worst self only to you and me. Her 'girls' think she's wonderful, generous, and self-sacrificing. Her minister adores her. We have to convince her to see a psychiatrist, for her own good. And, Heaven, we can play our own game until then, and in the meanwhile I'm putting away extra dollars so you'll have enough money to escape this hell-hole.'

I stepped to the door, then said in a calm voice, 'I'll help myself, in my own way, in my own time.'

He stood for a moment looking back, like a small boy who'd lost his way, before he closed another door, softly.

Seventeen

Saving Grace

Our lives in Candlewick took an unexpected turn after Chuckles died. Mr Taylor naively accepted my excuse about Chuckles dying in childbirth. One day passed, and in the cage I'd brought back there was another hamster, also pregnant (and little different from the one Kitty had killed), again named Chuckles. It hurt, really hurt, to see that one life more or less really didn't make any difference.

I'm not going to love this one, I told myself. I'm going to be careful not to love anything while Kitty is still in my life.

After this incident, as if the murder had done something to shame her spirit, Kitty slipped into a deep, prolonged silence, sitting for hours in her bedroom just staring into space and combing and brushing her hair, teasing it until she had it standing straight out like a wire brush; then she'd smooth it down again, and repeat and repeat the entire process until it was a wonder she had any hair left.

She seemed to have undergone a drastic personality change. From loud and abrasive she became brooding and too quiet, reminding me somewhat of Sarah. Soon she stopped brushing her hair and doing her nails and face. She no longer cared how she looked. I watched her throw out the best of her lingerie, including dozens of expensive bras. She cried, then fell into a dark pit of reflection. I told myself she deserved whatever she was going through.

For a week Kitty made excuses for not going to work, staying in bed, staring at nothing. The more Kitty withdrew the more Cal lost his abstract quality, forgot his moodiness, and took on a new, confident air. For the first time, he seemed in control of his life as Kitty gave up control in hers.

Strange, so strange, I couldn't stop wondering about what was going on. Could it be guilt, shame, and humiliation, so

Kitty didn't have the nerve to face another day? Oh, God, let her change for the better – for the better, Lord, for the better.

School ended, hot summer began.

Temperatures soared over ninety, and still Kitty was like a walking zombie. On the last Monday in June, I went to find out why Kitty wasn't up and ready to rule over her beauty-salon domain. I stared at Kitty lying on the bed, refusing to look my way or respond to her name. She lay there as if paralyzed. Cal must have thought she was still sleeping when he got up. He came from the kitchen when I called to tell him Kitty was desperately ill. He called an ambulance and had her rushed to the hospital.

At the hospital she was given every test known to medical science. That first night at home, alone with Cal, was very uncomfortable. I more than suspected Cal desired me, and wanted to be my lover. I could see it in the way he looked at me, feel it in the long, uncomfortable silences that came suddenly between us. Our easy relationship had flown, leaving me feeling empty, lost. I held him off by setting a daily routine that wore both of us out, insisting we spend every second we could with Kitty in her private room in the hospital. Every day I was there doing what I could, but Kitty didn't improve, except that she did begin to say a few words. 'Home,' she kept whispering, 'Wanna go home.'

Not yet, said her doctors.

Now the house was mine to do with as I pleased. I could throw out the hundreds of troublesome houseplants that were so much work, could put some of those gaudy ceramic pieces in the attic, but I did none of this. I carried on exactly as I'd been taught by Kitty, to cook, to clean, dust, and vacuum, even if it did wear me out. I knew I was redeeming my sinful acts with Cal by working slavishly. I blamed myself for making him desire me in a way that was not right, I was dirty, as Kitty had always said I was. The Casteel hill-scum filth coming out. And then, contrarily, I'd think, no! I was my mother's child, half Bostonian – but – but – and then I'd lose the battle.

I *was* the guilty one.

I was bringing this on myself just as Fanny couldn't help being what she was, I couldn't either.

Of course I'd known for a long time about Cal's smouldering passion for me, a girl twelve years younger than he, thrust at him in a thousand ways by Kitty herself. I didn't understand Kitty, probably never would, but since that horrible day when she burned my doll his need and desire had become ten times more intense. He didn't see other women, he didn't really have a wife, and certainly he was a normal man, needing release of some kind. If I kept rejecting him, would he turn from me and leave me totally alone? I both loved and feared him, wanted to please him and wanted to reject him.

Now he could take me out more often in the evenings, with Kitty in the hospital, the object of every medical test an army of doctors could dream up, and still they could find nothing wrong with her. And she'd say nothing to give them any clue to her mysterious ailment.

In a small hospital office, Kitty's team of doctors talked to Cal and me, seeking clues, and neither of us knew what to say.

All the way home from the hospital Cal didn't say a word. Nor did I. I felt his pain and his frustration, his loneliness – but for me. Both of us from different backgrounds, struggling to live with our battle scars delivered by Kitty. In the garage he let me out, and I ran for the stairs, for the safety of my room, where I undressed, put on a pretty nightie, and wished I could lock the door. No locks in Kitty's house, except in the bathrooms. Uneasily I lay on my bed, frightened that he'd come up, talk to me, force me . . . and I'd hate him then! Hate him as much as I hated Pa!

He did none of that.

I heard his stereo downstairs playing his kind of music, not Kitty's. Spanish music . . . was he dancing by himself? Pity overwhelmed me, a sense of guilt, too. I got up, pulled on a robe, and tentatively headed for the stairs, leaving an unfinished novel on my nightstand. It was the music that drew me irresistibly down the stairs, I kept telling myself.

Going nowhere in reality, poor Cal, marrying the first woman who appealed to him. Loving me was another mistake, I knew that. I pitied him, loved him, distrusted him. I felt choked with my own needs, my own guilts and fears.

He wasn't dancing alone, though the music played on and on. He was just standing and staring down at the Oriental rug, not seeing it, either, I could tell by the glaze in his eyes. I drifted through the door and stood beside him. He didn't turn to speak, to give any kind of sign that he knew I was there; he just continued to stare as if he were looking into all the tomorrows with Kitty as his wife, useless to him, except as a burden to care for. And he was only twenty-seven.

'What's that song you're playing?' I asked in a low, scared voice, forcing myself to touch his arm and give him comfort. He did better than just tell me, he sang the lyrics softly; and if I live to be two hundred and ten, I'll never forget the sweetness of that song and the way he looked at me when he sang the words about a stranger in paradise.

He took my hand in his, staring down into my eyes, his luminous and deep in a way I hadn't seen them before, appearing lit by the moon and stars, and something else, and in my mind I saw him as Logan, the perfect soul mate who would love me all the days of my life, as I wanted and needed to be loved.

I think the music got to me as much as his voice and his soft eyes, for somehow my arms stole up around his neck when I didn't send them there. I didn't wilfully place one hand on the back of his neck, my fingers curling into his hair, the other cupping his head to gently pull it down to where he could find my lips eagerly waiting for his kiss. No, it just happened. Not my fault, not his, either. Fault of the moonlight snared in his eyes, the music in the air, the sweetness of our lips meeting, all that made it happen.

His hand cupped my head, treasured it, slid down my back, shaping it to fit his need, and then it was on my hip, hesitating there before he moved it to caress my buttocks, fleetingly, lightly, his hand darting to briefly touch my breasts, discovering me again, trying to wake me up as his lips found mine.

I shoved him away.

'Stop!' I slapped his face. Cried out 'no, no!' and ran up the stairs, slamming my door behind me, wishing again it had a lock, wishing I had more of what came naturally to Fanny, and despising myself for even thinking that. For I loved him now.

Loved him so deeply, so much, it hurt to think of my hand striking his beloved face. A tease, the boys in Winnerrow would call me, or much worse. Cal, I'm sorry, I wanted to scream out. I wanted to go to him in his room, but I was held back by all the words Kitty had said to make me feel foul, unclean, unwholesome.

Again, some powerful force pulled me to the top of the stairs. I looked down. He was still there, glued like a statue to the floor in the living room, the same music still playing. I drifted down the stairs, caught up in some romantic notion of sacrificing myself to please him. He didn't turn or speak when I reached his side. My hand slid into his tentatively, tightened around his fingers. He failed to respond. I whispered, 'I'm sorry I slapped you.'

'Don't be. I deserved it.'

'You sound so bitter.'

'I'm just a fool standing here and thinking of my life, and all the stupid things I've done – and the dumbest of all was to allow myself to think you loved me. But you don't love me. You just want a father. I could hate Luke as much as you do for failing you when you needed him; then maybe you wouldn't be needing a father so much.'

Again my arms went around him. I tilted my head backward, closed my eyes, and waited for his kiss . . . and this time I wasn't going to run. It was wrong and I knew it, but I owed him so much, more than I could ever repay. I wasn't going to tease him, then scream no, as Kitty had been doing for years. I loved him. I needed him.

Not even when he swept me up and carried me into his room and laid me on his bed and began doing all those frightening wrong things did I realize what I'd started, and it was too late to stop him this time. His face was smeary with bliss, his eyes glazed, his actions making the bedsprings creak, and I was bounced, my breasts jiggling with the pure animal force of his lovemaking. So this was what it was all about. This thrusting in and out, this hot, searing pain that came and went – and if my conscious mind was shocked and didn't know how to respond, my unconscious physical side had innate knowledge, moving beneath his thrusts as if in other lives I'd done this ten thousand times with other men I'd loved. And when it was over, and he was curled up on his side holding me clutched tight in his embrace, I lay stunned with what I'd allowed him and myself to do. Tears were on my cheeks, streaming down to wet the pillow. Kitty had burned the best of me when she burned my doll in the fire.

She'd left only the dark side of the angel who went to the hills and died there.

He woke me up in the night with small kisses on my face, on my bared breasts, and asked his question. No, no, no, I could almost hear Kitty yelling, as she'd screamed at him so many times when he must have asked her the same thing. I nodded and reached for him, and again we joined as one. When we finished I, again, lay stunned and sickened by my actions, by my too-enthusiastic response. Hill-scum! I could hear Kitty shouting. Trashy no-good Casteel, I heard all of Winnerrow shouting. *Just what we expected from a Casteel, a no-good scumbag Casteel.*

The days and nights swiftly passed and I couldn't stop what had begun. Cal overrode all my objections, saying I was being silly to feel guilt or shame when Kitty was getting what she deserved, and I was doing no worse than many girls my age, and he loved me, really loved me, not like some rawboned boy who'd only use me. Nothing he said took away the shame, or the knowledge that what I was doing with him was wrong, totally wrong.

He had two weeks alone with me that seemed to make him very happy, as I pretended to have let go of my shame and guilt. Then one morning Cal drove off early to bring Kitty home. I had the house sparkling and filled with flowers. She lay on her bed blankly staring at all I'd done to make the house pretty, and she showed no signs of recognizing where she was. Home was where she'd said she wanted to be . . . perhaps just so she could pound on the floor overhead with a walking cane, and demand our attention. Oh, how I learned to hate the sound of that cane pounding on the floor that was the living-room ceiling.

Once every week one of Kitty's beauty-salon operators came and shampooed and set her red hair, gave her a manicure and a pedicure. I suspected Kitty was the best-looking invalid in town. At times I was touched by Kitty's helplessness, lying in her pretty pink nightclothes, her hair long and thick, and beautifully groomed. Her 'girls' seemed devoted to Kitty, coming often to sit, chat, and laugh while I served them treats I made on Kitty's best china, then raced about trying to keep the house clean, be a companion to Cal, and also keep his books and, using Kitty's chequebook, pay household bills.

'She wouldn't like me doing this,' I said with a worried frown, then chewed on the end of a ballpoint pen. 'You should be doing this, Cal.'

'I don't have time, Heaven.'

He took the stack of bills from the small desk that had been Kitty's and put them back in a filing cabinet. 'Look, it's a beautiful summer day, and it's been almost a month of constant caring for Kitty. We need to do some serious thinking about what to do with Kitty. Paying those nurses to help you is costing a fortune. And when you go back to school, I'll need another nurse . . . around-the-clock nursing. Have you heard from her mother yet?'

'I wrote and told her Kitty was very ill. But she hasn't replied yet.'

'Okay . . . when she does, I'll call and talk to her. She owes Kitty a great deal. And perhaps before school starts, we can work out some permanent solution.' He sighed and glanced at Kitty before he said, 'At least she does seem to enjoy the TV.' I'd never seen him look so miserable.

Was this retribution – did Kitty deserve to be stricken with whatever she had? She'd asked for it, and God in his mysterious ways did prevail after all. And my own exhaustion made me say yes, going back to Winnerrow and turning Kitty over to her mother was a fine idea, and it would give me the chance to see Fanny, check on Grandpa . . . and hunt up Tom, to say nothing of Logan. Beyond that I couldn't think. For how could I even look at Logan now?

Finally a letter came from Reva Setterton, Kitty's mother.

'I hate going back there,' he said after he read the short letter that showed no real concern for a sick daughter. 'I can tell from the way they look at me they think I married her for her money, but if we don't stay with them, they'll think you and I have some kind of relationship going on.'

He wasn't looking at me when he said this; still, I heard something wistful and yearning in his voice that made me feel guilty again. I swallowed, quivered, and tried not to think about what he might be implying.

'Besides, you need a break. You work too hard waiting on her, even when the nurse is here. If we stay I'll go broke from paying for nurses. And I can't let you quit school to tend to her. The worst thing is, nothing at all seems wrong with Kitty but her desire to stay home and watch TV.'

'Come back to life and love him before it's too late,' I yelled at Kitty that day, trying to make her understand she was losing her husband. She'd driven him to me with her coldness, her cruelty, her inability to give.

Later when he was home: 'Cal,' I began in a low, scared voice, not wanting to desert him now when he had no one, 'Kitty wouldn't want to lie there all day and night without moving if something weren't terribly wrong.'

'But I've had the best doctors in the country look at her. They've made every test they can think of, and found nothing.'

'Remember when those doctors gave you their diagnosis? They did admit sometimes the body is as much a mystery to them as it is to us. Even though the neurologists said she seems perfectly healthy, they don't know what's going on inside her brain, do they?'

'Heaven, taking care of her is ruining both our lives. I don't have you as much as I need you. I thought at first it was a blessing in diguise.' He laughed, short and hard. 'We've got to take Kitty back to Winnerrow.'

Helplessly I met his eyes, not knowing what to say.

Kitty was in her bed, wearing a hot pink nightgown under a hot pink bedjacket trimmed with row upon row of tiny pleated ruffles. Her red hair was growing longer and longer, and appeared remarkably healthy.

Her muscle tone didn't seem as flabby as it had, nor did her eyes seem quite as stark or apathetic as they turned our way when we entered together. 'Where ya been?' she asked weakly, showing little interest.

Before one of us could answer, she fell asleep, and I was stricken with the pity of such a strong, healthy woman lying still all the remaining days of her life.

I was also filled with excitement, with relief, with a rare kind of anticipation, as if Winnerrow had once given me something besides pain.

'Cal . . . there are times when I think she's getting better,' I said after we left Kitty's room.

His brown eyes narrowed. 'What makes you think that?'

'I don't know. It's nothing she does, or doesn't do. It's just that when I'm in her room, dusting the things on top of her dresser, I feel she's watching me. Once I glanced up and I could swear I saw some fleeting emotion in her eyes, and not that blank look she usually wears.'

Alarm sprang into his eyes. 'That's all the more reason to move fast, Heaven. Loving you has made me realize I never loved her. I was just lonely, trying to fill the void in my life. I need you; I love you so much I'm bursting with it. Don't pull away and make me feel I'm forcing you.' His lips on mine tried to give me the same kind of passion he experienced; his hands did what they could to bring me to the pitch of excitement he reached so easily – why couldn't I let go of the sense I was drowning myself? Going under each time we made love.

He possessed me with his body, with his will, with his needs, so much that he began to frighten me as much as Kitty once had. Not that he'd ever hurt me physically . . . only mentally and morally I felt damaged beyond repair. Regardless, I loved him, and I had that same insatiable, aching hunger to be cherished tenderly.

Going home would save me, save him, save Kitty, I convinced myself.

I'd find Tom, see Grandpa, visit Fanny, find Keith and Our Jane. I brainwashed myself with this litany I repeated over and over. I made of Winnerrow a kind of refuge, believing it held all the solutions.

PART THREE
Return to Winnerrow

Eighteen

Winnerrow Family

Cal and I made a bed for Kitty in the back seat, loaded our suitcases in the boot, and set off on a fine sunny day in mid-August, a few days before her thirty-seventh birthday. Kitty her been incapacitated for two months, and seemed likely to stay that way from the vacant way she acted.

Yesterday her 'girls' had shampooed and set her hair, had given her a fresh manicure and pedicure, and this morning I'd given her a sponge bath, put on her pretty pink bra, then dressed her in a brand-new pink summer pantsuit. I'd styled her hair as best I could, and done a pretty good job before I put on her makeup so she looked pretty. But for the first time during a trip, Kitty didn't say a word. She just lay as if dead, like the doll she'd burned so ruthlessly.

All the things we should have said on this return to West Virginia remained unsaid as Cal and I sat in the front seat enough room between us to have put Kitty, if she could have sat up. Soon Kitty and Cal would be established with her family and no longer could he come to me with his needs. Pray God that the Settertons never learned about what we had done together. It troubled me so much I felt almost ill. Was Cal thinking the same thing? Was he regretting now his declarations of love for a hill-scum girl?

This was our moment of truth, or soon would be. His eyes stayed on the road ahead, mine on the passing landscape. In another few weeks school would be starting again, and before that we had to decide what to do with Kitty.

I couldn't help but compare this sumnmer's trip with the winter one, more than two years ago. All that had been impressive then now had become commonplace. McDonald's golden arches no longer commanded my awe or admiration, and hamburgers no longer pleased my palate since I'd eaten in the best restaurants in Atlanta. What was Cal going to do with me now? Could he turn off his love and need, as Kitty could so easily turn off what she used to be? I sighed and forced myself to think of the future, when I'd be on my own. I had already taken my exams and applied to six different universities. Cal had said he'd go with me to college, and acquire his own degree while I began my higher education.

It wasn't until we were halfway to Winnerrow that I knew why Miss Deale had come to our range of mountains, to give the best of her talents to those who needed it most. We were the forgotten, the underprivileged of the coal-mining regions. A long time ago I'd told Tom in jest I'd be another Miss Deale; now, looking around, I knew I wanted more than anything to be her kind of inspiring teacher. Now that I was seventeen Logan would be in college, home for summer vacation, but soon to leave. Would he see guilt and shame on my face? Would he see something to tell him I was no longer a virgin? Granny had always said she could tell when girl was 'impure'. I couldn't tell Logan, about Cal, could never tell anybody, not even Tom. I sat on and on, feeling heavy with the burden of shame I carried.

Miles and miles and miles slipped by. Then we were in the hill country, steadily climbing, winding around and around. Soon the petrol stations became more widely spaced. The grand new sprawling motels were replaced by little cabins tucked away in shadowy dense woods. Shoddy, unpainted little buildings heralded yet another country town off the beaten track, until those too were left behind us. No fast motorway to take us up into the Willies. How scary that name sounded now.

I was seeing the countryside as my true mother must have seen it seventeen years ago. She'd be only thirty-one if she'd lived. Oh, what a pity she had to die so young. No, she hadn't had to die. Ignorance had killed her, the stupidity of the hills.

How had my mother had the nerve to marry Luke Casteel? What insanity had driven her away from a cultivated place like Boston, so she'd end up here where education and culture were scorned, and the general opinion was *who the heck cares . . . life's short . . . grab what ya can and run, run, run*. Running all through life, trying to escape poverty, ugliness, brutality, and never succeeding.

I glanced back at Kitty. She appeared to be sleeping.

A fork in the road ahead. Cal made a right turn that took us away from the dirt road leading to our small, pitiful cabin in the high country. How familiar everything seemed now, as if I'd never left. It all came rushing back, filling me with memories, tingling my nostrils with the familiar scents of honeysuckle and wild strawberries, and raspberries ripe on the vine.

I could almost hear the banjos playing, hear Grandpa fiddling, see Granny rocking, Tom running, hear again Our Jane wailing, while Keith stayed in close, loving attendance. Out of all this mountain ignorance, all this stupidity, still came the gifts of God, the children, not blighted by their genes, as some might have thought, but blessed in many ways.

Mile by mile I was growing more impatient, more excited.

Then came the broad green fields on the outskirts of Winnerrow; neat farms with fields of summer crops that soon would be harvested. After the farms came the houses of the poorest in the valley, those not much better off than true hillbillies. Beyond them, higher up, were the shacks of the coal miners dotting the hills along with the moonshiners' cabins.

The deepest part of the valley was reserved for the affluent, where all the richest mountain silt was driven downward by the heavy spring rains, to end up eventually in the gardens of Winnerrow families, providing fertile soil for those who needed it least, producing lavish flowers and gardens, so the rich grand houses of Winnerrow could grow the best tulips, daffodils, iris, roses, and every other flower to flatter their beautifully painted Victorian homes. No wonder they called it Winnerrow. All the winners in this area lived on Main

Street, and all the losers in the hills. On Main Street, long ago, the owners of the coal mines had constructed their lavish homes, and the owners of the long-ago gold mines that had stopped producing. Now those homes were owned by the cotton-factory owners or their superintendents.

Down Main Street Cal drove carefully, past all the pastel homes of the richest, backed by the lesser homes of the middle class, the ones who worked in the mines, holding down some overseer or manager position. Winnerrow was also blessed, or cursed, with cotton gins that made the fabric for bed and table linens, fancy knobby bedspreads, carpets and rugs. Cotton mills with all their invisible airborne lint breathed into many a worker's lungs, so they coughed up their lungs sooner or later (as did the coal miners), and no one ever sued the mill owners – or the mine owners. Couldn't be helped. A living had to be made. Was just the way things were. *Ya took yer chances*.

All this was in my mind as I stared at the fine homes that had commanded my childhood admiration, and in some ways, I had to admit, they still did. See all the porches, the remembered voice of Sarah was saying in my head. Count the floors by the windows, the first, second, and third. See all the cupolas, some houses with two, three, four. Houses pretty as picture postcards.

I turned again to check on Kitty. This time her eyes were open. 'Kitty, are you all right? Do you need anything?'

Her pale seawater eyes moved my way. 'Wanna go home.'

'You're almost there, Kitty . . . almost there.'

'Wanna go home,' she repeated, like a parrot speaking the only phrase she knew. Uneasily I turned away. Why was I still afraid of her?

Cal slowed, then pulled into a curving driveway leading to a fine home painted soft yellow and trimmed with white. Three levels of gingerbread grandeur, perhaps built around the turn of the century, with porches on the ground and second level, and a small balcony on the third that must be the attic. The porches went around the house on four sides,

Cal explained as he drew the car to a slow stop, got out, and opened the back door so he could lift Kitty from the backseat and carry her toward the high porch where her family stood motionless and waiting.

Why didn't her family come running to welcome Kitty home? Why did they just stand up there, bunched together, watching Cal with Kitty in his arms? Kitty had told me they'd rejoiced when she ran off and married at the age of thirteen. 'Never did love me, none of em,' I could remember Kitty saying more than once. And apparently from their lack of enthusiasm, they were not glad to see her again, especially sick and helpless – but could I blame them, could I? If she could do what she had to me . . . what had she done to them? They were very generous to agree to take her back, more than generous.

Hesitatingly, I just sat there, reluctant to leave the cool isolation and safety of the car.

Up the five broad steps of the porch Cal carried Kitty, to stop at the top between the white balustrades. That family stared at Kitty as I finally made up my mind that Cal needed some support, and it seemed I was the only one he was going to get it from.

It was like the story Granny used to tell of how she and Grandpa had just waited when Pa brought home the bride he called his angel, and they hadn't wanted her . . . not at first. *Oh, Mother, how painful it must have been for you. How painful it could be for Kitty.*

I ran to catch up, seeing the way they flicked their eyes at me. They weren't friendly eyes, nor were they hostile; all four stood staring as if Cal carried some unwanted alien in his arms. It was clear they didn't really want her, but still they had agreed to take her in and do their best . . . 'until it's all over, one way or another . . .'

The large, formidable-looking woman whom Kitty resembled had to be her mother, Reva Setterton, dressed in tissue-thin bright green silk, with huge gold buttons parading single file down to her hem. Her shoes were also green, and of course, foolishly, that impressed stupid me.

'Where can I put her?' Cal asked, shifting Kitty's weight, as Kitty stared at her mother with a blank expression.

'Her old room is ready and waiting,' said the woman, who quirked her thin lips in an imitation smile, then thrust forth her strong, reddened hand and briefly shook mine in a limp, halfhearted way. Her auburn hair had wide streaks of white, making it appear that a peppermint stick had melted and formed a fat blob on her head. The short, portly man at her side had a horseshoe ring of grey hair around his pinkish bald pate. Cal introduced him as Porter Setterton, 'Kitty's father, Heaven.'

'I'm going to take her right up to her room,' said Cal. 'It's been a long trip. Kitty had to be uncomfortable and cramped in the back seat. I hope I sent enough money to rent all she'll need.'

'We can take care of our own,' said Kitty's mother, giving her daughter another hard look of contempt. 'She don't look sick – not with all that gook on her face.'

'We'll talk about that later,' informed Cal, heading for the house while I was eyed up and down by Kitty's sister, Maisie, a pale, insipid imitation of what Kitty must have been when she was seventeen. The pimply-faced, sandy-haired young man named Danny couldn't take his eyes off of me. I guessed his age to be about twenty.

'Ya must have seen us lots of time,' said Maisie, stepping up and trying to act friendly. 'We sure did see ya and yer family. Everybody always stared at the hill – I mean the Casteels.'

I stared at Maisie, at Danny, trying to remember, and couldn't place them anywhere. Whom had I ever seen in church but the Reverend, his wife, and the prettiest girls and best-looking boys? Miss Deale . . . and that was about it. The best-dressed had also drawn my eyes, coveting what they wore for myself. Now I was wearing clothes much better than any I'd ever seen in Winnerrow's one and only church.

So far Danny hadn't said one word. 'I've got to go and help

Kitty,' I said, glancing back at the car. 'We have our things in the boot of the car . . . and we'll be needing them to take care of her.'

'I'll bring them up,' offered Danny, finally moving, as I turned to follow Reva Setterton into the house, closely followed by Maisie, as Mr Setterton followed Danny to Cal's car.

'Ya sure got some dilly of a name,' Maisie said as she trailed up the stairs behind me. 'Heaven Leigh. Sure is pretty. Ma, why'd ya go and name me something so dumb as Maisie? Ain't ya got no imagination?'

'Shut yer mouth, and be grateful I didn't name ya Stupid.'

Squelched, Maisie blushed and hung her head. Perhaps Kitty's tales of a nightmare childhood, told long ago to Cal, had been true after all.

What I could see of the house seemed spacious, neat, and rather pretty, and I was soon led to a bedroom where Kitty had already been put on a hospital bed and was stretched out in her modest pink nightgown. As Cal pulled up the sheet he glanced at me, smiled, then addressed Kitty's mother. 'Reva, I truly appreciate your offer to take Kitty in and do what you can for her. I've been paying nurses around the clock. But if you can manage with one night nurse, I'll send you a weekly cheque to pay for her services, and the expenses of Kitty's medical needs.'

'We ain't poor,' stated Reva. 'Done already said we can take care of our own.' She glanced around the pretty room. 'You can call me Reva, girl,' she said to me. 'This used to be Kitty's room – ain't so bad, is it? Kitty always made it seem we had her in a pigsty. A jail, she used to call it. Couldn't wait to grow up and run off with some man . . . first one who'd take her . . . and now look at her. That's what comes of sinning, and never doing what she should . . .'

What could I say to that?

In fifteen minutes I had Kitty refreshed with a sponge bath and slipped into a clean, pretty pink gown. She stared at me sleepily, with a kind of wonder in her fuzzy gaze, then drifted off into sleep. What a relief to see those strange eyes closed.

Downstairs in a pleasant living room we all sat while Cal explained Kitty's strange illness that no doctor could diagnose. Reva Setterton's lips curled upward to display contempt. 'Kitty was born complaining about everything. Never could fix nothing up right enough for her to like. She never liked me, her pa, or nobody else – unless they were male and handsome. Maybe this time I can make up for all my failures in the past . . . now that she can't answer back, and make me madder'n hell.'

'True, true,' volunteered Maisie, clinging like a burr to my side. 'Ain't nothing but trouble when Kitty comes to stay. Don't like nothing we do or nothing we say. Hates Winnerrow. Hates all of us, yet she keeps coming back . . .' And on and on Maisie rattled, followed me to my room, watching me as I unpacked, and she soon was gasping at the display of all the fancy lingerie and pretty dresses that had filled my cupboard once Kitty was too sick to care how much money Cal spent on me.

'Bet she's awful hard to live with,' pried Maisie, falling flat on the yellow bedspread and staring at me with admiring green eyes. She lacked something that Kitty used to have, the vitality, and the toughness. 'Kitty's never been much of a sister. She was off and married up time I was old enough to remember. Never liked Ma's cooking. Now she'll have to eat it, like or not.' Maisie smirked like a satisfied cat. 'Never liked nothing we do or say. She's a queer one, our Kitty. But it makes me feel sad to know she's lying on a bed, unable to move. What did it to her?'

That was a good question, a very good question that the doctors had asked many times.

When Maisie left, I sank into a tub chair covered with a chintz yellow print and gave it more thought. How had it all begun? After Chuckles was killed? I thought backwards, closing my eyes and concentrating, trying again to find a clue. Perhaps it had started the day when Kitty came storming home, furious because half her clients had shown up late for appointments. 'Damn crappy women!' Kitty had bellowed. 'As if they thinks they're better than me, and can keep me waiting like I don't have nothing better to do. I'm hungry, got me the worst kind of appetite – and I keep losing weight! Wanna eat, and eat, then eat some more.'

'I'm hurrying as fast as I can,' I'd answered, racing from sink to stove.

'Going up to take a bath . . . ya be finished time I'm back.'

Clickety-clack went her high heels up the stairs.

I could almost see Kitty up there, ripping off her pink uniform, letting it fall to the floor, stripping off her undergarments, letting them fall as well. Clothes that I'd have to pick up, wash, and take care of. I heard the water in the tub running. Heard Kitty singing in a loud voice, the same song she always sang when she was bathing.

> Down in the valley . . . valley so low . . . owww, owww . . .
> Late in the evening . . . hear the train blow . . . owww, owww . . .

Over and over again, until the song ate into my brain, chewed on my nerves. Just those two lines, repeated until I wanted to stuff my ears with cotton.

Then the scream.

That long, horrible scream.

I'd gone flying up the stairs, expecting to find Kitty had slipped in the tub and cracked her head on the tiles . . . and all I found was Kitty standing nude before a bathroom mirror, staring with wide, appalled eyes at her naked right breast. 'Cancer, got me a breast cancer.'

'Mother, you'll have to go to a doctor. It could be just a benign cyst, or a benign tumor.'

'What the hell does 'benign' mean?' she'd yelled. 'They're gonna cut it off, slice me with one of those scalpel knives, mutilate me . . . and no man will want me then! I'll be lopsided, half a woman, and I've never had my baby! Never gonna know what it feels like to nurse my own child! . . . Done told me, they have, I don't have no cancer. But I know I do! Just know I do!'

'You've already been to a doctor . . . Mother?'

'Yes, damn you, yes! What do they know? When yer on yer deathbed, that's when they know!'

It had been crazy and wild, the way Kitty had carried on, screaming until I had to call Cal, asking him to come home immediately, and then I'd gone back up the stairs to find Kitty lying on her wide bed, eyes fixed on the ceiling, just staring at nothing.

Darn if I could really remember . . .

After our first meal in the Setterton home, which was really very good, I helped Reva and Maisie with the dishes; then all three of us joined Mr Setterton on the porch. I managed to remind Cal of that day while Reva Setterton bustled about upstairs, forcing food down Kitty's mouth. 'She ate it,' she said when she was back, sitting stiffly in a reed rocker. 'Ain't nobody in my house gonna starve to death.'

'Reva, a few months ago, Kitty said she found a lump in her breast. And she said she went to a doctor who reported she didn't have a malignant growth – but how can we know if she really went? However, when she was in the hospital for two weeks, they went over her thoroughly and they didn't find anything suspicious.'

For some odd reason, Kitty's mother got up and left the porch.

'And that's all, all?' asked Maisie, her green eyes wide. 'What a dope to clam up until she knew . . . but then again, she's sure got some great ones, ain't she? With that kind, could hardly blame her for not wanting to know.'

'But,' said Cal, sitting close at my side, 'her doctors checked her over, Maisie.'

'Wouldn't make no difference to Kitty,' Maisie said with surprising complacency. 'Breast cancer runs in our family. Got a whole long history of it. Ma's had both hers taken off.

Wears fake ones now. That's why she walked away. Can't stand to hear people talk about it. Never would know it, though, would ya? Our ma's mom had one off. Pa's ma had one off, then died before they could cut off the other. Always Kitty's been scared to death of losing what she's so proud of.' Maisie looked thoughtfully down at her own small breasts. 'Ain't got much myself, compared to hers, but I'd sure hate losing one – sure would.'

Could this be it, explained so simply?

Something neither the doctors nor I nor Cal had thought of. Her secret to brood over. The reason why Kitty had retreated into a solitary world – where cancer didn't exist.

Two hours passed, and that was enough for me to sense that something about Cal was different now that he was in the home of Kitty's parents; something that put a distance between us. I didn't quite understand what it was, though I felt relieved and grateful, sensing he no longer needed me as much as he had. Maybe it was pity for Kitty that softened his eyes when he sat beside her bed and tried to hold her hand. I stood in the doorway and watched him trying to console Kitty before I turned and walked away.

What had happened between Cal and me would stay my most shameful, terrible secret.

When I was downstairs and on the porch wondering what to do next, I thought of Tom. Was this the day I'd feast my eyes on him – and Fanny as well?

And Logan – when will I see you again? Will you know me now, be happy I'm back . . . or will you turn away as you did that last time, when your parents were beside you? He'd never said a word to explain his action, as if he thought I hadn't noticed.

That first night Maisie and I slept together in her room, and Cal was given a cot to sleep on in the room with Kitty. Very early the next morning I was up and fully dressed while the others were still in bed. I had one foot on the step going down when Cal called from behind me, 'Heaven, where are you going?'

'To visit Fanny,' I said in a whisper, fearing to turn and meet his eyes, feeling a thousand times more ashamed in Winnerrow than I'd felt in Candlewick.

'Let me go with you. Please.'

'Cal,' I implored, 'if you don't mind, I'd like to do this myself. My relationship with Fanny has always been difficult. With you there, she might not talk honestly. And I need to hear the truth and not a pack of lies.'

His voice was gruff. 'How swiftly you run, Heaven, the moment you are on familiar territory. Are you running from me? Using any excuse to escape me? You don't need an excuse; I don't own you. You go on, and I'll stay here to tend to Kitty, and make plans for her care with her parents – but I'll miss you while you're gone.'

It hurt to hear the pain in his voice; still, it felt good to escape the house and leave all that behind. Each step I took away from the Setterton home made me younger, happier.

I was going to see Fanny.

My feet chose a roundabout way so I'd have to pass by Stonewall's Pharmacy. My pulse quicked as I neared the familiar store. I was just strolling by, truthfully not expecting to see Logan just because I was thinking about him and wondering what kind of boy he was by this time. I glanced inside the wide glass windows, my heart almost in my mouth, and didn't see him. I sighed, I caught the interested stare of two dark blue eyes belonging to a handsome young man who was stepping out of a sporty dark blue car. I froze, staring back at – Logan Grant Stonewall.

Oh, gosh!

He seemed caught in the same dream I was, both of us staring, disbelieving.

'Heaven Leigh Casteel . . . is that you, or am I dreaming?'

'It's me. Is that you, Logan?'

His face instantly brightening, he came quickly to me, grasping both my hands and holding them tightly as he stared into my eyes, then pulled in his breath. 'You've grown up . . . really grown up to be so beautiful.' He blushed, stammered, and then smiled. 'I don't know why I'm surprised; when I always knew you'd grow more beautiful.'

I was shy, snared in a spider's web of my own making, wanting to fling myself into his arms as he held them out inviting me to do just that. 'Thank you for answering all my letters . . . or most of them.'

He looked disappointed because I didn't make the next move. 'When I got your note saying you were bringing Kitty Dennison back here, I wrote and told Tom.'

'So did I,' I whispered, still staring at how handsome he was, how tall and strong-looking. I felt shamed and sick that I'd not held Cal off, to wait for this clean, pure, shining kind of love that would have been so right. I lowered my eyes, terrified he might see something that I didn't want him to see. I tembled with the guilt I felt, then backed off a foot or more so as not to contaminate him with my sins. 'Sure will be wonderful to see Tom again,' I said weakly, trying to pull my hands from his grip as he stepped forward to hold them even tighter.

'Not so wonderful to see *me* again?' Gently he tugged me closer, until he released my hands only to slide his arms about my waist. 'Look at me, Heaven. Don't look down. Why are you acting as if you don't love me anymore? I've been waiting so long for this day, wondering what I'd say, and what you'd say, and how we'd act . . . and now you're not meeting my eyes. All the time you've been gone I've thought of no one else. Sometimes I go to your cabin and wander about in those abandoned rooms, thinking of you and how tough you had it, and how brave you were, never complaining or feeling sorry for yourself. Heaven, you're like a rose, a wild, beautiful rose, sweeter and more lovely than any other. Please, put your arms around me. Kiss me, say you still love me!'

Everything I'd ever dreamed he'd say, he said, and again I was flooded with guilt – if he knew the truth – and yet I couldn't resist the pleading in his eyes, or the urging of my own romantic nature that said, yes, Logan! I flung my arms about him and felt myself lifted up and swung around. My head lowered so I could put my lips on his, and I kissed him so passionately I think it took his breath away, though he returned my kiss with even more fervor. His eyes shone when we separated, and he was breathing heavily.

'Oh, Heaven, this is the way I knew it would be . . .' he whispered breathlessly.

Now we were both speechless, our young bodies calling to each other. He pulled me against him so I could feel his excitement. It reminded me of Cal. This wasn't what I wanted! I tried to draw away, cringing as I shoved against him, shuddering and overwhelmed with a wild kind of terror, not only of Logan but of every man. Don't touch me that way! I wanted to yell. Just kiss me, embrace me, and let that be enough!

Of course he didn't understand my resistance. I could tell from the startled way his eyes widened, but he let me go. 'I apologize, Heaven,' he said in a low, humble way. 'I suppose I forgot it's been two years and eight months since we'd seen each other – but in your letters you sounded as if we'd never feel like strangers . . .'

I tried to sound normal and not terrified. 'It's been great seeing you again, Logan, but I'm in kind of a hurry . . .'

'You mean you're leaving? And we're only going to have these few minutes together? Heaven, didn't you hear me say I love you?'

'I have to go, really I do.'

'Wherever you're going, I'm going too.'

No! Leave me alone, Logan! You don't want me now!

'I'm sorry, Logan. I'm going to see Fanny, and then Grandpa . . . and I think it's best if I see Fanny alone. Perhaps tomorrow . . . ?'

'No perhaps, definitely a date. Early tomorrow, say eight o'clock, so we can spend the day together. You said a lot in your letters, but not nearly enough. Heaven –'

I whirled around, trying to smile. 'I'll see you tomorrow early. See you all day, if that's what you want.'

'If that's what I want? Of course that's what I want! Heaven, don't look at me like that! As if I frighten you! What's wrong? Don't tell me nothing is! You've changed! You don't love me now, and you haven't for the nerve to tell me!'

I sobbed, 'That's not true.'

'Then what is it?' he demanded, his young face taking on a more mature look. 'If we don't talk about it, whatever it is will put up a wall that sooner or later we'll never be able to climb.'

'Good-bye, Logan,' I threw out, hurrying away.

'Where?' he called out, sounding desperate. 'Here or the Setterton place?'

'Come there. Any time after seven,' I said with a nervous laugh. 'I'll be up early to help with Kitty.'

If only I'd come back to him still innocent, still a girl he could teach . . . and yet, even so, it felt good, really good, to walk away knowing his eyes were following me with admiration so strong I could almost feel it reaching out and touching me. His devotion warmed my heart. Then I heard him running to catch up. 'What will it matter if I walk with you to the parsonage, then disappear? I can't wait until tomorrow to hear the truth. Heaven . . . you told me that day in your cabin that your pa sold Keith and Our Jane, Fanny and Tom – were you sold?'

'Yes,' I said shortly, putting too much misdirected anger in my voice because he could still doubt, even now. 'Sold, like an animal, for five hundred bucks! I was carted away to work like a slave for a crazy woman who hates Pa as much as I do!'

'Why are you yelling at me? I didn't sell you! I'm terribly sorry that you've suffered – but damned if I can see that you have! You look terrific, wearing expensive, beautiful clothes, like a debutante, and you come and tell me you've been sold and treated like a slave. If all slaves end up looking like beauty queens, maybe all girls should be sold into slavery.'

'What an insensitive remark to make, Logan Stonewall!'

I snapped, feeling as mean as Kitty at her worst. 'I used to think you were so kind and understanding! Just because you can't see my scars doesn't mean I don't have them!' Now I was crying, my words breaking. And only a few minutes ago he had been so sweet. Unable to say more, and angry at myself for always losing my control and breaking into childish tears, I turned away again.

'Heaven . . . don't turn away. I'm sorry. Forgive me for being insensitive. Give me another chance. We'll talk it out, like we used to do.'

For his own good, I should run off and never see him again, and yet I couldn't let go of a boy I'd loved from the moment I'd first seen him. And with differences forgotten for the moment, side by side we walked until we came to the fine house of Reverend Wayland Wise.

He held my hand as I stared at the parsonage.

A pure white house, a pious house, a grand house, surrounded by two acres of beautiful flower gardens and manicured lawns. This house made Kitty's home in Candlewick seem a shack. I sighed. Sighed again for Fanny, who was now a young lady of sixteen and four months, and Tom, like me, was seventeen, and Keith would soon be twelve, Our Jane eleven. Oh, to see them again, to know they were healthy, happy.

But first Fanny.

Now that I was here, I could only stand and stare at the grandest house in all of Winnerrow. Corinthian columns lined the long porch. The steps up were made of intricately laid red bricks. Red geraniums and red petunias grew in huge terracotta planters. On the porch were sturdy-looking white wicker chairs with high fancy peacock backs.

In the huge old trees birds were chirping; a yellow canary in a white wicker cage hung from the porch ceiling began its cheerful song. It startled me to hear that singing from such a high place; the bird had been put there, I guessed, to keep it safe from cats and draughts. All her life Fanny had wanted a canary in a white cage; now she had one.

But for the singing of the birds, there were no other noises.

How silent this great house that gave no hint of its inhabitants.

How was it that such a lovely house could appear so threatening?

Nineteen

Found Casteels

Several times I jabbed at that doorbell. As I stood and waited for what seemed an eternity, I grew more than impatient. Every so often I looked to see if Logan had gone away as I hoped he would, but he hadn't. He leaned against a tree, smiling when I glanced his way.

Faint footsteps sounded inside the house. I stiffened and listened more closely. Slow, sneaky steps . . . then the heavy oak door opened just a wee slot. Dark sloe eyes peered out at me, glittering narrowed eyes that appeared suspicious, unfriendly. Only Fanny had almost black eyes like that, only Fanny – and Pa. 'Go away,' said the voice that was undeniably Fanny's.

'It's me – Heaven,' I called excitedly. 'I've come to see you, to find out how you are. You can't send me away.'

'Go away,' Fanny whispered more insistently. 'Can do what I want. And I don't wanna see ya! Don't know ya anymore! Don't need ya anymore! I'm Louisa Wise now. I've got everything I ever wanted. And I don't want ya coming round to mess it up.'

She could still sting me with her mean, selfish words and ways. Always I'd believed that, underneath all her hostility and jealousy, Fanny loved me. Life had warped her in ways different than it had me.

'Fanny, I'm your sister,' I pleaded in a low voice, ashamed Logan would overhear her 'welcome'. 'I need to talk to you, to see you, and know if you've heard anything about Keith and Our Jane.'

'Don't know nothing,' whispered Fanny, opening the door a bit wider. 'Don't want to know nothing. Just go away, leave me alone.'

I could see my younger sister had grown into a very pretty

girl with long black hair and a figure shapely enough to break many a man's heart. That Fanny would break many hearts without remorse had always been my expectation. Still, I was hurt that Fanny would refuse to let me enter the house and showed no interest at all in how I'd been, or where I'd been.

'Have you seen Tom?'

'Don't wanna see Tom.'

I winced, again stung. 'I wrote you time and time again, Fanny Casteel! Didn't you receive my letters?' I demanded, forcefully holding the door open so she couldn't slam it in my face. 'Damn you, Fanny! What kind of person are you anyway? When people are kind and thoughtful enough to write letters, the least you can do is answer – unless you just don't give a damn!'

'Guess ya got the picture,' snapped Fanny in reply.

'Now, you wait a minute, Fanny! You can't slam the door in my face! I'm not going to let you!'

'Ya never wrote to me, not once!' she cried, then turned to look over her shoulder with alarm. Her voice lowered to a whisper again. 'Ya gotta go, Heaven.' Urgency was in her eyes, a look of fright. 'They're upstairs sleeping. The Reverend and his wife hate to be reminded of who I am. They've done warned me not to ever talk to ya, or any other Casteel. Never have heard from Pa since I came.' She wiped at a tear that came to the corner of one eye and slid like a dewdrop on her cheek. 'I used to think Pa loved me best; seems he don't.' Another tear formed that she didn't wipe away. 'Glad ya look good.' Her eyes swept over my face before her full red lips thinned a bit.

'Gotta go now. Don't want them to wake up and scold me for talking to ya. Ya just taske yerself out of here, Heaven Leigh – don't wanna know ya; wish I'd never known ya; can't remember nothing good about ya and those old days when we were young ones in the hills. Only remember smells and hunger, and cold feet, and never enough of anything.'

Quickly I thrust my foot in the door when Fanny would have slammed it shut with more force than my hands alone could resist. 'You wait a minute, Fanny Louisa Casteel! I've thought about you night and day for more than two long years – you can't tell me to go away! I want to know how you've been, if youve been treated fairly. I care about you, Fanny, even if you don't care about me. I remember the good times when we lived in the hills, and try to forget all the bad. I remember when we used to snuggle up together to keep warm, and I love you, even if you always were a damned pain in the neck.'

'Ya get off this porch,' sobbed Fanny, crying openly now. 'Can't do nothing for ya, can't.'

She brutally kicked my foot out of the way and slammed the door. The inside lock was turned, and I stood alone on the porch.

Almost blind with tears, I stumbled down the steps, and Logan was there, sweeping me into his arms and trying to comfort me. 'Damn her for talking like that to you – damn her!'

I yanked away, hurting so much from Fanny's indifference I could hardly keep from screaming. What good did it do to dole out so much love to people who turned against you the moment they no longer needed you?

What did I care if I'd lost Fanny? Shed never been a loving sister anyway . . . why did I hurt so much? 'Go away, Logan!' I yelled, swinging my fists at him when he tried to embrace me again. 'I don't need you – don't need anybody!'

I turned from him, but he seized me by my arm and swung me around so this strong arms drew me against him. 'Heaven!' he cried. 'What's wrong? What have I done?'

'Let me go,' I pleaded weakly.

'Now, look,' he urgently pleaded, 'you're taking out your anger on me when it's Fanny who hurt you. She's always been a hateful sister – hasn't she? I guess I knew all the way here she'd act like she did, I'm sorry you're so hurt, but do you have to turn on me? I wanted to hang around and be here when you needed me. Need me, Heaven! Don't slap out at me! I haven't done anything but admire, respect, and love you. I could never really believe your pa would sell his kids. I guess I do now. Forgive me for not fully believing until today.'

I pulled away. 'You mean in all this time you haven't talked to Fanny about me?'

'I've tried many a time to talk to her about you . . . but you know how Fanny is. She takes everything and turns it around until she makes herself believe it's her I want to hear about, and not you. Fanny doesn't care about anyone but herself.' He blushed and stared down at his feet. 'I've found out it's better to leave Fanny alone.'

'She still comes on strong, right?' I asked bitterly, guessing that Fanny must have been her usual aggressive self with him . . . and I wondered if he'd fallen, like all the others.

'Yeah,' he said, raising his eyes. 'Takes a lot of resisting to hold Fanny off . . . and the best way to do that is to stay miles away.'

'From temptation?'

'Stop! I do what I can to keep girls like Fanny out of my life. Since you went away, I keep hoping someday a girl named Heaven will be the one to really love me. Somebody sweet and innocent; somebody who knows how to care and how to give. Somebody I can respect. How can I respect anyone like Fanny?'

Oh, God help me! How could he respect me . . . now?

We walked away from Reverend Wise's home and didn't even glance back. Obviously Fanny had adjusted well to her new life.

'Logan, now Fanny's ashamed of her old family,' I said with tears in my voice. 'I thought she'd be glad to see me. There were times when she and I did nothing but fight, but we're blood kin, and I love her just the same.'

Again he tried to hold me, to kiss me. I held him off and turned my face aside.

'Do you happen to know where my grandfather is?' I asked in a small voice.

'Sure I know. I visit him from time to time so I can talk

to him about you, and often I help sell his whittled animals. He's good, you know, really an artist with that knife of his. And he's expecting you. His eyes lit up when I told him you were coming. He said he was going to take a bath, wash his hair, and put on clean clothes.'

Again my throat constricted . . . Grandpa was going to take a bath without urging? On his own going to wash his hair and change his clothes?

'Have you seen or heard from Miss Deale?'

'She isn't here anymore,' he said, keeping my hand tightly in his. 'She left before you did, remember? Nobody's heard from her since. I go by our old school every once in a while, just for old times' sake, and sit on a swing and remember how it used to be. Like I said before, I've even been up to your cabin, and walked in your empty rooms – '

'Oh, why did you do that!' I cried, so ashamed.

'I went there to understand, and I think I do. To think that someone as smart and beautiful as you could come from such as that cabin, and Tom as well, fills me with awe, and so much respect. I don't know if I could have come out of that with all the courage, and all the drive which you have, and when I see Tom – '

'You've seen Tom? When?' I asked eagerly.

'Sure, and soon you'll see him too.' He smiled sadly when he saw my expression. 'Don't cry. He's fine, and quite a guy, Heaven. You just wait and see.'

We were approaching Martin's Road, which was one of the lesser, poorer areas, about twelve blocks from where Fanny lived in the grandest house of all. 'Mrs Sally Trench runs a nursing home, and she's the one who takes care of your grandpa. I've heard that your father sends money once a month to pay for his stay there.'

'I don't care what my father does.' But it surprised me to know he could be that caring . . . sending money to support an old man he'd seldom noticed.

'Of course you care about your father, but you won't admit it. Maybe he did take the wrong road out, but you're alive and well. Fanny seems happy enough to me, and so does Tom. And when you find Keith and Our Jane, no doubt you'll be amazed at how well they both are. Heaven, you've got to learn to expect the best, not the worst; that's the only way you'll give yourself a chance to be happy instead of miserable.'

My heart felt heavy, my soul wounded, as I glanced his way. Once I'd believed that kind of philosophy . . . now I didn't. I had tried his way of thinking with Kitty and Cal, doing my best to please both of them, and fate had tricked me, maybe tricked all of us. How could I restore the trusting innocence I'd lost? How could I turn back the clock and this time say no to Cal?

'Heaven . . . I'm never going to love anyone as I love you! I know we're both young and inexperienced and the world is full of others who might attract us later on, but right this minute you've got my heart in your hand, and you can throw it down, step on it, and crush it. Don't do that to me.'

I couldn't speak, made dumb from all the guilt I felt, all the shame of not being the girl he thought I was.

'Please, look at me. I need you to love me, and now you don't let me touch you, hold you. Heaven, we're not kids anymore. We're old enough now to feel adult emotions – and share adult pleasures.'

Another man who wanted to take from me!

'My family gives me lots to worry about. I wonder how I managed to grow at all,' I managed to say.

'Seems to me you did a super job of growing – and shaping up.' His tentative, troubled smile faded as his eyes went serious, and for a moment I thought I saw in those stormy blue eyes all the devotion and love an ocean could hold. For me, for me! An eternity of love, caring, and faithfulness. A deep throb stabbed me and made me feel for a moment there was hope, when there couldn't be, not ever.

'What's the matter?' he asked when I began to stride onward at a faster pace. 'Have I said something wrong? Again? Remember the day we pledged ourselves to each other?'

I remembered just as much as he did that wonderful day when we'd lain by the river and made our childish vows to love each other forever. Now I knew nothing lasted forever.

Then it had been easy to make pledges, thinking neither he nor I would or could ever change. Now everything *had* changed. I wasn't worthy of him anymore, if ever I had been. Funny how being a hill scumbag wasn't nearly as humiliating as being what I was since first I had allowed Cal to touch me, just another trampy girl who'd allowed herself to be used by a man.

'I guess you've never had any girlfriend but me?' Bitterness was in my voice that he didn't seem to notice.

'Just dates, casual dates.'

We'd reached Martin's Road. And there on the corner was a huge monster of a house, painted a sickly sea-foam green, like froth on the sea, like Kitty's eyes.

The yard about the house was wide, mowed to perfection. It was hard to picture Grandpa shut up in such a big house as that. Every last one of the old rockers on the porch was empty. Why wasn't grandpa on that grand front porch, whittling?

'If you want, I'll wait out here while you visit with him,' Logan said thoughtfully.

I stared at all those tall thin windows, all those steps there had to be inside, and Grandpa might now be as feeble and lame as Granny had been.

The home was on a tree-lined street. All the houses looked well kept up. Each had a front lawn, and morning newspapers lay on porch steps, or near the doors. Husbands in morning disarray were out walking dogs on leashes.

Many a night I'd visited Winnerrow in dreams when all the streets were dim, empty, and dogs didn't bark, and birds didn't sing, and not a sound was to be heard. Terrible dreams in which I walked alone, always alone, searching for Our Jane, Keith, and Tom. Never for Grandpa, as if my subconscious had truly believed he'd always be in that hill cabin, somehow surviving, just because I wanted him to.

Logan spoke again. 'I've heard that your grandfather helps with the cleaning to pay for his room and board, when your father forgets or is late paying Sally Trench.'

The sun, hardly over the horizon,was already blazing-hot, smothering the valley. No refreshing cool breezes blew as they did up in the Willies. And to think all my life I'd believed the valley represented paradise.

'Let's go,' Logan said, taking me by the elbow and guiding me across the street and up the brick walk. 'I'll wait out here on the porch. Take your time. I've got all day – all my life – to spend with you.'

A fat, frowsy-looking woman in her mid-fifties responded to my timid knock, stared at me with intense interest, then swung the screen door wide and admitted me.

'I've been told my grandfather, Mr Toby Casteel, is staying here with you,' I announced.

'Sure, honey, he's here – and ain't ya a pretty thing though. Really a pretty thing, ya are, ya truly are. Love that colour hair, those pretty lips – kissing lips, ya could say.' She sighed, glanced in a nearby window, and scowled at her own reflection before she turned back to me. 'Dear old man, got a soft spot in my heart for such as him. Took him in when nobody else would. Put him in a nice room, and fed him better meals than he's ever had before. Lay ya ten to one on that, twenty to one. Betting fool, I am. Have to be. Can't stay in this kind of business if ya don't gamble. People's tricky, real tricky. Young ones come and put their parents in here and say they'll pay, and they don't. They go, never show up again, and some old daddy or momma sits all their lives away, awaiting and awaiting for visitors who never come, and letters nobody writes. It's a shame, a crying shame, what kids can do to parents once they're too old to do them any good.'

'I understand my father sends money every month.'

'Oh, he does, he does! A fine man, yer father, a real fine looking and acting man. Why, I remember him from way back when he were a kid, and all the gals were hot to catch him. Can't say I blame them none – but he sure turned out a lot different than most folks thought he would – he sure did.'

What did she mean? Pa was a rotter through and through, and all of Winnerrow had to know that.

She grinned, showing false teeth so white they appeared chalky. 'Nice place, ain't it? Yer Heaven Casteel, ain't ya? Saw yer mom once or twice, a real beauty, really too fine for this hateful world, and I guess God must've thought the same thing. Ya got the same kind of look as she had, tender, like ya can't take much.' She rested her small but friendly eyes on me before she frowned again. 'Get ya gone from this place, honey. Ya ain't meant for the likes of what we are.'

She would have rambled on all day if I hadn't asked to see my grandfather. 'I haven't got much time. I'd like to see my grandfather now.'

The woman led me through the dim foyer of the house. I glimpsed old-fashioned rooms with beaded lampshades, browning portraits hanging from ceiling mouldings on heavy twisted silken ropes, before I was led up the steep stairs. This huge house seemed terribly old now that I was inside. All the glory of new paint and refurbishings was on the outside. There was nothing fresh and clean inside but the scent of Lysol.

Lysol . . .

Take yer bath now, hill scum.

Use plenty of Lysol, stupid.

Gotta rid ya of Casteel filth.

I shivered.

We passed a room on the second floor that seemed a page straight from a thirties Sears catalogue.

'Ya can have five minutes with him,' I was informed as the woman became more businesslike. 'I've got sixteen people to feed three meals a day, and yer grandpa has to do his share of the work.'

Grandpa hadn't ever done his share of the housework!

How abruptly some personalities could change. Up three

more flights of steep, twisting stairs. The buttocks under that flimsy cotton dress seemed twin wild animals fighting each other – I had to look away. Oh, how had Grandpa managed to climb these stairs, even once? How did he ever go outside? The higher we went, the older the house appeared. Up here no one cared if the paint was chipped and peeling off, if roaches scuffled over the floor. Spiders spun webs in dim corners, draped them from chair to table, from lamp to base. What a fright all this would give Kitty!

On the top level, we followed a narrow hall with many closed doors, to reach the door at the very end, and when it was opened, it revealed a pitifully small, shabby room, with a sagging old bed, a small dresser - and there sat Grandpa in a creaky old rocker. He'd aged so much I hardly recognized him. It broke my heart to see the second rocker – both chairs had been taken from our pitiful cabin in the Willies, and Grandpa was talking as if Granny sat in her rocker. 'Ya work too hard on yer knitting,' he murmered. 'Gotta get ready for Heaven girl who's coming . . .'

It was unbelievably hot up there.

There was no beautiful scenery all around, no dogs, cats, kittens, pigs, hogs, or chickens to keep my grandpa company. Nothing here at all but a few pieces of beat-up old furniture. He was so lonely he'd turned on his imagination, and put his Annie in that empty rocker.

As I stood in the open doorway hearing that landlady stomp away, an overwhelming pity washed over me.

'Grandpa . . . it's me, Heaven Leigh.'

His faded blue eyes turned to stare my way, not with interest as much as with surprise at hearing a different voice, seeing a different face. Had he reached a certain kind of miserable plateau where nothing really mattered?

'Grandpa,' I whispered again, tears welling, my heart aching to see him like this. 'It's me, Heaven girl. That's what you used to call me – don't you remember? Have I changed so much?'

Slow recognition came. Grandpa tried to smile, to show

happiness, his pale eyes lighting up, opening wider. I threw myself into his arms that slowly opened to receive me . . . and just in the nick of time. While he silently cried, I held him in my arms and wiped away his tears with my handkerchief.

'Now, now,' soothed Grandpa, finding a rusty voice to use while smoothing my rumpled hair, 'don't ya cry. We ain't sufferin, not Annie, not me. Never had it so good before, huh, Annie?'

Oh, dear God! . . . He was looking at the empty rocker and seeing Granny! He even reached to pat where her hand would have been if she'd been sitting there. Then, almost with relief, he leaned over to spread sheets of old newspaper on the floor at his feet, and began with his sharp knife to shave a piece of tree limb free of bark. It was so good to see those hands busy.

'Lady here pays me and Annie to work, help with the cooking, and to make these creatures,' Grandpa said in a low whisper. 'Hate to see them go. Never thought I'd let even one go, but it means nice things for Annie. She can't hear so good nowadays, either. Gonna buy her a hearing aid. But I can hear good, real good. Don't need no glasses yet. . . . That is ya, Heaven girl, that really ya? Yer looking good, like yer ma who came. Annie . . . where did Luke's angel come from? Can't seem remember much of nothing lately . . .'

'Granny's looking fine, Grandpa,' I managed to say as I knelt by his side and put my cheek on his old gnarled hand when it was momentarily still. 'Are they good to you here?'

'It's not so bad,' he said vaguely, looking lost and bewildered when he moved his eyes over the room. 'And I'm mighty glad to see ya looking so fine and pretty; pretty as yer own true ma. And here ya are, Luke's angel's Heaven. Gladdens this heart to see yer face looking like yer ma come back to life.'

He paused, looked at me uneasily before he went on. 'Know ya don't love yer pa, know ya don't even want to hear about him, but still he's yer father, and there's nothing to be done about that now. My Luke's done gone and got himself some kind of crazy, dangerous job, so I hear tell, but don't know what it is, except he's making lots of money. Luke set Annie and me up here with his money, didn't leave us to starve.'

How grateful he seemed for nothing! This horrible small room! And then I felt shamed, for he was better off here than alone in the cabin.

'Grandpa, where is Pa?'

He stared at me blankly, then lowered his eyes to his whittling. 'Like the dead rising from the grave,' he muttered. 'Like God tried once and made a mistake, and is trying again to do it right. God help her.'

It sure did make me feel strange, his saying that. I knew he didn't realize he'd said those frightening words aloud. Still, I felt sort of doomed. And even worse, he kept on speaking in that strange mumbling way, as if to his Annie. 'Would ya look at her, Annie, just would ya?'

'Grandpa, stop mumbling! Tell me where Pa is! Tell me where I can find Keith, Our Jane! You see Pa . . . he must have told you where they are.'

Vacant stare into nowhere. No voice to answer a question like that.

It was no use.

In time he said all there was to say, and I stood to go.

'I'll be coming back soon, Grandpa,' I said at the door. 'Take care, now. Ya hear?'

Then I joined Logan on the porch.

There was someone with him. A tall young man with dark auburn hair who turned when he heard the clickety-clack of my heels. I stared . . . and then my knees went weak.

Oh, my God!

It was Tom!

My brother Tom, standing and grinning at me, just the way he used to do . . . only thing was, in two years and eight months, he'd grown to look almost exactly like Pa!

Tom stepped toward me, grinning broadly and holding

out his arms. 'I can't believe my eyes!' I ran to him then and was caught up in his strong embrace, and we were hugging, kissing, laughing, crying, both trying to talk at once.

Soon all three of us walked down Main Street with arms locked, me in the middle. We stopped at a park bench that just happened to face the church, and of course the parsonage was across from the church. Fanny could have looked out and seen us there, even if she was too cowardly to join her own family reunion.

'Now, Tom,' I gushed, 'tell me everything your letters didn't.'

Tom glanced at Logan and seemed a little embarrassed. Immediately Logan was on his feet, making excuses that he had to hurry back home. 'Sorry about this, Logan,' Tom apologized, 'but I've only got ten minutes to visit with my sister, and years of filling in to do, but I'll see you again in about a week.'

'See you tomorrow in church,' Logan said to me in a significant way.

Logan left, while I feasted my eyes on Tom. His sparkling green eyes locked with mine. 'Good golly, if you ain't a sight for sore eyes.'

' "If you aren't" is the way you should say it.'

'I should have known. Still the schoolteacher!'

'You're no skinnier than you used to be, but so much taller, and so good-looking. Tom, I never guessed you'd grow to look like Pa.'

What did he hear in my voice to take the smile from his eyes and lips? 'You don't like the way I look now?'

'I like the way you look, of course I do. You're handsome – but did you have to grow up to look so much like Pa?' I almost shouted. Now I'd gone and hurt his feelings when I hadn't meant to do that. 'I'm sorry, Tom,' I choked, laying my hand on his huge one. 'It's just that you took me by surprise.'

He had an odd look on his face. 'There's many a woman who thinks Pa is the best-looking man alive.'

Frowning, I glanced away. 'I don't want to talk about him, please. Now, have you heard anything about Keith and Our Jane?'

He turned his head so I saw his profile, and again I felt stunned that he could be so much like Pa. 'Yeah. I heard they are fine, and Our Jane is alive and well. If Pa hadn't done what he did, no doubt she'd be dead.'

'Are you making excuses for him?'

Again he turned to me and grinned. 'You sound like you used to. Don't hold on to hate, Heavenly . . . let go of it before it eats you up and makes you worse than he is. Think of those who love you, like me. Don't go spoiling everything good that will come along in the future because you had a cruel father. People change. He's taking care of Grandpa, isn't he? Never thought he'd do that, did you? And Buck Henry isn't nearly as mean as he looked that first time we saw him; as you can see, I'm not starved, not sick, not worked to death. And I'll be graduating from school same time as you do.'

'Your hair isn't as red as fire anymore . . .'

'Sorry about that, but I'm glad for it. Tell me if my eyes still shine with devilment.'

'Yes, they still do.'

'Then I haven't changed so much after all, have I?'

He had a clean, honest face, with clear, shining eyes without secrets, while I had to duck my head and hide my eyes, so scared he'd see my terrible secret. If he knew, he wouldn't respect me as he always had. He'd think I was no better than Fanny, and maybe even worse.

'Why are you hiding your eyes, Heavenly?'

I sobbed and tried to meet his gaze again. If only I could tell him everything right now, and say it all so that he'd see I had been as trapped by my Candlewick circumstances as Fanny had been by her hill genes. I began to tremble so much that Tom reached to pull me into his arms where I could rest my head on his shoulder. 'Please don't cry because you're so happy to see me, and make me cry, too. I haven't cried since the day Buck Henry bought me from Pa. But I sure did cry a lot that night, wondering what had happened to you after he drove me away. Heavenly, you are all right, aren't you? Nothing bad happened, did it?'

'Of course I'm all right. Don't I look all right?'

He studied my face as I tried to smile and conceal all the guilt and shame I felt. What he saw apparently satisfied him, for he smiled as well. 'Gee, Heavenly, it's great to be here with you. Now tell me everything that's happened to you since the day I went away – and say it all fast, cause I'll have to go in another few minutes.'

The urgency in his voice made me look around – was Buck Henry with him?

'You first, Tom. Tell me everything you didn't in your letters!'

'Don't have time,' he said, jumping to his feet and pulling me up as I saw a familiar stocky figure coming down the street. 'That's him looking for me. Just one fast hug, and I've got to go. He's here in town buying vet supplies for two sick cows. Next time you've got to tell me more about your life in Candlewick. Your letters say so little. Too much talk about cinemas and restaurants and clothes. By gosh, it seems to me all of us were blessed the day Pa sold us off.'

There were shadows in the emerald depths of his eyes, dark shadows I suddenly noticed, putting doubts in my mind as to his happiness; but before I could question, he was off, calling back: 'I'm joining Mr Henry, but be looking for me next Saturday, and I'll bring Laurie and Thalia with me . . . and we'll all have lunch or dinner together – maybe both if we're lucky!'

I stood staring after him, so sad to see him going already; he was the one and only person who might understand, if only I could tell him. Tears were streaking my face as I watched him join that man I just couldn't believe Tom could like. Still, he looked fine. He seemed happy, big, and strong. The shadows in his eyes were only there because of the shadows he caught from me, as always he'd been my reflection.

Next Saturday I'd see him again. I could hardly wait for the day!

Twenty

The Love of A Man

Cal was waiting for me when I finally returned to the Setterton home. 'Heaven!' he cried when he saw me on the steps. 'Where the devil have you been? I've been worried sick about you.'

He was the man who loved me, who'd given me so much happiness when he gave me kindness and care, who gave me shame when he gave me love; put all together, it added up to feeling trapped. As I surrendered to his quick embrace and his hasty kiss, I was enveloped in a heavy fog of despair. I loved him for what he'd done to save me from the worst of Kitty's meanness, and yet I wished desperately that he'd just stayed my father, and not become my lover.

'Why are you looking at me like that, Heaven? Can you love me only in Candlewick, and not in Winnerrow?'

I didn't want to love him in the way he wanted me to! I couldn't let him overwhelm me again with his needs. I whispered hoarsely; 'I saw Tom today, and Fanny, and Grandpa.'

'And you're crying? I thought you'd be happy.'

'Nothing is ever quite what you think it's going to be, is it? Tom has grown to be as tall as Pa, and he's only sixteen.'

'And how was Grandpa?'

'So old and pitiful, and pretending Granny's still alive, sitting in the rocker next to him.' I half laughed. 'Only Fanny was predictable. She hasn't changed at all in personality, except she has turned into a beauty.'

'I'm sure she can't hold a candle to her sister, ' he said in a low, intimate voice, lightly touching my breast. At that moment Maisie opened the screen door, and her eyes were huge. She'd seen! Oh, God!

'Kitty's been calling for ya,' said Maisie in a small voice.

'Ya better run on and see what she wants. Ma can't do nothing right for her.'

Sunday morning we were all up early preparing to go to church. Kitty had to wait until Monday to see the doctors. 'We're all going to church,' said Reva Setterton when she saw me in the hall. 'Ya hurry and eat yer breakfast so ya can go. I done took care of my daughter early, so she's all right to leave alone for a few hours.'

Cal was in his bedroom doorway, staring at me in a disturbing way. Did he realize now that it was better that he and I would never be alone again? Surely he had to know Logan was the right one for me, and he'd let me go without making further demands. I pleaded with my eyes, begging him to restore our proper relationship . . . but he frowned and turned away, seeming hurt.

'I'll stay here with Kitty; the rest of you go on,' I said. 'I don't like to leave her alone.' Instantly Cal turned to follow Kitty's family out the door. He glanced back to give me a long, appraising look before his lips quirked in a wry small smile.

'Be good to your mother, Heaven.'

Was that sarcasm I heard in Cal's voice?

Here I was, stuck in this house, when Logan would be waiting for me in the church. How stupidly blind of me to presume Reva Setterton would stay home with her daughter, and how indifferent she'd been to suggest leaving her alone.

Slowly I climbed the stairs to check on Kitty.

Kitty lay on the wide bed, her face scrubbed so clean it shone. Not only was it red and chafed, as mine had been after that bath in scalding water, her thick red hair had been parted in the middle and was tightly braided in two long plaits that just reached the swell of her bosom. Her mother had put her in a plain white cotton nightgown such as old ladies wore, buttoned up to the throat, the very kind of nightgown Kitty despised, a plain, cheap nightgown. I'd never seen Kitty look so unattractive.

Her mother was wreaking her own revenge, as Kitty had hers when she put me in boiling water . . . and yet I felt overwhelming rage rising. I hated Reva Setterton for doing this to a helpless woman! How cruel when Kitty was so defenseless. Like a protective mother I gathered what I needed to undo what Reva had done. I pulled out Kitty's prettiest nightgown, and took off the plain ugly one, before I soothed her chafed skin all over with lotion; then gently I eased the lacy pink nightie over her head. Then I began to undo her tightly bound hair. When I had it styled as best I could, I carefully soothed her irritated face with moisturizer and began to apply her makeup.

As I worked to repair the damage I talked on and on. 'Mother, I'm just beginning to understand how it must have been for you. But don't you worry. I just put a good moisturizing lotion all over your body, and cream to help your face. I know I won't make your face up as well as you do it yourself, but I'll try. We're taking you to the hospital tomorrow, and the doctors are going to give your breasts a more thorough examination. It isn't necessarily true that you have to inherit tumours, Mother. I hope to God you really told me the truth, and you did go as you said you did – did you really go?'

She didn't answer, though it seemed she was listening, and a tear formed in the corner of her left eye. I went on talking, using blusher, eyebrow pencil, adding lipstick and mascara; and when I'd finished, she looked like herself again. 'You know something, Kitty Dennison, you are still a beautiful woman, and it's a damned shame you're lying there and not caring anymore. All you had to do was reach out and tell Cal you love him, and need him, and stop saying no so much, and he'd have been the best husband in the world. Pa wasn't meant to be any woman's husband. You should have known that. He's a born rogue! The best thing that ever happened to you was when he walked out and Cal walked in. You hate my mother, when you should have pitied her – look what he did to her.'

Kitty began to cry. Silent tears slid down her face and ruined her freshly applied makeup.

Early Monday morning an ambulance drove Kitty to the hospital. I rode beside her, and with me was Cal, while her mother and father stayed home. Maisie and Danny had gone on a hayride into the mountains.

For five hours Cal and I sat on hard, uncomfortable hospital chairs and waited for the verdict on Kitty. Sometimes I held his hand, sometimes he held mine. He was wan, restless, chain-smoking. When Kitty ruled her house, he'd never smoked; now he couldn't leave cigarettes alone. Finally a doctor called us into an office, and we sat side by side as he tried to tell us without emotion:

'I don't know how it was overlooked before, except sometimes a tumour is very difficult to find when a woman has such large breasts as your wife, Mr Dennison. We did a mammogram of her left first, since for some reason women seem to have them more frequently on that side than the other, and then her right. She does have a tumour, set deep under the nipple in the most unfortunate place, for it's difficult to discover there. It's about five centimeters in size. That's very large for this type of tumour. We are absolutely sure your wife has known about this tumour for some time. When we tried to do the mammogram, she suddenly came out of her lethargy and fought us. She screamed and yelled, and shouted out "Let me die!" '

Stunned, both Cal and I. 'She can talk now?' he asked.

'Mr Dennison, your wife could always talk. She chose not to. She knew she had a growth. She's told us she'd rather be dead than have her breast removed. When woman feel this strongly about losing a breast, we don't push the issue; we suggest alternatives. She's refused chemotherapy, for it would cause the loss of her hair. She wants us to try radiation . . . and if that fails, she says she is ready to "meet her Maker." ' He paused, and something that I couldn't read flickered through his eyes. 'In all honesty I have to tell you that her tumour has gone beyond the size that can be treated by radiation . . . but since that's all she'll do to help herself, we have no alternative but to do our best – unless you can convince her otherwise.'

Cal stood up and seemed to quiver. 'I have not once in my life convinced my wife of anything. I'm sure I can't now, but I'll try.'

He did his best. I was with him when he pleaded at her bedside. 'Please, Kitty, have the operation. I want you to live.' She clammed up again. Only when she glanced at me did her pale green eyes shimmer, with hate or something else, I couldn't tell.

'You go home now,' ordered Cal, settling in the only chair in her room. 'Even if it takes me a month, I'll convince her.'

It was three o'clock on Monday, and my heels made clicking sounds on the pavement. I wore blue button earrings Cal had given me only a week ago. He gave me so much, everything he thought I could possibly want. He'd even given me Kitty's jewellery box, but I couldn't force myself to use anything that belonged to her. The sweetness of this beautiful afternoon made me feel younger and fresher than I had since that first day Kitty had made me feel like hill scum. Whatever happened to Kitty would be of her own making, in a way, for she could have saved that breast if she'd acted sooner, and ended up with only a tiny scar that no man would ever notice.

With every step I took I prayed Cal would convince Kitty to have that operation. I prayed, too, that she'd see him for the fine man he was, and when she did, I knew he'd let go of me. It was Kitty he loved, had always loved, and she'd treated him so poorly, as if she couldn't love any man after what Pa had done to harm her.

Pa! Always full circle back to Pa!

Footsteps were following. I didn't look around. 'Hey,' called a familiar voice. 'I waited for you yesterday.'

Why did my steps quicken when all along I'd hoped he'd seek me out? 'Heaven, don't run. You can't run fast enough and you can't run far enough to escape me.'

I spun around and watched Logan approach. He'd grown to be everything I'd ever dreamed he could be – and it too late to claim him now for my own. Much too late.

'Go away!' I flared. 'You don't want me now!'

'Now, you wait a minute,' he growled, catching up and grabbing me by the arm, forcing me to walk with him. 'Why are you acting like this? What have I done? One day you love me, the next day you push me away . . . what's going on?'

My heart ached so much I felt weak. Yes, I loved him, had always loved him, would always love him; and yet I had to say what I did. 'Logan, I'm sorry, but I keep remembering how you ignored me that last Sunday before Pa sold me to the Dennisons. I wanted your help, and you looked right through me, and you were all I had after Miss Deale went away. You were my white knight, my saviour, and you did nothing, absolutely nothing! How can I ever trust you after that?'

Pain was in his eyes as he reddened. 'How dumb can you be, Heaven? You think you're in this world all by yourself with your problems, while nobody else has any. You knew I had trouble with my eyes that year. What do you think I was doing while you were starving up there on your mountaintop? Down in the valley I was almost going blind, so I had to be flown to a special hospital to have eye surgery! That's where I was! Far from here, sick in a hospital with my head in a clamp, my eyes heavily bandaged until they healed. Then I had to wear dark glasses and take it easy until my retinas were securely attached again. That day when you thought I saw you in church, I was only trying to see, and all I got were blurry images – and I was looking for you! You were the reason I was there at all!'

'Do you see all right now?' I asked with a lump in my throat.

He smiled, then stared into my eyes until *my* vision blurred.

'I'm seeing you with twenty-twenty eyes. Say I'm forgiven for that long-ago Sunday?'

'Yes,' I whispered. I swallowed all the tears that wanted to come again, bit on my lip before I bowed my head and rested my forehead briefly on his chest. I said a silent prayer for God to let him forgive me when or if I ever had to tell him. Useless to him now that I wasn't what he believed me to be – untouched, no longer a virgin. Yet I couldn't bring myself to tell him, not here. With resolve I began to lead him toward the woodsy area of Winnerrow.

'Where are we going?' he asked, his fingers intertwining with mine. 'To see your cabin?'

'No, you've already gone there by yourself and discovered all I wanted to hide from you. There's another place I should have shown you years ago.'

Hand in hand we strolled on towards the overgrown trail that would take us up to the graveyard. I glanced at him from time to time; several times our eyes met and locked, forcing me to tear my eyes away. He did love me. I could tell. Why hadn't I been stronger, shown more resistance? I sobbed and stumbled, and quickly he reached to balance me. I ended up in his arms. 'I love you, Heaven,' he whispered hoarsely, his warm, sweet breath on my face before he kissed me. 'All last night I lay awake thinking about how wonderful you are, how faithful and devoted you stay to your family. You're the kind of woman a man can trust; the kind you can leave alone and know will stay faithful.'

Gone numb from the misery I felt, I tried not to let too much sunshine come into the shadows of my heart as he rambled on and on, making me familiar with his parents, his aunts and uncles and cousins, until we came to the riverbank where we'd sat for so many hours a long time ago. Here time had stood still. Logan and I could have been the same adolescents falling in love for the first time. We sat again, perhaps in the very same place, so close our shoulders brushed, his thigh next to mine. I stared at the water that rippled over the stones. And only then did I begin the most difficult story of my life. I knew he'd hate me when it was over.

'My granny used to say my real mother came to that spring over there,' I said, pointing to the water that jetted from a crack in the rock face, 'and she'd fill our old oak bucket with the spring water since she thought the well water wasn't good for drinking, or for making soup, or for the dyes Granny used to make to colour old stockings she'd braid into a rug to fit under a cradle and keep out the draughts. She was fixing up the cabin as best she could for my birth . . .'

He sprawled on the grass at my side, playing idly with long tendrils of my hair. It was romantic sitting there with Logan, as if we were both brand-new, and nobody had ever loved before but us. I could see us in my mind's eye, young and fresh, unwrinkled and bright, in the prime flowering of our lives – but other bees had already flown to me. He played with my hands, first one, then the other, kissing my fingertips and palms before he folded my fingers on the kiss gifts he'd put in my hands. 'For all the days when I wanted you so much, and you were gone.' He pulled me down so my upper half lay on his chest, and my hair was a soft shawl that covered both our faces as we kissed, and then I lay with my cheek on his chest, his arms enfolding me. If only I were what he thought I was, then I could really enjoy this. I felt like a dying person on the last picnic of my life; the sun in all its glory couldn't keep the rain from my conscience.

I closed my eyes, wishing he'd talk on forever and wouldn't give me the chance to ruin his dreams – and mine.

'We'll marry while the roses are still in bloom, the year I graduate from college. Before the snow falls, Heaven.'

I shook my head, half caught up in his fantasy. My eyes closed, my breath regulated to coincide with his. He was caressing my back, my arms – and then, tentatively, my breast. I jumped, cried out as I jerked away and sat up. My voice shook as I said, 'Let's go now. You have to see, if you're to understand who and what I am.'

'I already know who and what you are. Heaven, why are

your eyes so wide and frightened-looking? I wouldn't hurt you, I love you.'

He wouldn't, not when he knew the truth. It was Cal who knew what I'd been through and Cal who understood. I was a Casteel, born rotten, and Cal didn't care, not the way the perfectionist Stonewalls would. Time and again Logan had turned from Fanny because she was wild and too free with herself.

Logan's bright eyes clouded with worry, seeming to sense I had a secret that wouldn't make him happy. I felt so small, so tainted, so alone.

'I've got a strange desire,' I said in a small, quivery voice. 'If you don't mind, Logan, I'd like to see my mother's grave again. When she died she left me a portrait doll I couldn't save from a fire, and I needed it to prove who I am when I return to Boston to find my mother's family.'

'You plan to go there?' he cried in a deep, troubled voice. 'Why? When we marry, my family will be your family!'

'Someday I've got to go there but also for my mother. She ran from her parents and they never heard from her again. They can't be too old, and must have worried about her for so many years. Sometimes it's better to know the truth than to go on forever wondering, speculating . . .'

He drew away from me now, though he matched his steps to mine as we climbed upward.

Soon the leaves would flame into a witch's brew of bright colours, and autumn would flare briefly in the mountains. Down in the valley where the wind didn't blow, two Stonewall parents would resent this Casteel girl who wasn't worthy enough for an only son. I reached for his hand, loving him as only the very young can love. Instantly he smiled and stepped closer. 'Must I say I love you ten million times before you believe me? Should I go down on my knees and propose? You can't tell me anything that would make me stop loving and respecting you!'

Oh, yes, there was something I could say, and eveything would change. I held his hand tighter, leading him on, always ascending, curving around tall pines, thick oaks and hickories, until all the trees turned to evergreens . . . and then we were there, in the cemetery. Room for only a few more now. Newer, better graveyards down lower, where it wasn't so much trouble to haul up machines to mow the grass, and men to dig up the graves.

No one mowed the grass where my young mother lay, all alone and off to one side. Just a narrow mound that was beginning to sink, a cheap headstone in the form of a cross.

Angel
Beloved wife of Thomas Luke Casteel

I released Logan's warm hand and sank to my knees, and bowed my head and said my prayer that someday, some wonderfully kind day, I would see her in paradise.

Along the way here I'd plucked a single red rose from the garden of Reverend Wayland Wise, and this I put in a cheap glass jar I'd buried at the foot of her grave years and years ago. No water nearby to put in the jar to keep the rose alive and fresh. A red rose to wither and turn brown. As she had withered and died before I ever had a chance to know her.

The wind whipped up and lashed the long arms of the evergreens as I knelt there and tried to find the will to say what I had to.

'Let's go now,' Logan said uneasily, glancing up at the late-day sun that began a swift descent behind the mountaintops.

What was he sensing?

The same thing I was?

All the little evening sounds bounced back and forth, echoing across the valleys, singing with the wind through the canyons, through the summer leaves, whispering the tall grass that hadn't been cut in years.

'It looks like rain . . .'

Still I couldn't tell him.

'Heaven, what are we doing here? Did we come just so you

could kneel and cry, and forget the pleasures of being alive and in love?'

'You're not listening, Logan. Or looking, or understanding. This is the grave of my real mother who died when I was born, died at the tender age of fourteen.'

'You've told me about that before,' he said softly, kneeling beside me and placing his arm over my shoulder. 'Does it still hurt so much? You didn't know her.'

'Yes, I do know her. There are times when I wake up and I feel as she must have felt. She's me, and I'm her. I love the hills, and I hate them. They give so much, and they rob you of so much. It's lonely here, and beautiful here. God blessed the land and cursed the people, so you end up feeling small and insignificant. I want to go, and I want to stay.'

'Then I'll make up your mind for you. We're going back to the valley, and in two years we'll be married.'

'You don't have to marry me, you know that.'

'I love you. I've always loved you. There's never been anyone but you. Isn't that reason enough?'

Tears were streaking my face now, falling to make raindrops on the red rose. I glanced up at the storm clouds swiftly drawing closer, shuddered, and started to speak. He drew me against him. 'Heaven, please don't say anything that will spoil what I feel for you. If what you're planing to say is going to hurt, don't say it, please don't say it!'

And I went and said it, as I'd planned all along, to say it here, where she could hear.

'I'm not what you think I am –'

'You're all I want you to be,' he said quickly.

'I love you, Logan,' I whispered with my head bowed low. 'I guess ever since the day we met I've loved you, and yet I let another –'

'I don't want to hear about it!' he flared hotly.

Because he jumped to his feet, I jumped to mine, and then we faced each other. The wind snapped my long hair so it brushed his lips. 'You know, don't you?'

'What Maisie's been spreading around? No, I don't believe anything so ugly! I can't believe gossip! You're mine, and I love you . . . don't you try to convince me there's a reason I can't love you!'

'But there is!' I cried desperately. 'Candlewick wasn't the happy place I wanted you to believe when I wrote those letters. I lied about so much . . . and Cal was –'

He wheeled about and ran!

Ran for the path to take him back to Winnerrow, calling back, 'No! No! I don't want to hear more! I don't want to hear – so don't tell me! Never tell me!'

I tried to catch up, but he had much longer legs, and my little heels dug into the mushy earth and slowed me. I headed back up the trail, to visit the cabin again. It stunned me with its bleakness. There on the wall was the pale place where Pa's tiger poster used to hang, and underneath, when Tom and I were babies, our cradle had sat. I stared at the cast-iron stove covered with rust where it wasn't green with fungus, and gazed with tears in my eyes at the primitive wooden chairs fashioned long ago by some dead Casteel. The rungs were loose, some were missing, and all the little things we'd done to pretty this place were gone. Logan had seen all of this! I cried then, long and bitterly, for all I'd never had, and all I might still lose. In the silence of the cabin the wind began to howl and shriek, and the rain came down. Only then did I get up from the floor to make my wet way back to Winnerrow, which was no home at all.

Cal was on the porch of the Setterton home, pacing back and forth. 'Where have you been that you come back wet, torn, and so dirty?'

'Logan and I visited my mother's grave . . .' I whispered hoarsely as I sat wearily on the top step, not caring that it was still raining.

'I thought you were with him.' He sat beside me, as heedless of the rain as I; he bowed his head into his hands. 'I've been with Kitty all day, and I'm beat. She won't eat. They're putting intravenous tubes in her arm, and beginning the radiation treatments tomorrow. She didn't go to a doctor as she told you she had. That lump has been growing steadily for two or three years. Heaven, Kitty would rather die than lose what represents her femininity to her.'

'What can I do to help?' I whispered.

'Stay with me. Don't leave me. I'm a weak man, Heaven, I've told you that before. When I saw you walking with Logan Stonewall, it made me feel old. I should have known that youth would call to its own, and I'm the old fool caught in my own trap.'

He tried to sit beside me. I jumped up, a wild panic in my heart. He didn't love me. Not as Logan did. He only needed me to replace Kitty.

'Heaven!' he cried. 'Are you turning away from me too? Please, I need you now!'

'You don't love me!' I cried. 'You love her! You always have! Even when she was cruel to me, you made excuses for her!'

Wearily he turned, his shoulders sagging as he headed for the front door of the Setterton home. 'You're right about some things, Heaven. I don't know what I want. I want Kitty to live, and I want her to die and get her off my back. I want you, and I know it's wrong. I should never, never have let her talk me into taking you into our home!'

Bang!

Always doors were being slammed in my face.

Twenty-One

Without A Miracle

A week passed. Every day I tended to Kitty in the hospital. I hadn't seen Logan since the day he ran from me and left me in the rain, and I knew that in just one more week he'd be returning to college. Many a time I strolled by Stonewall's Pharmacy, hoping to catch a glimpse of him, even as I tried to convince myself he'd be better off without someone like me. And I'd be better off without someone who'd never forgive me for not being perfect. Too flawed, Logan must have been thinking – too much like Fanny. If Cal noticed I was miserable from not seeing Logan anymore, he didn't say anything.

Hours spent in the hospital at Kitty's bedside made all the days seem exceptionally long. Cal sat on one side, I on the other. He held her hand most of the time, while I kept my hands folded on my lap. As I sat there, almost feeling her suffering as my own, I pondered the complexities of life. At one time I would have rejoiced to see Kitty helpless and unable to deliver slaps and insulting words to take away my self-esteem. Now I was full of compassion, willing to do almost anything to ease her pain, when there was little enough I could do to make her comfortable. Still, I tried, thinking I was redeeming myself, forgetting, as I struggled to find myself worthy and clean again, just what Kitty had done to make me hate her.

There were nurses to give her medications, but I was the one who gave her baths. She made signs to hint she'd rather have me do for her all the pampering things the nurses didn't have time for such as smoothing lotion all over her body, or brushing and style her hair as she wanted. Often as I teased, then smoothed her hair, I thought I could have truly loved her if she'd given me half a chance. I made up her face twice a day, dabbed on her favourite perfume, painted her nails, and all the time she watched me with those strange pale eyes. 'When I die ya got to marry Cal,' she whispered once.

I looked up, startled, and started to question, but she closed her eyes again, and when she did that, she wouldn't speak even if she were still awake. *Oh, God, please let her get well, please!* I prayed over and over. I loved Cal and needed him as a father. I couldn't love him in the way he wanted me to.

Other times, as I tended to her needs, I rambled on and on, talking as much to myself as to her; talking about her family and their great concern for her welfare (even though they didn't have any), trying to lift her spirits and give her hope as well as courage to fight the thing that was controlling her life now. Often her eyes were shiny with tears. Other times those dull, seawater eyes riveted on me without expression. I sensed something in Kitty was changing, for better or for worse, I couldn't tell.

'Don't look at me like that, Mother,' I said with a kind of nervous resentment. I was afraid Maisie might have visited and told her tales of seeing some touch or small bit of affection between Cal and me. *But it wasn't my fault, Kitty, not really,* I wanted to say as I pulled on her pretty, new gown and arranged her arms so she didn't appear so lifeless.

No sooner had I finished with Kitty than her mother came in, scowling disapprovingly, her large, strong arms folded as shields across her fake swelling bosom, her scowl deep and menacing. 'She'd look better without all that paint on,' she grumbled, giving me another sour look. 'She's done taught ya rotten ways, ain't she? Done made ya into what she is. Gave ya all her own faults, ain't she? And I licked her many a time to take the evil out of her. Never did. Never could. She's got it in her yet, festering, killing her . . . and the Lord in the end always wins, don't he?'

'If you mean we all have to die, yes, Mrs Setterton, that's true. But a good Christian like you should believe in life after death –'

'Are ya mocking me, girl? Are ya?'

In her eyes I saw some of Kitty's meanness shining forth. My indignation rose. 'Kitty likes to look pretty, Mrs Setterton.'

'Pretty?' she queried, staring down at Kitty as if seeing an abomination. 'Don't she have no colour gowns but pink?'

'She likes pink.'

'Just goes to show she's got no taste. Redheads like her don't wear pink. Done told her that all her life, and still she wears it.'

'Everyone should wear whatever colour they like. It's her choice,' I insisted.

'Ya don't have to make her look like a clown, do ya?'

'No, I paint her face so she looks like a movie star.'

'A whore is more like it!' Reva Setterton stated flatly before she turned her stony eyes on me. 'Know what ya are now. Maisie done told me. That man of hers, knew he couldn't have been no good or he wouldn't have wanted her. She's no good, never was even when she were a baby – and neither are ya! I don't want ya in my house! Don't ya show up there again, hill-scum filth! Take yerself to the motel on Brown Street, where all yer kind of trash hangs out. I've made her man move all yer stuff out along with his.'

Astonishment and anger widened my eyes before my shame and guilt made me blush. She saw and smiled cruelly. 'Don't wanna see ya again, not ever – ya hide when ya see me coming!'

Trembling, I spread my hands wide. 'I have to keep visiting Kitty. She needs me now.'

'Ya hear me, scumbag! Come no more to my place!' And she stormed out of the room, having come and looked at Kitty without one word of sympathy or encouragement or compassion. Had she come just to let me know what she thought of me?

Kitty was staring at the door, an unhappy pale fire in her eyes.

Tears coursed a crooked way down my cheeks as I turned

again to Kitty, arranging her bedjacket so she looked neat, before I fiddled again with her hair. 'You look lovely, Kitty. Don't believe what you just heard. Your mother is a strange woman. Maisie was showing me the family photograph album, and you look a great deal like your mother when she was your age . . . except you are prettier, and no doubt all your life she's been jealous of you.' (Why was I being so kind, why, when she'd been so cruel? Perhaps because Reva Setterton might have done many of the things to Kitty that Kitty had done to me.)

'Get out now,' Kitty managed when I was through with her.

'Mother!'

'Not yer mother.' Some terrible pain fleeted through her eyes, the agony of frustration so horrible I had to duck my head and hide my pity. 'Always wanted to be a mother, more than anything else, wanted my own baby. Ya were right when ya told me what ya did. Ain't fit to be a mother. Never was. Ain't fit to live.'

'Kitty!'

'Leave me be!' she cried weakly. 'Got the right to die in peace – and when the time comes, I'll know what to do.'

'No, you don't have the right to die! Not when you have a husband who loves you! You've got to live! You and Cal, and he needs you. All you have to do is will your body to fight back. Kitty, please do that for Cal. Please. He loves you. He always has.'

'Get out!' she yelled with a bit more strength. 'Go to him! Take care of him when I'm gone. Soon I will be! He's yers now. My gift to ya! Only took him for my man because he had something about him that made me think of Luke – like Luke could have been if he'd been brought up by some nice family in the city.' She sobbed low in her throat, a hoarse, raw sound that tore at my heart. 'When first I saw him after he came and sat at my table, I squinted my eyes and pretended he were Luke. All the time I been married to him, I could only let him take me when I played my pretend game – and made him Luke.'

Oh, Kitty, you fool, you fool!

'But Cal's a wonderful man! Pa's no good!'

The pale fire flared hotter. 'Heard that all my life about myself, and I'm not bad, I'm not! I'm not!'

I wouldn't take any more. I went out into the fresh September air.

What kind of trick did love play on common sense? Why one man when there were thousands to choose from? Yet here was I, hoping to find Logan. Almost wild to find him and have him tell me he understood and forgave me. But when I passed Stonewall's Pharmacy, Logan wasn't to be seen. In the drizzling rain I stood in the shadow of a huge elm and stared across the street at the windows of the apartment over the corner store. Was he up there looking down at me? Then I saw his mother at one of the windows just before she pulled the cord and closed the curtains, shutting me out. I knew she'd like to keep me forever out of her son's life. And she was right, right, right . . .

I walked toward Brown Street to the only motel in town. The two rooms Cal had rented were both empty. After I'd refreshed myself and put on dry clothes, I went out into the rain again and walked all the way back to the hospital, where I found Cal sitting dejectedly on a waiting-room sofa, staring moodily at a magazine held loosely in his hand. He glanced up when I came in.

'Any change?' I asked.

'No,' he answered gruffly. 'Where have you been?'

'I was hoping I'd see Logan.'

'Did you see him?' he asked dryly.

'No . . .'

He reached for my hand and held it firmly. 'What do we do, and how do we live with something like this? It could last six months, a year, longer. Heaven, I thought her parents were a solution. They're not. They're withdrawing their financial support. It's you and I or no one, until she's well, or gone . . .'

'Then it's you and I,' I said, sitting down to hold his hand in mine. 'I can go to work.'

He didn't say anything. We continued to sit, our hands joined, as he stared at the wall.

For two weeks we lived in that motel. I didn't see Logan. I was sure he'd gone back to college by now without even saying good-bye to me. School started, and that told me only too clearly I might never again enter a classroom and college was only a dream cloud drifting off into the sunset. And the job I'd thought would be so easy to find when I could type ninety words a minute didn't materialize.

The first real signs of winter came, and although I'd seen Tom twice, his visits were too short for us to really say all we needed to say. Buck Henry was always waiting for him, glaring when he saw me, and forcing Tom to hurry, hurry. I went every day to visit Grandpa, hoping just once pa would be there, but he never was. I tried time and again to see Fanny, but she wouldn't even come to the door anymore. A black maid responded to my demands. 'Miss Louisa don't talk to strangers,' was what she said every time, refusing to recognize I was her sister, not a stranger.

I hated the motel, the way people looked at Cal and me, though he had his room and I had mine, and not since we'd come to Winnerrow had he made love to me. When we went to church, we drove to another town and prayed there, knowing by this time that the Reverend Wise wouldn't allow us in his.

One morning I woke up cold. The strong north wind was blowing leaves from the trees and fanning out the curtains as I got up and began to dress. A walk before breakfast was on my mind.

It was a cloudy, rainy day, with fog covering the hills. I stared upward toward our cabin; through the mists I saw snow on the mountain peaks. Snowing up there, raining down here . . . and here was where I'd longed to be so many times.

I heard footsteps following, making me walk faster; a tall figure came to walk beside me. I expected to see Cal, but it was Tom! Instantly my heart gladdened. 'Thank God you're back again! I waited and waited last Saturday praying you'd show up. Tom, are you all right?'

He laughed as he turned to hug me, thinking all my concern for his welfare was silly and unnecessary. 'I can stay a whole hour this time. I thought we could have breakfast together. Maybe Fanny will join us and it will be like old times, almost.'

'I've tried to visit Fanny, Tom, and she refuses to talk to me. A black maid comes to the door, so I never even see her, and she doesn't stroll the streets.'

'We got to try,' said Tom, frowning. 'I don't like what I'm hearing in whispers. Nobody sees Fanny anymore, not like they used to before you came. There was a time when Fanny was everywhere showing off her new clothes, and bragging about all the Wises gave her. Now she doesn't even attend church on Sundays, or go to any of their social events – and neither does Rosalynn Wise.'

'To avoid me, I suspect,' I guessed with some bitterness, 'and Mrs Wise stays home to see that Fanny stays in her room. Soon as I'm gone, Fanny will come out of hiding.'

At the restaurant that served lorry drivers, we ate a hearty breakfast, laughing as we reminisced about all our poor meals when we lived in the Willies. 'Have you decided yet which sister you want?' I asked when he insisted on picking up the bill.

'Nope.' He threw me a small, shy grin. 'Like them both. However, Buck Henry says if I marry Thalia, he'll send me on to college and leave Thalia the farm. If I select Laurie, I'll have to make it on my own . . . and so I've decided not to marry either, and leave soon as I finish school, and set out on my own.' Until now his tone had been light; suddenly he was serious, his voice heavy. 'When you leave for Boston, how about taking me along?'

I reached for his hand, and laughed to think he'd say the

very words I'd been hoping to hear. People in Boston wouldn't be as prejudiced as they were here; they'd see our true worth. There I could easily find a job, and then I could mail Cal money to help pay for Kitty's care. He had put the house in Candlewick up for sale, but even if he did sell it, that money wouldn't last if she didn't recover soon, or . . . .

'Don't look like that, Heavenly. Everything will work out, you'll see.' Arms linked, we strolled on toward the nursing home to visit Grandpa.

'He ain't here,' said Sally Trench when she responded to Tom's loud knocking. 'Yer father done come and took him away.'

'Pa's been here!' cried Tom, seeming unbelievably happy. 'Where did he take Grandpa?'

Sally Trench didn't know. 'Left about half an hour ago,' she informed us before she slammed the door.

'Pa could still be in town, Heavenly!' Tom cried excitedly. 'If we hurry, maybe we can find him!'

'I don't want to see him, not ever!' I flared.

'Well, I do! He's the only one who can tell us where to find Keith and Our Jane.'

Both of us began to run. Winnerrow was an easy city to search, one main street with twelve side roads. As we ran we looked in shop windows, questioned those we saw walking. The sixth man we asked had seen Pa. 'Think he was going to the hospital.'

Why would he go there? 'You go on alone,' I said tonelessly when Tom insisted.

Helplessly Tom spread his large, calloused hands. His expression was miserable. 'Heavenly, I've got to be honest. I've been lying to you all the time. In those letters, and those pictures I enclosed, those were only school friends named Thalia and Laurie. Buck Henry doesn't have any children but ones who're buried in a churchyard. That fine house belongs to Laurie's mother and father, six miles down the road. Buck Henry's house might once have been nice, but now it's run-down and needs repairing. He's a slave driver who works me twelve to fourteen hours a day.'

'You mean you lied? All those letters when I lived in Candlewick – all lies?'

'All lies. Lies made up to make you feel good about me.' His eyes pleaded. 'I knew what you had to be thinking, and I didn't want you to worry, but now I have to say I hate that farm! Hate Buck Henry so much sometimes I feel if I don't escape I might kill him . . . so please understand why I'm going to run away from him and find Pa. I have to do this.'

To help Tom have what he wanted, to see Keith and Our Jane again, I'd do anything, even face the man I hated most in the world. 'Hurry!' Tom kept urging, and soon we were both running toward the hospital.

'Maybe Cal will be with Kitty by this time,' I gasped breathlessly when we were in the hospital lobby looking around.

'Sure,' said a nurse when Tom asked about Luke Casteel, 'he was here . . .'

'But where is he now?'

'Why, I don't know . . . been an hour ago since he asked the room number of Mrs Dennison.'

Pa had come to see Kitty . . . or me?

Grasping my hand tighter, Tom began to pull me along.

All the nurses and attendants had grown to know me by this time, and they greeted me by name as I took over and led Tom toward a lift that would take us up to Kitty's room. I felt strange, almost numb, and so fearful of what I'd say and do when I saw Pa. Still, when I was in Kitty's room, and she was pale and weak-looking, and Cal was kneeling by the side of her bed crying, it took me momentst to adjust to the disappointment of not seeing Pa, and then I was again shocked to see how happy Kitty looked. She lay on the narrow bed, beaming at me, at Tom. Why?

'Yer pa done come to see me,' she whispered in a frail voice I could hardly hear. 'He asked about ya, Heaven; he said he hoped to see ya. Said he were sorry for what he did in the past, and hoped I'd forgive him. Ya know, I never thought in a million years I'd hear Luke Casteel sound – Cal, what way did he sound?'

'Humble,' Cal said in a hoarse voice.

'Yeah, that's it. He were humbled, sorry-sounding.' Her eyes were bright, as if she'd seen a miracle. And for days she hadn't spoken. 'He looked at me, Heaven, and he never did that before. When I loved him, and would have died for him, he never saw me . . . just took me like I was a thing, and left. But he done changed, he has . . . and he's gone and left this here note for ya.'

Hers was a feverish kind of happiness, frenzied, as if she had to hurry, hurry. For the first time I saw she was dying, dying, right before our eyes, maybe had been for months before we even came here, and both Cal had I had grown too accustomed to her erratic swings of moods to recognize they were manifestations of depression, of frustrations . . . and fearful secret anxieties about that lump. Her thin hand seemed gaunt, her nails long and witchy like, as she handed me the envelope with my name on the outside. But her smile, for the first time, seemed warm, loving.

'Did I say thank ya for all ya've been doing for me, Heaven? Got me a daughter, at last – and ain't it something, though, ain't it, that Luke would come to see me? Were ya the one who sent for him – were ya? Ya must have, because he came in and he looked around, like he expected to see ya. So go on, Heaven, go on, read what he says in his letter.'

'This is Tom, my brother,' I finally said.

'It's good to see you, Tom,' said Cal, standing up and shaking his hand.

'Why, yer like Luke when he was yer age!' Kitty cried with delight, her pale eyes glowing strangely. 'All ya need is black hair and black eyes . . . and ya'd be just like yer pa! Ya would, ya would!'

She was touching, this devil-woman with her red hair and her long nails which had raked my skin many a time. Images of how she used to be flashed in and out of my brain; my ears rang with all the insults she'd thrown my way without regard for my feelings; and here she was putting tears in my eyes when I should have been feeling glad God was delivering to her just what she deserved. Yet I was crying. I sat in the chair that Cal pulled out for me and, with tears streaming down to wet my blouse, I opened the letter from Pa and began to silently read.

'Daughter, read it aloud,' whispered Kitty.

Again I glanced at her, sensing something different, then I began in a small voice:

'Dear Daughter,

Sometimes a man does what he feels is necessary and lives to find out his problems could have been solved in better ways. I ask you to forgive me for things that can't be changed now.

'Our Jane and Keith are happy and healthy. They love their new parents, and Fanny loves hers.

'I have married again, and my wife insists that I try and put my family back together again. I have a fine home now, and earn a great deal of money. There is very little hope that I can buy back Keith and Our Jane, or Fanny, but I am hoping you and Tom will come to live with us. Your grandfather will also be there.

'Maybe this time I can be the kind of father you can love instead of hate.

'Father'

There was an address and a telephone number beneath his name, but I could hardly read by this time. He'd never called me daughter before, never referred to himself as my father before – why now? I balled up the note and hurled it into the trash can near Kitty's bed.

Anger overrode all my other emotions. How could I trust a man who'd sell his children? How did I know for sure Tom and I would be all right in his care? What could he possibly do to earn a lot of money? Or had he married it? How could I believe anything he said? How could he know that Keith and Our Jane were truly happy where they were? Or Fanny? How could I know until I found out for myself?

Tom ran to retrieve the balled-up letter, and carefully he smoothed it out and read it silently. Each line he read made his face brighter.

'Why did ya do that?' asked Kitty with softness in her eyes. 'It were a nice letter, it were, weren't it, Cal? Heaven, ya take it up and save it, because there'll come a day when ya'll need to see him again – ' And then she failed and began to cry.

'Tom, let's go.' I turned to leave.

'Wait a minute,' whispered Kitty. 'Got something else for ya.' She smiled weakly and took a small envelope from under her pillow. 'Had a good talk with yer pa – and he gave me this here to keep for ya, and give to ya when the time comes. It's my way of trying to make up for what I did . . .' She floundered, glanced at Cal, then added, 'I think the time is now.'

I was trembling as I took the second small envelope. What could Pa say in this one to make up for all he'd done? Maybe Our Jane and Keith were fine – but how could I be sure, when that horrible farmer had worked Tom like a slave, as Kitty had worked me? Then I glanced up and saw with his eyes fixed on me, as if I held his life in his hands . . . and maybe I did. Oh, what harm would it do to read more lies?

Again I read his small handwriting. My eyes widened even as my heart began to race.

Pa'd come to the hospital hoping to find *me*.

Your grandpa has told me you have your heart set on going to Boston to find your mother's parents. If that is your choice, to go there, instead of coming to live with me and my wife, enclosed is a plane ticket I bought for you to use, and I have called your Boston grandparents to tell them you might be coming. Here is their address and telephone number. Write to me to let me know how things go.

My muscles tightened from the shock I felt. Why was he doing this? To get rid of me a second time? There were two addresses at the bottom of the letter, one written hurriedly in pencil. I stared at the names: Mr and Mrs James L Rawlings.

I looked up. 'Heaven,' Cal said softly, 'it was Kitty who persuaded your father to put the names of the couple who bought Our Jane and Keith in that note you hold. Now you know where they are, and someday you can go to see them.'

I couldn't speak, could hardly think.

Tom was reading over my shoulder. 'Heavenly, you see, you see, he's not as bad as you think! Now we can visit Our Jane and Keith. But I remember that contract the lawyer made Pa sign . . . we can never take them away –' He stopped short, staring at my face. I felt odd, my knees weak, all my emotions draining into the floor. I'd so wanted to find Keith and Our Jane, and now it appeared I could. But the plane ticket in my hand seemed blackmail to force me to stay out of their lives. Trembling still, I jammed the small envelope and its contents into my pocket, and said good-bye to Kitty before I strode out into the hallway, leaving Tom still talking to Cal.

Let Cal stay. I didn't care

In the hall outside of her room I called 'Tom!' impatiently, tired of waiting when he continued to talk in a low voice with Cal. 'I'm not going to wait forever.'

I turned and walked away. Tom hurried to catch up, and outside the hospital I headed for the motel, thinking that right now, today, I'd head for Boston . . . 'Are you going with me to Boston, Tom?'

His long strides shortened to keep in step with me. He had his head lowered against the wind and rain. 'Heavenly, we've got to talk.'

'We can talk as we walk to the motel. I'll pack my things. Kitty's happy . . . did you see her face? Cal didn't even look at me. Why aren't you delighted to be going with me?'

'Everything has changed! Pa's different! Can't you tell by

his letters? He went to see that woman, and she sees he's changed – why can't you? Heavenly, I want to go with you, you know I do, and Mr Dennison said he'd pay my way, if that's what I wanted . . . but first I have to see Pa. I'm sure he's gone on to the Setterton home to look for you, and perhaps he's already been to visit Buck Henry, and suspects I am with you. We can catch him if we hurry.'

'No!' I flared, feeling my face burn with anger. 'You go if you feel you have to, but I never want to see him again! He can't write two short notes and wipe the slate clean!'

'Then promise to stay put until you hear from me!'

I promised, still feeling numb from all that had happened to confuse my hatred. 'Tom . . . you will go with me to Boston? Come with me, and together, after we're established, we'll go for Keith and Our Jane.'

He was striding away from me! Turning at the corner to wave and smile. 'Heavenly, hold on. Don't you dare go anywhere until you hear from me!'

I watched Tom walk away with a certain joy in his stride, as if he believed he'd find Pa, and with Pa he'd have a better life than with Buck Henry.

In the motel room, I lay down and gave in to a weird crying spell that left me weak and completely drained. I resolved before I slipped into sleep, never to cry again. When the telephone rang I woke up to answer it, and heard Tom on the other end saying he'd found Pa, and now they both were coming to see me. 'Heavenly, he was in Stonewall's Pharmacy asking for you, and for me. He's changed. You're not going to believe it when you see him! He's sorry for all the mean things he did and said, and he's going to say that when he sees you . . . so you be there when we drive up. Promise?'

I hung up without promising.

Tom had betrayed me! Again I left the motel, to sit alone in the park. It wasn't until dark, when I felt Tom would have given up, that I returned to the motel and fell into the bed.

Tom wasn't going with me to Boston – he'd rather stay

with Pa, and after all the vows we'd made to one another!

And Logan had flown off to college without making any effort to see me again. What did I have left but my mother's parents in Boston? Even Cal seemed indifferent to me now he was so taken up with Kitty. I needed someone. Maybe this was Fate's way of seeing I went on to Boston to my grandparents.

I was packing my clothes when Cal came in and told me what he knew about Tom finding Pa, and Pa driving Tom to the motel to pick me up, only I'd gone. 'They looked all over town for you, Heaven. Tom presumed you'd already flown to Boston, and he looked so hurt. Anyway, he and your father gave up their search. Where were you?'

'Hiding in the park,' I admitted. Cal didn't understand; still he held me and rocked me as if I were seven instead of seventeen. 'If they call to check on me, you tell them you haven't seen me,' I pleaded.

'Yes,' he agreed, his eyes troubled as they tried to meet mine. 'I do think, though, you should see Tom again, and talk to your father. Heaven, maybe he has changed. Maybe he is sorry. Maybe you don't have to fly to Boston, and you will like living with your father and his new wife.'

I turned my back. Pa hadn't changed.

Cal left me alone, and I continued to pack, thinking of what a sorry mess I'd let myself in for when I chose Kitty Dennison and her husband. I had almost packed all my clothes when Cal opened the door and stared at me, his eyes narrowed. 'You still going to Boston?'

'Yes.'

'What about me?'

'What about you?'

He blushed, had the decency to bow his head. 'The doctors examined Kitty a little while ago. I know this sounds incredible, but she's better! Really better. Her white-cell count is almost normal. Her platelet count is rising. The tumour has shrunk just a bit, and if this keeps up, they think she will live. Heaven, that visit from your father gave her the will to go on. Now she says it was always me she loved most, and she didn't know it until she was on the brink of death – what can I do? I can't turn away from my wife when she needs me so much, can I? So perhaps it is for the best that you go on to Boston with my prayers and all my love – and someday you and I will meet again, and maybe then you can forgive me for taking advantage of a young and sweet and beautiful girl.'

Stunned, I widened my eyes in astonishment. 'You never loved me!' I yelled accusingly, brokenly. 'You used me!'

'I do love you! I will always love you! I hope wherever you go you'll always love me just a little. You were there when I needed someone. Go and forget Kitty and what was done, and don't step into Tom's life when he'll have everything going fine for him. Fanny is happy where she is. Leave Keith and Our Jane where they are. Your mother's people in Boston might object if you come with others. And forget me. I made my bed when I married Kitty. It doesn't have to be your bed too. Go now, while I have the strength to do the right thing. Go before she leaves the hospital a well woman, and her old self returns to seek you out and destroy you for taking what she thinks belongs solely to her. Kitty'll never truly change. She's been on the brink of death, afraid of what's on the other side . . . but once she recovers, she'll come after you. So, for your own sake . . . go now, today.'

I didn't know what to say, or what to do. I could only stare with teary vision as he paced back and forth.

'Heaven, when your father was in the room with Kitty, she was the one who pleaded for him to tell you where Our Jane and Keith are. It was her gift to you to make up for all she's done.'

I didn't understand, and yet my heart-throbs hurt so much I wanted to run from my body. 'How can I believe anything Kitty says, or Pa?'

'Your father sensed you were running from him, and he guessed you'd never see him again, so he turned over to Tom more photographs of Our Jane and Keith so he could give them to you. I saw them, Heaven. They've grown since the last pictures sent to you. They have parents who adore them, and they live in a fine home, and attend the one of the best schools in the country. If you have an idea of going there, remember you will take with you sad memories they might want to forget . . . think of that before you walk into their new lives. Give them time to grow up a bit more, Heaven, and give yourself time to mellow.'

He said many things that I refused to hear.

Cal gave me cash that Pa had given him to pass on to me. I stared at the bills in my hand. A stack of twenty-dollar bills – amounting to five hundred dollars, the price Kitty and Cal had paid for me. My wide bleak eyes raised to meet Cal's – and he turned away.

That was all I needed to really decide me. I'd go! I'd never come back! Not even to see Logan again! I was finished with Winnerrow and the Willies, and everybody who'd said they loved me.

The first flight to Atlanta, from where I could transfer to a plane for Boston was the next day at nine. Cal drove me to the airport and carried my bags for me. He seemed nervous, anxious to get away, before he kissed me good-bye; then his stark eyes fleetingly swept over my face, scanned down to my shoes, then up again, slowly, slowly. 'Your plane takes off in twenty minutes. I'd like to stay and wait with you . . . but I really should get back to Kitty.'

'Yes, you really should,' I said dryly. I wasn't going to say good-bye, wasn't . . . yet I did. 'Good-bye . . . good-bye . . .' I wasn't going to cry or hurt inside to see him walk away without looking back, yet I did, though I saw him slow and hesitate before he shrugged, stood taller, and then walked off even faster. Going back to Kitty, and whatever the future held.

Twenty minutes to wait. How could I pass the time? I didn't have anyone now that Logan had run from me, now that Tom preferred Pa to me; and Fanny had long ago decided she didn't need me. . . . New doubts washed over me in great fearful waves. How did I know my mother's family would want me? But I had five hundred dollars, and even if things didn't work out right in Boston, I'd find a way to survive.

'Heaven! Heaven!' I heard a faimiliar voice call. Turning, I stared at the lovely young girl running my way. Was that Fanny? Fanny running in a slow and awkward way? 'Heaven,' she gasped, throwing her arms about me. 'Tom came and told me ya were leaving, and I couldn't let ya go way thinking I don't care, when I do, I do! So scared we'd be late and miss ya! Sorry I was mean to ya, but they don't want me to talk to ya!' She drew away and, with a broad, happy smile, threw open her heavy fur coat to display her bulging middle. Then she whispered in my ear. 'Got the Reverend's baby in there. It's gonna be so sweet, I just know it is. His wife is gonna pass it off as her own, and give me ten grand for it . . . then I'm heading on to New York!'

Nothing could surprise me anymore. I could only stare at her. 'You'd sell your own baby, for ten thousand?'

'Ya'd never do that, would ya?' she asked. 'Don't ya make me sorry I said yes when Tom came and said I had to come and say good-bye.' Tears shone in her dark eyes. 'Do what I feel I gotta, just as ya do.'

She backed off, and only then did I see Tom, who was smiling at me in the sweetest, most loving way. He stepped forward to take me in his arms. 'Cal Dennison called and told me you were leaving for Boston today, Heavenly . . . and he asked me not to bring Pa.'

Pulling away, I cried out, 'You're not coming with me, are you?'

He spread his large hands wide in a supplicating gesture. 'Look at me! What do you think your grandparents will feel when they see you've brought your half brother with you? They won't want me! I'm a hillbilly! Like Pa! Haven't you said that many times since you came back here? I'm not refined and dainty the way you are, with culture and manners. Heavenly, I'm thinking of your welfare when I say

I've got to stay with Pa, even though I'd much rather go with you.'

'You're lying! You'd rather stay with Pa!'

'Heavenly, please listen! You can't go to your mother's family hauling along all your hillbilly relatives! I want your life to turn out right, and it won't if I go with you!'

'Tom, Please! I need you!'

He shook his head, his wild red hair flying. 'If you need me later on, after you're settled in, write and I'll come, I swear that. But for now, start out afresh.'

'He's right,' vouched Fanny, coming closer and looking around nervously, as anxious to leave as Cal had been. 'It was Tom who made me come, and I'm glad I did. I love ya, Heaven. Didn't want to close the door in yer face . . . but I do what I have to. Mrs Wise is taking me away so my baby can be born where nobody will know who we are; and when it's over, she'll go back to Winnerrow with *her own* baby, and she'll tell everyone it's hers, and I was just a no-good Casteel and ran off with a no-good fellow.'

'And you won't care?'

'Nope. Can't afford to.' She smiled and backed off. 'Tom, we got to get back before I'm missed. Ya promised me, ya did.'

Fanny, who'd always said she wanted a baby so much, was selling hers, just as Pa had sold his.

Again I turned to Tom. 'So you're going to stay with Pa and his new wife. Why don't you tell me about her – one of the girls from Shirley's Place?'

He flushed and looked uneasy. 'No, not that kind at all. Right now I've got to drive Fanny back home. Good luck, Heavenly. Write . . .' And with those words he kissed my cheek and seized Fanny by the arm and hurried her away.

'Good-bye, good-bye!' I was calling again, waving frantically to Fanny, who turned and smiled through her tears. Oh, how I hated good-byes! Would I ever see Fanny or Tom again?

And why was Tom turning around to smile at me in that

odd, sad kind of way? I watched him and Fanny until they were out of sight, then turned and sat again, thinking now I had ten more minutes before my flight.

It was a small airport with a nice little park outside where I could watch the planes as they landed. I paced back and forth in the frail autumn sunlight, with the wind whipping my hair and stealing all the neatness and making it wild again. I almost felt I was back in the hills.

My eyes swam in tears.

Then it was time for me to go to my plane, which was boarding passengers. For the first time in my life I was boarding a small plane, climbing the ramp, taking a seat and buckling my seat belt, as if I'd done this many times before. In Atlanta I transferred to another, larger plane that would land in Boston.

I'd begin a new life in a new place. My past would be unknown.

Strange that Kitty could be so happy just because my pa came to see her one time, and brought her roses, and said he was sorry, when Cal had bought her roses a hundred times, and he'd said he was sorry a million times, and that hadn't given her peace or happiness – or the will to survive. Who would have ever believed Pa could inspire that kind of lasting love?

But I'd asked myself that before, and hadn't found the answer. Why ask again?

I closed my eyes and determined to stop thinking about the past and clear the way for the future. Kitty and Cal would go back to Candlwick when she was released from the hospital, and they'd live on in her pink-and-white house, and somebody else would water all those plants. I reached in my pocket for a tissue to dry my eyes and blow my nose. To distract myself I opened the Winnerrow newspaper which I'd picked up in the airport just before I left and casually flipped through its pages.

It had only four sheets. On the fourth one I stared at an old photograph of Kitty Setterton Dennison, taken when she was about seventeen years old. How pretty she'd been, so fresh-faced and eager and sweet-looking. It was an obituary!

> Kitty Setterton Dennison, age 37, died today in the Winnerrow Memorial Hospital. The deceased is survived by her husband, Calhoun R Dennison, her parents, Mr and Mrs Porter Setterton, her sister, Maisie Setterton, and her brother, Daniel Setterton. Funeral services will be held at the Setterton family home on Main Street, on Wednesday, 2 p.m.

It took me a while before all that sank in.

Kitty was dead. Had died the day before I left Winnerrow. Cal had driven me to the airport, and he must have known and didn't tell me!

Why?

He'd rushed away . . . why?

Then I guessed why.

I bowed my face into my hands and sobbed again, not so much for Kitty as for the man who'd finally gained the freedom he'd lost at the age of twenty.

Freedom at last, I could almost here him shouting, to be what he wanted, do what he wanted, how he wanted – and he didn't want me to deprive him of what he had to have.

What kind of crazy world was this anyway, that men could take love, then throw it back? Cal wanted to go on alone.

Bitterness overwhelmed me.

Maybe that's the way I should be, more like a man, take 'em and leave 'em and not care so much. I'd never have a husband; only lovers to hurt and discard, as Pa had done. Sobbing, I folded the paper and stuffed it into the pocket on the back of the seat in front of me.

Then, once more, I slipped a photograph out of a large brown envelope the one Tom had handed me just before he pulled Fanny away, and at the time I hadn't even considered it important. 'Hold on to this,' he'd said in a low whisper, as if he hadn't wanted Fanny to know. There they were, Our

Jane and Keith, looking older, stronger, happier. I stared and stared at Our Jane's sweet, pretty face, and then it came to me who she looked like. Annie Brandywine Casteel! Granny born again in Our Jane, just as I could see a bit of Grandpa in Keith's good-looking young face. Oh, they did deserve the best, the very best, and for now I'd do nothing to bring unhappy memories to them. My tears dried. I knew without doubt that someday Fanny would reach her goals, no matter what she had to do to gain them.

What about me? I knew now that every event in anyone's life changed some facet of them – what was I now? Even as I thought that, my spine stiffened. From this day forward I'd step boldly, without fear or shame, not timid, nor shy, nor to be taken advantage of. If you gave me nothing else, Kitty, you did give me true knowledge about my strength; through thick and thin, through hell and back, I'd survive.

Sooner or later I'd come out the winner.

As for Pa, he'd see me again. He still had a huge debt to pay, and pay he would before I quit this world that had shown me so little mercy.

As for now – Boston. The home of my mother. Where I'd change, as if magically, into all that my mother had been – and more.

Virginia Andrews
The Casteel Family Saga

HEAVEN
DARK ANGEL
FALLEN HEARTS
GATES OF PARADISE
WEB OF DREAMS

Virginia Andrews' second compelling series is the heart-breaking story of four generations of the Casteel family and their desperate fight for happiness. Again and again tragedy threatens to overwhelm them as they struggle to escape the awful shadow cast over the family by the Tattertons and their mysterious, magical home, Farthinggale Manor.

Virginia Andrews
The Dollanganger Series

FLOWERS IN THE ATTIC
PETALS ON THE WIND
IF THERE BE THORNS
SEEDS OF YESTERDAY
GARDEN OF SHADOWS

When *Flowers in the Attic* was first published, it rapidly became an international publishing sensation, establishing Virginia Andrews as one of the most popular and biggest selling authors in the world.

Her spellbinding story of four children who spent days, and then years, imprisoned in an airless attic – just so that their mother could gain her inheritance – proved so irresistible that it was made into a chilling film, and was soon followed by four more bestselling books continuing the story of those loveless, forgotten children and the terrible effect their harrowing ordeal had on them and their own families . . .

My Sweet Audrina
Virginia Andrews

The house in the wood was picturesque and charming. The family who lived there were happy and affluent. So what was the secret of that room – empty of everything but the rocking chair?

Audrina wanted to be as good as her sister. Audrina knew her parents could not love her as they loved her sister. Her sister was perfect, much loved – and dead.

But how did she die? Who was Audrina and who did she have to become? What was the secret that everyone knew? Everyone except sweet Audrina . . .

ISBN 0 00 616757 8

Forbidden Garden
Diane Guest

Journalist Patrick Kaiser arrives for a holiday on Nantucket Island to forget a crushing divorce. But late one night, from across the garden, he hears the sounds of haunting sobs. Curiosity draws him to investigate – and he becomes irrevocably entangled in the dark lives of a mysterious family.

What powerful and unnatural hold does the celebrated conductor Julian Ferrare have over his terrified wife and children? Is their attic sanctuary or prison?

Kaiser vows to protect the children from the growing evil of their home. But as each new horror unfolds he becomes enmeshed in a shocking legacy of heated desire, stark fear, and secrets too monstrous to share . . .

ISBN 0 00 647052 1